ANOTHER KIND OF LOVING

When journalist Mike and his wife Sara decide to foster a 12-year-old Bosnian refugee, they have no premonition of the far-reaching consequences. Jasminka evolves from a traumatised child of the bitter ethnic conflicts of besieged Sarajevo into Minkie, an English schoolgirl-with-a-difference in a village in Middle England. She also becomes the daughter Mike has always wanted and Sara cannot have, and one of the excuses for Sara to resume an old affair. Mike's assignments continue to take him to Bosnia and Serbia and he finds himself emotionally drawn into the conflict for reasons he could never have imagined and which have a profound effect on the deepening rift at home. As shifting international tensions are about to change the world forever, Minkie returns to Sarajevo to seek her roots and decide her future, just as Mike and Sara must decide on theirs in these early days of September 2001.

By the same author

The Young Traveller in Finland	Phoenix House, 1962
The Young Traveller in Yugoslavia	Phoenix House, 1967
Travellers' Guide to Yugoslavia	Cape, 1969
Travellers' Guide to Finland	Cape, revised 1977
Welcome to Yugoslavia	Collins, 1984
Welcome to Scandinavia	Collins, revised 1987
The Big Muddy – a canoe journey down the Mississippi	Oriole Press 1992

Educational aids

Assassination at Sarajevo	Jackdaw Publications 1966
Caxton and the Early Printers	Jackdaw Publications 1968
Scott and the Antarctic	Jackdaw Publications 1971
The Vikings	Jackdaw Publications 1976

ANOTHER KIND OF LOVING

Sylvie Nickels

Antony Rowe
Publishing Services

This book has been printed digitally and produced in a standard specification in order to ensure its continuing availability

Published by Antony Rowe Publishing Services in 2005
2 Whittle Drive
Highfield Industrial Estate
Eastbourne
East Sussex
BN23 6QT
England

ISBN 1-905200-12-9

Printed and bound by Antony Rowe Ltd, Eastbourne

to my Yugoslav friends,
especially Sveto and Ksenija

PROLOGUE

Extracts from guidebooks on former Yugoslavia in the 1980s:
"Yugoslavia is one country with two alphabets, three religions, four languages, five (main) nationalities, six republics, seven frontiers...."
"If ever East meets West it is here among the magnificent mineral-rich mountains of (its) central republic Bosnia-Hercegovina. And nowhere is this more true than in its capital Sarajevo, where buses and trams rumble past mosques, bazaars and supermarkets, and minarets share the skyline with Orthodox towers and domes and Roman Catholic spires."

In 1991, first Slovenia, then Croatia, declared their independence, deaf to foreign warnings and threats of retribution from Serbia on behalf of the hundreds of thousands of Serbs living within Croatia's boundaries.

By early 1992, a six-month civil war had left over 6000 dead and uprooted a million people. Unrest grew in Bosnia and Macedonia.

On March 1ˢᵗ 1992, following an overwhelming vote (boycotted by Bosnian Serbs) in favour of Bosnian independence, Serb snipers opened fire on civilians in Sarajevo.

1

SARAJEVO - MAY 1992 - *Extracts from the personal diary of a Bosnian Serb during the early days of the siege*

' When we heard that the younger part of the family was safe and sound – telephone connections were still operative – my wife and I were greatly relieved. We could go back to patching up our broken dreams of living together in a multi-cultural society. This was helped by our mixed neighbourhood, the bonds of horrors and suffering and, finally, shared awareness of the inevitable self-destruction of at least two of the major participants, Moslems and Serbs, in a lunatic outbreak of violence.

'Some days later: .... heavy bombardment, most telephone lines destroyed, public transport, trams and buses systematically shelled, and hundreds of apartments hit ... more and more paramilitary looting and beating up of people on national grounds; ... growing hatred on all sides; family quarrels on national and political grounds; and yet enormous solidarity in small, everyday matters, in sharing food, gas, coal, wood....

'27th May.... We go to the market, buy a jar of beetroot for a thousand million dinars; the price of matches has gone down so we buy three boxes. And some toothpaste. We meet two elderly, in fact very old friends, Austro Hungarian style (and probably origin, both professional people who retired years ago). The old gentleman proudly informs us ... they had seen a man setting up scales on a counter, rushed up before any goods were in sight. And what appeared: spinach! Only a thousand million dinars a kilo! ....

'29th May ....After the 'breadline massacre' yesterday, tonight the shelling horrors start on a larger scale. We are in the cellar, from eight o'clock in the evening until two in the morning; mortars, heavy artillery, multiple rocket launcher, horrifying destruction of many parts of Sarajevo.... I could feel horror and fear creeping into my bones, and I remained there throughout the next day.'

MIKE – October 1992

The steep narrow lane was strewn with debris: bricks, shards of glass, a table with three legs, a T-shirt abandoned in the gutter. Mike Hennessey bent to retrieve it. A jagged tear across the front of it severed the slogan *I love Sarajevo* in English across a blood-red heart. Christ, there was even symbolism in the gutters of this benighted city. He dropped the T-shirt thinking *well at least the children's home is on the right side of town:* the side least vulnerable to the barrage of death pounding out from the encircling Serb artillery.

Instinctively he drew into the relative shelter of a doorway, then saw it opened into the shell of a house. But the view was magnificent over the city, late autumn sun slanting on to minarets and spires and towers too distant to reveal their scars; and the steep slopes beyond still too densely forested to hint at what they concealed.

"It's un*real*," he had said quietly, those fifteen, sixteen years ago when it had still been Yugoslavia and the world mostly remembered Sarajevo – if it remembered it at all – as the place where that chap shot an Archduke and started the First World War. Or something like that.

He was on holiday then, had fallen in love with the city, and with a girl called Marija with smooth high cheekbones and green eyes. "Sarajevo has always welcomed persecuted people," Marija had said. "People with different blood feelings from ours." She meant blood ties, but back then Mike thought her expression got it about right.

God help 'em.

He had looked for her of course, but in this mayhem it was a forlorn hope, even supposing she still lived here and had survived. She had stopped answering his letters quite soon after his return to England. Or had he stopped writing first, caught up in the self-important busy-ness of his first reporting job? He couldn't even remember her full name and anyway she would be

3

married by now. As he was. He pictured Sara briefly, the stable constant in his life for eleven years: at home in the rural, well-ordered quiet of Middle England. And longed to be there.

"Get a story about how the kids are coping," was the latest instruction from Canary Wharf.

He had sent a message to the director of the orphanage the previous day and she was waiting for him. Her name was Jovanka and she looked exhausted. But she smiled as she said, "I wondered if you would come. The shelling was bad last night."

She led him down a long corridor that was very cold and smelt of institution. "We have no heating," she said. "Little food or water, and light for only two hours. Some days. Soon we will have no candles."

"I'll get you some."

She raised her eyebrows politely. "And most of the staff have gone: to safety, or to fight, or to take care of their families."

There were about 50 small children. They had been collected into one large dormitory to make the most of whatever warmth and light were available. Most were in bed but some of the smallest had clambered out and were squatting on the floor, sucking their thumbs, rocking to and fro. But noiselessly. It was the silence of so many children in one place that was unnerving: a kind of resignation more suited to a home for the elderly.

Jovanka spoke sharply in Serbo-Croat to a girl standing in the middle of the room. Her head was down, her face concealed by a dark lank curtain of hair and she clutched a book. Jovanka sighed. "She is supposed to be helping me, that one. I ask her to make sure they stay in bed where it is warm now that it is dangerous to play outside. But..." She shrugged.

Mike went over to the child, crouching down beside her. Instinctively he pushed back the curtain of hair. She flinched but did not draw away until he tried to look at her book when she stepped back, clutching it harder and glared ferociously at him. She had dark eyes, a sallow unhealthy complexion and he saw then that she was older than he had first thought – perhaps eleven, twelve? Then he noticed with surprise the title of the book: *Winnie the Pooh.*

"It was in a parcel from your country," Jovanka said.

"And what's *her* story?"

"Her father was killed by a sniper; Branka, her mother is now very sick. She is an old friend, from long ago and asked if Jasminka should come here. To be safer. To help me...." She paused. "Branka is a Serb. Jasminka's father Ismet was a Bosniak, a Moslem. She was playing outside and he had gone to fetch her. She was holding his hand when he was shot." She shrugged. "I forget to make allowances. But when tragedy is the norm ..."

But tragedy wasn't the norm in Mike's life, and he ached with compassion for the girl with unkempt hair. As he followed Jovanka out of the room, he looked back and saw the child was still glaring after him.

"I'll get those candles," he repeated later as he took his leave of Jovanka. The shelling had started again and, across the valley, fresh puffs of smoke and dust rose where missiles struck with distant, gentle, harmless-sounding thuds. "And some things for the children. I'll come back in a few days."

He did return, but he never intended to get so involved with the girl with the uncombed hair.

5

SARA – October 1992

Sara Hennessey was just finishing her editorial for the village magazine when Mike's call came through that October Saturday morning. It had been a particularly tiresome issue. The Parish Council had turned down an application for a nature reserve in favour of plans for new housing - 'executive' so-called - on a piece of local wasteland owned by them. The Postbag was seething with outpourings from protagonists on both sides. Editing out the vitriol without losing some often very valid arguments had taken most of the morning; likewise concealing her own preferences (for the reserve), though she had allowed herself to slide off the fence in her editorial.

Her computer, an extremely new toy, had crashed twice that week– thankfully without the loss of anything vital – and the duplicator on which 950 copies of the magazine were about to be reproduced was beginning to show its age. OK so the *Daerley Green Chronicle* was hardly the Times or the Washington Post, but to a sizeable number of Daerlians it was the voice of the community. It also these days occupied a substantial portion of her, Sara's, life. With Mike away so much, she welcomed this. Everyone said she did a great job, no doubt largely because no one else was willing to take it on. Still, she was prepared to accept that under her stewardship the *Chronicle* had become an ever more important repository for all things Daerlian.

"Though don't let it take you over completely, dear girl," Justin said quite regularly, usually when he delivered his copy as Clubs Editor. Sara grinned as her eye caught a sheaf of papers bearing his sprawling scrawl. At 78, Justin could get away with calling a 35-year-old 'dear girl' and would almost certainly achieve his stated goal of being the ultimate dinosaur to die uncontaminated by either computer or mobile phone. She was very fond of him.

The thought of Justin lightened her mood and was reflected in her flip "Hello World," as she answered the telephone's second ring.

"Hi Darling," crackled Mike's voice across an appalling line. "That's the most cheerful sound I've heard in days in this God forsaken place."

"Just put the adjectival magazine to bed. Total euphoria," Sara said. And then registered what he'd said and where he was. "Sorry, lover. You sound bushed."

He started to tell her about a children's home. She pictured his face, squarish, serious: mostly serious except when his delicious sense of humour triggered a network of crinkles that make him look distinctly puckish. And very attractive. She hauled her attention back to what he was saying: something about a girl and what sounded like *Winnie the Pooh,* but the line kept breaking up and she must have mis-heard. Then for a few seconds the line cleared and his voice, as clear as if he were in the next room, said "... so many tragic stories. In the end you feel desperate to do something. Anything. I thought ... well, just may be she could come and live with us for a while."

In a lengthening silence Sara's mind scrabbled to interpret these words.

"Darling are you there?"

There was only one possible interpretation. Sara took a deep breath. "Yes, but I don't think I heard ..." The line began crackling again.

"Be home next week with luck. We'll talk about it ...." The line broke up altogether.

Sara went on staring at the white receiver in her hand, as though staring at it long enough would make everything clear. Then she put it back on its cradle.

"Don't start jumping up and down," she said aloud. "Mike's not a fool." No, but he was a compulsive collector of strays. He'd also been under a lot of pressure lately - that was blindingly obvious from his calls and from his reports in the paper.

And he'd always wanted a child. No doubt to compensate

7

for his own disordered upbringing, as he'd implied more than once.

She snapped her mind shut. It was a reflex she had developed when faced by uncertainty and she had become good at it. With a conscious straightening of shoulders, she slipped the master copy of the *Daerley Green Chronicle* into a plastic folder and headed across the market place to the church hall. Amanda Heyforth was already there, heaving reams of paper from a cupboard to a trestle table. Over three years they had fine-tuned the routine to a wordless procedure as they wheeled the duplicator out from its alcove, fed it with paper, ran a couple of test pages. But Amanda was not a great one for long silences, even those disguised by the rhythmic clank of the duplicator. It was not long before she said: "So what's up then? And don't say 'nothing' because you're looking distinctly broody."

Sara chose her words carefully "Oh Mike just rang. Sounded sort of hyped up."

"For God's sake, he's entitled to sound hyped up isn't he – assuming he's still in that horrendous place? Well, you know what *I* think."

Amanda was deputy head at a local Prep School and, yes, Sara was well aware of her views: *Can't think why we don't just leave them all to kill each other off until they've run out of puff – or people.* Amanda was an 'eye-for-an-eye' person, whether it was Northern Ireland, the Middle East, any one of half a dozen African states, the Balkans - and without too much regard for causes and effects as Mike was keen to point out. With a good friendship at stake, they'd given up arguing about it a while ago. This suited Sara who loathed confrontation of any kind. It wasn't that she held strong views on the international scene, but she certainly did not want Mike's challenged, least of all on the Balkans, which had long been his special patch.

So "Not that sort of hyped-up – I can't really put my finger on it," was all Sara said. Then "Here comes Justin for his caffeine fix. I'll put the kettle on."

It had become a ritual on what they grandly called Press Day for Justin to look in and usually stay, ostensibly to help patting the untidy sheaves of duplicated pages into regimented piles ready for collation. The proceedings were well laced with the latest village gossip and Sara had never felt more grateful for this welcome diversion of the surface of her mind. That afternoon discussions mostly centred on the P.C.'s latest decision.

"Good editorial dear girl," Justin said. "Though in this case I think you're wrong. The P.C. should, must, put people first. Even above feathered and little furry things."

"People yes," Sara said firmly. "It's not people being considered here; it's the unadulterated lure of more dosh. Now if it had been low-cost housing to keep the younger generation from moving out, that would have been something else. But executive houses – I ask you!"

"Executives – business – more work opportunities – more customers for local shops…?" suggested Amanda.

"Rubbish – they'll all commute like mad to Banbury or Oxford. Even London. And clutter up the market place with their cars because they won't be bothered to walk the half-mile to the shops. That's if they're not piling out to the supermarkets."

They wrangled amiably for a while, moved on to the imminent retirement of the vicar and the usual chaotic plans for the annual Christmas fair. It was well into dusk by the time a couple of paper jams had been cleared, the duplicating completed and more trestles set out with pages stacked in the right order, ready for the collating team on Monday morning.

"Time for a jar at The Trumpet?" Justin suggested, as he always did at the end of Press Day. Amanda had already rushed off to catch some esoteric TV analysis of the current art scene.

"Better not tonight, Justin" Sara said. "A few things I need to check in the shop –Polly's been stuck there on her own all day." Also by now she was really beginning to need headspace.

They locked up the hall and he followed her across the

market place, quiet in this early evening period with the commuters' cars gone, the three pubs not yet busy, most Daerlians at home preparing meals, watching the news, doing homework. Though these days it was a market place in name only, Sara loved this small hub of her universe: the jumble of 18th and 19th century houses and shops round it, the triangle of green with the chestnut tree in the middle. The lights were out in the small dress shop and adjoining florist. The estate agents were just locking up, but some one was still glued to a computer screen in DG Publishing which had recently taken over from the greengrocers ("bloody supermarkets", Sara had ranted at the time). The village store was still open and would be for another couple of hours and, straight ahead, she could see Polly's fluffy fair head bent over a book, at the back of *Sara's Collectibles*, her own contribution to the local economy.

"Not a bad place to end your days," Justin said, his thoughts obviously running along a parallel track "Not, of course, that you're anywhere near the end of yours. Though I do worry about you. All these village involvements, the shop, Mike away so much ... Time he came home to look after you. How is he by the way?"

Not the time to voice nameless concerns. "Just heard he'll be home in a week. Can't wait. It's been a particularly long stint, but the poor love doesn't have much choice." She raised a hand in farewell as she pushed open the door into *Sara's* and clicked her attention from Mike-unknown-orphans-the-*Chronicle*-Justin-Parish-affairs to young Polly Cuttle. Who was looking exceedingly pallid, as well she might four months into her first pregnancy and still coping with morning sickness.

Sara felt a twinge of contrition. "Home Polly," she ordered. "Immediately."

"I'm fine, really." Polly pushed the book into her bag and stood up. Despite the baggy fisherman's smock, the baby was definitely apparent now. "You know I love working here with all these nice things." She paused, surveying the imaginative display

10

of locally produced arts and crafts that Sara had made her speciality. "Anyway, all this creative stuff – I reckon it's bound to rub off on junior...."

Yuck. Fond though Sara was of young Polly, this mother-in-bloom stuff was getting a bit much. She pushed her gently towards the door. "Out!" she said firmly.

She closed up after her. Whatever needed doing could damned well wait till the morning. Suddenly Sara felt weary to the marrow – literally as though, with very little encouragement, her bones would simply disintegrate right here in view of the evening patrons beginning to trickle passed the window towards The Trumpet. If she were going to melt into a pile of mush, it might as well be in the privacy of her own living room. After a quick final check, Sara locked up and turned away from the Market Place, down a lane, into an alleyway. It had been Mike's idea to call the house Abel's Yard after the earliest recorded occupant. He'd always had a great sense of order had Mike – perhaps partly due to his own disrupted upbringing. It had offended him that so many changes had completely altered the original 17th century character of the house: walls knocked down to make larger rooms, small leaded windows replaced by modern panes in the days before stricter planning regulations might have obstructed such sacrilege. Sara, appreciative of greater space and more light, didn't share his views, but compromised by conceding to the odd name which, Mike said, would go a little way towards restoring the place's psyche. After all, she'd always been good at compromise, and it didn't do any harm.

The house felt unexpectedly chilly. Or perhaps it was her mood. Sara flicked the central-heating switch on, flung her coat over a chair, got some ice from the fridge, poured herself a stiff malt. She stood for a moment in the middle of the living room and listened. Distant village sounds, immediate quietness. A waiting sort of feeling. Mike had this weird theory that houses could reflect circumstances.

She curled herself into a corner of the sofa and felt the

first sip of malt head straight for the solar plexus, then diffuse into a blessed release of tension. It was followed by a surge of the anxiety that had been lurking in the shadows of her mind all day. In one bound the potential enormity of what she thought Mike had said leapfrogged every intervening scrap of the day's minutiae: " ... *just may be she could come and live with us for a while ...*"

She? Who? What the hell's going on, Mike?

Something about a child in an orphanage and *Winnie the Pooh*. A newsreel began to unwind through Sara's head of refugees, sad, unkempt, weeping, and landscapes spattered with gutted houses: scenes distant and quite unconnected with the quiet ebb and flow of Daerley Green's seasons. Unconnected enough at any rate to allow her the luxury of compassion without involvement. Until now.

Was it a bit of this that Mike wanted to transplant to Daerley Green?

Why?

The effect of the malt was hugely comforting, helped her to think, brought clarity. She noticed the glass was empty, poured another, went off to get more ice from the fridge.

Her mind probed back, reconstructing the conversation. It had been such a lousy line there was frustratingly little to reconstruct. Something about so many tragic stories and feeling desperate. Did all the correspondents in Sarajevo feel the same desperation, have a need to bring home an orphan?

It was then, sipping at her malt, that Sara saw with a new insight close to revelation that the whole shebang was nothing to do with correspondents and Sarajevo, but with the complex psyche of this particular correspondent

For some time now her mind had been tiptoeing round a deepening unease; this morning's phone call and a little alcoholic assistance had merely brought it into sharper focus. So how did you bridge a sense of apartness so subtly insinuating you had barely noticed its coming? It wasn't anyone's fault. Mike was a first class journalist and other people's dramas were his stock in trade. Sara's Collectibles and a growing involvement in Daerley Green's affairs had become hers. Being useful, needed, important in a large-fish-in-small-pond way could be heady stuff she had discovered. In the process she had evolved into one of what Mike teasingly referred to as Daerley's Great and Good.

With a few exceptions, she knew he did not feel at ease with them. This safe, comfortable, attractive corner of middle England must seem a galaxy away from the fear and tragedy that were currently daily features of his life. When he came home she tried, she really did, to bridge that yawning space between the two; equally she tried to suppress a niggling resentment that such efforts appeared to be one-sided. After all, community commitments *were* commitments. They had become as important to her as Mike's were to him. It was hard to imagine life without them.

Perhaps if they'd had children....

Ah, children.

Which brought her to that other even more deeply suppressed source of concern: the remembered flicker of raw envy on Mike's face when he first heard the news of Polly's pregnancy.

"OK for a couple of kids?" he had said long ago.

Of course she'd said it was OK. They were deeply in love and kids were an OK idea. Some time in the future. Say three, five years.

After three years she'd stopped taking the pill. "It's supposed not to be good to get anxious about it," Mike reassured her when she began to mutter on nature's tardiness. She hadn't explained that the anxiety was more on his behalf than hers.

It was around that time he had started getting heavily involved in other people's wars. Occasionally they had talked of checking things out, maybe giving nature a helping hand. Somehow they had never got around to it.

Mike had been in some unpronounceable part of East Europe when she'd had that routine appointment for a cervical smear. Almost in passing she'd mentioned to the doctor that she didn't seem to be very good at conceiving. How long had they been trying? Well, it wasn't so much they had been trying as they hadn't been not-trying. And they'd been married then seven years. They said they'd do some tests.

She hadn't mentioned it to Mike at that stage; not much point when there was nothing to report, and anyway he was up to his eyeballs in collapsing Iron Curtains. In any case she hadn't been that concerned. She still remembered how casually pleased she'd been when the appointment at Gynae came through, thinking how nicely it would fit in after an earlyish morning shop at Sainsbury's; and how great it would be if the medicos could speed the creative process up a bit. Motherhood still wasn't that high on her agenda, but she could probably get used to the idea. And time was getting on.

After a preliminary shuffling of papers the young Registrar looked up and said, "The problem is there seems to have been some damage to your fallopian tubes, Mrs Hennessey."

She had looked at him expectantly, said "So what can be done about that?"

"I'm afraid it's not that simple." He pulled a sheet of paper across and began drawing on it, curves and squiggles merging into each other. "You see... " He pointed with his pencil "the damage is just here, preventing the eggs travelling from the ovaries to the uterus. Under some circumstances we could try microsurgery, but in this case I'm afraid it's not appropriate ..."

At that point Sara had switched off. She had gone on staring at the squiggles and at the Registrar's pencil wavering over it, but the only thought in her head was *so that's that. I'm barren. How on earth am I going to tell Mike? What on earth is the* point *of someone like me?* The thought jangled on and on and on, meaningless, without beginning nor end, until she interrupted

"You're sure there's nothing that can be done?"

He'd said "So sorry Mrs Hennessey," which she had taken to mean "no", and she stood up and walked away.

She had driven home on auto pilot, put away the shopping, stuffed some washing into the machine, cleaned out the fridge and was in the middle of hauling out the vacuum cleaner when she registered what she was doing. She put the cleaner away again, put on a coat and walking shoes and headed for the short cut across the fields that led to Whirling Wood. It was where she always headed when she needed to think: a rare piece of surviving native woodland bordered by a sinuous minor tributary to the Thames.

It was the finality that was so shocking: the abrupt confrontation with a life-altering circumstance over which she had absolutely no control. And not only life-altering for her.

She had no idea how long she walked and did not remember stopping. Then *"Malva sylvestris,"* a voice had said from somewhere above and behind her. "A much prettier name than common mallow I always think. But then the Latin names have a resonance which appeals to me."

Bemused, Sara glanced up at the bulky figure towering above her, and then down at the pink flowers strewn over her lap. What on earth was she doing on her knees in a hedgerow with pink flowers in her lap?

"If you'd prefer me to go away, just say."

She shook her head, remembered now seeing him in the Post Office. Recently moved into Daerley Green. A retired civil servant someone said.

"Apparently the Romans ate it, both as nourishment and as preventative medicine – the whole lot: flowers, leaves, seeds. According to old Pliny a daily dose would keep all ills at bay. Sort of 'apple-a-day' panacea."

Sara got to her feet. "I'm not very good on plants, I'm afraid." She brushed herself down. "I'm Sara Hennessey by the way."

"Yes, I know." She saw now that he had nice twinkly blue eyes and an amazing amount of quite long silvery hair that curled up at the edges. "I've made purchases in your excellent shop – you have an exceptional flair if I may say so. A charming idea to display your wares in the form of an art nouveau drawing room – exceedingly seductive for this oldie anyway."

Sara said "Thanks. That's improved the day a bit."

He smiled. "I'm Justin Wytham-Smith. Recently took over the Old Bakery on the High Street. But I daresay your bush telegraph is as good as mine and you already know that. In fact I'd welcome some ideas for presents for a clutch of great-nieces of whom I seem to have an inordinate number. Perhaps I can persuade you for a drink one evening? With your husband, of course, next time he's back from Bosnia. You see I know quite a lot about you. " It was a very nice smile.

But he didn't know she was barren. Or that perhaps she might not have been if she hadn't had that abortion all those years ago.

JASMINKA – October 1992

Dear Franko – Jovanka has promised to bring this letter to you. I'm very frightened and wish I could see you. It is safe and quiet here, but there is no one to talk to and my head is bursting with bad thoughts. But I also think about the promise we made. That whatever happened we would always help each other. That one day people in Sarajevo will be living together as before. You said we are the future. Do you remember?

But now I can't remember Father's voice in all the noise in my head. And Jovanka says Mother is very sick and I can't go home. Please go and see her and send me a message.

An Englishman came here, a journalist. He came twice, the second time with candles and fruit and chocolate. Then Jovanka asked me if I would like to go to England with him. What would I do there? I only want to stay here and for everything to be normal again. Tell me how you are. – Love and kisses, Jasi.

Dear Jasi – You must be brave little cousin. Auntie Branka is very sick but the one thing that helps her is knowing you are safe. If this journalist can find a way it would be good for you to go to England for a while. It's getting worse every day here in the city. But I have made some contacts and can sometimes get some of the foreign food; also wood they are bringing down at night from the forests. I'll make sure Auntie Branka has some.

Yes, I remember what I said. And we *are* the future, but just now, Jasi dear, we have to live in the present. There is no more time to be children. Go to England with this journalist. You can tell them how it is. And later we will make Sarajevo a good place again, I promise you. – Love and kisses, Franko

MIKE – *February 1993*

It was February. A month earlier a convention banning chemical weapons had been signed by 120 nations including the United States and Russia. In New York, the United Nations had voted to set up an international tribunal to try war crimes in the former Yugoslavia. And in Daerley Green, the snowdrops were making whiter-than-white splashes under the old oak tree at the bottom of the garden.

Mike paused to examine them on his pre-breakfast tour of the estate as he called his ritual wander round their modest and distinctly under-nurtured plot. Sara was no gardener. He might have been, given more time at home. It was Mike who had planted the snowdrops and watched them multiply and in the process discovered that getting earth under his fingernails was extraordinarily satisfying. It also gave him a sense of contact with the past: with Abel whose yard was now Mike's garden and in which from time to time he came across some discarded or partly worked piece of his predecessor's stone masonry. The daily tour was one of the things he missed most when he was away: a time also when he ordered his thoughts for the day.

They needed ordering. What had seemed the right – indeed the only decision a few weeks ago in war-ravaged Sarajevo looked a bit different in the thin February sun of Daerley Green. Of course he had known it would, but knowing and feeling were two different things. Jasminka had been with them now for four weeks. She certainly looked a different girl, with a new shine to her hair and a glow to her skin. But how she felt. It was impossible to get behind that closed expression.

"Breakfast!" Sara called from the kitchen window.

He waved in acknowledgement. He was aware of a distance between them and unsure of how to deal with it. On his return last October they had, of course, discussed Jasminka's situation at length. Indeed, ad nauseam. He'd already acknowledged to himself that perhaps his first instincts to help

18

the child were based on too much heart and too little head. Not so Sara. She had produced a barrage of unanswerable questions: was it in the girl's best interests; might not the mother bitterly regret decisions made under such stress; what about the rest of her extended family; and how would she cope with the language and the loneliness?

In the end events had left no time for measured decisions. Jovanka had accompanied him on his first and only meeting with Jasminka's mother in that bleak tenth floor flat overlooking what had come to be known as Sniper Alley. The woman had some chest infection, could hardly breathe, and there were no drugs. And she looked terrible. He had brought with him some typed lines for her to sign, giving her agreement that he could take Jasminka with him should the opportunity arise. Jovanka had propped her up while she signed, and then added her own name as witness. "I thank God for this," Jasminka's mother had whispered in English.

Then, between one hour and the next, he had been told of a place available on a safe Red Cross convoy – or as safe as anything could be deemed in the then-and-there of Sarajevo. If he had not brought her out then there was no knowing when the next opportunity might arise. He had brought her out. He would never forget the journey to the coast with its rough roads and deviations through magnificent, stricken, snow-bound countryside of towering mountain ranges and deep gorges and burned out farms and villages and checkpoints with trigger-happy and rarely very sober soldiers of whatever ethnic group. Beside him, the child Jasminka, silent and expressionless, stared out of the window. When he rang from Split airport to announce their imminent arrival, Sara had said little. Indeed, what was there to say once the choice had been removed from her?

He took off his shoes in the back lobby and padded through to join her at the breakfast bar.

"She's in the shower as ever," Sara said brightly. "I reckon she must be the cleanest kid in middle England."

The cleanest and the most silent. Jasminka had discovered the shower on the first evening and disappeared into it for an hour. Water had been at a premium in Sarajevo. Many had died in their efforts to collect it from the improvised standpipes. A constant supply of clean, hot water was unimaginable. Afterwards Sara noticed that Jasminka had experimented with some of the flasks, tubes, phials of hair conditioners, body lotions, shower gels. She told Mike it seemed an encouragingly normal thing for a just-teenager in a strange house to have done.

Perhaps it was as encouragingly normal for her to be slumped for hours at a time in front of the box. At first Sara had agonised over shielding the girl from the regular scenes of her ever more devastated homeland that featured on most news bulletins, but her expression never flickered. And at least one anticipated problem did not materialise. Jasminka's mother Branka, had taught English in one of Sarajevo's schools, and had drummed a solid foundation of English grammar into her daughter. On top of this her hours of television gazing – Mike sometimes doubted that she was doing anything so active as watching - built up a considerable vocabulary. Not that she made much use of it, but at least it was clear she understood everything they said.

Now, over breakfast, Sara suddenly stopped being bright and asked "Have you thought of how we're going to handle this in a few weeks', months' time? She can't simply be left to her own devices. You're due back at work in a couple of weeks; Polly's baby is getting imminent and I can't leave her in charge of the shop much longer. And then there's the *Chronicle*." She ran a hand through her hair. "I'm feeling a bit desperate Mike."

"We have to give her time, love."

"That's all very well, but you won't be here and have to cope for much longer."

Mike was aware of guilt and irritation in about equal measure. She was right, of course – the reality of Jasminka here in Daerley Green was very different from the theory, and Sara was the one in the end lumbered with dealing with it on a daily basis. But *was* it such a lot to ask?

"You've always said what a community-minded place Daerley is. Surely amongst your gaggle of friends you can find some helping hands with the shop? And what about Amanda, couldn't she share a bit more of the *Chronicle* load?"

"Amanda has a full time job. People have their own commitments."

"We have to give the poor kid time," Mike said again. "We can't begin to imagine what it's like to see your whole world disintegrate as her's has." And so the questions were left hanging unresolved.

There was no doubt they had done everything – Sara as much as he – to try and make Jasminka feel at home. With some weeks of leave, Mike had made it his business to take her around. They had 'done' Oxford several times, driven hours through the rolling wintry Cotswold countryside, walked the twisty streets of countless honey-coloured villages, probed into low-ceilinged pubs and high vaulted churches.

His attempts to draw her out were met by polite, terse responses. Usually he ended up taking refuge in tapes or the car radio, and felt Jasminka likewise relax beside him.

"Did you enjoy your day?" Sara would ask on each return.

"Was very nice," was the usual response.

A few days after the unresolved breakfast discussion, Polly rang from the shop. "In case you've lost Jaz, she's here."

Sara was out shopping in Banbury "Who? Oh, I'll come and get her," Mike said.

"She doesn't need 'getting'," Polly sounded surprised. "We're having a nice chat. Just thought you should know where she was."

So, through Polly, they had begun to know a little more about Jasminka who, with her new name, seemed also to acquire a more accessible personality. Or at least a personality that was accessible to Polly.

"Poor kid's just been overwhelmed. I guess she feels comfortable with me," Polly said, then laughed. "After all you can't really feel intimidated by someone who looks like a beached whale!" She was now eight months pregnant and enormous. "Jaz said her newest cousin was born in the middle of a mortar attack. Can you imagine?"

Mike had never regarded himself in the least intimidating, but then he wasn't a thirteen-year-old refugee. And Polly was always so patently herself, never assuming emotions she didn't feel, just genuinely interested in a world that had been a closed book to her before the advent of Jasminka. It was from Polly they also learned about Franko.

"Her cousin. I gather he's four years older, and she obviously has a massive crush on him. This Franko is from her father's side of the family, so he's a Moslem; and apparently that makes life very complicated because Jaz's Mum is Serbian Orthodox or something. Beats me why it matters, but there you go. Anyway, Franko and Jaz made a sort of pact that they would never let it come between them, and when all the fighting is over they're going to join up with other people who feel the same, and bring the communities together again." Polly was frowning at the effort of trying to unravel such an incomprehensible set of circumstances. "If everyone thought that way I guess the world would be better for it."

Polly wasn't the only one discovering new insights into their silent guest. Amanda came round the following Sunday morning. "Looked in at the shop yesterday," she said, without preamble. "Met your Bosnian child. Very bright I thought, if rather scowly. So what are you going to do about her?"

"Do about her," Sara repeated blankly.

"Do about her education," Amanda said impatiently. "You can't have brought her all this way to leave her sitting around your shop indefinitely."

It was typical of Amanda's bossiness, but Mike had to

admit she had a point. He said "The overriding priority at the time was getting her to safety. The long term didn't come into it I'm afraid."

"Well you're hardly likely to send her back to a war zone, are you?" Amanda looked from one to the other. "So I suggest she comes with me to Brendon Hall – attends the classes when appropriate, and I'll settle her in the library with suitable things to do at other times." A pause. "I've cleared it with the school of course." Of course.

Mike looked across at Sara. It made a lot of sense. It would also reduce Sara's day-to-day involvement. "That's a generous offer, Amanda."

Sara said doubtfully, "Do you think she's ready to cope with a lot of other kids?"

"My judgement is young Jasminka is more resilient than you give her credit for."

"I think Amanda's right," Mike said.

"OK," Sara said. "Let's see what she has to say about it."

Amanda's eyebrows rose. "I don't think this is a decision for the child to make, do you?"

"I'll say one thing for Bossy-boots," Mike said when she had gone. "She has absolutely no doubts about her own judgement. But in this case I think she's right. Could be we've been swamping the poor girl with too many choices?"

"Or is it simply that it will be so much more convenient to have her out of our hair during the week? Or I should say out of my hair, since you won't be around much longer. Am I really doing what's best for Jasminka or what makes life much easier for me?"

"I think that *is* what's best for Jasminka." Mike felt a sharp twinge of impatience. "Which includes being with other kids and having her mind usefully occupied. It'll also provide what I thought you wanted - to be let off the hook."

He heard the sharpness in his own voice and regretted it; but living with Sara had its difficult times. The diffidence that had seemed so refreshing in their early days together began to lose some of its charm with its constant need for reassurance. The self-confidence gained by her involvement in Daerley Green affairs had frankly come as something of a relief. Even worth being dragged from time to time into a social scene that was fundamentally alien to him.

As indeed Jasminka's arrival must have been to Sara.

That night in bed he put his arms round her and apologised, after which they made particularly good love. Then they talked more than for a long time about the difficulties of maintaining a normal relationship with so many interruptions and disparate experiences, some too deep and complex to share.

"We always knew it would be difficult," Sara said. "But knowing isn't the same as feeling, is it? And now a bit of that world – your other world - has sort of catapulted into mine, without all the preliminary baggage that goes to create the right mindset."

"But you're brilliant with her."

"Come on Mike. She can talk to Polly easier than to me."

"Or me. The talking can come later. First she needs the stability, the space and time to find her own level."

"You're right," Sara said. "Somehow we'll make it all right for her." And then "Since we can't have one of our own we might as well do our best for someone else's."

"*...can't have one of our own....*"

So that's what all this was about.

Lying there long after Sara had gone to sleep, her breathing soft and relaxed against his shoulder, Mike remembered another time three, four years ago when he had returned from East Europe to find her in a state of near-hysteria. At last she made him understand that she'd had some tests and they wouldn't be able to have a child. Not ever. And then, from amongst the harrowing sobs, he'd finally understood she took full responsibility for this.

Sara had always understood – or said she did – his

profound wish to be able to give his own son or daughter, preferably both, the sort of ordered childhood he'd not had. It was no doubt deeply Freudian of him, but there it was. Sara's inability to have a child was a devastating shock, but at that point he would have said, done, anything to alleviate her terrible distress. They'd talked it through endlessly and he thought she'd at last accepted the reality that it was just something that happened to some people. It was not the end of the world. They had a huge amount going, not least each other. And may be one day they might look into adoption. The discussion had gone on for days. And nights.

They'd returned to the idea of adoption from time to time, but the moment never seemed right. Neither of them had broached the subject for a long while and, and with the shop and the *Chronicle* and all their ramifications, Mike had honestly thought Sara had settled for what she had. Until he had presented her with the *fait accompli* of a child with nowhere else to go.

Now there were echoes of that long ago first meeting when Sara had not impressed him at all.

"Meet Sara Matthews," his friend Plum Pleydell had said at some point in the late seventies. Their friendship had survived school and college and now, at the grand old age of 22, they were spending a weekend with Plum's colourful stepsister Jane in London. She ran a small art gallery, was a single Mum with two children. Sara was living in as an 'au pair'. The kids were a couple of little horrors, Mike recalled, but Sara seemed to manage them.

At the time it seemed the only positive thing about her. That and her amazing green eyes which brought a quiver of memory of a young woman called Marija he'd fallen for a few months earlier in Sarajevo. Otherwise he merely registered a self-preoccupied girl with a sulky mouth who spoke in monosyllables.

"Where on earth did Jane dredge her up?" he'd asked

Plum.

"Oh, their mothers were friends I gather and Jane is doing her's a favour. Farming family out in the north Oxfordshire sticks – not that far from where we had our own heady school days come to think of it. Seems Sara went a bit wild for a while, and a nannying stint at Jane's was prescribed as a cure...."

"Good Lord," Mike said, then forgot about Sara altogether.

Until three years later. It was soon after he had moved across from the Banbury paper to local radio. He was also on a health kick: 5 K, pre-breakfast. It was March, the daffodils at their best. He'd just done the stretch through Spiceball Park and was swinging out of it to join the canal towpath when he almost collided into a figure jogging across his route, nearly knocking it into the canal. They had both landed in a heap on the muddy bank.

"Sorry," he said when he had caught his breath, and began untangling himself. Then he saw it was a young woman with amazing green eyes.

"I know you," he said.

"I don't think so."

"Oh but I do; I couldn't forget those eyes." He grinned. "Sorry that's pure schmaltz. But I know now where it was: in London. You were looking after Jane Pleydell's kids I was visiting with her brother."

He noticed a shadow of wariness. "Sorry I don't remember." She got to her feet.

And suddenly he hadn't wanted her to go. "Look, we're both plastered in mud. How about we get a shower at the sports centre and I buy you breakfast in their cafeteria. It's what I normally do anyway." As she hesitated he said "Please. It's the least I can do after nearly knocking you into the canal."

Twenty minutes later she'd joined him in the cafeteria, long shiny hair falling on to the shoulders of an immaculate russet tracksuit and looking fantastic. At that moment Mike decided he was going to see her again, whatever it took.

Brendon Hall began to make its mark on Jasminka quite soon. Returning from her first day, she announced unprompted "It is like big country house, not like school." Mike started to point out that it was not a state school, but a public school, and then tied himself up in knots trying to explain the meaning in this instance of 'public'.

"It's OK," Jasminka said. "Mrs Heyforth tell me about that." Yes, she had found it interesting. It was very strange that there were only girls in the school. "This is not like in my country." They began to learn that quite a lot of things were not "like in my country". But she was talking.

According to Amanda, Jasminka was attentive but silent in class. She soon proved to be happiest in the library where she read voraciously.

Dropping her home at the end of the second week Amanda announced cheerfully "Jasminka is angry with us."

"There are no books about my country in the library," Jasminka said. "Not one." Amanda's explanation that the Balkans did not feature high on the Prep school curriculum made little impression. And then Mike remembered a book he had picked up in a long-ago closing down sale: a book that helped trigger his own interest in the heroic and bloody times of the clash between Christian and Turk in the medieval Balkans.

That evening he presented Jasminka with a small battered copy of *The Ballads of Marko Kraljević*. Her face lit up, as if a light had been switched on behind her dark eyes. It brought a snapshot memory of a girl called Marija, laughing as he tried to pronounce the name of Sarajevo's bazaar district. *"Baščaršija,* pronounced bashcharshiya," she had insisted. "You can say it. Go on, try." That same Slav quality of stillness made vibrant by a smile.

Then, during the weekend before Mike was due to return to his office, Jasminka disappeared.

JASMINKA – *February 1993*

I'm going to keep a diary for you Franko, so that I can remember all the things to tell you when I come home. And Mother, of course. It's awful not having news from you.

To begin with everything was so terrible I didn't think there would ever be anything I wanted to remember. For a start, it was so *quiet* and organised, and I couldn't get used to not being frightened. People kept asking me how I was and what I wanted, and all I wanted was to be home with everything as it used to be. Then when I tried to remember how things used to be, I couldn't remember that either: only waiting for the next shelling to start, and running from one place to another. And Mother being so ill. And Father holding my hand as he fell down, looking so surprised. Only now I can't even remember his voice.

Mike and Sara are very kind but I can't tell them things. Not how I feel. I can't explain to you how different it is here. Do you remember that film E.T.? It's a bit like that, landing on another planet. Of course Mike has been in Sarajevo, so perhaps that's like another planet to him. But most people talk about 'former Yugoslavia' as if it was a place that doesn't exist any more. Some don't even know where Bosnia is – can you imagine?

This is a nice house – old, a bit like Gran's cottage but bigger. I have a room to myself with a slopey ceiling, and my own television. That was amazing. To begin with I spent ages watching it. A lot of the time it was just looking at changing pictures, but I suppose my English got better and sometimes there were quite interesting things. They have a lot of nature films here, and quiz programmes. Then Mike said it was bad to stay in the house all the time and started taking me to different places. We've been to Oxford, which has a famous university – much, much bigger than Sarajevo's. There are lots of old buildings called colleges where the students live. They have beautiful gardens, and some of them are by the river Thames. I was surprised to find it was the same river as in London, only in Oxford they call it the Isis. I don't know why. We saw a lot of students, many of them from other countries. It would be wonderful to come here and study, especially if you were here too. We went into some old churches. I found these rather cold. I think our Orthodox ones are more homely, with people coming in and out all the time, lighting candles and saying a prayer. Well, you wouldn't know about that. I was trying to remember how it was in the mosques for you, but then I couldn't remember you ever going to the mosque. Mike has taken me for long drives too. The countryside is very pretty, but not like our wild mountains. And everything is so tidy: all the animals in fields so they don't need anyone to look after them. No chickens or geese running about the villages either. Not even dogs. But I did see a dead fox.

One day Sara asked me to go shopping with her. We went to a big supermarket in Banbury. While she looked for things I pushed this trolley between shelves stacked with food – as much food as you could possibly imagine or dream of – enough you would think to feed the world. And suddenly I remembered how it is for Mother and all of you, waiting for hours for a few leaves of spinach or a jar of pickled gherkins. I couldn't bear it.

Next time Sara went shopping I made sure I wasn't in the house. I went to visit the shop that Sara has in the middle of the village – it sells hand-made things and stuff. If Gran lived here she could make a fortune with her embroidery. Sara has someone called Polly working for her in the shop; I was really surprised to find she was quite young and absolutely enormous because she's having a baby soon. It was weird how I could talk to her as if I'd known her all my life. She didn't seem to know anything about Bosnia and looked horrified when I told her how baby Branka was born in the middle of the shelling, but she was interested and asked a lot of questions. There were quite a few I couldn't answer, especially about why Serbs and Bosniaks and Croats had been living together all that time and were now fighting. But I told her about how you and I and our friends were going to put things right when the fighting is over.

Then a couple of weeks ago, I started school! Sara's friend Mrs Heyforth, who's my teacher, is a bit like Aunt Jovanka at the children's home, always seems to know what's right for everyone. And actually it's OK. It's more like a big country house than a school. Mrs Heyforth explained that it's a public school not a State school. Apparently 'public' means 'private' in England. Don't ask me why. Anyway I'm one of the oldest and spend a lot of the time in the library doing exercises Mrs Heyforth has given me on history and geography. But it's all different here. Do you know there isn't one book on Yugoslavia in the school library!

Another amazing thing is that people here often don't know really simple things. Polly was saying how awful it must be for us having to eat wild plants instead of proper vegetables during the siege and when I explained that even before the war Mother often made soups from wild plants and they were really good, I could see she didn't believe me. So I thought I'd try and make some. I took this book about wild flowers from the school library and went for a walk in the fields to find some sorrel because I knew that makes a great soup. Only identifying plants from pictures in a book wasn't as easy as I thought it would be.

I was sitting by a hedge with a heap of plants all round me trying to work out what they were, when this old man came up behind me. He was very tall and big, with lots of silvery hair. And the great thing was he knew all about plants. He seemed to know who I was and when I told him what I was trying to do, he really understood. But the most amazing thing is that when he was my age, his father was a diplomat in Montenegro; Justin – this old man – remembers going there for his holidays, walking in the Durmitor Mountains where his father was collecting plants. And it got Justin interested in them too. So he was able to find lots of sorrel for me without any problem. He even had a big plastic bag to put it all in - I'd forgotten to bring anything. Then he came home with me, which was just as well as Sara was pretty cross because I'd gone out without telling her. But Justin is a friend of hers, and that made it all right.

What a lot I've written. I'm going to sleep now.

SARA – May 1994

Following the February cease-fire, the Serbs had begun to withdraw their heavy artillery encircling Sarajevo. The tenuous peace brought a flourish of cultural activity, especially in music and art. Foreign reporters spoke of the amazing survival of the Obala Gallery in which Bosnia's leading artists exhibited their work created from salvaged debris – soot, charred wood, broken glass, shattered stone. "What is the good of living if our brains are dead?" asked the Gallery's director Miro Purivatra.

In Daerley Green, Mike's magnificent display of late tulips was over. He had planted them in scarlet clumps in their minuscule front garden, creating around them a carpet of deep purple aubretia. The combination had been one of the sights of Daerley Green.

Now he was back in Sarajevo. They had decided against telling Jasminka of this latest assignment, knowing it would only raise wild hopes and fears. After months of abortive attempts to get news, they had finally received a message from Jovanka at the Children's Home. No, she had had no contact with Jasminka's mother for a very long time. She had made several visits to her flat and on the last occasion had coincided on the stairs – for of course the lifts had long since stopped working – with one of Branka's neighbours. He was one of the influxes of refugees who had moved in from the countryside and taken over the many abandoned flats in the increasingly devastated outskirts of the city, so he was not able to help much. Except to confirm that Branka's flat had received a direct hit from a Serb mortar and been gutted. No, he didn't know whether she had been in it at the time, though he thought he'd seen her heading for the market a few days later.

Jovanka had then called on Branka's Bosniak in-laws who said they knew no more than she did. This could mean anything or nothing. They had been tight-lipped, unsure whether they were more relieved that Jasminka had been sent to safety or angry that their Ismet's child was beyond their reach. The rift between Bosnian Serb and Bosniak deepened daily with escalating deaths, fear, exhaustion, deprivation of all the norms of life. Branka might have sought refuge with friends, even found her way to her parents in the countryside; she might have been killed at any moment crossing one of the many street intersections that were in a direct line of fire from the artillery in the encircling hills, or while queuing for food or to collect water. Jovanka had done the rounds of the hospitals and makeshift clinics. Nothing. The only blessing was to know that Jasminka was safe.

This report had been drastically censored for Jasminka. "We've heard from Jovanka at last," Mike told her casually. "She thinks your mother has gone to stay with some of your relatives in the countryside."

In the past fifteen months Jasminka had changed beyond recognition, at least in most aspects of her outward appearance. In her school uniform – navy skirt and jacket, white blouse – she looked the archetypal English school girl, providing you didn't look too closely at her features. She had grown a couple of inches, her skinny figure now rounded and firmed up by a proper diet, regular exercise and puberty. Her curtains of hair had been cut and shaped into a gamine style, and she had got rid of her hunched look. Some of these improvements were due to a friendship forged the previous September when she transferred to the Comprehensive in Banbury. It was, as far as Sara knew, the only close friendship with a girl of her own age: an Iranian child called Azita. Jasminka referred to her as Azzie and was in turn referred to by her new friend as Minkie. How curious it was, Sara mused, that the young's first contribution to their own identity was to distort their own names.

Azzie had come to live with an English auntie a few years ago, as the Iran-Iraq war ended and the Gulf War was about to begin. It didn't take a degree in psychology to appreciate how the two girls, washed up like human flotsam on a tide of inhumanity, found a mutual empathy. Azzie had the slender build, small bones and grace characteristic of her race. Sara was grateful that Jasminka had chosen, however unconsciously, to use her new friend as a model rather than mimic the average untidy slouch of her English peers.

Both girls adored Polly and chubby, cheerful Billy, now fourteen months. When Azzie came to stay they'd announce at breakfast they were off to see Billie and disappear for hours.

"So what did you all get up to?" Sara would ask on their return.

"Nothing much," was Jasminka's usual noncommittal reply. It was always Azzie who enlarged on this characteristically terse response with titbits about small tasks accomplished in Polly's garden, or their walk down to the waste ground where plans for the executive housing had been thwarted by groundwater and potential subsidence problems, and there was now a major rethink.

There had been times in recent months when Sara had felt quite sharp flashes of resentment at such a permanent and uncommunicative presence in the house. However hard she tried she never felt totally at ease with the girl, as though she, Sara, were herself on trial. This was especially true in her more tired moments and when she saw the developing empathy between Jasminka … Minkie … and Mike on his irregular visits home. She was a different child when he was around; unarguably 'Mike's girl'.

"It's not that I want her to be grateful," Sara had exploded in exasperation to Amanda on one occasion. "Just an acknowledgement that I'm more than a board-and-lodging machine."

"We all need to be needed," was Amanda's response, shrewd and to the point as always. Now Amanda had departed on a sabbatical to the States. Sara missed her.

Jasminka's other favourite remained Justin.

"She's so relaxed with Polly and with you," Sara told him. "What am I doing wrong?"

They were heading for the Trumpet, another *Daerley Green Chronicle* safely bedded. "Absolutely nothing, dear girl," Justin said. "It's quite simple – she assumes that she found me rather than the other way round. While she's no doubt aware, though perhaps not in those terms, that you were lumbered with her, as it were." After a moment he added "And I don't suppose it's too deeply Freudian to assume that any demonstration of feelings towards you might be construed as disloyalty to her mother. Construed by Jasminka herself, I mean."

Sara nodded, remembering that day when she had reached a crescendo of anxiety following Jasminka's disappearance and the relief when Justin delivered her home, complete with a large plastic bag full of limp weeds.

"Jasminka wants to make you some of her mother's sorrel soup and rather forgot the time," Justin had said, adding under his breath "She thinks she's going to get a bollocking, so surprise her."

Jasminka's enthusiasm for soup making had fortunately waned rather quickly, but not her attachment to Justin.

"And I'm afraid," Justin mused now, once they were settled on their favourite window seat, respectively confronting a half lager and a large malt, "you may have to accept that she'll never really understand what you've done, are doing for her. She's a different child; indeed before long will be a rather attractive young lady."

"Her friend Azzie is more responsible for that than me."

Justin took a sip of his malt and peered at her over the rim of the glass. "This self-deprecation is becoming a bad habit, Sara. And a mite tedious."

"Sorry. Mike's been away a lot recently, and I suppose there's too much chewing things over in my own head. At the moment he's back in Sarajevo and it's quite hard work not letting it slip to Jasminka. As you know we've had no luck at all contacting her mother and I can't help assuming the worst. I mean, surely the woman would have tried to get in touch.

Through the Red Cross or something? Anyway Jasminka hasn't talked about home for a while, and I don't want to raise false hopes."

"Hmm, it could be ... " Justin began, then stopped.

"Could be what?"

"This is rather difficult, Sara. Betraying a confidence, you know ... "

"You're worrying me. Get on with it, Justin."

"Very well. About three months back Minkie had a bit of trouble with a few of the older children at school. You know how wretched youngsters can be to each other, especially if they find an easy victim. It was when that mortar bomb was lobbed into the middle of the busy market in Sarajevo: all those people killed, awful scenes of carnage on television. A small group of the older children started hurling obscenities at Minkie, led by one boy whose grandfather apparently was a Croat. He said all Serbs ought to be strung up, or words to that effect. Of course the children know nothing – don't stop to think or even realise that many of the victims were themselves Serbs; and would certainly be unaware of Minkie's personal loss. Fortunately one of the teachers heard it all and gave them a pep talk. But of course it upset the child."

"And she couldn't tell me?"

"She was terrified you would take it up with the school." Justin put a hand over hers. "And you would, wouldn't you?" Sara nodded reluctantly. "Added to which Minkie is well aware by now that I'm a history freak, and seemed to think I might be able to throw light on the whole mystery of what is happening in her country. If only I could! But I can perhaps provide a modicum of perspective."

Sara lent forward and gave him a peck on the cheek. "And all because you were born on Armistice Day 1918." It had been almost the first thing Justin had told her after that meeting in the fields on the way to Whirling Wood. "It means," he'd said quite seriously "that I have a compulsive, even pathological sense of history which can be exceedingly boring for my friends: a truly tiresome awareness that there is no straightforward reason for anything; that all things are inextricably linked in chains and cross-chains of cause and effect. This is a dreadful burden for any honest politician, and not much less for a civil servant." She knew he had become something quite high up in the Board of Trade before he retired: about as high as you can go without compromising your principles he had told her once after a few shots of malt. For a while she wished her own sense of history had been rather better developed. Mike had often teased her saying she was an irredeemably here-and-now person, and tried for a while to instil into her some of his own enthusiasm for the past. Not with much success.

Now Justin said, "It helped of course that I was there as a small boy, in that post-Habsburg limbo before even there was a Yugoslavia. In those days it went under the name of the Kingdom of the Serbs, Croats and Slovenes – not exactly conducive to a good sound-bite." Justin made a wry face. "They were killing each other then of course, but in Minkie's eye I'm at least able to be a little more even handed in meting out blame."

"Which lies …?"

"In a word or two, outside interference is probably as big a culprit as any: interference, that is, by the great powers protecting their interests over the best part of a millennium. Which, of course, is precious little consolation to the likes of Minkie's family." Justin paused. "And perhaps that also gives you a little perspective too on what *you* are offering Minkie herself."

Sara ran a finger round the rim of her glass. "I suppose I've let things get out of proportion lately. You know how it is when everyone else's life seems immensely purposeful – Mike out there putting the world to rights, and even when he's back in the UK he's spending more and more time in London. His bosom chum from school days, Plum – he's got himself a fancy penthouse in Dockland, and Mike uses it as his own. Of course

I'm pleased for him in a way – not least because it saves a lot of late night drives. But we'll soon be needing to make appointments to meet. Then there's Polly, waist deep in Pampers and baby talk, and Amanda ... Oh you probably don't know Amanda took off for the States last month. A sabbatical to study behavioural adjustments in teenagers to the impending Third Millennium, or some such rubbish."

"... while Sara runs her shop, local magazine, home, foster child, not to mention several other irons in the community fire?" Justin finished for her. "It seems to me that what is missing from that list is an element of fun. Which reminds me – though it probably doesn't quite fit under the heading of riotous living – you will be getting an invitation through your door very soon for a little soirée I'm arranging. It's to meet a newcomer to the village. Name of Beresford. He's just moved into the Old Schoolhouse –something to do with running a new golf course just over the Warwickshire border."

Sara smiled. Everyone else had 'a few people in for drinks-and-nibbles' or 'just an informal gathering'. Only Justin had soirées. She gave him a hug. "You're wonderful," she said.

"Dear girl," Justin murmured, looking surprised.

Mike telephoned the evening of Justin's soirée while she was getting ready. The line was quite good and he sounded unusually upbeat. However, Jasminka's mother seemed to have vanished without trace, though there was no record of her death. The children's home where Mike had first met Jasminka had closed down and Jovanka was now living in Belgrade, so this main line of contact was broken. Another problem was that in the case of many mixed marriages such as Branka's, the couples had split and returned to their original ethnic group so that the community as a whole was totally fragmented. He had a couple of leads, but wasn't hopeful. Still, the ceasefire seemed to be holding, and a semblance of normal living returning though the increasing international presence and foreign aid had fuelled a rampant blackmarket and sent prices rocketing. On the other hand, it was truly inspirational to see how the cultural life of this amazing place survived – a flicker kept alive in underground cellars, now fanned into a flame – concerts, art exhibitions, shows. Mike paused. "I *am* rattling on. How are you? And Minkie?"

A soirée to meet a newcomer seemed small beer after that. "We're fine," Sara said.

She had brought the cordless telephone into the bedroom, out of Minkie's hearing. Ending the call, her glance caught her own reflection in the dressing table mirror. She noted that it looked ungroomed. She thought it was probably a long time since she had paused to notice her appearance.

"Right," she said firmly.

It was also a long time since she had been to an event that was purely social, unconnected with the *Chronicle*, the shop or fund-raising for one of innumerable good causes. She dressed carefully: an emerald green trouser suit with a waft of bronze chiffon at the neck, short high-heel boots. Casually elegant. Well, Justin would appreciate it even if no one else did.

"Wow - you look really cool," Minkie said looking up from a magazine. She was lying on her bed as Sara went passed the open door.

Sara noticed the slight lilt of surprise. "Thank you Minkie. Shan't be long – back around nine I imagine."

It was only a few hundred yards to Justin's: three cottages knocked into one by his predecessors and rendered long ago unrecognisable to their original farm labouring tenants. She was late and the buzz of voices had already reach the pitch of party-in-full-swing.

"Come in, Sara, come in. Good gracious, you look quite magnificent. Enough to make me wish I could lose three or four decades ..." Justin beamed at her, took her elbow guiding her into the room she loved with its oak table and Jacobean settee, its collector's items from a life time of travel, its walls lined with books.

A group of people was gathered round a tall man who had his back to her. "Beresford, let me introduce you to one of Daerley Green's most sparkling leading lights."

He turned. Sara looked into a face, nearly twenty years more mature than when she last looked into it, but still totally recognisable.

"Sara ...dear God."

"Brett." She stared at him aghast. Never in her worst nightmares had she thought she would see him again: the man who would have been the father of her child.

Brett Tremayne. He'd managed to keep the 'Beresford' well and truly under wraps, presumably because it hardly matched the image of the youth who entranced the whole of the female element of Form VI. Almost the whole. A few of them found him, or pretended to find, him a bit of a pain. No real person should be quite so outrageously good looking, have such wealthy parents, live in such a fab house in the rolling farmlands of south Warwickshire, as well as being the school's best runner and swimmer, *and* no mean drummer for a small group that did the rounds of local gigs.

As far as Sara was concerned he was way out of her league.

Then came the day of A-level results. She had been pretty pleased with hers – an A in art history, Bs in Sociology and English – and was crossing People's Park on the way to join her classmates in celebration or commiseration when she saw a familiar figure on a park bench. A familiar figure in unfamiliar pose – Brett Tremayne slumped in despondency. Her first instinct was to enjoy a bit of a gloat, the second and more instinctive to play ministering angel She dropped on to the bench beside him. "Come on Brett, they can't have been *that* bad."

"What?" Blue eyes met her . "Oh hi." He ran his fingers through his thick blonde mop of hair. "No the results were OK. It's the parents ..."

It came tumbling out in uncharacteristic confusion from which Sara finally gathered that Brett's parents lived in a permanent state of war with each other. Living at home was hell with incessant arguments about his future. His father was determined Brett should follow him into some obscure and exceedingly unattractive-sounding branch of international finance. The prospect was dire and he couldn't wait to get away, but since he didn't have a bean of his own he didn't have any choice.

Trapped in a gilded cage, Sara thought. *Who would have imagined?,* - and found herself giving him a comforting hug.

They had drifted into dating, become briefly an item. He was amazingly dishy and Sara enjoyed the envious looks cast her way. She also became more than a little smitten. When he stopped bemoaning his lot, which was most of the time, he was great company, had a car and a generous allowance. And anyway the exams were over and she'd earned some fun. In a few weeks she would be heading for London to get work experience in an art gallery run by a friend of her mother's.

It was towards the end of summer Brett suggested a valedictory lunch in a special pub he knew to mark the impending parting of their ways– she to London, he to a business colleague of his father's in Frankfurt. They'd got quite maudlin and nostalgic. Sara had never been a great drinker, but he had teased her into a gin, after which another one seemed a good idea and a third even better.

They had ended up having sex in the back of the car. Sara's memory was hazy, only that he seemed to know exactly what he was doing: that pleasure had rather rapidly turned to desire and then urgent, imperative demand, and by the time she'd panicked, he was thrusting into her and she wasn't enjoying it one little bit. As they readjusted their clothing, she was too appalled and embarrassed to say anything; only desperate to get home and into a bath.

"That was fantastic," Brett had said when he dropped her

home. "Didn't dream you'd be such hot stuff." It was obviously intended as a compliment, but she could hardly bear him to kiss her and was terrified of bursting into tears of shame. "I'll keep in touch." Thankfully, he hadn't.

And now, nearly twenty years later, Justin looked from one to the other and said "Am I about to hear something about small worlds?"

"More likely about the attraction of one's roots," Beresford said, his eyes still on Sara. "And what stunning surprises that can bring."

"Well, be aware ...." began Justin as the doorbell rang.

The first impact of shock was passing. Sara said with elaborate casualness "The 'Beresford' bit remained a well-kept secret."

He made a face. "Yes, well it didn't seem the greatest name for a teenager with ambitions to shine. But things move on, don't they? Beresford carries an aura of reliability, good connections, vision for the future, don't you think?" He had his head on one side. The blonde mop, still thick, had darkened, no doubt with some artificial assistance; and he'd put on a bit of weight. But the charm was still there. "So what was old Justin about to make me aware of?"

"Probably that I'm happily married," Sara said evenly.

"Ah well, you would be, wouldn't you? You always were the level-headed one, I remember. And is he another pillar of society?"

"Mike's a journalist, a foreign correspondent. A good one."

"And away foreign corresponding at the moment, since he's not with you?"

Sara said reluctantly. "In Bosnia actually. What about you?"

"Twice married. I left the first one for the second. And the second one left me for another. I suppose you might say fair do's, eh? Anyway for the moment, I'm a hundred-and-ten percent committed to this new Club. I hope you're a golfer."

"Afraid not."

"Pity. Still there'll be plenty of opportunities to catch up with the past twenty years I'm sure. Perhaps over dinner? Some time when Mike is away so we don't bore him stiff with our 'do-you-remembers?'"

"We can hardly fail to meet in a community the size of Daerley Green," Sara said.

He turned up at the cottage next day. Jasminka answered the door and let him in, and he was comfortably settled in Mike's favourite chair by the time Sara came downstairs.

"You didn't tell me about this charming young lady," Beresford said, rising to greet her.

"Minkie is staying with us for a while. And Minkie, aren't you supposed to be looking after Billy this morning while Polly's at the dentist?" Sara said crisply. She waited until Minkie had removed herself with obvious reluctance. "What can I do for you Beresford?"

"Be my lunch companion I hope. Fill me in on all the great and the good of Daerley Green. And the last twenty years."

"Sorry I'm tied up with the magazine most of this week."

Beresford looked at her thoughtfully. "Something tells me that I'm not flavour of the month. Any special reason? I seem to remember we got on … rather well once; were both simultaneously quite wild for a while."

Which was obviously all that had meant to him. Sara said, "It *was* rather a while ago Beresford. Hopefully we've both grown up a bit. As I said last night, our paths are bound to cross. Let's leave it at that, shall we?"

JASMINKA – *May 1994*

Dear Franko – I started a diary for you *aeons* ago, but it's a dead loss writing without knowing when and where it will be read. So I'm sending you this proper letter to your home address. For ages after I came here I waited every day for a letter. Even though Mike and Sara kept telling me that it was impossible to get news from Sarajevo. But now there's this cease-fire it *must* be possible. I just can't bear to think of everything going on without me and not knowing what's happening, except what we see on the news. Sometimes when I see those pictures on the television I can't believe it's the same place. Then I thought you'd get so used to me not being there that you'd forget I existed. But then I haven't forgotten about any of you and never, ever will, so I hope it's the same for you

After a lot of trying, Mike finally got a message from Auntie Jovanka through the Red Cross. She thinks Mother may have gone to stay with Gran in Mislići. This was a big relief at first, then I thought if she had left Sarajevo she ought to be able to send a message or even telephone. Please Franko, try and find out where she is.

I've just thought that of course you won't know any more about me than I do about you, like who Mike and Sara are. Mike is the journalist who arranged for me to come here – perhaps Mother told you that? Sara is his wife and she has a shop in this village, selling hand-made things. Gran's embroidery and Uncle Marko's wood carvings would make a fortune here. Mike is away at the moment and I'm not telling Sara about this letter because she would make a worried face and tell me I shall only be terribly disappointed because you won't get it so there won't be a reply. But I don't believe that. If you want something so much that it hurts, then I think God will help it to happen.

I really need to talk to you because you're the only person who will understand some of the things in my head. It's not that I'm unhappy, not like I was. A lot of things are quite nice here but that only makes it more difficult. To begin with I just hated everything which wasn't a nice feeling at all, but it was uncomplicated. But now it's like being two different people: the 'me' I was before I came here, and the one I am now. And suddenly it's become quite hard to put the two together and feel it's the same person. Most of the time I forget about it because there's a lot going on. Then I remember and find I just can't make myself feel how it was to be the original me, however hard I try. It's an awful feeling, not being sure where you really belong. And wondering about all those plans we made and how we are going to make them happen. Or even if you still want them to happen like I do. But I have to believe that you do or there wouldn't be any point in anything.

Everyone in the village here is very nice to me, especially Polly who used to work in Sara's shop before she had her baby Billy, who is fat and laughs a lot. Then there's Justin who's terribly old, only he doesn't talk like an old person, so I forget that he is. He used to work in the government here or something; but the really magic thing is that he came to Yugoslavia when he was a little boy, before it was even Yugoslavia, because his father was a diplomat. He remembers a holiday in Montenegro and has old photographs of the king's palace in Cetinje, and some of himself walking in the Durmitor Mountains. Do you remember when we went to the summer camp there and did that raft trip down the Tara river? It was the most frightening thing that ever happened to me. Until the war.

But what I wanted to explain, however nice people are, life here is so normal there's no way they could understand what it's like living in a war. I mean, the wars they had here are right back in history. Justin did try to explain how it was then, but even he said it was different because ours is a civil war, which isn't like everyone being on the same side against a common enemy. Then he went on about *our* history and the way it's made people take sides against each other. To be honest, I didn't really understand what he was on about, except that he wasn't blaming

Serbia for everything. So you probably wouldn't agree with him anyway.

When I first moved to my new school, some of the kids wanted to know what it was really like to be in a siege. Then there was an awful boy whose grandfather came to work in England from Croatia after the big world war, and decided to stay. This boy kept shouting at me that I was a Četnik and telling everyone that Četniks had always been bad and killed a lot of people. So I shouted back, what about the Ustaše and the trillions of people they'd killed in terrible concentration camps in the big war. Well, you know that Gran's two brothers were sent to one and never heard of again. This boy was furious and some of his friends joined in and started pushing me about and it was really terrible till my friend Azzie came rushing in to help me screaming like a banshee. One of the teachers came to see what was going on and we were all given a real talking to: about learning from history and if people didn't move on from the past then there was no hope for the world. I talked to Justin about it later and that helped a lot.

Azzie is another person I can talk to a bit about these things. Her real name is Azita – and she comes from Iran. I met her when I moved to this new school. You'd be surprised how good my English is now, so there are no problems with the lessons. The only thing is that it's really strange how some of the kids mess about, interrupting and things. They wouldn't get away with it at home, and Azzie says the same.

Azzie came to stay with an English auntie a few years ago after her country was at war. She says she can't remember much about it, except there always seemed to be a lot of people shouting and holding up banners. And a lot of prayers for soldiers that had been killed. Her uncle says it's the best thing you can do, killing people and dying for God. He has big arguments about this with her English auntie. Azzie and I don't think God would like this at all. In fact, Azzie's God sounds a bit like mine, which is pretty confusing. We decided it didn't matter as long as they both wanted good things. Supposing it was the same God with a different name? I wish I could talk to you about this.

Sara is very nice to me, but somehow I just can't seem to find the right words to talk to her about important things. I find it easier to talk to Mike – well, of course he's been to Sarajevo and knows a lot; but he's not here very often. As well as running the shop, Sara organises a monthly magazine for the village, so she knows pretty well everyone and everything that goes on. You wouldn't believe how excited everyone's getting about what should be done with a bit of land near the village. Sara's dead keen that they should plant some trees on it. In fact I think she likes trees more than she likes people. Isn't that weird?

Of course she and Mike don't have children – I don't know why. In a way it's an advantage because she doesn't seem to mind what I do, as long as I tell her where I'm going and when I'm coming back. And when Azzie comes to stay, which is quite often, we go off for most of the day, usually to see Polly and Billy or for a walk. The countryside is quite nice round here, but there are no mountains and they don't have any forests like we have, so perhaps that's why Sara thinks there aren't enough trees. Or we spend a lot of time watching TV or playing the stereo in my room. Sara gets mad if we have it too loud. I guess she's a bit lonely with Mike away so much. The other evening she dressed up for a party that Justin was giving and I was amazed how great she looked. Quite beautiful.

Then next morning this dishy man came to see her. Actually I opened the door and I think Sara was pretty cross because I invited him in; but he said they'd met at the party so how was I to know? I think they knew each other a long time ago.

But I suppose it's pretty boring hearing about all these people you've never met so I'll stop and send this off now. I can't wait to hear from you.

MIKE - *July 1994*

It was a few days since Mike had returned from several weeks in Sarajevo and soon time, he decided, to cut back the *clematis montana*. And then: *if only all problems could be solved by such clear-cut decisions..*

In the past three months there had been a subtle shift of emphasis in his concerns. Minkie, to a quite remarkable degree, was developing into her own person. It was Sara who really worried him. Even granted the fact that Polly's evolution into motherhood had brought problems in keeping the shop competently manned, Sara seemed to have become quite manic about it. In a short time she had worked through quite a list of part-time staff. Now at last, a relative newcomer to Daerley was proving reliable, though it hadn't stopped Sara continuing to look like a worried hen.

In the end they had decided to tell Jasminka of Mike's assignment in Sarajevo and his failure to find any trace of her mother. They had expected disappointment, even upset, but her initial explosion of rage was quite dumbfounding. "I'm not a small kid," she shouted and slammed off into her room. Later they discovered the true cause of her anger was that she had written to her much loved cousin and "if only I'd known, you could have taken the letter." Mike managed to convince her that delivering letters in Sarajevo wasn't quite as easy as it sounded.

She was surprisingly relaxed about her mother. "Well, there wouldn't be any trace of her would there, if she's gone to Gran's at Mislići? I mean Mislići is, like, *remote* - down a dirt track off a lane off a minor road off the main road to Mostar. It's not like getting on the bus to Banbury." Her expression suddenly became sad. "If I'd stayed I'd be there too, probably looking after the cows on the summer pasture above Mislići – right up high on the mountain near the sky. They've got three cows, or they did the summer before .... before the war. Uncle Marko said the next girl calf would be called Jasminka after me. But they were all boys. I expect they've been eaten by now."

Mike's heart went out to her. After some weeks away in a place where so many kids had reminded him of her, he'd been startled to return and find her quite different from the image he carried in his mind. In the way she spoke and acted, if not the way she looked, she was such a typical English schoolgirl, it was at times quite funny, until he remembered again why she was here. And then there would be that sudden glimpse beneath the façade of the vulnerable, uncertain child he had first seen nearly two years ago.

Would he have made the same decision had he remotely realised how long the commitment would be? And had it been the right decision for Jasminka? She was right. She might well this minute have been with her mother in that rural backwater, looking after a few cows on a mountain pasture, a long way from the shelling and the deprivations.

Or she might have been dead.

What he had not mentioned of course and only now, in retrospect, was it beginning to seem seriously important, was his renewed search for Marija. It had begun with a whim that came out of nowhere.

The expansion of the city's devastation since his last visit was quite appalling and the whole place felt stricken with what he could only describe as a soul-sickness. Both the combined Muslim-Croat parliament in Sarajevo and the Bosnian Serb legislature in Pale had rejected proposals for the partition into three ethnic republics. Solutions and lasting peace seemed as elusive as ever. The city was also full of UN vehicles and multi-national personnel who seemed like the alien beings they were, until their ubiquitous presence ceased to shock. But it was easier and certainly less dangerous to get about and it was on one of his solitary probings into the narrow streets above the old bazaar that he was momentarily swamped by a sense of déja-vu.

A derelict sign over the entrance to a courtyard caught his eye: *Dve bela goluba*   "It means 'Two White Doves'," said

Marija's voice from eighteen years ago. "The owner and cook is my friend. He is very good cook. You will see."

They had met a few days earlier in a coffee bar. In fact, she more or less picked him up. He suspected it had been a dare because there were a couple of giggling friends in the background. He was sipping thick strong Turkish coffee, reading an English newspaper, and she slid on to the bar stool next to him. "May I practise my English with you?" she had asked, scarlet with embarrassment. He had bowed his head and said it would be an honour, and perhaps she could tell him about her beautiful city. She had visibly relaxed and the giggling friends had soon disappeared. It was her amazing green eyes he noticed first. But he soon discovered she was also a very nice girl, nineteen or twenty, to his just twenty-two. And then that they liked a lot of the same things. They agreed to meet again the next day, and the next. And he felt himself falling a little in love with this girl called Marija.

That particular evening she had brought him to this, her favourite restaurant. The young man who was juggling with pans and grills and chopped vegetables and spices was an old school mate. He prepared a selection of Bosnian specialities for them: pastry layers of *burek*, so light you could blow them away, filled with cheese or spinach or potato; and *sarma,* vine leaves stuffed with meat and rice. There was a pale golden wine from Mostar to go with it, and then the finest Turkish coffee Mike had tasted, served in tiny cups from a long handled copper pot, with a dish of sweet, sticky Turkish delight.

That evening a deep sense of peace had combined with the huge attraction he now felt towards the girl with the green eyes sitting across the table from him; and the call to prayer from a nearby minaret, echoing from mosque to mosque across the old city, seemed like a blessing. They had made love for the first time that night in Marija's tiny bedsitter. She was studying at the University. Her parents lived far away in the mountains, she said, though she had other relatives here in the city. Her mother had wanted her to stay with them, but this was her first taste of freedom and she was revelling in it, though there always seemed to be some aunt or family friend checking up on her. Mike prayed that no one would be checking up on her that night. She had added, looking at him very seriously, that she did not offer her body lightly. She had actually used that funny old-fashioned expression that would have caused hysteria among his friends at home, and Mike was surprised at how angry that thought made him.

And now, eighteen years later, he picked his way over the rubble where the building had collapsed into the courtyard. Someone shouted from behind and he turned to see a man waving a warning, admonishing hand. The man only had one leg but with the aid of his crutch, approached Mike at surprising speed. "Are you crazy?" the man said angrily.

Mike saw he was right: there was plenty more unsteady brickwork where that rubble came from. He said "Thanks, that was stupid of me. I was thinking of when I came here many years ago. Good memories."

"You came here? This was mine. My restaurant." He smiled bitterly. "My life."

Mike looked at him more closely; he had aged far more than warranted by the intervening years, but not beyond recognition. He felt a shaft of compassion, remembering the cheerful, energetic young man who had flaunted his culinary skills with such pride. "Of course, now I recognise you. I was here with a friend of yours. Marija, a very lovely girl with green eyes."

The man stared at him. "Marija, my beautiful Marija. You knew her?"

Mike nodded, hardly able to breathe. "What happened to her?"

"What happened? The same that happened to all Sarajevans. Her life destroyed." As Mike gave a small shocked cry, he added "No, she still lives. I think she still lives. But her man, her two children, all dead. A mortar to their apartment. Marija, she is sick a long time. In the head you know? Then she goes with Red Cross out. I think she is in Novi Sad. In Serbia."

She was alive. Marija alive. Mike could barely control his elation. It was hard to feel sadness for an unknown husband and children. Only sadness for her. When this bloody war was over .....

"Thank you, thank you," he said.

He made his way back through the bazaar to the main Serbian Orthodox Church and, almost without thinking, turned into it. A steady stream of people came and went, lit candles, murmured prayers. He became aware of a benign quiet, rare in this city that had been through so much. He thought of Marija and how she had suffered, but it was the sort of suffering beyond imagination. It was only then that he realised he had long forgotten her surname, though with all his contacts it shouldn't be impossible to track her down.

Not impossible, but perhaps not too sensible either.

He found himself remembering how he had really, really meant to keep in touch with her, arrange for her to visit England. And then, who knew? But almost immediately after his return, his first job on the Banbury paper catapulted him into a world of smaller but more immediate local dramas. They had exchanged a few letters, he and Marija, but then she had stopped. Or did he stop first? And he'd met a girl, and then another. And in due course Sara.

Ah, Sara.

He had arrived home from Sarajevo just as she was finalising the next issue of that confounded magazine. Apparently her computer had crashed, she had lost a lot of copy and spent most of the previous night resurrecting it.

Admittedly his arrival home had been unexpected. On this occasion he had not even rung from the airport; just turned up as, hopefully, a pleasant surprise. He found Sara in the kitchen in her pyjamas preparing a mug of herbal tea to take up to bed. At nine o'clock in the evening, for heaven's sake! She'd managed to replace the look of dismay with a half-convincing smile of welcome, but she looked tired and middle-aged and, when he shied away from that thought and put his arms round her, he felt the resistance.

They had gravitated to the living room where he'd poured himself a malt while Sara sat hunched over her herbal tea looking even more tired and middle-aged as she catalogued the previous night's disasters. Mike could only think how much he wanted to make love to her, exorcise the soul sickness of Sarajevo and may be even his elation over Marija's survival, and slip back into the normality of Sara's world. Then he thought *for Chrissake it's only a village rag.* But he hadn't meant to say it out loud.

He might as well have slapped her face. But after staring at him blankly for a moment, she said "You could have put it better, but you're right. Daerley Green can get quite claustrophobic at times and then you lose track of the big world out there."

They had made love. Mike sensed it was not what Sara wanted just then, but he needed it ... her ... the affirmation of their unity. It ended up OK and he'd slept like a child. When he awoke, he rolled over to take her in his arms again, but she was already up, had been for a couple of hours, putting the final touches to the *Chronicle.* He had stifled his resentment, trying to convince himself it wasn't fair to shoot in and out of her life and expect her to drop everything instantly to accommodate him. But the resentment didn't go away.

In contrast, he had been surprised and touched to overhear Minkie on the phone as he came downstairs. "Sorry, can't make it this morning. Mike came home last night and I've got loads to tell him."

She had, too. An enthusiastic stream-of-consciousness poured over him as he made toast, grilled bacon: school gossip, titbits about Polly and Billy and the new plans for planting trees (why was it everyone in England kept going on about trees?) and the movie *Schindler's List* she'd seen with Azzie, and how she'd cried and cried; and the walks she'd done with Justin, whom Mike thought of as a boring old fart but whom she seemed to adore as Sara did. Mike had watched her changing expressions, contrasting them with memories of the sad sullen child he had brought with him from Sarajevo; thinking, too, that she was going to be quite a beauty in a few years – not in the conventional sense, but head-turning with those high smooth cheekbones and expressive eyes. Not green as a mountain torrent like Marija's, but a sunlit autumnal russet-brown.

He heard himself ask "Is it all right for you here Minkie? Are you happy?"; then thought *what sort of question is that to ask a 15-year-old from her background?* But Jasminka poured him out a mug of coffee and said cheerfully "It'll be absolutely magic to go home, but it would be stupid not to be happy when everyone is so kind: especially Polly and Justin, and you. And Sara of course. It's just that sometimes I feel guilty to be so lucky; and then more guilty because a lot of the time I forget how bad it was – and still is for them at home."

Mike reached across and gave her arm a squeeze. What a great kid she was becoming. Good company for Sara, too, he would have thought; and was puzzled why it didn't seem to be working out that way.

Several times he had asked Sara if anything were wrong, most recently the previous evening.

"Why are you keeping on about it?" she asked.

"I thought it was called showing an interest. Concern. I know it's not been easy trying to juggle the shop and the *Chronicle* and everything since Polly left."

"It's OK now. Jean, this new person, is really reliable. A bit sort of middle-aged and not exactly a ball of fire; but you can't have everything. Anyway Polly's murmuring about coming back, says she misses it, and apparently one of her near neighbours is starting a crèche."

"Hey, that's good news. You hadn't said."

"No, well, it's not the sort of thing for a crackly line in the middle of someone's war." She shrugged. "I suppose that's the only 'wrong' thing: that we spend most of our lives doing separate things. It's the nature of your job."

"I could change. There are always plenty of subbing jobs going."

"Mostly at highly unsociable hours I seem to remember."

"But at least I'd be here."

"You'd hate it. Not being in the thick of the action."

Yes he would. But it might be better than becoming a stranger to your wife.

That morning, prodding at a fresh molehill in the lawn near the oak tree at the far end of the garden, Mike went over the previous evening's conversation again. "...the only 'wrong' thing is that we spend most of our lives doing separate things," Sara had said.

And suddenly he had the answer. Why on earth hadn't he thought of it before? He was long overdue for a good stretch of leave, Minkie would soon be breaking up for the summer holidays, and the confounded *Chronicle* didn't publish in August. It surely wouldn't be unthinkable to close Collectibles for a short time, or perhaps this Jean person would agree to hold the fort? So why wouldn't they take off, the three of them, for a totally unplanned jaunt across the Channel – combining a little gentle French culture with attractive scenery, laced with cheap wine and a large dose of good gastronomy. And, above all, time to stop and stare and be together.

He hurried back up the garden. Sara, sorting recipes in the kitchen, looked up and began "Sorry I've been grumpy ..." but he waved the apology aside, caught up with the immediacy of his own enthusiasm for his new plan. As he unfolded it to her, he saw her expression light up, his enthusiasm contagious.

"And we could take Azzie to keep Minkie company?"

"Brilliant idea." Mike enveloped her in the sort of hug

they hadn't had for a long time and thought *that's all that was needed – time together for all of us. It's all going to be all right.*

He arrived home early that Friday evening a few days before their departure. Holding a steady 70 mph down the M40 he consciously closed the door on everything connected with Canary Wharf and concentrated on a sense of pleasant anticipation for the coming venture. He even began to compose a packing list in his head.

It was a bit of an anticlimax to find the cottage empty. A note on the kitchen table reminded him that supper would be late as it was parents' evening at the school, ending with *should be back by eight.* The table was set and there was an enticing waft of casserole from the oven. Mike checked his watch. Seven-thirty. Time to relax with a drink, he thought. And because he did not feel like drinking on his own, he scrawled at the bottom of Sara's note: *if I'm not back, am imbibing in the Trumpet – come 'n get me.*

At this time of the evening the bar was still fairly empty. Mike's heart sank a little as he saw Justin at a window seat talking to a tall man he did not recognise. But while Mike was still ordering his pint of lager, Justin clapped him on the shoulder in greeting on his way out, pausing only to say "Delighted to hear you're taking the girls off for a holiday to *la belle France*, dear boy."

Mike took his pint to another window seat and looked out. The light was turning to evening gold and the market place was looking good. It was a long time since he had simply stopped and stared at this small civilised rural corner that was his patch. He relaxed back into the window seat. He really was a lucky sod.

"Mind if I join you a moment?"

"Sorry?" Mike glanced round to find Justin's tall companion looking at him with a friendly expectant expression.

"You're Sara's Mike aren't you. Mind if I join you?"

Mike tried not to sound reluctant. "Sure. We haven't met before have we?"

"No, but I've been looking forward to it. I'm Beresford Tremayne, though Sara may have referred to me as Brett, if she referred to me at all."

"I'm afraid not." Mike ended with a note of enquiry.

"Ah. Well she always did imply I was a big-headed prat." The tall man made a self-deprecating face. "It was a very long time ago. We were at school together."

"Oh I see." Odd, though, that Sara hadn't mentioned it. "So you've just moved into Daerley?"

"Mm. The Old Schoolhouse. After a couple of career changes and knocking around the universe for a dozen years or more, it's a bit like returning to the old roots. I'm taking over the new golf course. Other side of Banbury?" He paused. "But why should you know about that either? Not quite in the same league as civil wars in the Balkans."

Mike inclined his head. "I see you're well informed."

"The Daerley Green grapevine rarely fails. Added to which I really admire what you and Sara are doing for that Bosnian child. Fact is I have quite a special interest in that part of the world. My second wife was a Slovene, so I've dipped a toe, as it were, in the complex currents of Balkan affairs – and experienced just how unfathomable they can be. Though I daresay I was as much to blame. Never was very strong on relationships."

What an extraordinary confession to a complete stranger. "I expect most of us have our problems with those," was all Mike could think of saying.

Beresford shook his head. "Lord, I'm sorry. Here you are, in for a quiet pint after a hard day's graft, and some wretched stranger starts baring his soul. It must be the association with Sara. But my interest in the Balkans is quite sincere I promise you, quite apart from the 'ex'. I really would like to tap the opinions of someone who has genuine knowledge of what's going on. Perhaps you'd come for a drink one evening, you and Sara. When you get back from France?"

"I doubt if anyone has genuine knowledge of that part of the world. Except for the good Lord Himself, if He hasn't entirely abandoned it. But yeah, I'll be happy to share what perspective I have."

Beresford looked pleased. "I look forward to it. Must be off now. Say hello to Sara – and have a good holiday."

Over supper Sara said, "Glowing reports about this young lady."

"Except for Maths," Jasminka said.

"OK except for Maths. And Environment Studies. But all the rest way above average. And the Art. I wish you'd seen her art project. I'd no idea she was so good. Talk about lights under bushels."

"Father had several art exhibitions in Sarajevo."

Mike and Sara looked at each other. Mike said quietly "What a lot we still don't know."

"I don't hide anything," Minkie assured them. "It's – like – I don't think to talk about all that stuff from home."

"It's all right Minkie. We can understand that. And talking of hiding things, I've just shared a pint with a ghost from your past, darling: Beresford something. Seemed surprised you hadn't mentioned him."

Sara began collecting plates with a clatter. "Nothing to mention, except that he's a creep."

Mike looked surprised. "A bit full of himself at first, but improved on acquaintance. A bit lonely I thought. Wants us to go for a drink when we get back from France."

"Nothing to stop you," Sara said as she went to collect the dessert.

Jasminka - April 1995

Franko, I want to die. This morning they told me Mother has been killed. I have gone quite dead inside, but I want to die outside too because there's no reason to be alive if you don't feel anything. So I have to speak to you even if it's only on paper you will never read, because there is no one here who knew her: how gentle she was, but also how strong. I can understand that better now I am older: how strong she was to go on after Father died, and after the family turned against her. Except you of course.

They told me she was badly wounded in the street and died in hospital the next day. I try and feel her pain but can only think that I was not there to hug her. Then I think perhaps it's not true. With how things are at home there will be a lot of mistakes. And no one has explained why she came back from Mislići.

But most of the time I know it must be true.

I don't understand how I ever believed there was a God who wouldn't allow this to happen; but I was just a child then. It's quite weird but now that I know God isn't there, it's stopped a lot of the shouting in my head. Somehow I will go on alone, with the strength that Mother taught me to have. And perhaps later you can help me too.

Sara and Mike are very kind. They talk to me gently as though I am sick and tell me it's better if I can cry. But you can't cry if you don't feel anything.

Later: I started this message on Thursday when they told me about Mother. My head is in such a terrible muddle that I'm going to try and sort it all out on paper. This is what Beresford suggested. I'll explain who he is in a minute.

Part of the muddle is that before the news of Mother, I was really feeling that everything was going to be OK in the end. It started last summer when we had that holiday in France and it seemed to change everything. I sent you a postcard but I don't suppose you got it. There was Mike and Sara and Azzie and me.

We went through the new tunnel under the Channel to France; you put the car on a train and just sit there. It's magic. We were in France for three weeks, staying in small hotels in villages. A lot of the time we were in an area called the Dordogne where there are rivers and steep gorges that reminded me a lot of home. You can hire canoes in some places on these rivers, and it's really exciting travelling on such fast water, sometimes between rocks and through rapids; then you come to another place where you leave the canoes and they take you back on a minibus to where your car is. Sara got terribly worried about us falling in the river, or the canoe turning over. But it was real kids' stuff after some of our trips on the Vrbas and the Neretva – and that time on the Tara in Montenegro. But I think Azzie was pretty scared.

I was really surprised how Mike and Sara were though. They suddenly seemed so much younger, laughing and fooling about and playing jokes on each other, and on Azzie and me. Sometimes it felt as though we were all about the same age! Back in England they never seemed to talk to each other very much, and of course Mike is away a lot; but sometimes when we were in France, if Azzie and I went off somewhere on our own, we'd come back and find them in a café or sitting somewhere, talking their heads off. When we weren't canoeing or sightseeing and things, we played some games they'd brought with them; especially one called Scrabble in which you have to make up words to score points. They were amazed at how good I was sometimes. Personally I think Mike cheated with words that he made up in his head, and of course we didn't have a dictionary with us, so sometimes he got away with it.

It was a lovely holiday, and I was quite surprised to find how pleased I was to come back to Daerley Green. Like coming home, only of course it will never be that. Mike wasn't away so much last winter, so we did quite a lot of things like a normal family: going to London, and to the Shakespeare Theatre in Stratford which isn't far from here. And once we had a weekend by the sea.

Then in the autumn, I had some pictures in an exhibition in Oxford. Art is the thing I'm best at. Sara found some paintings I'd done in my room – I was mad at the time because they were paintings I'd done for me, not for anyone else. They were trying to remember home and what it was like. Sara asked if she could show them to one of her artist friends. She has something to do with arranging exhibitions and said she'd put three of mine in one she was doing in Oxford showing young people's view of conflict. It was really weird seeing my pictures up in that big gallery and looking at people looking at them. I didn't like it at first. Some of them made very stupid comments, but then others seemed to understand what I was saying. One day there was this young man, an American, who stood in front of one of my pictures for a long time. It was one I'd done when the mortar hit the market place. He turned to me and said "Don't you think that's really cool?" And I said no I didn't, because when mortars explode it's noisy and frightening and smelly and not cool at all. He told me I was bizarre, and I said may be, but I was also a Serb devil refugee from Sarajevo, then walked away. He came rushing after me and apologised and asked a lot of questions.

In the end we went off to The Pizza Hut and talked for simply ages, and he was really nice. He's called Jesse, which I thought was a girl's name, and is doing international business studies in Oxford. He's the first American I've spoken to properly and has some bizarre ideas, like he thinks Europe is old-fashioned and quaint compared with America – his parents are diplomats so he's travelled an amazing amount. He said everyone was much more wired up at home, especially in California where he was born, and that things here are rather slow and unexciting. He made me realise how quiet and ordinary life is at the moment, and talking to him started a lot of new ideas in my head. I don't suppose he'll stay here long if he finds it so boring; but he asked a lot of questions about how it was living with Mike and Sara

Then at Christmas, one of Sara's sisters came with her family. Sara got a big Christmas tree and put it in the conservatory and decorated it with real candles like she said her mother used to do. You can't imagine how beautiful it was, and peaceful. I felt very homesick, but almost in a happy way because about that time we heard a cease-fire had been agreed at home. Even Sara thought it might be possible I would be able to come home some time this year.

Only now Mother is dead. And even if it's possible, where will I go?

After the news about her, I stayed in my room nearly all the time, except when Mike or Sara were going out and wouldn't go without me. Then yesterday it felt as though the walls were falling in, so I went for a walk. Then I walked and walked without noticing where I was going, until suddenly I felt so tired, and found I was in a place called Whirling Wood near here. There's an old wooden seat in a clearing and I was sitting there feeling dead when this dog came rushing up to me. He was so excited and friendly it was impossible to ignore him. Then a man called out very crossly and the dog suddenly flattened its ears and looked at me so sadly. I started to hug it and before I knew what was happening I was crying so hard I couldn't stop.

The man's voice said "Why it's Jasminka isn't it?" and I felt him sit down beside me. But I couldn't look up or stop crying. He just went on talking quietly, I don't really know what about, except he said he had never been so unhappy as when *his* Mother died, so he must have known about Mother – but then everyone knows everything about everybody in Daerley Green. When I looked up I saw it was this Beresford Tremayne, though I didn't remember his name then. He moved here a few months ago, and it turns out that he and Sara went to school together. He came to visit her once and she was really rude to him, though I don't know why. Anyway, apart from seeing him around in the village, I hadn't spoken more than a few words to him since then. He has something to do with a new golf course near here, and must have lots of money because has the latest BMW as well as a Land Rover.

Well, sitting there in Whirling Wood, he pushed a handkerchief into my hand. After ages the crying stopped and I just felt terribly tired. The dog seemed to have cheered up and started licking my hand. Beresford told me it was called Rus, and he'd recently bought it from an Animal Rescue place. People here are mad about animals as well as trees; especially dogs. Though not all of them can be, because the animals that go to the Animal Rescue place have often been badly treated, which is why Rus looked so scared when Beresford shouted at him. Rus is a Collie, a bit like the ones at Mislići that look after the sheep; only I don't think Rus would be much good at that. He's a really soppy dog and just sat looking pleased while I hugged him, which made me feel better too.

It's amazing how you can get the wrong idea about people. I thought Beresford looked a really boring person, only interested in making money and talking to the important people in the village. I guess that's what Sara thinks too. But he was so kind. I found myself telling him and Rus all about Mother and coming here and how sometimes it's difficult to know where I belong and even remember what it was like at home before the war. He said when he got in a muddle he found it helped to write things down just as the thoughts came. So that's what I've been doing. And later I'm going to write down everything I remember about home.

We walked back to Daerley Green together. When she first saw Beresford, Sara looked really mad. Then she must have noticed I'd been bawling, and Rus started licking *her* hand, and she asked Beresford to come in. He said he wouldn't but if I ever wanted to take Rus for a walk it would do him a great favour. I think that's what I'll do.

Sara – January 1996

In Afghanistan the Taliban were tightening their grip. In Sarajevo, in the wake of the Dayton agreement, nearly four years of siege were about to end. And in Daerley Green, Sara stood at the kitchen window looking out at the garden. Mike had left a week earlier for some international bonanza in New York. Minkie and Azzie were at a weekend rave near Abingdon with that young American who seemed to have become very much part of their scene in recent weeks. It was Sunday morning and the best kind of English winter's day, low sunlight gleaming on the golden fluffy balls of witch hazel in a corner of the lawn, and catching the lemon spikes of winter jasmine against the south-facing wall. Sara hardly saw them.

When the phone rang she flinched, though she was expecting, waiting for the call. As always eight-thirty on the dot. As always her pulse quickened.

"Hi," she said into the receiver.

"Has anyone ever told you that you have the sexiest 'hi' in Christendom?" said Beresford's voice quietly.

Sara smiled "Shut up Berry." She felt the ripple of pleasure that came with the sound of his voice these days; like a teenager. Like the teenagers they'd once been together.

"So what's it to be today? Walk, drive, movie....?" A pause, then hopefully "A quiet snog?"

"Shut up Berry," Sara said again, wanting him badly, right there and then. It was getting increasingly difficult to think of places to go where the risk of seeing mutual acquaintances was minimal. Not long ago it would not have mattered, but then there were no feelings to disguise. She drew a deep breath. "Let's go for a walk. Along the canal, north of Banbury. How about meeting at Cropredy around half-nine?"

After she put the phone down, she went into the hall cupboard to get her small knapsack, pausing to stuff a waterproof into the bottom of it. No English winter's day was that predictable. Then she took the knapsack up to the bedroom, rummaged around for a scarf, gloves, spare pair of socks. Back downstairs, she shoved her wallet and a couple of chocolate bars into the side pockets. All this she did with full concentration, as she also did when she checked the back door, switched on the answering machine. It wasn't that she was consciously pushing out other thoughts. No, she'd finished with the guilt trip, re-travelled it endlessly through sleepless night after sleepless night. It was because these small preparations were part of the pleasure, part of the confirmation of the on-goingness of something that had brought her alive, something so totally unforeseen and unforeseeable; like waking after a long half-sleep.

Her first reaction was of annoyance that afternoon last spring when Beresford had brought Minkie home from Whirling Wood. In the year since their first re-encounter, she had successfully come to regard him with indifference: just a newcomer to the village with whom she had nothing in common. She gathered by the usual osmosis from village gossip that he had done wonders with the new golf course, was beginning to appear on village committees for this or that. Occasionally there was some elegant female companion in tow, but never the same one for long.

But then on that April afternoon she saw Minkie's face, swollen from crying; the trusting expression on her face as she looked up at her companion, the intensity with which she knelt down to hug the dog Rus. Beresford had rung Sara later to describe in more detail his encounter with Minkie. "If it's all right with you, I think she would enjoy taking Rus for a walk sometimes – and it would save my old legs!" He had laughed self deprecatingly. Sara was surprised. Self-deprecation was not a characteristic she would have associated with Beresford Tremayne. But she agreed that taking Rus for walks might prove good therapy.

After that he rang occasionally to see if Minkie and Azzie could go on some outing he was arranging for the village youth club with which he'd become slightly involved. That was another surprise. Sara was always included in such invitations and always declined. But somewhere in the lower levels of consciousness she began to re-adjust her assessment of the man that the boy Brett had become.

In any case she was better placed for making more generous judgements. The holiday in France seemed to have provided them all with a new perspective. Subsequently Mike's assignments had been far more UK-based for a while and because he was home much more they had been able to plan things together. Just like a real family. For Sara observing Mike and Minkie together on a theatre trip to Stratford, or a shopping jaunt to London, the sense of father-daughter was at times almost tangible. Then briefly she would recall that her child would have been much the same age, then that it would not have been Mike's child, then that the child's real father was even now only a few hundred yards away. Then that this way lay madness, and better by far to slam the mind shut against it, her proven best means of defence.

Was it sod's law that soon after the news of the death of Minkie's mother, Mike's work schedule had suddenly sent him into overdrive? There were rumours of take-overs and redundancies. Mike became thoughtful, then taciturn.

"Talk about it for heaven's sake," Sara said in exasperation after yet another evening redolent with silent desperation.

"What's there to talk about? Either they keep me or they don't."

It wasn't just the financial security that she knew worried Mike far more than it did her; it was the potential obliteration of the main focus of his life. "Sticking my nose in other people's business, and making sense of it – that's what I'm good at," he said once. "And what the hell else does that qualify me for in the real world?"

He was determined to be sorry for himself.

"He really is insufferable," Sara informed Justin over a post-Press day lager. "In fact about the only person he's civil with these days is Minkie. Bet he's not like this with Plum or his Canary Wharf cronies." She did not add *with whom he seems to be spending more and more time.*

Justin said, "When you have a particular skill it can be extremely difficult to accept there are alternatives. I'm afraid you'll have to let him find his own way through this, Sara."

For once she'd found Justin irritating. To her, Mike's behaviour felt increasingly like rejection of any comfort she tried to offer, in or out of bed.

She found she was missing Amanda more than she could have imagined: that special talent she had for summing up a situation, usually a touch caustically but always to the point. And for putting things into perspective. The study of teenage behavioural patterns that had taken her to the States had been crap, she announced cheerfully. But through it she'd made a contact that led her to New York and a library job which focussed on translations of foreign literature in which she was in her element. The said contact had other attributes too it seemed, for she had moved in with him for a while. Sara could almost hear Amanda's voice telling her it was time for her to get a life. Or perhaps it was wishful thinking.

And then she found the letter from Marija.

She was in the loft rummaging in old boxes of photographs. Minkie had prompted this by an unexpected show of interest in her and Mike's past, partly triggered by a school project on the Sixties. It was then late summer, about six months ago, and Minkie was sixteen and a half. She had matured quite startlingly in the few months since the news of her mother's death: physically of course, but even more emotionally. In the summer she had announced that she was now convinced her mother was still alive, that in the on-going mayhem of Sarajevo reality and rumour were virtually interchangeable.

Nothing would shake her conviction. Mike had exploited

every contact to try and obtain proof one way or the other. The now impenetrable alienation between the Bosniak and Serb sides of the family left very few leads. It filtered back that Branka's elderly parents in Mislići, completely disoriented by the disintegration of their world, were confused about when and for how long their daughter had taken refuge with them, but she was certainly no longer there. A Bosniak sister-in-law confirmed uninterestedly that she had heard of 'that woman's' death. Nothing conclusive.

For the moment it seemed simpler to assume that Minkie was as likely to be right as anyone else.

The box of photographs in the loft proved very seductive. An hour vanished as Sara picked her way through a series of junior school sports days frozen into black and white glossy perpetuity. She saw herself in the 100 yard sprint and relay races, looking skinny, agile and earnest. She picked out long forgotten bosom pals, others she had admired for their aplomb or scorned as pathetic. She fished out a few to show Minkie; they would make her laugh. They were all pre-Brett.

She had paused to make herself a coffee and returned to the loft determined to be more systematic. There was a big batch of pictures from their early married days which she put aside to take down and check through at more leisure. A miscellaneous collection featured relatives and family friends during World War Two and even earlier. A handful went back to the Great War, sepia tinted on thick card: unknown young faces gazing steady-eyed at the camera from above scratchy looking army uniforms. Part of a lost generation. Sara felt a twinge of guilt and sadness because she would never know who they were or what had happened to them.

Then she found a bundle labelled 'Mike pre-Us'. There were yellowing cuttings from his days on the Banbury paper; group pictures of young people with Mike somewhere amongst them always managing to look rather more serious than the rest; a few of his parents in their flower-power days, fey and a little absurd; a collection of Mike and Plum 'doing Europe' during their gap year; one or two portrait photos of pretty girls with meticulously groomed hair posing for the professional camera; a few dog-eared theatre programmes and letters. One in particular.

It was folded outwards, the first page exposed. Her eye caught the word 'Sarajevo' scrawled in the top right hand corner, and underneath the date July 7, without a year. And underneath that 'My darling – I never have wrote these words before …'

It was a letter of a first love folded round a small snapshot of a girl standing on a street corner. However hard she peered, Sara could only make out a pale blob of face under a cloud of dark hair. In the background there was the minaret of a mosque. She skimmed through the letter to the signature 'your Marija, always'. Then she read it through slowly again. And again. She felt a flush spread through her: of shame at intruding on this unknown girl's passion for it was certainly that, of empathy with that exquisite painful rawness of first love, and then of deep resentment. She had believed they had shared it all, she and Mike, made the mutual confessions, wiped slates clean.

Except for Brett. And now Marija.

Gradually she worked it out. Mike would have met Marija when he'd returned alone to Yugoslavia on holiday after that gap year. When the siege began he would have tried to trace her, of course he would. She could not believe that anyone could get such a letter with all it implied, however long ago, and not become desperate to know what happened to its writer under the terrible circumstances. Certainly not Mike who had more compassion than was comfortable for anyone. For the first time, Sara found herself trying to project into that stricken city, hearing the screaming shells, smelling the dust, sensing the fear.

Think, *think, **think.*** She remembered his phone call on his second visit to Sarajevo: how up-beat it had been, how admiring of the resilience of the Sarajevans. Had he somehow tracked her down or, at the very least, had news of her? She remembered how different he had seemed on his return: a new lightness of spirit and at the same time an uncharacteristic lack of empathy with her own moods. That trip to France had come at just the right moment.

And now? Well, the obvious thing would be to get things out in the open, tell him of her discovery. Be adult.

She hadn't of course. Slamming the door shut had become too deeply entrenched a solution to all potential conflict. And easy to justify, especially now with Mike so at odds with himself.

The thought of the unknown Marija became a presence stalking her through each day. It was like being haunted by someone else's shadow. Absorbed in his own preoccupations Mike did not appear to notice.

Shortly after, Sara was standing outside the post office, staring without seeing at the notices requesting domestic help; appeals for a lost cat; offers of a nearly-new computer, garage space, part-time secretarial assistance. Beresford's amused voice said "Are you learning them all by heart!" As she half turned, the amusement turned to concern "Sara, you look terrible. Is something wrong? Minkie all right? Mike?"

She managed to produce a smile. "We're all fine – bit of a bad night that's all."

"Then I know just the cure: a pick-me-up and a bite to eat." He nodded at the Trumpet across the Market Place. "Unless you're on your way somewhere." As Sara stood indecisive he added, "I owe you anyway. It's been a real pleasure getting to know young Minkie."

Sara said "Well, that was your own doing," but she let him lead her across the Market Place.

He was a good companion. Once he said, "I hope this has buried whatever hatchet I sense needed burying from the past. I guess I was a pretty obnoxious youth, but hopefully there has been an improvement." Otherwise he spoke amusingly of the tribulations of dealing with local planning restrictions in places as far flung as Benidorm and Bermuda. It was like a gleam of light in a dark tunnel.

"I had a bar snack with Beresford Tremayne today," Sara told Mike when he rang that evening.

"Who? Oh, I thought he was supposed to be a creep."

"He seems to have improved."

"Good." Mike sounded exceedingly uninterested. "I think I'd better stay in town this week-end. JP seems to be flexing his muscles now he's got promotion."

And so a lunch time bar snack with Beresford became first an occasional, then a regular mid-week event. After a while Sara noticed that she had totally ceased to think of him as Brett and was grateful for the change in both of them. All the same she said early on "I really can't call you Beresford. So absurdly pretentious."

He inclined his head. "I'll take that as a compliment. A favoured few know me as Berry." So Berry it was. Occasionally she would catch him observing the scene with that quizzical appraising look that brought an uncomfortable twinge of déja vu. Mostly he was just an intelligent and humorous companion. And life with Mike these days was exceedingly short on humour. Thankfully the ghost of Marija had disappeared.

Then came a long-promised day on the canal.

"Leave everything to me," Berry said. "Just turn up with the girls as early as you can."

The rendez vous was a marina on the Oxford Canal a few miles south of Banbury where friends of Berry's had left a longboat in his charge for the summer while they were abroad.

Sara awoke early to an English summer's day at its best: light breeze, blue sky punctuated by small fluffy clouds that held no threat. Mike was in London for the weekend yet again, but odd clatterings from below indicated that Minkie was already up and about. Sara found her in the kitchen pressing a pair of vividly striped stretch jeans.

"Hey, where did those come from?"

"Azzie found them in a Banbury charity shop. Too small

for her." Minkie held them against herself and wiggled her hips. "What do you reckon?"

"I reckon you'll have every fisherman from here to Oxford plunging into the canal in hot pursuit," Sara laughed.

Azzie arrived, white chinos and splashy golden top setting off her olive complexion. "Wow!" Berry exclaimed as they approached along the towpath half an hour later. "Can any other man in Middle England be blessed with three more outrageous beauties?"

He had thought of everything: a fridge full enough to feed an army of gourmets, with smoked salmon, cold meats, salads, crisp French baguettes, rye loaves stuffed with olives, pitta bread, a battery of sauces and a basket of fresh herbs. There was fresh fruit and ice cream. There was coffee, three varieties of tea including Minkie's favourite blackberry herbal, white wine, elderflower cordial. There was even a small library of books for identifying flowers, trees, birds, insects along the way.

It was a wonderful day: a quintessentially English day of cattle grazing quietly in pastures, of the distant throb of a combine harvester, of bees humming and the cascading trill of rising larks, of the sudden waft of honeysuckle from banks tangled with dog rose, blackberry, hawthorn, wild cherry. Not a car in sight; not even a road. A family of moorhens scuttled into reeds and there was the sudden azure flash of a kingfisher.

"You wouldn't believe we were in the heart of one of the most populated corners of the world," Sara said.

"If you overlook the distant friendly hum of the M40 and the gentle chug of Chiltern Railways," Berry observed dryly.

They grinned at each other. The two girls were sunning themselves on the cabin roof, exchanging banter with the youthful occupants of the occasional passing vessel. Berry was at the wheel, Sara perched on the gunwale behind him. There was a lot of companionable silence into which Berry suddenly said, "You must be very proud of her."

Sara followed his gaze. They had reached a lock in the

middle of nowhere and the girls had jumped on to the towpath to go ahead and open it. Azzie was giggling uncontrollably at something Minkie had said.

"Avast such mirth my hearties or it'll be up the mainsail before eight bells," Berry bellowed after the girls rendering them even more helpless.

"I think," Sara said, "you're mixing a metaphor or two."

"What's a mixed metaphor or two among friends," Berry leaned back, his lips brushed her cheek, slipped down to her mouth as though by accident. "Sorry," he said.

They moored for lunch by a disused quarry just west of Kirtlington, now a nature reserve where nothing much stirred except a dancing, darting population of butterflies and damselflies, an army of ants on some intense and unfathomable mission; and a grebe fussily herding its brood beyond visible range of the intruders.

"Let's go and identify plants," said Sara, when it was impossible to eat any more.

"Creepie-crawlies for me," said Azzie.

"Good idea," said Berry.

"Yes, let's" said Minkie.

But in the full heat of the early afternoon no one stirred except to reach for a book (Azzie), a sketching pad (Minkie) or to curl up more comfortably for a snooze (Sara) until reluctantly Berry said it really was time to go.

"It was a truly heavenly day," Sara said as he helped them pile their belongings back into the car. "Thank you Berry." She gave him a light hug, conscious of the memory of that supposedly accidental kiss.

"My best day ever in England," Minkie said, her hug more vigorous.

"One does one's best," Berry said modestly, but looked pleased.

As she wallowed in herbal foam that evening, Sara thought back over the day. It was a long time since she had felt so at ease with the world. She explored the idea of Marija and found it irrelevant. Then she turned to thoughts of Mike and felt a flicker of guilt.

Was this friendship with Berry becoming marginally less casual than was sensible?

Absurd. It had been a fab day out with a good friend.

Unbidden the thought came: *and how would said friend react if he knew he was responsible for an aborted foetus?*

Sara shot out of the bath, horrified at her own train of thought and where it was leading. Suddenly she wanted the familiar shape and feel of Mike; or at least the sound of him. Enveloped in a bath towel she reached for the cordless phone and rang him at the flat.

It was Mike who answered. "Hello darling." He sounded pleased, surprised. And cheerful.

"Been missing you. We had a great day with Berry on the canal, Minkie, Azzie and I; but we missed you." When did a white lie ever hurt?

"It's good of him to take such an interest in Minkie." A pause. "Miss you too. I'll be home in a couple of days. We'll celebrate."

Great. Mike wanted to celebrate.

Encouraged by the thought Sara said, the idea taking shape as she spoke, "How about celebrating with a few days away? Just the two of us? Minkie's always glad of an excuse to stay with Azzie." The idea took on a momentum of its own. "We could go back to some of those places in France." Where they had been so happy, at one with each other.

There was a pause that went on a bit too long before Mike said "Yeah. Great idea. May have to wait a bit though." Another pause. "I'm being sent back to Sarajevo."

Sara felt stillness. "Oh." So that accounted for the cheerfulness.

"Well yes. With the cease-fire finally taking place, it's the obvious place to be."

"Couldn't someone else go?"

He laughed as though she'd made a joke. "Sure. I'll just tell JP sorry, I know I'm the Balkans specialist, but could you please send someone else as my wife wants a few days away."

Hiding the hurt Sara said briskly "Well it would have to wait anyway till I've completed the make-over for Collectibles."

"Well yes, that would make sense." Mike sounded relieved. "Must say I'd forgotten about that."

"I've only recently been mulling it over. With Polly four months into her second pregnancy, it ought to be sooner rather than later." A pause. "But you probably didn't know about that either. See you in a couple of days then." She replaced the receiver, sat glaring at it sullenly. And then said, "Sod you, Mike Hennessey."

It was at least true that the shop was well overdue for a thorough makeover. Sara became exceedingly busy doing the rounds of all her usual suppliers, checking out new ones. Minkie began to take interest and came up with some plans. They were good. Evenings were spent crouched on the floor poring over sketches, debating this and that detail of colour, fabric, lighting.

"Rather more Chelsea ... or perhaps Islington, than north Oxon?" Mike suggested, glancing at the sketches on the eve of his departure. "Still I'm sure you girls know best."

Spiritedly Minkie agreed that they probably did. Sara found herself wishing Berry hadn't chosen just now to check out the golfing opposition in the south of France. Azzie and a couple of friends were hauled in to help. The result a few weeks later was a total re-design: the art nouveau drawing room transformed into a modern penthouse, focussing on a dozen items to show that good taste could be as much a matter of imagination as of money. Leading off it were side displays showing a range of products from the best local talent.

The local press were enthusiastic; a regional tv station gave her three minutes of prime time. At a packed launch day guests were lavish with praise as they sipped and nibbled their way through vast quantities of Chilean *Cabernet* and table-loads of finger food. She hoped their admiration would translate into sales.

"I began to wonder if you were avoiding me," observed Berry a couple of weeks later as their paths crossed in the north aisle of the Parish Church after a concert.

"You're the one who's been away," Sara pointed out. "And it has been hellishly busy – you know, re-organising the shop – and with Polly pregnant again. Then the usual on-going crises with the *Chronicle.* Copier on the blink this time. Then Minkie's school is preparing a new art show...."

Berry held up his hands in mock-surrender. "OK, OK. I know life has a habit of taking over. Still you've made a magnificent job of the shop. You're on to a winner there."

Sara was surprised and pleased. "I didn't know you'd even seen it. You approve?"

"Absolutely. And of course I've seen it – first thing when I got back. Hoping to see you. But as you say, you've been busy. I've just missed our chats that's all."

Yes, she'd missed them too. "Perhaps we can catch up on bonfire night? I'm running the Charity raffle."

Minkie stayed at home on bonfire night. Such celebrations for a historic terrorist baffled her, and anyway she said she'd had her lifetime's fill of explosions. Jesse came over to keep her company for the evening. He'd become quite a regular visitor in recent weeks. Mike had expressed reservations over the growing friendship, but Sara had really taken to the young American: his slightly brash openness, eagerness to please. She'd also noted the switch in his priorities as his plans to head off and do a dozen countries of Europe in about as many weeks were replaced by "guess I'll stick around the old UK for the summer, after all."

The bonfire on the edge of the school playing fields flared and crackled to satisfying effect. The sky briefly sparkled with coloured cloudbursts of stars to the accompaniment of appreciative 'oohs' and 'aahs', and a team from the PTA did their stuff with hot sausages wrapped in rolls, cans of fizzy drinks and urns of steaming coffee.

The usual hard core stayed behind, collecting litter, damping down embers.

"Feel like a jar or two at The Trumpet to wind the evening up?" asked Justin.

Sara shook her head. "Lovely idea, but I'm shattered Justin. Anyway Jesse's keeping Minkie company this evening; I ought to get home."

Berry heaved a final bag of rubbish on to a trailer. "The young American? You're surely not going to spoil their fun!"

In the end they were the last to leave. The rain that had miraculously kept off so far began to fall in a misty drizzle as they turned into the narrow short cut at the back of the school. Sara pulled her collar up, tucked a hand in Berry's arm. "Wasn't that lucky? The rain keeping off, I mean."

When he didn't respond she turned and looked up at him. "Berry?"

As he pulled her towards him, Sara's first startled reaction was to push against him, but the warmth of him, the softness of his mouth, the gentleness of his hand cupping her face seemed to home straight in on a well of loneliness that she had barely allowed herself to acknowledge. Just for a moment she let it happen, then breathing hard she pushed him away.

He said "I've been wanting to do that ever since you walked back into my life that first evening at Justin's party; but never more so than since our day on the canal. Don't tell me it's not what you've wanted too, Sara. Don't tell me everything's fine between you and Mike."

"I'm married to him Berry. He's a great guy who's been having a hard time and lost his way a bit. We both have." She put her hands over her face. "This should never have happened."

He let go of her and stood back. "Tell me you didn't enjoy it, and I'll never touch you again." Sara did not move. "Or we could meet from time to time well away from here, when Mike's away, with no one getting hurt. Or we can remain the friends we've become. You and I and Minkie. You can't deny me that Sara."

"I can't ... we can't ..." Sara began, then turned and ran for home.

She had forgotten about Jesse until she saw his vivid red banger parked outside the cottage. He and Minkie were at the kitchen table playing Scrabble and looking extraordinarily settled: a Darby and Joan in the making. Sara was too distressed to find it amusing.

"He's cheating and using American spellings," Minkie said indignantly.

"And some of hers are sur*real*!" Jesses's blonde head waggled in mock disbelief as he turned to her. "Hi Mrs Hennessey. Did the Fawkes guy burn nicely?"

"We could hear the fireworks from here," Minkie said and then registered Sara's expression. "Are you all right?"

"Thumping headache, that's all." Sara shrugged out of her coat. "I'll get off to bed."

She didn't sleep for three nights. There was no word from Berry, nor from Mike come to that. The head conversations went on incessantly. So did the head games. If I meet him in the market place, then it's meant to be. If Mike rings tonight it'll be a sign. If... if ... if ... Dear God, was this the rationalising of a forty-something-year-old, or an infatuated schoolgirl? But suddenly she was discovering that all she wanted was to be wanted. Was that such a crime? And Berry wanted her, that was for sure. And Mike seemingly didn't.

On the fourth morning the phone rang at eight-thirty on the dot a few minutes after Minkie had left for the school bus. "I'll keep ringing," Berry said. "I need you to answer one way or the other." After the third time they arranged to meet in a pub in Banbury.

"Well?"

"We'll try the friendship option," Sara said, knowing it was sheer wishful thinking.

"OK."

"I'm not sleeping with you."

"OK."

And then she stopped caring whether it was right or wrong.

Mike returned briefly from Sarajevo for Christmas. It became a challenge to guard this precious new secret, not least to prevent any hurt though Sara by now was convinced Mike wouldn't really care. Why else would he have lost interest in making love except for a couple of occasions when they had both had a particularly alcoholic evening?

And why did he wait so long to announce "By the way it'll be Belgrade in the New Year. It's pretty obvious things are festering in Kosovo and that we haven't finished with this Milošević guy. It'll be a great opportunity to look up Jovanka."

And who else? But it didn't seem to matter any more.

Christmas became a desert of dutiful enjoyment, punctuated by half a dozen village events at which she and Berry coincided. His friendly detachment on these occasions was worse than not seeing him at all. Patently he was much better than she was at this sort of thing. More practice? She dismissed the thought, not even caring what practice he might or might not have had. In the here and now he wanted *her* and that was all that mattered. It was a huge relief when Mike left.

And now a few days later on that early January morning in 1996, Berry was waiting for her on the little hump-back bridge over the Cherwell near which Royalist had done battle with Roundhead 350 years earlier.

They walked, holding hands, talking little until Berry stopped suddenly, put his arms round her and said, "This is driving me mad, Sara. We must get away from Daerley. Soon." Well it had always been inevitable. He went on "Minkie can stay with Azzie. You'll be invited by an old school friend. It won't even be a lie."

"OK," Sara said.

Briefly Berry looked startled at her lack of protest. She smiled at his expression. "Time to stop messing about," she said.

"On the contrary, time to begin," he corrected. He ran his hand gently over her face, then more probingly under her hair at the back of her head, his mouth tantalising, promising, close to hers as he said "God, Sara, if you knew how much I want this."

She could hear the desire in her own voice as she said, "Let's make it soon."

He knew a gem of a place, Berry said. A small hotel on the Dorset coast, which would be virtually empty at this time of the year. A cosy bar, good food, views over the sea and the cliffs where they could work up an appetite and get rid of any excess energy. Pre-supposing they had any to get rid of.

There were no more reservations in Sara's head. She'd been through all the arguments, had stopped looking for justifications. She and Berry wanted each other, full stop. Mike clearly had another agenda, and anyway she had no intention of leaving him. She just wanted for a while to be fully part of someone's life. Yes, and the sex that went with it, but not just that: the being with and the sharing. May be, above all, the wanting and being wanted. And just now she wanted Berry like hell.

They made their way slowly back to the village.

"Let's go in and drink to us," Berry fatally said as they reached the pub.

She was holding his hand, laughing her agreement as they went in. Then turned towards the almost empty bar. But only almost empty. From a corner by the window Azzie looked up in surprised recognition.

Extract from a letter of Lady Wortley Montague to Alexander Pope, 1717, on her travels near Novi Sad and to Belgrade, the latter still then in Ottoman hands

Crossing the battle-strewn plains that were to become shared by Hungary and Yugoslavia, Lady M. wrote "... we pass'd over the feilds of Carlowitz (Karlovci), where the last great Victory was obtained by Prince Eugene over the Turks. The marks of that Glorious bloody day are yet recent, the feild being strew'd with the Skulls and Carcases of unbury'd Men, Horses and Camels. I could not look without horror on such numbers of mangled humane bodys, and refflect on the Injustice of War, that makes murther not only necessary but meritorious. Nothing seems to me a plainer proofe of the irrationality of Mankind (whatever fine claims we pretend to Reason) than the rage with which they contest for a small spot of Ground, when such vast parts of fruitfull Earth lye quite uninhabited."

And a little later "We came to Belgrade, the deep snows making the ascent to it very difficult. It seems a strong City fortify'd on the east side by the Danube and on the south by the River Save (Sava), and was formerly the Barrier of Hungary." She comments on undisciplined soldiers and their forays to "burn some poor Rascian (Serbian) Houses."

Extract from the diary of Michael Quin, a passenger on a Danube steamer, in the 1830s

The boat did not land at Belgrade "in obedience to the quarantine laws", but gazing at it from the deck Quin saw that the "... city, which is associated with so many interesting recollections of the wars between Austria and the Ottoman empire, looks a splendid collection of mosques, with their white tall minarets, palaces with their domes, gardens, cypresses, and shady groves. The citadel, which is strongly fortified, occupies a lofty hill that overlooks every part of the town, and is well calculated for its defence. The palace and seraglio of the pacha were pointed out to me by our captain; they cover a considerable space of ground, and exhibit an imposing appearance ... It (the Danube) does, indeed, present a most magnificent sheet of water, upon which, if it were deep enough, the whole British navy might ride with safety; but with the exception of a few small wherries, in which some dirty Turks were fishing lazily in the sun, there was scarcely a symptom of animation around us. Belgrade itself looked at a distance like a city of the dead."

Mike - January 1996

Up in the sunlight, somewhere above Europe and several layers of cloud, Mike felt himself relax for the first time in weeks. Away from Daerley Green, he could now admit that Christmas had unfolded like an interminable charade. In the past it had quite often been difficult to adjust to the normality of rural middle England after an assignment at the heart of someone else's disaster; but never as difficult as this time.

His last stay in Sarajevo had extended longer than usual and he'd been entirely responsible for that. There had been a kind of awful fascination about the city's developing double life. As always in the wake of terrible events, a minority had trampled its way to the top of the heap and were illicitly making serious amounts of money; not to mention the vultures homing in from outside. Below them a far larger layer of opportunists made themselves ready to service their needs, while at the bottom the bulk struggled to survive.

By now the forested slopes above the city were denuded. The resulting firewood had earned small fortunes for those with the tools and nerve to brave the night and the mortars to harvest it. Foreign aid intended for basic rations for the whole population had increasingly found its way into the black economy where it exchanged hands at prices far beyond the reach of the most needy. It didn't take a clairvoyant to foresee that here were strong foundations for future trade routes in drugs, arms, prostitution, along with all the human flotsam that went with it.

Mike knew that his outrage at the widening chasm between the 'haves' and 'have-nots' was rooted in those memories of a waif-like Jasminka, her face closed against the world. It had come to represent for him the struggling soul of Sarajevo. And what of that other memory: of Marija of the green eyes? Several times he returned to The Two Doves restaurant. The block had been demolished and was now waste ground, a parking lot for abandoned and rusting machinery. There was no sign of the man with one leg.

He'd written some strong pieces on the black economy; researched them carefully interviewing some of those who thrived on it as well as its victims; local and United Nations officials; foreign aid workers. Heaven knows he ought by now to be unshockable, but the connivance and indifference he encountered appalled him. Canary Wharf, however, was not interested, informing him that Sarajevo was no longer top news, and the time was overdue for his return home.

So – reluctantly because he felt he had failed the real Sarajevans – he had returned to Daerley Green. It was mid-December. The Christmas tree donated annually by local businesses twinkled in its usual corner of the market place. DG Publishing had filled a display window with prints depicting Yuletide across the centuries, with packs of Christmas cards to match. Tinsel glittered in shop windows and, as dusk fell, Advent candles glowed in the house windows of the more traditionally-minded. Wall-to-wall carols pursued him round every supermarket. Goodwill burst from every pore. It felt obscene.

And Sara was in very strange mood. She had always been good at 'doing' Christmas: the tasteful decoration of both shop and home, the logistics of catering, gift-buying and wrapping, the several small drinks parties with the right mix of people. In this she hadn't changed. But it seemed to Mike he was observing a well-programmed automaton, relaxed, efficient, cheerful, considerate, impossible to fault at any surface level; but beneath that surface with a preoccupying agenda of her own. The feeling did not go away on the few occasions they made love.

Early on he'd said "It's not easy re-adapting to all this surfeit after seeing so much deprivation."

"Well, try and not wear your hair shirt too publicly," was Sara's almost absent-minded response. For a moment he thought she was going to pat him on the cheek; it would have been more appropriate if she had slapped it.

Yes, people with missions could be a real pain when everyone else was concentrating on a good time. But for Chrissake ... Then he had acknowledged that, after all, Sara had always shown a curious detachment with regard to his overseas assignments. No that wasn't quite fair. She regularly read and commented on his reports but always with a kind of unquestioning approval. He could not remember her once challenging his point of view or the processes that led him to it. On the whole that was understandable. He didn't go in for analysing the *Chronicle* or her sales strategies at Sara's Collectibles. Maybe cumulatively over the years that was where they had gone wrong.

He thought back to that determinedly good time over Christmas with its round of festive parties. He didn't dispute he was the odd one out, found it hard to believe he'd ever been part of such explosions of *bonhomie*. Mostly there was the same mix of people or, more accurately, the same *type* of people. Justin was always there. And that Beresford guy who in an odd way came to epitomise all that Mike found so difficult to meld with. Not that he had anything against the fellow. He was patently successful at whatever it was he did with golf courses, and no doubt had earned the comfortable, slightly self-satisfied affluence that he exuded. Certainly he'd been generous in many ways to Minkie who was obviously devoted to him. Mike also noted the occasional glance that showed he, in turn, had taken a bit of a fancy to Sara. Not so long ago he might have teased her about it; now it didn't feel like a good idea.

And Minkie herself? Her friendship with that blonde American boy showed no signs of ending. On the contrary. But at least he seemed wholesome and unthreatening; and very polite, though Mike judged him much less mature than his Minkie. He smiled a little, acknowledging in himself undeniable signs of 'proud, protective Dad' syndrome.

Not something to which he had ever been subjected himself. The next moment he was hurtling back through the tunnel of memory: to his seemingly perfectly nice, ordinary parents who, abruptly and inexplicably, had turned their backs on safe jobs and suburbia and thrown themselves into flower power in the early 1960s. Only eight or nine at the time Mike could recall no reason for it, only remember life thereafter as a haze of communes and muddy fields and eventually a tumbledown cottage just over the border in Warwickshire. What made it worse was that all the other kids had revelled in so much freedom and lack of order.

Once in the cottage, some kind of normality returned. His father had set up an odd-job enterprise; his mother took in ironing. He couldn't remember any sense of poverty: never any shortage of food or clothing, just strange meals thrown together at odd times, the impossibility of finding a quiet clear space to do his homework, and a school uniform that was clean but rarely ironed. Ironing was something you did for money for other people.

At school he had desperately tried to hide from his peers the chaos of his home life. Then he met Plum Pleydell, whose real name was Peter but everyone called Plum because of the way he spoke. Plum's father was in banking, his mother appeared to run everything in the village as well as being a fabulous cook. The house was steeped in a quiet order offering everything that was lacking in Mike's home life. He spent more and more time there.

Plum would have adapted with infinitely more easy to the commune life, Mike reflected now, for Plum was the sort that would adapt to pretty well any circumstance. A bit like a chameleon. Perhaps that's why his relationships never lasted and why he seemed equally able to survive happily without them. Yet, in that way of attracting opposites, he and Mike had become – and stayed – best mates. It was still to Plum's that he tended to head if he had any wounds to lick.

So, between Christmas and New Year he'd found an excuse to sneak off to London for a couple of nights with Plum on the town. He'd got drunker than usual, and managed to persuade the News Editor it would be a good idea to have a correspondent trawling the Belgrade scene for the former Yugoslavia's next move. Clearly the Balkans saga wasn't finished yet.

Which is why he was here in the sunlight, somewhere above Europe and several layers of cloud, being handed a small glass of *slivovica* by a handsome young woman who might have been Minkie in a few years' time.

He consciously relaxed his shoulders into the seat and took his first sip. Any resemblance between this firewater and the plum from which it originated was purely in the imagination he thought, as his senses absorbed the first onslaught. He took the opportunity to redirect his thoughts. So what did it taste like? Mike pursed his lips round the lingering feel of it – for it *was* far more a sensation than a taste – and gave it his full consideration. Soil … sun … limestone crags rearing from a purple sea … horizons filled with sunflowers … dark, smoke-stained medieval frescoes in hidden valleys . courage … pride … unspeakable barbarism … unimaginable sacrifice … a girl with green eyes.

No more purple seas, he reminded himself. Those belonged to the days of the so-called former Yugoslavia: well, except for the little Montenegrin bit.

"Why do you like my country?" Minkie had asked in those days when she had begun asking questions.

He had tried to give her a proper answer, better thought out than merely 'because it's beautiful and interesting'. Such epithets seemed meaningless when applied to that primeval splendour of rock coast and ravine, of mountain and plain, of human imprints from Neolithic times onwards, and disparate cultures that had survived two millennia-plus of power struggles from within and without. Especially from without.

In the end he had said something to the effect "because it is the sum total of so much that has survived in spite of everything." At which she had looked pleased with him, and added fiercely

"And *will* go on surviving."

His thoughts were interrupted by an announcement from the captain: they were about to descend on Belgrade.

He checked in to the large, modern glassy hotel in New Belgrade, overlooking the Danube; noted the shady characters hanging around the marbled spaces of the foyer. The vultures were gathering. Then he had a shower, changed, took a cab into the old town and went to walk in Kalemegdan.

Whenever he was in Belgrade he came here to this park created round the remains of a succession of fortresses. It was a microcosm of the country's history. He dawdled his way up through the labyrinth of paths, passed the art gallery, passed the restaurant, passed the Military Museum. Despite the cold there were plenty of people about, taking advantage of a watery winter sun: old men – still a few Partisans from World War Two among them no doubt – smoking, yarning, watching the grannies and the Mums with the kids rushing around on scooters or roller-boards as they would be in any major city in the West. At the highest point, beyond the broken stonework of Illyrian, Roman, but predominantly Ottoman and Habsburg times, he stopped as if at the end of a pilgrimage, and sat on a wall overlooking the confluence of the Sava and Danube rivers. Up here almost everyone else was part of a couple, deeply engaged in public displays of affection that would have scandalised their parents' generation. Certainly they had no eyes for the scene that always totally absorbed him: the centuries of history represented by the banks of the merging rivers.

Belgrade … Beograd … the Beli Grad or White City of the early Slavs, that was destined to straddle a political faultline splitting Europe for centuries. Across the Sava, there in New Belgrade where his hotel was, had been Habsburg territory. Here on the wall where he sat he was on the first defence line of the Ottoman Empire. Of the long Ottoman occupation of Belgrade only some fortifications, the odd mausoleum and a late 17th century mosque remained. But in the resulting conflicts across the political chessboard of Europe, few consulted the Slav inhabitants. And as hundreds of thousands of Serbs were encouraged to settle in the Krajina, becoming valuable guardians of those Habsburg borderlands with the Ottomans, who could have foreseen the explosion of tit-for-tat killing that would result three or four centuries later as the second millennium drew to a close?

Another young couple came to install themselves on the wall near Mike. Well, they certainly had not come to this spot for a history lesson. Likely as not the young man had more immediate conflicts to preoccupy him. Any number of young Serbs were disappearing to where hopefully no conscription machinery could ferret them out. Perhaps if it had been left to their generation .... Minkie's generation ... ? What a mess.

Next morning he set out to track down Jovanka. It was surprisingly easy. There were a number of places – cafés, church halls, libraries – that had become favoured meeting places for the dispossessed Bosnian Serbs. Some had family connections or friends in Belgrade; the rest made do with handouts and makeshift accommodation.

He found Jovanka teaching folk songs to a class of small children in a community hall. When he looked in, she had her back to him and, without understanding what she said, he saw that she was cheerful but firm with her charges. There was no heating and the children were wrapped like multi-coloured footballs as if for the Arctic. He retreated to wait outside with a growing group of women, presumably mothers collecting their offspring. They glanced at him without interest though his way of dress, let alone his masculinity, made him out of place. He was quite familiar with this Slav trait: telltale reactions instinctively kept under wraps until the situation could be more fully assessed.

When the singing had stopped and the mothers had gone in to claim their own, Mike followed them. Jovanka, still with her back to him, was being engaged by a tense, anxious young woman with two small boys clutching an arm each. He hovered in the background until they had finished and moved forward as Jovanka turned, noticed him, frowned questioningly, and then gave a flash of recognition.

He held out his hand and said, "I'm Mike Hennessey if you remember. Jasminka ..."

Her hand was firm and cool. "You brought us candles and chocolate. How can I forget?" He saw the mask of cheerfulness had also gone and there was a hardness about her handsome features that had not been there before. She looked stronger though than she had in Sarajevo; better groomed, better dressed, more determined. "You are welcome. We do not have the pleasure of many English visitors in Belgrade these days." The hall seemed strangely silent as the last of the Mums and children departed.

"I'd like to talk to you. If you have time, perhaps I could take you to lunch."

There was a *čevap* kiosk round the corner and a small park nearby where they found a bench in the sunshine and shared out the spicy minced meat morsels, onions, bread, like travellers on a journey far from home. He had wanted to take her to a restaurant, but she shook her head saying she only had half an hour before the next class, and she needed a breath of fresh air. She seemed oblivious to the cold.

"Tell me about Jasminka," she said now. Mike had brought photographs of her and passed them to her silently. He watched her face softening. Without looking up she said "A real little English schoolgirl. And not so little. And how pretty! But I'm happy she has not lost her Bosnian looks." Then she looked up. "If you want news of her mother, I cannot help you."

Mike nodded. "It was just a small hope. After all, I've been twice to Sarajevo and found nothing."

"You have been back? But of course you are a journalist, it is your work to go back to places, especially places where terrible things happen. Even to come here, to this – how do you say –

pariah? This pariah place of Europe." She straightened and said defiantly, "I shall never go back. I will stay in this pariah place." Her expression became sardonic. "So how is it in beautiful, multi-ethnic Sarajevo?"

Mike said simply, "A broken place full of broken lives, and I weep for it. It's not what I tell Jasminka, of course. She still has an astonishing faith that Sarajevo will rise from its ashes again; not just the bricks and mortar, but the spirit of it – that concept that despite all evidence to the contrary people can learn tolerance towards each other …"

Jovanka gave a bitter laugh. "That extravagant illusion on which we once all based our lives."

"Maybe - just maybe – it will be possible for the young, for the children?"

"I think you would have different opinion if you heard them crying in their sleep, the look of fear if there is a sudden noise. Or saw their paintings – the black shapes in the sky with open jaws and sharp teeth dripping red, the body parts scattered across the page like broken sticks, the little groups of houses by lakes of blood." Jovanka stopped. "You are a good man Mike. I wonder how do you describe these things in your newspaper; not just what you see now, but how anger and hate make ripples that don't stop at any boundaries." No point in telling her that Canary Wharf wasn't too bothered about tomorrow's news. She went on "After Bosnia, it will be Kosovo, and then Macedonia, and then … who knows?" She shrugged. "And wherever it is it will be the fault of those terrible Serbs."

"And Srebrenica?" He had to have her reaction to that vicious massacre by the Serbs the previous summer: thousands of Bosniak men and boys separated from their families, taken away, shot, in a supposed UN safe-enclave.

She snapped "Why do you not ask about the thousands of Serbs murdered by Croats in Knin, and the 200,000 Serbs attacked as they fled from the Krajina where most had families going back three, four hundred years? You did not speak of ethnic cleansing then." She fell silent, shaking her head as if beyond any hope of understanding. Then she straightened again, gave a determined smile. "You have done a wonderful thing for Jasminka. And you are right. Perhaps, just perhaps, with her genes from two devastated peoples she may hold the key. What a terrible responsibility, poor child. Will you be able to keep her?"

"If her mother really is dead, we will apply to adopt her of course. Though the bureaucracy will certainly be a nightmare."

She nodded. "And your wife is happy about this?"

Was she? "She's very fond of Minkie – that's what Jasminka calls herself these days." Mike launched into more detail of Minkie's life, her Iranian school friend, her American boyfriend, her art achievements and her undiminishing Bosnian patriotism. Then he asked Jovanka about her life in Belgrade. She said it was all right; she had work, a room to live in, she was independent. The Serbs of Serbia, she added, were not always as sympathetic as they had first been. There were too many – hundreds of thousands of refugees from Croatia, Bosnia, and now a growing number from Kosovo fearful of what was to come.

Mike said, "There is someone else I would like to find. A girl, a woman, I met many years ago in Sarajevo. Before the war. She was studying English then. A girl called Marija. I know she's in Novi Sad."

Typically, Jovanka showed no curiosity. "There are places in Novi Sad, like Belgrade, where the Bosnian community meet." She delved into her bag, found a pen and wrote on the back of an old envelope. "Here is the name of an old friend who will help you."

Mike took a visiting card from his wallet, scrawled his home address and telephone number on the back, and passed it to her. "Perhaps you could drop a line to Jasminka."

"I think it is better if she gets on with her new life. But if I hear news, anything about Branka I will write to you." She stood up, held out her hand. "I was happy to meet you again Mike. It is good to know not everyone has forgotten us." She walked away, straight and brisk, without looking back.

He rented a car from the hotel and drove the eighty kilometres to Novi Sad the following morning. The wintry sunshine had given way to thick cloud graded from ash-grey to blue black. You could tell just by looking at them that they piled up in mega layers for tens of thousands of feet, the weight of them almost a physical pressure on the flat Danubian plains of Vojvodina. They looked well husbanded those plains. In a few months they would be a bright patchwork of maize and wheat and sunflower, geese and chickens squawking and scuttling on the road verges through the villages. For now the scene was inanimate, earthy, drab.

On an impulse Mike turned off the main road into the little town of Srem Karlovci. It was a charming and typical community from its Habsburg heyday: no echoes of the bloody conflicts that had raged in the surrounding fields as the Ottoman Empire was finally forced to relinquish its hold. The Peace of Carlowitz signed in the little town in 1699 wasn't the end of it of course, but as Churchill famously said of a much later conflict it was "perhaps, the end of the beginning." Soon Sremski Karlovci became the mecca of a much earlier flood of dispossessed Serbs, finally abandoning their old medieval-heart-of-empire in Kosovo; and a few miles away the Austrians built Petrovaradin, their own Gibraltar on the Danube, to ensure victory remained theirs.

Mike stopped the car on the far side of the bridge in Novi Sad and leaned on a wall looking back at the massive fortress of Petrovaradin. Even its great size did not hint at the 77 kilometres of passages that burrowed down through eleven underground levels. Near the bridge was a gaunt memorial to many thousands of Serb and Jewish civilian victims in World War II. He noticed the fresh flowers. In this part of the world martyrs were not forgotten: from generation to generation, from century to century. Perhaps that was one of their weaknesses. And strengths.

He got back in the car and went in search of the address Jovanka had written down. And struck gold. It was a café just

93

off a main street, run by the man whose name she had given him: a sort of unofficial one-man lost persons facility. He was elderly, with a leathery face and sharp blue eyes and his English was almost too impeccable.

"A woman called Marija you say?" he repeated. "That's a bit like seeking a woman called Mary in Birmingham! Wait while I put on my thinking cap. And have a nice cup of Serbian coffee. We used to call it *turska* because it was made in the Turkish style. But now it's more politically correct to call it coffee. Though I can assure you the style is the same."

Mike smiled politely, wishing he would get on with it.

The man served him the coffee, disappeared into a back office, came out surprisingly soon. "I think – though I cannot guarantee it – that your Marija is a Kostić. She came here two years ago, after her husband had been killed. He was a Croat I should tell you. I think there was also a child, possibly two children who died. A shell hit the apartment while she was at the market."

The tone was so matter-of-fact it was quite chilling. Except that Mike knew, had learned that a daily diet of tragedy creates its own impenetrable walls.

"The last information I had of this Marija Kostić is that she is working in a restaurant called *Dva ribara*. That means The Two Fishermen. One wonders why only two? Here, I will show you where it is on your map."

And then Mike was out again in the grey afternoon with the first spots of rain driving in across the river. He left the car where it was. The restaurant was only a few minutes walk away, and he needed time to adjust to the thought of a possible encounter that would have seemed inconceivable a few hours earlier. In the event, all he could focus on were his own footsteps leading him towards it.

It was quite a large restaurant attached to a hotel. There was a bar leading off it where he could sit and sip more coffee and watch. Within five minutes he saw her. It was too far to distinguish those green eyes, but the dark cloud of hair and the way she walked and held her head were quite unmistakable. With a sense of total unreality, he moved to another seat so he could see her better without being seen, and he watched for two hours as she took orders, came and went through the squeaking swing door into the kitchens, served drinks, meals, took money, gave change. Clamouring pangs of hunger eventually reminded him that he had not eaten since breakfast in Belgrade, but terrified that the barman might delegate Marija to serve him, or that she might disappear while he was eating, he ordered a beer at the bar as a stop-gap.

It was just after five o'clock when she finished her shift and he followed her out on to the street, to the tram queue, on to a tram, swaying and rattling interminably through deepening dusk and ill lit streets, and eventually a short walk amidst a maze of high-rise blocks. She appeared lost in thought; how could she otherwise not have noticed this stranger dogging her footsteps? He let her go ahead in the lift, noting that it stopped for her on the eighth floor and came down immediately to his summons. And then he was there on her landing, looking at the tiny notices with their typed names. Number 831 – Kostić.

Mike could hardly breathe, his heart thundering in his throat. He stood, willing it to quieten so that he could think, think, think. Apart from a distant hum of traffic it was very quiet. He made himself look round the landing, notice the cracked plaster, the stale smell of cooking. Then behind him there was a clank of the lift as it began its journey down to pick up another passenger. Supposing they came to this floor, found him lurking there like a thief. He took a step towards Marija's door, put his ear close to it. Faintly he heard a man speak, then clearly a child's voice, bright and questioning. And finally a laugh – Marija's laugh – quite short, but unmistakable.

As the top of the returning lift came into view, Mike turned for the stairs and began the long journey home.

Jasminka – April 1996

Minkie had fallen in love with Jesse Maynard. And was missing Mike. And had made up with Azzie after a terrible row. And was confused.

In his absence she found herself adopting Mike's pre-breakfast patrol of the garden. It had become a tradition to join him on this soon after his brief return from Serbia the previous month. On the first occasion she had glanced out as she opened her bedroom curtains and seen him towards the bottom of the garden near the old oak tree. He was standing, hands on hips, looking down – at the first signs of some precious plant she assumed. Rus, who had become a temporary part of the household in Berry's absence, was squatting beside Mike, tongue lolling, looking up at him expectantly. But he went on standing for a long time, not moving, head down, shoulders bowed, and eventually Rus got bored and mooched off.

There was something about Mike's stance that reminded Minkie, with a sharp stab of pain, of her mother: that motionless slump, sunk in her own dark world, in those last days before Minkie had been dispatched to the children's home. And then her stomach clenched as she remembered what Azzie had told her only a couple of weeks earlier.

She finished dressing and slipped downstairs. Mike looked up and smiled at her approach. "'Morning Princess. A bit crack-of-dawnish for you, isn't it?" He'd taken to calling her Princess sometimes since he'd wolf whistled her new outfit for some rave a few months back.

"I thought it was time I learned something about all your plants."

Mike grunted sceptically. "And what's the real reason?"

She'd never been one to avoid a direct answer. "I thought you looked ... a bit ... sort of lost-ish."

"I'm absolutely fine."

Exasperated she said, "I'm not a kid, Mike."

He looked at her seriously. "No you're not." He ruffled her hair. "OK, so I found my recent trip quite difficult. It was wonderful to see Jovanka in Belgrade of course and she looked ... well, much better than when I saw her in Sarajevo. But her outlook has changed completely and talking to her made me realise where the real enduring effects of war lie. Rebuilding houses is one thing; lives are another matter. I don't think Jovanka will go back...." He paused, shaking his head. "Of course it's inevitable people's lives and attitudes get re-written in such circumstances; but when you apply it to someone you know and then multiply it hundreds of thousands of times ..." He stopped and gave her shoulder a squeeze. "And who should know better than you, Princess?"

Well, thanks heavens, at least it didn't seem to have anything to do with Azzie's unspeakable bombshell. Minkie slipped an arm round his waist. "You sound a bit like Justin, with all this cause and effect stuff."

Mike laughed. "Heaven forbid!"

"Seriously. Sometimes I think there could be something in it. You see Jovanka left Sarajevo and has given up on it, so it would change her feelings, wouldn't it? Yes, I know I left it too; but that was to please Mother, and I *know* it's possible for us to make things all right again. May be all right in a different way from before, perhaps even a better way? Don't you see? Especially my generation, mine and Franko's." She was silent for a moment, her mind working in overdrive on the thought that had been in the back of her head for a long time, but was now becoming more persistent with each passing month. Before she could think herself out of it she said, "You know I shall go back one day? To Sarajevo? You know I have to do that? I have to see what happened for myself, make bridges with the family. Look for Mother." She paused. "Or see her grave." It was a huge relief to have got it out.

He gave her shoulder another squeeze. "I suppose we've always assumed you'd want that – once we've sorted out the paperwork. And you've sailed through your exams of course." After a pause he went on "Don't get your hopes up that it will be soon though, will you Princess? It's not a good situation out there." They moved off round the garden, pausing to admire the golden flutter of daffodils, just passed their best, and the fattening heads of tulips on their tall straight stems.

"By the way, what's all this about you and Azzie? I wouldn't have imagined anything ever coming between you two. Or should I mind my own business?"

Minkie felt her face flare with embarrassment. He was the last person she could discuss it with. She muttered "We'll get it sorted," and he nodded and said, "OK. Let's head for breakfast then."

She hadn't told him – or Sara come to that - about being in love with Jesse either because that was still a precious private thing whose magnitude she couldn't fully grasp herself. He'd rung her quite soon after that first meeting at the art exhibition, and they'd started meeting on a regular basis, usually with one or two of their friends. To begin with Mike had driven her in to Oxford a couple of times, she was pretty sure in order to check Jesse out. But usually she went in by bus. After a while she noticed Jesse had stopped complaining about life being slow and unexciting. When she teased him about it, he said that things had been looking up recently. Minkie knew this had something to do with meeting her, and felt pleased.

They met most weekends, going for walks, doing a rave or a film, having a Balti or a Chinese take-away. Usually there was a small gang, nearly always including Azzie. And then one day they were on their own in a favourite spot by the Cherwell river and she had caught him looking at her in a way that made her feel like jelly inside. Just like in some of those yukky stories in magazines, only now it didn't seem yukky at all. He'd said in a funny voice "I guess you're the best thing in my life, Minkie." Then he kissed her, which hadn't been a great success because their noses got in the way and she couldn't breathe and she'd started giggling nervously. So he stopped kissing her and held her in a gentle warm hug that was the most wonderful feeling she had ever had. So wonderful and safe and caring that she'd had quite a struggle not to burst into tears because no one had made her feel safe in that way for a very long time. Then after a while they had another go at a gentle, not-quite-chaste kiss which she had relived a thousand times since.

The school week became an interminable limbo between meetings; and there was the huge problem of getting time on their own. It wasn't just the kissing – though how come she had never realised how amazing that could be? It was the getting to know this extraordinary being, this object of her love whom she'd taken for granted for months, but now had a thousand new facets that needed to be explored and possessed and understood.

The thought that Sara or Mike or both might not approve, might try and interfere in some way, was too awful to contemplate. And even before their awful row she'd sensed Azzie hadn't exactly taken to Jesse for some reason. No, the only solution was to keep this magic thing a precious secret. "It's the first big thing, really big thing, in my life that isn't the result of someone else making it happen. I'll die if anyone spoils it," she explained to Franko in her head.

Just filling even a small part of every day with each other's voices was soon a top priority. This was impossible to achieve from telephones that could be overheard, and Minkie could come up with no plausible reason for suddenly needing a mobile. So she went on a much discussed health kick which involved a daily cycle ride immediately after supper. Her circuit would include one of a number of public call boxes far enough away for it to be unlikely she might be spotted by curious eyes.

Jesse had needed some persuading. "It's not right me sitting in a warm apartment," he protested, "while you hang around call boxes." But Minkie could be very persuasive and Jesse was on the whole a follower rather than a leader. That much she instinctively sensed and she had no hesitation in exploiting her new-found sense of power.

The whole devious plan was fraught with exquisite peaks of anticipation and agonising chasms of anxiety. There could be the frustration of finding someone already in occupation of the selected call box at which Jesse was to ring at a pre-arranged time. Or there was the flood of relief to find it unoccupied, and the heart-thudding wait in that confined place with the smell of old coins and stale smoke and faint sweat, and the willing that no one would want to use the call box in the meantime. And finally the first ring which made her jump however much she expected it, and the sound of Jesse's voice with its soft transatlantic twang that made her want to smile as well as desperately want the feel of his arms round her. There was the daily risk that circumstances might forestall her outing: indeed one stormy evening Sara had put her foot down with the result that a frantic Jesse had rung in the middle of supper. The deviousness became an end in itself, transforming each telephone call into a heady daily adventure. She needed one almost as much as the other.

When Mike left again on some assignment, she began to undertake the garden tour alone. It was a time totally her own to re-run the previous evening's telephone interlude, remembering every intonation and pause and the magic of such total empathy with another human being. Sometimes she felt so explosively happy she couldn't believe that Sara would not notice and comment on it. But then with adolescence she had come to accept that she didn't feel, indeed had never felt, the same rapport with her as she did with Mike, so it was quite likely that Sara hadn't noticed.

Then for a while after that row with Azzie, she wondered if Sara would somehow guess the reason for it. Except there was no believable reason. The whole thing was outrageous. Nor was there a flicker of evidence to be detected in Sara's manner or bearing.

It had taken Azzie quite a while to come out with it but

when she did it was blurted out in a rushed, crude gabble: "I think Berry Tremayne's screwing Sara." Defiant and awkward, Azzie looked almost triumphant in her possession of such preposterous knowledge.

The two girls were walking Rus down by the canal at the time. Minkie stopped in her tracks, spun round to face her friend and croaked "*What* did you say?"

Azzie fumbled for better, more convincing words. "I saw Sara and Berry together. At Cropredy the weekend before last. They came into the pub there, holding hands and looking … well, you know."

Clinging to the irrelevant Minkie snapped "And what were you doing in the pub at Cropredy?"

"I went for a cycle ride. That weekend you and Jesse were at that rave near Abingdon. Remember I had my period and felt awful? Then I felt better and went for a bike ride. And there they were."

Minkie was choking with indignation. "You're making it up Az. That's an absolutely dire thing to say. Why should Berry … Sara …?"

Azzie went on looking awkward and defiant. "I'm not making it up. Why on earth should I?"

Minkie heard her voice getting shriller, couldn't stop it or the angry, unfair words that were spewing out in her distress at this threat to the only security she knew. "Because you never really did like Berry. Even though he's always really nice to you. You're dis*gust*ing, making up something like that…."

Then Azzie was angry, blazing back "It's not me that's disgusting – it's your precious Berry …. People are always having affairs – Uncle says in the West they have the morals of alley cats …"

Minkie's shrillness rose. "Well, perhaps your Uncle should go back to where he came from. And you as well. How dare you talk about Berry and Sara like that! You just want more attention, that's what. Because you're jealous of Jesse too aren't you? How *could* you? Rus! Rus! ***Rus!***" She looked round frantically for the dog that appeared through a gap in a hedge and came loping amiably down the canal path towards them. Minkie grabbed him by the collar, clipped on his lead and headed back towards the road.

She had taken a long circuitous route back to Daerley Green, her head full of shouting arguments and counter-arguments. Eventually she found herself in Whirling Wood and collapsed on to the seat, releasing Rus who went bounding off in happy relief into a world of familiar shapes and smells. And there she sat in an emotional storm of anger and bewilderment and sense of betrayal and, finally, a deep down fear that even the tiniest grain of truth would make the security of her life here disintegrate like blossom in the wind. Azzie was right, of course. Lots of people had affairs. But not people she knew. Not Sara, who called her in every morning from the garden with 'breakfast's up' and put her head round the bedroom door to say ''Night, love' each evening when Mike wasn't there to do it himself. Not Berry who had tapped into her deepest sorrow and given her hope.

Suddenly he was standing there, cross and anxious   "I guessed I'd find you here. What the hell's going on Minkie? I've had Azzie in floods of tears, convinced you're about to do something stupid and dramatic."

Minkie said sullenly "Azzie always goes over the top. We had a row that's all."

Berry sat down beside her. "Do you want to talk about it?"

"No!" No way.

"She's very upset."

"Yes, well ..." Minkie stood up She couldn't look at him. "I want to go home. I'll sort it later."

But she hadn't 'sorted it later' because she didn't know how. What Berry said to Sara when he delivered her home she didn't stop to hear. "If you want to talk any time let me know," was all Sara said later that day and gave her a little hug. Then she had chatted quite normally about all sorts of village things and even mentioned meeting Azzie in the pub that time, saying that she and Berry were out for a walk. Minkie became more and more convinced that the whole thing was a creation of Azzie's imagination, though for the life of her she could not begin to imagine why. In due course she also acknowledged that, while Azzie had made unforgivable accusations, she too had said some awful things.

It was Jesse who pointed out that it had been really brave of Azzie to take her concerns straight to Berry.

"I mean if she can't stand the guy like you say..."

"Well may be I exaggerated a bit," Minkie admitted. "It's not that she can't stand him; she just thinks he's sort of creepy for some reason." They were walking hand in hand along the river below Wolvercote.

"That's your specialty," Jesse agreed. "Exaggerating a bit." He pushed his shades up over his blonde hairline and looked down at her briefly in mock severity before sliding them down again. Shades were his speciality, worn regardless of season and light levels. Azzie said it was a stupid affectation; Minkie thought it looked really cool. He went on now "I think Berry's great and as you know I adore Sara almost as much as I adore you; and like you I don't buy this secret love stuff one bit."

"So why is Azzie being so awful? You're the psychobabble expert. You tell me."

Jesse looked quite serious. "You don't have to be a psychobabble anything to see that Azzie's gotten very lonely. You two had a real special thing between you. I never had a pal like you two have with each other. My guess is that Berry may not be her style of person, but the real problem is me. She must hate my guts for kinda getting in the way."

Minkie considered this new perspective in silence for a few moments. "But we're always including her in things we do. Even when we don't really want to."

"And that's the point. Azzie's not stupid. She'll be aware of that however much we try not to show it. And it's not just that, hon. She's gotta be missing the sort of girl talk you can't have with me around."

"Girl talk…" Minkie began, protesting. Then stopped, remembering the times beyond counting when she and Azzie had started on some thread of talk that slanted off into the ridiculous, then egged each other on into the ever more absurd until they were quite helpless with laughter. "So what can we do?"

"I guess the only thing we can do is stop being so darned selfish with this huge lucky thing we have going for us, and let her come and be part of it."

"That means letting everyone else in too."

Jesse stopped, turned her gently round and put his arms round her. "If this is as real for you as it is for me, that's gonna have to happen. Let's make Azzie the first so she feels special too."

As Minkie sat on the bus going home that evening, the full meaning of what Jesse had said slowly began to sink in: … *if this is as real for you as it is for me.* Suddenly this wasn't boy-meets-girl stuff any more. Suddenly this wonderful, exciting adventure that felt as though it need have no end had become serious, urging consideration, requiring decisions, demanding commitment. She felt very alone.

Without warning she felt the tears welling, her throat tightening so that she could hardly breath. With all her being she longed for Mother, wanted her there sitting beside her with that steady quiet voice reassuring, the feel of her firm hand on her cheek.

"You're looking very serious young lady," Sara said coming out into the hall as Minkie let herself in a deeply thoughtful hour later. She stood watching her a moment "Not getting too fond of that American boy, are you?"

Minkie was startled out of her preoccupation. So Sara wasn't as unaware as she had assumed. She made a face and said

"We're both a bit stressed out, that's all. You know exams, things like that. Thought I'd give Azzie a ring." It was at once the only sane and highly desirable thing to do.

"Good. Glad you two have made it up. Whatever it was."

But supposing Azzie put the phone down on her? "Or perhaps I'll bike over and see her." Of course she might well be out. She might equally shut the door on her.

But Azzie was not out, nor did she shut the door on Minkie when she turned up on the doorstep half an hour later, cycle left propped against the hedge. Simultaneously they burst into tears, flung their arms round each other.

"Sorry, sorry, sorry!" Azzie drew back at last, gave a loud sniff. "I was awful. And it's been awful. Missed you. Dreadfully You wretch." She led the way upstairs to her room. Auntie it seemed was out.

Minkie blew noisily into a hankie, handed Azzie a spare. "I was awful too. And missed you too. Dreadfully."

They sat on the edge of Azzie's bed staring at each other's blotchy, tear-streaked faces. Then Azzie's mouth wobbled a bit as she began a grin and said "I suppose I must look as much of a mess as you do." She got up and began brushing her long dark hair. "And, yes, I probably was wrong about Sara and Berry. And you were right – I was jealous of Jesse. He's OK – just a bit .. well, American, and he can't really help that."

"And I was thoughtless ..." began Minkie, then grinned too. In their relief at the reconciliation both were competing in taking the blame. She went on "Yes, I was thoughtless – couldn't believe what was happening to me." She paused awkwardly. "Shan't go on about it, but I do love Jesse terribly Azzie; only it's getting complicated because he wants us to be serious ... I mean of course I want us to be serious too, but he wants us to sort of go public." She thought for a moment. "I'm not sure exactly what that means."

"You're too young for what I think you think it means," Azzie said. "And that's not jealousy, it's common sense. Sixteen for heaven's sake."

"Seventeen."

"Well only just."

Minkie said soberly "I can't lose him Azzie. He'll be graduating this summer and then ... he's talking about going back to the States. And then there's his father who sounds absolutely terrifying. And what Sara and Mike will say. And Mother if ... when she hears." She stopped, gave a gulp. "I'd give absolutely anything ... *anything* ...to be able to talk to her." She felt the tears returning.

Azzie came back to sit on the edge of the bed and gave her a hug. "Look, as I'm the only rational person around here at the moment, let's look at this sensibly. The first thing is you need to talk to Jesse, get it clear what he wants, what you want. After all he's yonks older than us .. than you. At least twenty-two. He's obviously crazy about you for reasons quite beyond me, so he's not going to suddenly change his mind. And you must talk to Sara and Mike. You *must*. After all they are responsible for you while you're here. As for Jesse's father, he's not the one you're going out with. And being serious about someone doesn't have to be a life commitment." She drew a deep breath.

Minkie gave her a wan smile. "How did I manage all these weeks without you?"

"By the sound of it, you didn't."

Aware they were starving they went down to the kitchen and raided the fridge, talking non-stop, interrupting each other in the vital business of getting up to date with each other's lives. In a rare pause Minkie said "What *was* all that about Sara and Berry that day you saw them."

Azzie said "Oh I can't remember the details after all this time. I thought they were holding hands, but he was probably giving her a hand while she took off muddy boots or something. And after all, they're old friends. Weren't they at school together?"

"Yes, though Sara didn't seem a bit pleased when he first turned up in Daerley." Minkie shrugged, disposing of the entire episode in favour of much more immediate and interesting concerns. "You're right, I must talk to them – Sara and Mike."

But how did you tell your guardians you were desperately in love? All the way home Minkie rehearsed phrases, discarded them.

"I'd better tell you," she announced more loudly than intended as she burst in on them in the middle of News at Nine. "I'm in love with Jesse, and he is with me."

Mike flicked off the TV. There was a small pause, then Sara patted the sofa beside her and said "Come and tell us all about it then."

It came out in a torrent: how well they got on, how they liked a lot of the same things, enjoyed being together; then quite out of the blue they wanted to be together all the time. Only it felt so special they wanted to keep it to themselves, in case anyone… anything spoilt it. But now Jesse felt it was time … Minkie abruptly dried up, looked from one to the other deeply anxious.

"Poor Princess," Mike said. "It was quite obvious that you and Jesse had more than a passing fancy for each other. Yes, I confess we did check up on him and his family – you mustn't be mad at us. It wouldn't be normal otherwise when we're so fond of you - not to mention responsible for you. And with you sneaking off on those cycle rides, clearly something was up. We didn't want to interfere but all this lurking round telephone boxes … well, we had to be sure."

Minkie looked from one to another of her foster parents, the beginning of a new awareness of what it really meant to be responsible for another human being; and felt suddenly much older herself. She said "Being committed is quite complicated isn't it?"

"Yes, Princess, it is. It's also quite rewarding if you're committed to the right person."

Sara added "Anyway at least you won't have to lurk round telephone boxes any more. Though with a perfectly good cordless I'm not sure why you felt the need." She leaned forward and gave her a pat. "You know I'm very fond of Jesse. How about his family? His father's something diplomatic I gather. And isn't there a stepmother?"

"I haven't met them yet, and I expect his father'll hate me, being foreign." Minkie pulled a face. "Jesse wants me to go there one evening soon. He sounds terrifying."

"Well it's not him you're going out with" Sara said, echoing Azzie.

But next morning, for all of several minutes, Jesse and his father were forgotten as Minkie picked up the morning mail. An envelope addressed to her in a large sloping hand had German stamps and a Hamburg postmark; and on the back the sender's name: Franko Simić.

In a surge of joy, Minkie tore it open, her glance skimming across the sprawly message in Cyrillic. Franko had written: *I got your letter at last and can't wait to see you dearest Jasi. I plan to be in England soon and hope you will be able to help me.*

Sara – September 1996

In Afghanistan the Taliban were about to overrun Kabul, depose the government and impose strict Islamic rule. In northern Iraq conflict between rival Kurdish factions continued to bring a heavy death toll. And in Daerley Green it had been, so far, a year of emotionally exhausting peaks and troughs. Mike had spent much of it commuting between London, Belgrade and Kosovo. Polly Cuttle was expecting her third child. Following Jesse's return to America, Minkie sank into a restless gloom. Justin had been extremely ill. And, indescribably above all, there was Berry.

That micro-moment of seeing Azzie sitting there in the corner of the pub in Cropredy back in January was an indelible memory. Sara could still hear her own false bright voice as she'd said, "Why, hello Azzie. So you're exploring fresh pastures, too?" And then Berry's over-genial "Fancy another of whatever you're having there?"

For long moments Azzie had stared at them, mouth opening and shutting soundlessly before she managed "Thank you – but I was just going anyway," which she patently wasn't.

As the door closed behind her Sara said "She was supposed to be with Minkie at some rave near Abingdon." She felt the anger rising. "It's so un*fair*, so bloody unfair. Of all the totally diabolical things to happen."

"You're over-reacting," Berry said, steering her towards a table furthest from the bar. "Just sit there while I order us a lager. Then we'll think this through"

But the anger and disappointment and sense of injustice had become a tightening knot in her head. It had taken her so long to reach this point, to talk herself out of guilt and into a commitment that she knew was one hundred percent self-indulgence. Couldn't she even get away with this one puny flaunting of convention? Other people were doing it. All the time. Already the guilt was back, chipping away at hard-won certainties.

"So that's that," she said flatly as Berry returned with the drinks.

"What's what precisely?"

She stared at him petulantly. "Come on, Berry. You saw Azzie's face. You don't seriously think she's going to believe some tale about Minkie staying with her while I visit a school friend, and you just happen to be away at the same time?"

He met her gaze steadily. He said "Sara, my love, there is no way I'm letting you go after all this. No way. Azzie is little more than a child. We only have to be as casual with each other as we've always been and she will soon think she must have imagined it. And what did she see? You were holding my hand and she knows we have been friends since ... since we were her age. What kind of a sin is that?"

The knot in Sara's head began to loosen a little. "She's not going to buy the coincidence of us both being away at the same time."

"Leave it to me," Berry said.

A month later Minkie announced that, through contacts with local parents, some open air outfit in Snowdonia was offering a modified Outward Bound course at half term to selected youth clubs and "please, *please*, can I go." Over the phone Mike expressed reservations until assured that one of the youth club leaders would be supervising the group. And Azzie was going too. Of course.

Berry's "gem of a place" was a small hotel tucked into a sheltered corner overlooking a sandy Dorset cove, its café and its hire facilities for every kind of beach paraphernalia shuttered for the winter. There was a snug bar, an attractive dining room with bay windows looking out over the coast. The hotelier and his wife were courteous, efficient and unintrusive. A couple of sales reps and a pair of dedicated walkers were the only other residents and in any case they were out most of the day. Much of which Sara and Berry spent in bed.

"It's never been as good as this," Berry said in one of the interludes when they lay back looking at each other, briefly satiated. "Sara, Sara, you're fantastic."

"It's not me. Nor you. It's the five-star combination."

They went on lying there, looking at each other, quietly waiting: Berry on his side facing her, propped up on one elbow, Sara lying back against the pillows. She saw his gaze drop from her face to her body, glanced down too, scanning herself in slight astonishment. Her figure seemed to have improved beyond recognition, filled out, become unashamedly voluptuous. Especially her breasts and the warm firmness of her inner thighs. Even without looking up she could feel Berry's eyes on her breasts, watched the nipples harden in anticipation as though they had an agenda of their own, sensed him reaching out for her. Then, with a small moan of pleasure, she rolled over towards him.

So it went on. Their love-making ... lust ... sexual gratification ... was mind-blowing as if the weeks, months, of postponement and uncertainty had built up a head of pressure that had become beyond the power of either of them to control. Having sought and found satisfaction in each other by no more subtle means than following their own preferences, they could not as Berry once gasped as he reached some new peak 'get enough of it'. Never in her wildest imaginings had Sara thought herself capable of such ecstasy, firmly shutting off the thought that it was on the basis of so little love.

In due course they discovered and explored other talents, especially during those interludes between the peaks: those moments in the eye of the storm, as Berry put it. They found that renewed arousal could begin as much with a glance as a touch or the sound of the smallest change in the pace of breath. And then that, almost intuitively, they could bring each other to matching levels almost at will as satiation melded from reality to memory and then to a mounting urgency for the satisfaction to come.

Once Berry said "I reckon if we'd carried on all those years ago we'd have burnt ourselves out before we reached twenty." It was the first time either of them had referred to their brief teenage affair.

"So perhaps it was as well you went to Frankfurt and put me out of mind."

"Is that what I did? I must have been mad."

Piqued that he could not even remember that much of an episode that had turned her own life upside down, Sara came close to lobbing the revelation of her abortion at him. There was a brief engulfing sense of power as she tried to visualise what might replace that look of self-absorption. But no, the possible repercussions were unimaginable and, anyway, for the moment she was too addicted to everything that Berry had come to represent.

In between their sessions in bed, they went for brief forays along the coastal path, lingered over the hotel's excellent meals, quietly watched each other over 'just another nightcap', hyping up each other's expectations for the coming hours.

They had three full days and four nights. For the first two days and three nights little existed beyond this mutual pleasure. Occasionally the thought of Mike emerged fleetingly from an existence that was otherwise totally disconnected with the here-and-now. In any case, Mike had another agenda equally disconnected from her: somewhere in a city she had never visited. She was sure of it.

It was on the third day that she saw in the distance a girl who reminded her of Minkie. Without thinking she said "What are we going to do when we get back to Daerley?" It was the first time she had voiced an acknowledgement of the future.

Berry had a hand wrapped round one of hers, comfortably tucked inside his pocket. "We'll find a way."

Sara felt the beginnings of panic. "I'm serious, Berry. We can't go on like this."

He laughed. "Well no, may be not quite like this. All that

huffing and puffing might get noticed...."

Sara stopped walking, turned to look at him. "You're not hearing me, Berry. I've been carefully keeping my head buried in the sand about the future."

"May be you have, but I haven't. So stop panicking. With Mike away so much, and with my golfing contacts round the country – let alone abroad. For heaven's sake there's absolutely no problem that a bit of ingenuity won't overcome."

She wriggled her hand out of his, clenching both fists in her urgency to make him understand what she was only just beginning to understand herself. "I can't do that Berry. I can't go on living that sort of lie."

He frowned. "You're seriously telling me that being a lying cheat is OK for a few days, but there's a time limit on it? And after that you'll go back to playing happy families with someone who doesn't even notice you're there half the time." As Sara flinched, he put his arms round her, bringing her back in from the cold. "Sorry, sweetheart. But it's true. And in case you hadn't noticed, I have something of a need for you. And I don't think I'm mistaken that it's mutual ..." He nuzzled into her ear. "Look, we still have some magic hours left. Let's not waste them. Just trust me that I can work something out."

So it had been easier to put her head back in the sand for a little longer, and swamp niggling doubt with the seismic fulfilment of sexual appetites she had only just fully discovered.

They had left Sara's car in a pub car park far enough from Daerley to be secure from any potential sighting. They'd had lunch there and asked the barman if they could do this; he'd managed to manifest just about everything except a knowing wink to show he understood very well what was going on.

"I don't think I want to face that man again," Sara said as they drove away from the hotel. But it turned out to be out of pub hours and there was no need.

Parking beside her car they sat for a few last minutes in Berry's, neither wanting to be the first to break out of the cocoon that had sealed them off from the rest of the world for the past several days.

"I'll ring you tonight," Berry said.

"Not tonight. It will be Minkie's first evening home." Already the rest of the world was out there, waiting.

"I'll ring late." Berry's face lost its normal composure. "You'd better go before I start tearing your clothes off. Go."

As she began the short remaining journey home Sara directed all her concentration to the mechanics of driving. She let Berry get well ahead, until the familiar silver shape was no longer in view, even on that long, empty, undulating stretch that was one of her favourites as it followed one of the Cotswold ridges with sweeping views on either side. It felt unexpectedly good to be alone and in total control, even of such simple processes as changing gear in response to the road's curves and gradients.

She could hear the telephone ringing as she closed the garage door behind her, and the answering machine cut in followed by a murmur of male voice as she bundled clothes over one arm, let herself in by the communicating door with her free hand. A persistent beep informed her there were several messages, but having dumped her things in a pile at the foot of the stairs, she consciously delayed the moment at which the world would finally be allowed to intrude.

There were four messages from Mike: three from Belgrade, the latest from London sounding increasingly surprised at her absence. "Give me a ring at Plum's," the last one said.

Among a miscellany of other queries, requests, invitations, greetings, mostly connected with Daerley affairs, two were from Minkie. One was from two days earlier exploding with enthusiasm about the good time they were having; the second from the previous day, ended with an aside "No you can't Azzie, she's still not there."

"Damn," Sara said aloud. And then noticed how cold the cottage was. And quiet. Like a waiting animal.

Why on earth had she not foreseen that half the world

would be ringing her, but above all Minkie? She said aloud "I don't think I'm very good at this," then reached for the phone and punched in Berry's number.

"Wonderful!" His voice deepened with pleasure as he recognised hers.

"I'm afraid it isn't," Sara said, and told him why.

There was a brief pause before he said calmly "Don't get paranoid sweetie. For heaven's sake you're allowed to be out sometimes aren't you? Shopping? A walk? Having a drink with me? Or with Justin if you think I sound too sinful? Anyway I can't believe Minkie's going to check up on you."

No but Azzie might. She urged him to keep a low profile, at least for a while. Reluctantly he agreed, adding that he couldn't help it if he happened to bump into her.

The priority now was to get the cottage looking homely and lived in, and a meal ready for the girls' return. It would be normal for Azzie to stop off for a bit of supper before she went home. An opportunity, too, for her, Sara, to be her usual self, annulling fears and suspicions. If only she could remember what her usual self was. What a mess! And she had just …Sara glanced at the hall clock – hell, only a couple of hours to get herself together.

She put the central heating on full blast, scurried back and forth emptying the car and putting away all signs of her travels, fished a casserole and Minkie's favourite chocolate pudding out of the freezer and put them to defrost in the microwave, scooped up the small pile of mail that had accumulated on the doormat. And then remembered Mike.

The familiar sound of his voice answering the phone was almost shocking, as though he had unexpectedly returned from an infinitely long and distant journey. The thought flashed: *but it's me that's been on a journey this time – and what a journey* just before he exclaimed cheerily, "Darling! At last! I thought you must have left me."

I did, Sara said in her head. Aloud she said a good deal

more casually than she felt, "Sorry - you know what this place is like for riotous living."

"I know what you're like. How's the Princess appreciating the great outdoors?"

"With enthusiasm according to her phone calls. She and Azzie are due back any minute. When are you coming home?"

"That's the problem, love. With the Balkans situation so volatile I'm heavily in demand. Off to Kosovo in the morning. Why the hell they couldn't have thought of that while I was still in Belgrade …" Sara was conscious of a huge sense of relief that she wouldn't have to face him. Yet.

She said "Any idea how long?"

"Inside of a week I reckon." A pause. "You sound … different. Are you OK?"

"Fine. As ever."

"Tell Minkie to call me when she gets back." Another pause, then a short laugh. "Let's try not to change beyond recognition, eh?"

Sara said lightly "We can always swap photographs."

"I wasn't just thinking of appearance," Mike said.

What a very odd thing to say. But this was no time for analysis. Sara took the mail into the living room and perched on the edge of the sofa riffling through it: a bill, a small forest-worth of junk mail, a couple for Mike – one with a Yugoslav stamp. She held it for several moments, turning it over in her hand. From the smudged postmark she could just decipher the place name of origin: Novi Sad. It meant nothing to her. Wasn't Jovanka in Belgrade? She examined the writing and decided it looked feminine. She thought, if only Mike were having an affair it would let her off the hook.

The thought was not appealing.

She toyed with the idea of opening it; after all she could claim to have mistakenly thought it was addressed to them both. But suddenly she didn't want to know one way or the other, as though the not-knowing was some kind of penance she must accept in return for her own infidelity. She turned to a letter with a US stamp for her. From Amanda in New York. She wrote marvellous letters, bringing life to places and people in a few words, and Sara tried to concentrate on her latest adventures in the Big Apple; and not least that she was planning to return to the UK in the autumn. "Think I've had enough of mega-everything," Amanda wrote. "Time I down-sized again."

But Sara's mind kept going back to the letter for Mike and then, by association, catapulted to Berry, the feel and the smell and warmth of him, his expression as he watched her before love-making, and an awareness of her own responses even to these thoughts. She closed her eyes and let the feelings wash over her. It was all developing into an almighty complicated mess – far beyond anything she might have imagined before she embarked on this self-indulgent escapade. And she was no more capable of giving it up than she imagined an alkie or druggie could give up their addiction.

Minkie's "Hi-i-i-i-i! - anyone at home?" and the slam of the front door brought Sara sharply back to the present. She stood up quickly, smoothing her hair, adjusting the scarf round her neck as though preparing to meet a stranger. Then Minkie was in the doorway, glowing with good spirits and well being.

"Welcome home, love." Sara looked beyond her. "No Azzie? I thought she'd stay for supper."

"No, for some reason she just grabbed her bike from the garage and said she'd better get home." Minkie shrugged. "She's been a bit odd. Probably PMT. I'm starving."

Sara's heart sank, aware of far more likely causes for Azzie's oddness than PMT. Her fears were confirmed only a few days later when she opened the door to Berry, Rus and a thunderous-looking Minkie who pushed passed her and stormed upstairs.

"For God's sake what's happened?"

"Probably not what you think," Berry said. "At least not in the way I think you think it."

In no mood for conundrums Sara said sharply "You'd better come in and explain."

He followed her into the kitchen from which Sara dispatched Rus into the back garden. Berry stood fiddling with his lead. "Azzie landed on my doorstep a couple of hours ago in near-hysterics. She and Minkie had apparently had the mother of all rows as a result of which Azzie was convinced Minkie was about to top herself or something equally unlikely. She – Azzie that is – demanded that I immediately go and look for her, but refused to come with me. She also refused to tell me what the row was about. It's rather surprising that she came to me as it's been clear to me for a while that I'm not her favourite person; but then she knows I'm devoted to Minkie ...."

Sara leaned on the sink watching Rus investigating some unseen treasure at the foot of the oak tree. "So it's pay-back time already."

"I'm not sure what that's supposed to mean but it sounds unhelpfully like a dose of self pity." The impatience in Berry's voice shocked Sara into silence. He said, "I think I'm as anxious not to lose Minkie's affection and regard as you, and exuding guilt is not the way to go about it. Yes, we've had some fantastic sex - for Chrissake it's not a criminal offence. And I have every intention that we shall have plenty more. But we're just going to have to cool it for a while, that's all. To protect Minkie – OK and Azzie too."

"Not to mention Mike ...."

"Who is not my first priority." Berry's expression softened. "Sorry. It's just that I can see you hyping yourself up for the guilt-trip of the century, and I'm selfish enough not to want to suffer from any fall-out. It's going to be difficult enough staying away from you."

Sara said in a subdued voice, "You're right. Minkie's the important one, and Mike is my problem."

"Well, maybe I have the solution, at least in the short term. I was going to tell you anyway - that there's pressure from above for me to test the golfing waters in some new tourist destinations in eastern Europe: the burgeoning Czech Republic in the first instance. Under the circumstances it makes sense to schedule this sooner rather than later."

Appalled Sara said "You're going away?"

"Oh my love, can't you imagine how much I wish I could take you with me?" They stood looking at each other, Sara leaning against the sink, Berry by the breakfast bar. In a voice so low she could just catch the words he said "God, if you knew how I want you this minute." As she wanted him. He did not move towards her.

She said shakily. "You're right. It's what's best all round."

Later, after he had gone and when Minkie eventually came down to pick at her supper, Sara said with all the casualness she could muster, "If you want to talk any time let me know. I don't like the idea of you and Azzie falling out." It had never been more difficult to haul her mind back from where it wanted to be, but somehow she had gone on chatting, dredging up every piece of local gossip she thought might draw Minkie out of her dark cloud, even daring to end with "By the way, you were pretty rude to Berry so you'd better go and make your peace with him before he goes off – next week I think he said. To the Czech Republic."

Minkie looked up at her. "Azzie doesn't like Berry."

"Oh? I wonder why." Sara began clearing the table. "Come to think of it she didn't seem that pleased to see us when we bumped into her in Cropredy. That week-end you were at the Abingdon junket. We'd gone for a walk Berry and I. We vaguely wondered then if you'd had a fall out."

"No, she just wasn't feeling very well." Minkie watched her for a while, then began to help her. Sara could sense her mood almost tangibly changing. "I think she's a bit neurotic. Anyway, you're right – I'll go over and see Berry in the morning."

Mike returned briefly in March. It seemed that the situation in the Balkans was not getting any better with festering hatred erupting ever more virulently in ever more places. Sara, watching through the kitchen window, noted that Mike seemed to be finding it easier to talk to Minkie than to her these days. She had tried sharing her concerns over the quarrel between the two girls, but he brushed it aside with "we must let them sort themselves out; they're not children anymore." As far as Sara was concerned, they were not adults either, but she kept her other major worry – that Minkie seemed to be getting too fond of that young American – to herself.

Before he went back to Kosovo, Mike returned from London one week-end with a box of paraphernalia that resolved into a computer and basic accessories, discards apparently resulting from one of Canary Wharf's upgrading exercises. "Brill," was Minkie's enthusiastic verdict, "Jesse's right into this sort of stuff. Can't wait to get on the Internet."

Soon after Mike returned to Kosovo, Justin was rushed into the Horton in the early hours of a Monday morning.

"Felt something was quite dramatically wrong," he explained to Sara when she shot into see him as soon as she heard the news. "Rang 999. Just like in that *Casualty* nonsense on the box. What a performance." He was attached to a monitoring machine and looked impressively frail for such a large man.

"I've been neglecting you," Sara said contritely.

"You have, dear girl" he agreed, "but I don't hold you directly responsible for this little adventure." He reached out a hand and patted hers resting on the bed. "Seeing too much of that Beresford fellow I reckon. You want to be careful. Thought he was rather splendid at first. Now not so sure." He began to sound breathless.

"You're talking too much," Sara said. "Anyway he's away on a long trip."

A very long trip as it was turning out: by then already a month as a short stay in Prague was followed by a succession of

Bohemian spas. "Steeped in faded Edwardian elegance," Berry reported in a postcard to Minkie, "which yours truly is attempting to adapt to meet 21st century ambitions." This apparently included the restoration or creation of a number of golf courses in places with unpronounceable names. So much Sara gleaned from a couple of other postcards addressed to Minkie and which she surreptitiously scanned en route from doormat to breakfast table. Berry was clearly sticking to their agreement that there should be no direct communication between them. She had been unprepared for the levels to which her sexual addiction to Berry had taken her, or rather the withdrawal symptoms when that addiction could not be fed. At times catching her reflection in the mirror, she was shocked by the raw misery she saw there. The physical ache was never far away; at times it was unbearable, except that it had to be borne.

Gradually it became easier; or at least less difficult. Without that first fix it seemed easier to manage without the next and the next. She embraced the intrusion of Daerley affairs and Sara's Collectibles' daily needs for her attention. The shop's new look had led to mentions in a number of local and specialist publications and a welcome boost in sales. Sara began to focus more on finding new local talent and promoting it with special weeks. For much of the time, thoughts of Berry retreated to a lower level of consciousness.

Mike's estimated 'within the week' in Kosovo had also proved open-ended. From one almost incomprehensible phone call and messages relayed from Canary Wharf, Sara understood that a repeat of Bosnia was in the process of fermentation. "Only this promises to be much worse," Mike's voice crackled over the atrocious line.

Trying to understand, Sara produced an atlas one evening. "Tell me about Kosovo," she said, "And why it's to important."

Minkie began riffling through the pages. "Well, it's a very beautiful area in the southern part of Serbia. It's where we have our oldest and most beautiful monasteries. Look, there. That bit squashed in between Albania and Greece. It's where we fought a great battle against the Ottoman Turks in order to save our empire, and our culture. June 28th, 1389."

"And what happened when you won?"

Minkic shook her head. "Oh we didn't win. That was a terrible tragedy, for Serbia. In fact, for all Europe because after that the Turks went on advancing more and more and more until eventually they came right to the gates of Vienna."

It was very baffling. "So why was it such an important battle if you lost it?"

Minkie looked at her in amazement. "So much Serb blood lost to save our country and the birthplace of our culture! Later many Serbs moved to the area we call Vojvodina, north of Belgrade, and rebuilt monasteries there. But Kosovo will always be our heartland. And now the Albanians want to take it from us."

Sara decided she would never understand.

A few days before Mike's return, she received a letter from Berry. Her heart began to race as soon as she saw his writing. She stuffed the envelope in her pocket until Minkie was out of the way, and then sat on the edge of the bed, looking at the envelope for minutes of anxiety and anticipation before ripping it open.

"Sara, my precious - This is one message I don't want to relay through Minkie. It seems, my darling, that we shall be apart rather longer than either of us ever anticipated. Through my work here, I've made a good many contacts in sport tourism in all the neighbouring areas, first of all in the Czech Republic and Slovakia, and now in Slovenia. There's the potential for a really superb site here not far from the Austrian border: near a place with the unlikely name of Ptuj, pronounced like a sort of stifled sneeze! As well as being a spa, it's incredibly old – back to Roman times, that sort of thing. When it's finished it will be one of the best courses in Europe, if I have anything to do with it.

"Anyway, my love, the point is that I've been offered the

job of overseeing its development for the rest of the summer: that means discussing the layout of the course, and all the allied buildings with the architects. The project is tied up with the UK consortium that employs me, so I can hardly say no. It's a great challenge too. But I ache for you. Is there any chance of you coming here for a trip. I can promise you days and nights we'll never forget."

There followed a postbox address where she could write to him and several more pages of impassioned exhortation that she should join him for whatever time she could manage.

Sara sat on the edge of the bed for a long time, reading and re-reading the letter, feeling the stirring of old desires. She had never been under any illusion that Berry would remain faithful to her, accepted that sleeping around was an intrinsic part of his life style. But she did believe that their ability to fulfil each other's needs was in a class of its own, sufficient to bring him back to her whatever other adventures he strayed into. '*...promise you days and nights we'll never forget... .*" She lingered over the words, wondering if there was a shelf life for animal magnetism. So much for the nobbling of her own addiction: one letter, a few suggestive phrases, and she was back to square one, wildly making plans that she knew could never be realised. She sat on the edge of the bed for a long time rocking to and fro, wanting Berry and furious at the wanting in almost equal measure. Later she wrote a short message: alas, no hope of getting away; Daerley Green as demanding as ever; of course she missed him but just think how they'd make up for it when the time came. She felt better for managing to keep the tone controlled.

And then Mike was back. An accumulation of leave meant that he had more time at home than for a long time, and unexpectedly he seemed to want to spend it with her.

"I think we need to get back in touch," he said one evening. "You look like you could do with some light relief."

At first surprised, Sara then grappled with guilt for several days, supposing this to be the ransom demanded as retribution for going against her own unwritten code. Fairly soon she noted that Mike appeared to carry no such burden. Berry certainly never would. If she were to become a fully paid-up member of the real world where cheating was OK if you kept the fall-out to a minimum, perhaps it was time to get rid of guilt, too.

They did a lot of things – trips to Stratford, Cheltenham, Bath, country runs for a pub lunch. It was like rediscovering a comfortable old friendship. They even took Justin with them once or twice on his return from hospital; Mike seemed suddenly to have taken to the old boy, encouraged him to talk about his early days, especially in the Balkans.

It was also a great relief when Minkie patched up her quarrel with Azzie and almost simultaneously confessed her love for the young American. A dinner arranged at Jesse's home so that Minkie could meet his father and stepmother had not been a great success. "I felt like a prize cow on show," Minkie reported, resentful and disappointed. "He obviously hated me."

For a while, following his unexpected message from Germany, she had been buoyed up by expectations of seeing her beloved cousin Franko. Then in June two brief emails from a cyber café in Prague assured her all was well and he would be seeing her very, very soon. A further silence was broken by a longer email, this time from Germany again, in August. He had had to change plans but it was absolutely certain he would be coming to England in the next few weeks.

"I can't wait to see him," Minkie said, but each time with a little less conviction that it was going to happen.

Jesse had graduated that summer with a First and been almost immediately dispatched by his parents "to go back home to show the rest of the folks what a great guy I am. But be sure I'll be back before you've noticed I'm gone." He was still emailing her daily, but on the whole it had not been a good summer for Minkie.

At the beginning of September an email arrived from

Amanda. DG Publishing had offered her the job of heading a new department to launch a series of school textbooks. New York had been a wonderful experience, but she couldn't wait to be back. She had come to an arrangement with the tenants of her cottage who would be out by the end of the October, so in the meantime she planned to bed down in The Trumpet. So would Sara please get out the red carpet?

It would be great to have her back.

Mike, Minkie and Azzie had gone to the cinema in Banbury that Saturday evening in late September when the phone rang as Sara was watching a TV documentary. Amanda's unmistakable voice with just the faintest new nuance of trans-Atlantic twang said breathlessly "Whatever you're doing, stop doing it. Your lager is lined up."

Five minutes later they were embracing, laughing, talking at the same time, standing back to look at each other appraisingly.

"You look a bit wan," Amanda said. She was stunning in a jazzy two-piece, her hair in a becomingly youthful fly-away cut. She gave a mischievous grin. "And I think I know someone who might help: sitting in the very place where you are now not half an hour ago. Says he's a good friend of yours, just back from some jaunt round Europe. A rather dishy guy. Name of Beresford. Ring a bell?"

Mike : March 1997

Early on a Saturday morning in late March, Mike stood at a twelfth floor window in Novi Sad staring out between tower blocks at a strip of grey Danube.

"Coffee?" said Jovanka behind him.

"Thanks." He turned away from the window. From the outside the tower blocks were of uniform and stupendous ugliness. Within, each apartment was a microcosm of its owners' history and aspirations. He remembered that Jovanka had once told him she would never go back to live in Bosnia. Instead she had frozen it in time and transposed it to her one-and-a-half rooms in Novi Sad.

The half-room was a slit of a study: lined floor to ceiling with books, just space for a small desk and a narrow bed. It was on this that she insisted on sleeping while he had the lumpy but broad sofa bed in the living room. After his initial protest he accepted this, knowing her sense of hospitality would be deeply offended by any other arrangement.

Woven woollen wall hangings in soft colours concealed a mesh of plaster cracks. A large oil painting captured the domes and spires and minarets of central Sarajevo's skyline caught in a drifting haze of smog between the wooded mountains. Smaller paintings filled in the detail: a carved doorway, a market stall piled with peppers, an Orthodox priest passing the courtyard entrance of a mosque. Statements of what Sarajevo had once been. The focal point of this pleasant room was the low circular carved wooden table she had somehow transported from Sarajevo. It was on this that she had set out the brass tray and was serving coffee from a long-handled copper *džezva* into tiny cups. Every item echoed *baščaršija*, the market of Sarajevo whose stalls and workshops were piled high with such crafted items. Or had once been, and probably would be again.

Mike wondered how much Jovanka was aware of the on-going metamorphosis of her city. Nearly a year into peace, the battle for the streets of Sarajevo had changed from the crash of mortar fire to the silent shadowy conflict of drugs and arms dealing. And, Mike suspected, it had also become potentially a springboard for the spread of Islamic radicalism in Europe.

He had arrived late the previous evening. Since Sara had forwarded Jovanka's letter to him over a year ago now, they had been in regular correspondence. What he had not shared with Sara was the fact that Jovanka had moved to Novi Sad. There was no reason for not sharing it, except for his sense of the significance of the presence of both Jovanka and Marija in Novi Sad. Or rather of the potential significance if he let it become so. The memories of that minuscule glimpse he had had into Marija's life, her laugh, the sound of the child's voice, the accompanying male murmur, the stale smells pervading the apartment block as he turned to hurry away, were lodged somewhere just beneath the level of daily living. It didn't take much to make them surface, especially in those strange vacuums between assignments when he so often felt himself alienated from the Daerley Green scene. Increasingly he became aware of his need to know: to fill in the blanks represented by the child's voice and the man's murmur.

"So tell me about the teaching job," he said now, joining Jovanka on the sofa that was also his bed. "Children with learning difficulties you said?"

"Not so much learning difficulties, as stability difficulties. They are the 7-11 year age group, local Serb and Bosnian Serb children, born at best into uncertainty, at worst into death and destruction. Many have lost at least one parent, some are orphans.

She went on at some length about the real challenge of triggering in them any sense of curiosity towards the world beyond their own claustrophobic confines; and the disproportionate feeling of reward on the rare occasions she achieved it.

"I'm sure you have read about the huge anti-government

demonstrations here. People are exhausted by war, shortages, uncertainty about the future. And what will happen in Kosovo..." Jovanka broke off. "But now you must tell me about life in your wonderfully normal and peaceful-sounding Daerley Green. And especially about Minkie. You wrote to me that she has an American boyfriend? You did not seem altogether pleased by him?"

Mike felt for his wallet, extracted a photograph, paused to look at it before passing it over to Jovanka. Who could have dreamed that wan, snotty-nosed child could evolve into such a stunner. Not pretty in the conventional sense, but with a classic kind of beauty. Almost Grecian. She had grown her hair in the last year, lost the gamine look, appearing if anything more mature than was really desirable for her eighteen years. Her brown eyes stared back at him from the photograph, dark hair framing wide cheekbones. The photograph didn't do justice to those shining curtains of hair.

He grinned self-consciously. "Fact is I was probably jealous. It's what fathers are supposed to feel about their daughter's boyfriends isn't it?"

"And that is how you feel, like a father?" Jovanka looked up from the picture. "She is certainly quite beautiful now."

"Yes that's how I feel." Though come to think of it he hadn't actually put it into words before. "Her beauty – that's a bonus. She's just a wonderful kid. Talented too, artistically. She's now in her first year of A levels: Art History and French. And very strong minded." Mike paused to sip his coffee, thick, sweet, Bosnian style. "But, yes, I fear for her Jovanka. Not for Jesse, the young American. He's turning out to be surprisingly all right. Awful, snobbish parents – diplomats of the worst kind - who packed him off back to the States as soon as he'd done his Finals to put as much distance between him and Minkie as possible. And then got posted to Paris. And presumably thought that would be the end of it. But the boy had other ideas, and is now back in Oxford working for some travel agency with US

128

connections. There's no doubt they're very much in love. Time will tell how it will survive the rocks that undoubtedly lie ahead."

"So, your fears ...?"

"Basically for how ... where she will find her place – the place where she belongs. I think I told you about her cousin Franko? How he suddenly got in touch and eventually turned up? You've met him haven't you?"

"He came to the children's home a couple of times. Minkie adored him – you know the way children get such deep passions. He was a very charming boy – about fifteen or sixteen at that time. Full of ideals." Jovanka shook her head sadly. "They thought the two of them they had all the answers to bringing peace back to Sarajevo, if they would be a few years older."

"Yes, well, I doubt if you'd recognise him now. Still, as far as Minkie is concerned, it seems to have been a real case of absence making the heart grow fonder. When she got the first letter, she was quite euphoric. Then she heard nothing more for months, followed by one or two emails, putting her on a roller coaster between hope and despair. Anyway, finally he turned up literally on the doorstep." He stopped.

"And?"

Mike grimaced. "To me he seemed a typical example of the young layabouts you can see hanging around bars almost anywhere in the world: you know, designer stubble, arrogant swagger, and a sort of American gangster English."

"You're right, I would not recognise him!"

"After her initial joy, I think Minkie was a bit disconcerted at first. But he's clever this Franko. And he can put on the charm. Not surprisingly he was quite bowled over by this cousin who had transformed from a duckling into a swan, and in no time they were jabbering away in Serbian. As you can imagine there was a lot of emotion – not least over Minkie's mother, though Franko had somehow got out of Sarajevo quite early on and couldn't add anything either way to news of what had happened to her. But he did succeed in assuring Minkie that in the end it would all work out, that he and his friends were already thinking ahead to the future. This all emerged over several days during which they were inseparable – he stayed with us of course. After a while he went off to London to meet some of his friends, then came back for a couple of days. That happened several times. Not surprisingly Minkie became very edgy and restless." Mike gave a short laugh. "That was probably the first time I really regretted Jesse wasn't around – he hadn't come back from the States at that stage. And I was away a lot, and Sara really involved with this new career she's launched into. Anyway in the end Franko had to go back to Germany, and by the time he came again in January, Jesse was back. You probably won't be surprised to learn that the two of them didn't exactly hit it off."

Jovanka had watched him intently as she listened. "This terrible war has deeply affected everyone who experienced it any way and no one more than the young people who have seen things no young people should see. Especially for them, for it replaced a time for learning to love with a capacity for hatred that will poison their whole lives. I know. I have felt it too. You have saved Minkie from that Mike, you and Sara."

"And turned her into a young woman with no roots. Generations of one culture overlaid by a crash course in another whose values are so different I wonder how she's going to cope."

Jovanka's expression softened. "If you really understand that Mike, you are a good man."

"A man with the best of intentions," he said wryly. "Not quite the same thing."

"And Sara – you haven't said how does she feel."

Mike met her gaze for a moment, then sighed and leaned back, his head cradled against the pile of cushions. "Sara is very involved in her own affairs. The truth is Jovanka, that I don't really know how she feels."

They'd had a good summer the previous year. He had even

convinced himself that the deepening sense of unease he felt with and within Sara was largely imagined; or at least largely the result of his own frequent and often long absences. Just as he felt resentful, even at times hurt, by her seeming lack of empathy with whatever assignment was preoccupying him at the time, he realised how he too had become detached from great chunks of her life and preoccupations. That summer he'd been home far more than usual. They had done things, a lot of things together. Sometimes at Sara's request they had invited Justin who was then getting over some major heart problem. To Mike's surprise he found himself quite enjoying this, once he'd got over the irritation of being addressed as "dear boy". Of course their mutual interest in the Balkans helped, and the old man really was very knowledgeable.

It probably helped too that the Beresford chap had taken himself off to the Continent on some long golfing venture. He had increasingly come to represent everything that Mike disliked most about his own comfortable patch of Middle England. Minkie seemed to think he was the best thing since sliced bread and one result of this was that they had become lumbered with the fellow's dog during his absence. Could it be that he was jealous, Mike wondered? Since he infinitely preferred the presence of Rus to his master's, he probably was.

There'd been that business of the shop, too. For a while Sara had seemed really keen on expanding its connection with local crafts people. But when young Polly announced they were moving away from Daerley Green following her husband's promotion, Sara appeared to take this as an omen and put the shop on the market. It was rapidly absorbed into the small antique shop next door. He had worried a lot that she would soon get bored – Sara had never really gone in for self-sufficiency. But in the event they'd had had a wonderful summer, a companionable summer in a new, almost exploratory way. Not only had he been home a good deal, but he'd actually wanted to be home.

And then in a very short time, everything changed again. In October Amanda had returned from New York, erupting back in Daerley Green like a Midwest tornado, and almost coinciding with Beresford's return from Europe. Amanda had taken a job launching a new department at D.G. Publishing, which for some reason seemed to make Sara very restless. The next minute she had booked herself on to a computer course in Banbury run by an extraordinary larger-than-life Aussie woman. In no time she had joined said Aussie to form a small desktop publishing outfit.

"I need something to get my teeth into," she'd said when he had protested that she was taking on too much. "Talking to Amanda has made me realise what a horrendous rut I've dug for myself over the past few years. And with you away again so much ..." To which there was not much he could say as the overseas assignments were snowballing once more. She added "Anyway Amanda's agreed to take over the *Chronicle*, which will make all the difference. It was part of my rut and as much in need of change as I am."

They seemed to see less of each other than ever, which was as much his fault as hers; but the new job suited her, it had to be said. She looked well, sounded upbeat, seemed to thrive on far longer hours than originally projected. And at least that Beresford chap wasn't hanging around any more. Early in the New Year he had sold up to move to a place nearer his precious golf course.

It was around then Mike had received that letter from Jovanka including one short sentence that leaped out at him from the page. *I think I have met that friend of yours, Marija.*

He had called Jovanka at the first opportunity from the London flat. The two women had met at mutual friends', she told him. She worked at a restaurant just round the corner from Jovanka's school: the same restaurant where Mike had seen her. No, she knew nothing about a child or a man. No, of course she had not mentioned Mike, had not even been sure that it was the same Marija. After further questions, Mike had no doubts at all.

"I suppose," he said now, "you don't approve of what I am doing."

"If you mean your plan to meet Marija, it's not my business to approve or disapprove, though if I had understood your feelings for her, I doubt if I would have mentioned our meeting. Perhaps it is better for you to exorcise ghosts when you have the choice."

"It's all right, I have no intention of barging in without very carefully assessing the situation first."

"And how do you intend to do that?"

"I was rather hoping you might have some suggestions."

Jovanka's expression managed to combine resignation with exasperation as she said "Well if it's going to stop you haunting her apartment block, the most likely place you will find her alone is in church." Mike raised a questioning eyebrow. "Yes it is so. Deep tragedy sends some people into angry rejection of God, and others into a despairing search for confirmation of His existence. Marija and I chose different paths."

"Any thoughts about which church and the best time?"

"You can start with the Uspenska in the centre of town, near the Post Office. I saw her going in a couple of times after work. Otherwise she has not felt it necessary to give me her daily timetable."

Mike leaned over and gave her shoulder a squeeze. "You're a star, Jovanka. I'll take you for a very special meal this evening."

She shook her head at him. "You Western people think there's a price for everything. And you're probably right. Mine is some English song books for the children when you get home." She got up briskly. "Anyway go now. I have lessons to prepare. The number eight bus will take you to the church."

It would be raining soon. Mike felt the dampness in the air as he came out of Jovanka's block of flats, down the broken steps and turned towards the main road. People's church-going habits had never been a part of his life study but if those of Daerley Green were anything to go by, he could be in for a long wait. For the moment he was certainly not ruling out other options. Then he remembered his visits to the Orthodox Church in Sarajevo, the constant comings and goings, the lighting of candles, the worried faces, concentrated expressions. No, Daerley Green did not provide valid criteria.

The rain started as he came off the bus: straight, steady rods of it undeflected by even the slightest breeze, and with no hint of remission. By the time he had found the shelter of the church porch he was already very wet. He saw there was a kiosk selling candles of different sizes. Nearby several trays flickered with their flames, each candle fixed in a bed of sand under a shallow covering of water.

The interior of the church was richly and darkly baroque, dominated by the huge iconostasis from which the stylised faces of the saints and the Virgin Mary stared back at him through sad eyes. There were several smaller shrines dotted about, each with its icon, each attracting its own devotees who came with bowed head to stand before it in prayer or contemplation, sometimes bending forward briefly to brush the icon with their lips.

Mike found a corner where he could wait without intruding on such privacy. There was the strangest sense of unreality, of time and life suspended. It was out of his hands now: whether Marija came or not - and what followed from that. Out of his hands. Into God's? Whatever. He'd never thought about it in sufficient length and depth to reach any conclusion he could defend with confidence, though on an emotional level he leaned towards Jovanka's view. Most of the time it was comfortable enough sitting on his fence. But the thought of Marija, of seeing her again, of what he would say to her or she to him, had been somewhere in the back of consciousness for so long that now he was here, with the encounter potentially imminent, the only awareness he had was of his own heartbeat and quickened breathing.

When she suddenly was there before him, it was moments before he recognised the fact as reality rather than as a hopeful expectation. He saw her bowed head first, draped in a dark shawl, and then as she looked up at the icon, a full face view with the candlelight picking out the highlights of her cheekbones, the soft mouth and pointed chin, those green eyes hidden in shadow. She had a handful of candles and lit them one by one, placing them in the watery tray in front of the icon: a tall one, two smaller ones, several more tall ones. Then she bowed her head again for a moment, turned and left.

Mike hurried after her. For an awful moment he thought he had lost her, for all he could see through the curtain of rain was a swarm of figures hunched and hurrying under a barrage of umbrellas. But as one of them stopped at the kerbside, turned to check the traffic, he glimpsed the unmistakable profile, watched her cross the busy road, head for a shop, and disappear inside. He followed her. It was not a shop but a restaurant attached to a hotel, its windows fogged with condensation. A waft of onions and French fries greeted him as he went in.

He saw her straight away, shaking off her wet coat, hanging it on one of several coat stands before crossing to a table where a man was already sitting. There were plenty of empty tables and Mike chose one that was not too close but from which he had an uninterrupted view. Marija had her back to him. As she pulled off her shawl, he saw she had cut her long hair: a gamine cut. Like Minkie's until recently. He switched his attention to the man. Even in a sitting position he was obviously tall. Certainly he was broad. Beefy was the word that came to mind. And ... and... Mike took in the heavy jowls due for a shave, the one visible large hand resting on the table. Coarse was the other word he sought.

What could she see in him?

His view was blocked by a waiter. *"Molim?"*

"Er.... *pivo,*" Mike said, as much because it was one of the few words he knew and could pronounce properly as because he really wanted beer.

And when his view was unblocked, he saw the child: eight or nine years old, her golden head of curls glowing like sunlight in the dim faded elegance of the place. Whatever it was she was saying in that piping little voice, it caused some amusement at nearby tables. The sound of this must have attracted Marija's attention for she suddenly looked round smiling, apparently straight at Mike. But without seeing, certainly without recognising. He heard her embarrassed laugh as she turned back to the child, and then the man's voice as he too smiled and leaned forward and touched Marija's cheek with his big beefy hand. And just for a moment there was a stillness between them that Mike recognised as unique and exclusive.

As his beer arrived several things happened in such quick succession that thinking back later he was not completely clear himself of their sequence. Marija's companion rose to leave, looking at his watch, obviously establishing some future arrangement with her. Standing, he looked even larger than Mike had estimated; but muscular rather than fleshy. As he went out of the door of the restaurant, the child suddenly ran after him and Marija hastily rose to stop her going out into the street. The child giggled, dodged and began to weave away from Marija through the tables, and the next moment was there by Mike, staring at him with that unblinking fascination children sometimes show when face to face with a stranger. Then Marija was there, scolding and worried, looking straight at Mike as she went into an incomprehensible stream of apology that gradually slowed into silence. She went on looking at him with a small puzzled frown.

Mike half rose to his feet. "Marija," was all he could say. As she began to talk questioningly in Serbian, he went on quietly "Please sit down. Please."

People at a nearby table glanced at them curiously and then away again. Serbs preferred to mind their own business. She sat down still staring at him. The little girl, silenced by this unexpected circumstance, stood sucking her thumb at Marija's side, clutching her arm.

"I didn't plan it to happen like this," Mike said. "I never meant to shock you." When she said nothing, her expression as uncomprehending as ever he had the extraordinary thought that she did not know who he was. He said "I'm Mike Hennessey."

"Mike Hennessey," she repeated. Automatically she removed the child's thumb from her mouth. She said again "Mike Hennessey."

He began to tell her quietly how it had all happened: how he had tried unsuccessfully to trace her; how he had met the man with one leg, outside the restaurant in Sarajevo; how he had come to Novi Sad, found where she worked and followed her to where she lived. Marija went on staring at him as she listened, those green eyes widening as the sequence unfolded. Then she interrupted him, speaking in rapid Serbian, hands agitated and gesturing. The torrent finally faded into a silence from which a long way away there came the clink of cutlery and the murmur of voices: a silence into which Marija said at last "I have forgot my English since ... since that other time. But *why* Mike? Why *now* are you looking for me so hard?"

"Because I had cared for you. Loved you. I thought perhaps I could help."

"Yes we loved once. For short time. But it was long, long time ago. And you did not answer my letters." She said it as a fact without accusation.

Mike bowed his head. "I'm sorry. There is no excuse, except I was young."

"We were both young. And I did not understand. But it was OK. I met Niko and became happy again. Very happy." Her eyes filled with tears.

He wanted desperately to comfort her but there was no way he could put his arms round her, or even touch her hand. "The man at the restaurant told me about your husband and the children. I can't begin to imagine ..."

She let the tears fall unchecked. "No one can imagine

such a thing. I was dead inside. For two years I was dead inside. Then Bogdan found me. He was Niko's brother-in-law, and his wife was killed too. Another mortar. But he had still this child, Snežka." Marija wiped the tears away with the back of a hand, took a handkerchief from her pocket and blew her nose. Hearing her name the little girl looked from one to the other anxiously.

"It's all right Snežka," Marija leaned down and stroked the child's cheek, began speaking to her in Serbian. When she looked back at Mike he saw she had made a decision.

"I would like you to meet Bogdan. We stay together because we do not need words. We are for each other the past and the future. And for this little one. Come tomorrow. For supper." For the first time she smiled. "I think you already know the address."

He really did not want to go. It was clear that he could do nothing for Marija, that her experiences, like so many he had spent his life reporting, were in a realm beyond his knowledge. Bogdan, with his burly shoulders and big beefy hands, could be for her all the things that he, Mike, could never be.

"I've been chasing something that didn't exist. Perhaps never existed," he told Jovanka.

"You've been chasing a ghost that's all, and I think you owe her the opportunity to put an end to an unfinished chapter in her life. Yours too," Jovanka said quite decisively.

The following evening when he got to the door of the flat where, a year earlier, he had listened from the landing to Snežka's voice and Bogdan's murmur, Mike nearly turned away. It was to all intents and purposes finished. He really did not need any additional fuel for his what-might-have-beens. But as Jovanka had said, he owed Marija.

She greeted him like a friend, took his coat and went off to do things in the kitchen, saying "Sorry, Bogdan can't English. But he will give you beer."

Bogdan brought a couple of bottles from the fridge,

produced two glasses. He handed a glass and a bottle to Mike, making a great show of how cold the bottle was. "England drink hot beer," he said, triumphantly dredging the words out one by one. Ah that old chestnut! Mike grinned dutifully, prodding the bottle with exaggerated enthusiasm.

"Sit," Bogdan said. And Mike sat in one of the two armchairs that faced the television set, while Bogdan stood looking larger than ever in these more confined surroundings. Mike thought he had never seen a room that told you less about its owners. Whereas Jovanka's small flat spoke in banner headlines of her Bosnian origins, Marija's and Bogdan's could have been any anonymous furnished flat from Islington to the Bronx: a sofa, two armchairs, a dining table already set for their meal and four straight chairs, the TV, a chest of drawers its drawers all firmly shut, a book case with more folders and files than books, all neatly stacked. It was almost uncannily tidy, even the child's toys neatly stowed in a cardboard box. Snežka herself was apparently visiting a little friend in a neighbouring flat.

"So what does Bogdan do?" Mike aimed his raised voice at the kitchen.

Marija put her head round the door. "He is driving *kamion.*"

"Truck-driver," Mike translated. Bogdan looked at him questioningly and Mike mimed the swivelling of a steering wheel. Bogdan nodded in comprehension, and they grinned at each other again: two men who couldn't speak to each other but cared for the same woman at an interval of nearly twenty years.

It was a farce, and Mike wished profoundly it was all over.

Marija came in bearing a large dish. Not a Bosnian speciality, but a goulash, a Hungarian one. It was extremely good and Mike tucked into it grateful for some legitimate occupation. He had rarely felt so ill equipped for making conversation, for the past felt like forbidden territory and that was all they had in common. He forced himself not to think of how he had held this woman in his arms; how she had said with touching simplicity that she did not offer her body lightly. He wondered what she had told Bogdan about him. Probably nothing since she seemed to have slammed the door on the past.

Or so he assumed until she began "Bogdan was working in Bulgaria when the war started. Afterwards it was not possible to come to Sarajevo. My Niko worked in a hospital in the city. He make ... how do you say when you make people to sleep?"

"Anaesthetist."

"Yes, that. And then one day a woman came for operation after mortar, and it was Anja his sister, Bogdan's wife. But she was too sick and died in operation. So we took Snežka to live with us, and with Sonja and little Niko."

"Those were your children?"

She nodded. "Bogdan did not know us so well before that time because he was away very much with his *kamion*. It was terrible because we could not find him to tell him about Anja. And then I was shopping in market and Niko was with the children at home on his free day when they were killed. Except Snežka who was only small then and with my friend."

They had all stopped eating now. Marija went on talking as though reading from a prepared script. "I don't remember nothing from that time, only that I must live for Snežka. It was a long, long time, perhaps two years. Then the war stopped and Bogdan came home. When he found me and Snežka we both cried. For days and nights." She looked across at him and again he put out his beefy hand and touched her cheek and Mike sensed that unique stillness between them. "Later we came here."

There was a long pause into which Mike said at last "I'm glad you have a good man to take care of you." It sounded trite and stupid.

She nodded, gave a sudden sigh and said "And you Mike? I have not asked about your children?"

"No children. It's not possible for my wife Sara. I ... we regret this very much." It did not seem an appropriate moment to mention Minkie.

"I'm sorry." Marija looked away, began collecting up the plates, Bogdan helping her. It was while they were both out of the room that he noticed a small table with two framed photographs on it, tucked away in a corner. He went over and picked them up. One was of a pretty young woman holding a baby: presumably Anja, Bogdan's wife. The other was of a younger Marija and a good-looking man in a boat with two children. Mike peered at them. The boy, little Niko, was about ten years old, his face screwed up in bright sunlight. The girl Sonja, perhaps thirteen or fourteen, was looking straight into the camera with a small smile. She seemed curiously familiar.

Puzzled, Mike went on scrutinising the small figure in the bows of the boat, with its squarish face and arched eyebrows. Finally he smiled in recognition. She might have been a carbon copy of pictures he had seen of his own mother as a child. Then the smile died and his stomach lurched as the significance of the likeness hit him with a half-knowledge that would change life for always.

Marija, coming from the kitchen with another dish, looked round when she saw he was no longer at the table. Their eyes met and she gave a sharp involuntary gasp. And then Mike knew without a doubt that Sonja was the daughter he would never hold in his arms.

Jasminka – April 1997

As she awaited Franko's arrival, Minkie was discovering how deeply confusing the state of young adulthood could be.

Events seemed to succeed each other with ever-growing momentum: beginning with that truly awful evening the previous June when she had been summoned for inspection by Jesse's Dad and stepmother. Or that's how it felt. She still cringed at the thought of how awkward and tongue-tied she had been in her anxiety to please. And how obviously she had not succeeded.

"They treated me like some alien half-wit," she wailed to Mike and Sara afterwards. "And the dire thing is that's just how I behaved."

They had both reassured her that it was all in her imagination and that anyway it was Jesse's opinion that mattered and he was quite obviously besotted. But it hadn't stopped him obeying the parental directive to go 'and see the folks back home' after his Finals. "I'll be back before you've noticed I've gone, you'll see," he said. A few weeks after he left, his father was posted to Paris which, in Minkie's book, only increased the unlikelihood of Jesse's return.

After that each day had succeeded the last in interminable and uniform greyness, though around her everything seemed to be changing. Disturbingly, Azzie had also headed across the Atlantic to visit an uncle and aunt on the banks of the Mississippi in Wisconsin. Mike and Sara went through a friendly period from which, in her present mood, Minkie felt excluded. Berry seemed to be staying away forever. Justin was disconcertingly frail after a heart attack. Polly and her family had moved out of the village, an event which prompted Sara to talk seriously of selling the shop. And then there was the endless waiting for another message from Franko which never came.

Her one consolation was Rus who became her constant companion and confidant, flattening or pricking up his ears in response to her moods as though he really understood all she said.

It was about the middle of July, on one of their almost daily long hikes, that she came upon Justin lost in thought on a bench in Whirling Wood. She was about to change direction and leave him at peace when he said, almost as though carrying on a conversation that had been interrupted, "You're bound to miss him, dear child. It's what happens when you're in love." He indicated the seat beside him. "So why haven't you been to see me?"

"I didn't want to disturb you after … after your illness."

"You think you know better than I do whether I should be disturbed? I've been screaming with boredom at my own company."

Minkie sat down beside him. "Sorry."

"So you should be." He patted her hand. "I suspect it's probably more to do with you feeling very sorry for yourself and thinking that someone as ancient as I am couldn't possibly understand. Let me tell you young lady, I have loved with a passion that would make the hairs of most people in dear old Daerley Green stand on end." It was the thing about Justin that had attracted her from their first meeting: the way he talked to her on the same level, person to person, never adult to child.

She said "Well, you can't just leave it there."

There was a longish silence before he gave a big sigh and said, "Over such a long life there have been quite a few romantic interludes, but there was one which will stay in my mind's eye until my dying breath. Indeed did so during my recent little escapade in hospital."

"Go on."

"She was a diplomat's daughter …" Justin saw her disbelief. "No, seriously. That is where any resemblance between your situation and mine begins and ends. She was the daughter of one of the attachés at the Soviet Embassy. It was long, long ago during the early days of the Cold War, so extremely inappropriate. At least you don't have that problem. You can't imagine the tricks we had to evolve to find ways to meet without attracting unwelcome interest. We loved each other – and it *was* mutual dear Minkie, I know it was … We loved each other for a year. And then I was posted to … well, let's say one of our embassies in a rather obscure little Middle Eastern state. When I refused, I was told in no uncertain terms that my career was on the line. And the next moment, my love and her parents had been whisked back to Moscow."

Minkie gave a small cry of protest in sympathy.

"Yes, it felt like the end of the world," Justin agreed, and she saw that just for a moment he had travelled back half a century.

She felt the prickle of tears as she leaned across and gave him a hug. "Poor, poor Justin. I think I'd have died. Did you … ever meet again?"

"Ten years later. I was in Moscow this time and was invited to this lavish reception by some junior minister. And there she was, looking absolutely exquisite: our hostess. She had married this very smooth and successful career diplomat. We had two minutes alone together, that's all. But it was enough to know that we both still felt the same." He paused. "I didn't see any reason to get married after that. Lots of nice women, beautiful women, intelligent women; but not one that matched up to .. well, matched up to her. And you're the first person in Daerley Green I've ever told." He patted her hand again. "So here I am, a tedious old bachelor boring everyone with the causes and effects of history. Which reminds me young lady, couldn't you usefully spend some of your moping time on your studies?"

Minkie grimaced. "I've got an unbelievably boring project on the effects of the market economy on global warming. Please give arguments for and against…"

"Then here's the solution," Justin said firmly. "I know even less about the subject than you do, so you can come and instruct me on the subject, say, once a week. Which will give you an objective and me an afternoon of stimulating company."

If the weather was bad, Minkie went to the cottage;

otherwise they met at Whirling Wood, or down by the canal. Justin took to bringing a thermos of tea for himself and a flask of his home-made elderberry cordial for Minkie. When they had finished discussing Minkie's project, she would get him up to date on the latest news from Azzie and Jesse. Sara had recently acquired an Internet connection for her computer and provided Minkie with her own password and email address. Azzie's news was sensational and a bit ominous. She'd arrived in Wisconsin to an euphoric reunion with her parents, recently arrived from Teheran and whom she had not seen for seven years. They hoped eventually to apply for US citizenship. "So she'll be disappearing out of my life next."

"Don't cross bridges," Justin said.

Jesse was doing the rounds of a seemingly boundless extended family and emailing her pretty well daily.

"I must say it's a great comfort to me that I do not need to learn about such unnatural processes," Justin said when Minkie launched into an enthusiastic explanation on the workings of cyber space. "Indeed I'm sure it will all end in tears. Just imagine all those negative thoughts and destructive instincts swilling around unfettered through the ether."

"Sara's right – you are a dinosaur," Minkie said affectionately.

In September the outlook began to look distinctly brighter. Azzie returned from America, bursting to share her experiences and with the reassuring news that there was no question of her joining her parents until they had been granted citizenship and, at a minimum, she had completed A levels. Jesse announced his plan to return to Oxford in the New Year despite his parents' relocation to Paris. Another message from Franko assured her he would be coming to England very soon, that he was involved in some really big project in which he was sure she would be able to help. Berry returned quite unexpectedly, almost at the same time as her former teacher and Sara's old friend Amanda Heyforth arrived back after a couple of years in New

York. Surprisingly Sara, rather than being delighted at these returns, became quite edgy. At about that time Mike started travelling a lot again, and before long the two of them were back in their more usual mutual state of civil indifference.

They were both out and Minkie had just finished drying her hair that early October evening when the doorbell rang. She still had a towel over one shoulder when she opened the door to a tall dark male shape silhouetted against a street light.

"Yes?" she said questioningly as she flicked on the porch light. Her first thought was that he was extremely good looking if you went in for bedroom eyes and designer stubble, her second that this wasn't the usual sort of door-to-door salesman. And then the shape said in wondering tones "Jasi ... can it be you?" and held out its arms.

For a moment Minkie could not breathe. Then she gulped in air in a big grateful gasp. "Franko?" He moved towards her, enfolding her in arms as hard as steel, so that her forehead was jammed against his rough stubble, her nose against his T-shirt that smelt of cigarette smoke and some kind of tangy after-shave , and his breath warm in her ear as he said, "I never imagined this moment would come. Or that my little cousin could be so beautiful."

He held her away gently and looked at her. "And I wonder why do we speak in English?"

Minkie had taken his hand and was pulling him into the cottage, wondering if you could burst with happiness. Laughing she said "I've probably forgotten all my Serbian."

"We call it Bosnian now," he said.

Glancing back, she saw he was serious, but for the moment there were more important things to discuss. "Where have you come from? How long can you stay? What are you doing?" She stopped dead. "And above all do you have any news of Mother. Anything at all?"

They were in the living room now. Speaking quietly in their own language, he touched her cheek and said "I have no

146

news little Jasi of your mother. I know only what you know already: that she went to Mislići for some months, and then came back to Sarajevo. By that time I had got out and much later heard that she had been killed. But that's all I know and I have not been back for three years now."

Minkie did not take her eyes off his face. "I know she is alive," she said. "And I shall go and find her when I have finished at school and have some money."

Franko's expression changed as though a switch had been thrown. With that huge teasing grin that she remembered so well from childhood he said, "Of course I have forgotten that my little cousin is now a proper English school girl. And can English school girls make food for hungry cousins? I am *starving*."

He followed her into the kitchen, looking round approvingly. "I must say you have found yourself a very comfortable pad."

Rummaging in the fridge for eggs, bacon, sausages Minkie said, "I didn't find it. Some very kind people gave me a home." She glanced at the kitchen clock. "They'll be home in about an hour. But now tell me about you. Everything."

So Franko had leaned against the breakfast bar watching her as she prepared a huge fry-up for him and told her how very soon after she had left Sarajevo, he had realised there was no future for him either in staying there, especially as he had no intention of fighting. He had teamed up with other young men and some older ones, and very quickly learned there were ways of making money, and that with money you could have power.

"So how did you do that?"

"Well, supposing you had the right contacts and enough guts, for instance, there was a fortune to be made from fetching firewood from the forest."

Minkie looked horrified. "But that meant going up into the hills; that was terribly dangerous."

"Of course it was dangerous; imagine at night when there was a lull in the shelling, but you never knew when it could start again, or who could be aiming at you from behind the next rock. I tell you, it really got the adrenalin pumping. But next day you could get a lot of Deutschmarks for a small bundle on the street. And with that you could buy some of the food rations coming in through the United Nations people, and make more money with that." It didn't seem the right moment to enquire about the people who couldn't afford those high prices. "And then soon it was possible to … let us say, to make arrangements to get away." Through his contacts he had found his way to Belgrade and then via Hungary into Austria and then Germany.

By now he was tucking into a plateful of food while Minkie made him toast and coffee. He paused to say appreciatively "I see that English school girls are very good cooks."

"Stop calling me that or you won't get any more. Everyone here calls me Minkie."

"Minkie, Minkie, Mi-i-i-n-kie," Franko repeated experimentally. "I think that goes well with your style."

"So what is this big project you are involved with?"

Franko put his fork down and leaned an elbow on the breakfast bar. "This is what I want to discuss with you, Minkie. Do you remember how long ago we said we wanted to change things, to make things better for people at home?"

"Of course I remember. I still often think about it."

"Well I guess we were pretty unrealistic. Or may be naive. You know how it was when you left, and it got worse. Much worse. Little food, often no heating or lighting, people going to get water or wood and just never coming back. Everyone was sick in some way – maybe not always their bodies, but in their minds."

Automatically buttering his toast, pouring out his coffee, Minkie listened stricken by what she already knew but now heard put into words by someone who was there, someone she could trust. "I don't understand how people could stay sane in such conditions."

"Many didn't. Others seemed to cope at the time and are now getting the after effects. Many are desperate to get away but don't know where to go. And this is where I ... we are trying to help. May be it's not possible to change things for a whole city, but it becomes more realistic if you think in terms of individuals, of smaller groups."

Minkie took a can of Coke out of the fridge and joined him at the breakfast bar. "How?"

"You can't imagine what possibilities there are for jobs in the West when you know the ropes."

"Such as?"

"All kinds. Agricultural work, making things – especially making things. Clothes, toys, gadgets."

Minkie remembered a TV documentary she had seen recently and frowned. "I hope you don't mean sweatshops."

She flinched as Franko crashed a fist down on the breakfast bar and said furiously. "I've seen some of your television programmes too. Here, and in Germany, with so-smug reporters who never in their life have known what it is like to be *really* hungry, *really* afraid – not just for yourself but for people you love. But you, Jasi. You have been hungry and afraid. I am shocked that you cannot see the reality behind what you are saying. That only people who are lucky --like you – who experience a miracle – that only such people should have the opportunities for a new life ...."

Minkie flared back "So it's lucky that my father was killed, that my mother ... that I don't know where my mother is ... that I don't belong anywhere ... that sometimes I'm not even sure who I am?"

Again that lightning switch of expression. Franko sank back wearily. "I'm sorry Jasi. Seeing you here in all this ..." He waved an arm in a gesture that indicated Daerley Green and all it implied "and thinking of others that I know ..."

And then there had been the sound of a key in the door and a moment later Mike's voice calling, "We're back Princess."

It was clear within minutes of their meeting that Mike and Franko were not at ease with each other. Thinking about it later, Minkie saw that Franko initially pigeon-holed Mike as one of those "so-smug reporters"; and Mike – well, it had to be said that on first appearances Franko did not slot comfortably into the Middle England scene.

"Minkie … Jasminka has been waiting for you so long. A pity you couldn't let us know – we'd have had the red carpet out for you, young man," were Mike's first words.

Franko had smiled, managing to look apologetic but with just a hint of defiance at the same time. "Yes, I'm sorry. Conditions have been a little … difficult since I left my country. When you come to the West, there are many questions, regulations, papers, uncertainties …" He shrugged and left the sentence hanging in the air. "But for you Mr. Hennessey … and Mrs Hennessey … I can speak only with all the gratitude in my heart for what you have done for my cousin."

And Minkie had watched full of admiration as Franko re-arranged himself to meet the expectations of these important people in her life. With gratitude, too, for she desperately wanted the two halves of her life to make a coherent whole.

If Mike wasn't won over straight away Sara certainly was. Smiling, she said, "It's wonderful to meet you at last Franko - we've heard so much about you. And of course you can stay here as long as you like."

In the event it was not for so long. There were people he had to see in London, Franko said after a few days; and then a quick trip to Germany. In between he returned to Daerley Green making sure to telephone in advance. When pressed by Mike, he explained that he was trying to set up an agency with some friends for importing Bosnian crafts in order to try and help "those in my country who have lost everything".

Minkie's joy in seeing him was tempered with unease. She suspected that his involvement in any import business came into a category very different from anything Mike envisaged, and that however altruistic the motives behind such movements of human cargo, it was intrinsically wrong not to mention illegal. And she felt, however innocently and unwillingly, she was being drawn into it if only by her silence.

"I trust you with my life," Franko said. "You must never, never speak of this to anyone."

Not to Mike or Sara, not to Justin, not even to Azzie. And not to Jesse when he returned?

On his second visit Franko said, "I need your help now Minkie. To find some accommodation. For twenty, thirty people, say. It will be good if it is in the countryside, far away from any big city. We can pay good money."

Minkie protested "But I don't know anything about any accommodation. And what will they do there?"

Franko smiled. "Life in England has made you so complicated Minkie. And worried ... about everything. They will only stay for a short time, so it can be very simple accommodation – like a big barn or shed. Somewhere where they can recover from their journey while we find more permanent accommodation and work for them."

He made it sound so reasonable. And that smile was straight out of her childhood, straight out of the meadows and forests above Sarajevo where they had roamed without a care for the future.

Feeling she was failing him Minkie said, "But I don't know anyone with accommodation."

"What about all those people you wrote me about. The old man Justin? That Berry person who has golf courses."

"Justin *is* old and has been very ill. And Berry doesn't own golf courses, he manages them ..."

"You will think of someone," Franko said. "From the train I see many old farm buildings, sometimes in a very bad state..."

Old farm buildings! Suddenly Minkie remembered Polly's cousin "three times removed and as mad as a March hare"

151

she had once described him. He had a farm about an hour's drive away which was so run down that one day, according to Polly, the environmental people would be after him. She'd taken Minkie to visit him once and he had seemed pretty mad. What was his name? Joshua? ...Joshua something. She remembered thinking it sounded like a character straight out of the Bible. But the farm buildings had been more like something out of a bad movie, a crumbling brick house with odd sheds and barns and outhouses tacked on over the generations. They were full of old machinery and stuff that no one had probably looked at for decades. But they could be cleared out.

"I can see you have thought of somewhere," Franko said. His eyes gleamed when Minkie told him reluctantly what she had in mind. "It sounds perfect. We shall go there together and speak to this man who is mad like a hare. But I think it's better not to mention it to your friend Polly."

Minkie had no intention of discussing it with anyone; would have much preferred to remain in total ignorance herself. But she could not let Franko down. Or those poor people looking for a decent life. Franko had his own transport now: a white van which his group used to move consignments of goods – or people? - to outlets round the country. On a bleak November Sunday afternoon, with Sara's attention engaged in one of her numerous commitments, the two cousins headed east through flattening landscapes to the Bedfordshire borders and a network of lanes that became progressively narrower.

Even from a distance Minkie could see that the place was far worse than she remembered it. She was about to apologise when Franko said, "But Minkie this is perfect. You are so clever. I knew you wouldn't let me down."

So she said nothing. When they eventually rooted the old man out from deep and noisy sleep in an armchair in the kitchen, he seemed barely surprised to be confronted by strangers wishing to rent his barn.

"He's not mad, he's drunk," Franko said with great

satisfaction. "So he'll be very happy to earn some extra cash with no responsibilities."

Indeed Joshua appeared to have given up on farming altogether. Several fields, he said vaguely, had been leased out for grazing or cash crops and this probably accounted for a semblance of maintenance at least of fences and gates on the property. But a quick tour of the farm and its outbuildings showed they were in accelerating decline.

"You can't put people to live in those!" protested Minkie.

"Stop worrying. I will arrange for them to be made dry and clean, provide some bedding and other furniture, make sure the outside lavatory is working ... Believe me it will seem like a palace after what they've been through."

A couple of weeks later he insisted she went with him to meet the first group "so you can see for yourself". She hadn't wanted to go one bit and dreaded what she would find. In the event it had been a pleasant relief. There were about twenty of them, mostly young men but two or three women. Franko's organisation had fitted out the barn with camp beds. The farm's two outside toilets had been cleaned up and a small shed converted to a primitive shower. A formidable woman acted as camp warden in charge of basic catering and strict discipline.

Franko introduced Minkie to Ivan and Vera; both his classmates in the long-ago days of peace. "We'll never forget you," Vera said, embracing him.

Franko said, "I'm not going to pretend it'll be easy. The idea is you'll be transported in a couple of days to a big farm in Lincolnshire. I guess the accommodation'll be pretty basic – a bit like this – and the work back-breaking."

"Better a broken back than a broken heart," Vera said.

Minkie thought she'd never seen anyone look so tired until she remembered her own days in Sarajevo, and how her mother looked, eventually all the time.

"Anyway, once we've got things better organised I should be able to get you into one of the factories. Boring work, but easier – and better pay."

Soon after, Franko left for Germany again and said he'd be away for several weeks. The visit to the farm had reassured Minkie. At least she'd seen for herself what it had meant to the camp's weary occupants and, once Franko had gone, she was glad to let it become someone else's problem. Occasionally she pictured those shadowy figures arriving in the night, consoled herself with the thought that at least they found somewhere to rest, something to eat. She remembered Vera's words "We'll never forget you..."and clung to the remembered hope in them.

Then there was Christmas and the New Year. And then Jesse was back. After that it was easier than ever to switch off the imagination. On a crest of euphoria Minkie took to living in the sheer joy of the here-and-now and the exquisite knowledge that there was no reason it should not be same the next day and the next.

Jesse found a job in a travel agency in Oxford and a bedsitter off the Woodstock Road. His salary was not high and the bedsitter not cheap. He did not hide the precariousness of the situation. "Pop is real mad at me. And I mean mad. I guess he thought we'd both get over it, find someone else … whatever. But Minkie, if you love me like I love you, then …"

For answer she leaned over and gave him a long and unchaste kiss.

"Wow." Jesse took a deep breath. "I'll take that as a 'yes'."

"But it feels different too. Doesn't it for you?" Minkie said slowly. "Sort of more serious. May be your dad did us a favour. He thought we'd grow away from each other; but the opposite's happened." She gave a big grin. "And that's inspite of the fact that you've changed a bit. Got more .. more American I suppose."

He looked startled. "What's that supposed to mean for heaven's sakes?"

She studied him a moment. "I'm not sure. I'm really not

sure. May be it's because I've got used to Franko's dark Balkan style."

"Ah the famous mysterious Franko. You haven't had much to say about him so far."

"There isn't much to say. We've both grown up. Changed." Minkie wished suddenly she had not mentioned him, not yet.

"Do I hear a note of disappointment?"

She shrugged. "Only about all those old dreams … when we were kids… You know, changing the world. All that stuff. We've both learned it doesn't work like that. But at least Franko is trying to help a few people." She stopped, aware of approaching shaky ground.

Fortunately Jesse did not pursue it and she was in no hurry to engineer an encounter between them. In the end, with Franko's erratic movements and Jesse's job commitments, it was a few more weeks before the two men met. And it was OK. Jesse was prepared to try and like anyone who had a place in Minkie's affections, and likewise Franko, at his chameleon best, played his part carefully in this first encounter with the man in Minkie's life.

"So what did you think?" Minkie asked eagerly of him when Jesse had left them to go back to work.

Franko pretended to give the question solemn consideration before presenting her with one of his old infectious grins. "I suppose he's OK …for an American."

"What exactly is he doing over here?" Jesse inevitably asked in due course.

Minkie tried to reproduce some of Franko's explanations about the Bosnian craftware, the difficulties of transporting it across Europe and finding outlets for it.

Jesse was quiet for a moment, began to say something, changed his mind. In the end "Just be careful what you get mixed up in," was all he said.

Now, on a Friday evening in late April, Minkie awaited Franko's arrival with unease. "I really need your help just this once," he'd said in a hurried call from London a couple of days earlier. "I have to meet a special consignment coming direct from the east coast. We've arranged for the take-over at the service station on the M40. If I come at six, can you fix me up with a small snack? There'll be plenty of time – it's better if we get there after dark." He'd rung off before she could ask any questions, including why her presence was so vital; or even protest that it would mean breaking a date with Jesse in Oxford.

"I'd completely forgotten about a special workshop at school. Don't be mad," she'd told Jesse on the phone, hating the way the lie came out so smoothly.

"Hopeless scatterbrain," he grumbled in his disappointment, then cheering up "OK, so I'll kiss you twice as hard and long on Saturday."

Mike was away, as so often these days. It was almost a relief. Since his latest return from Novi Sad he had been acting very strangely. For a while he was really demanding, wanting to know everywhere she went and what she did. He'd never been like that before. Then he became withdrawn to the point of churlishness. Minkie really missed the easy-going relationship that had grown between them over the years, but he was so grumpy she hesitated to ask what was wrong. Anyway it was probably better if he wasn't too aware of what was going on in her life at the moment.

Sara was working late that Friday. "Tell him he can stay as long as he likes," she told Minkie on learning that Franko was taking her out for the evening, but Minkie suspected social visits were not at the top of Franko's agenda just then.

He arrived early, looking great in a pair of designer jeans and a black T-shirt with scarlet lettering exhorting all comers to 'Save the Planet.' Over coffee and sandwiches laid out on the breakfast bar in the kitchen Minkie said, "I want to know what this is all about Franko. Now."

He nodded, looked serious, leaned across and touched her cheek as he had not done for a while. "I'm truly sorry Minkie to get you involved in this way. It will be the last time, I promise. More and more people want to come, and there are new arrangements all the time. On this occasion we have been helping someone important – the daughter of a man who is in some trouble with the authorities. Nothing bad – something to do with the wrong papers, and he is in hiding. She … and some friends … they're coming over to set up arrangements for when he is able to get here himself." He paused. "They said it was important that another woman should be involved – at this end I mean. So I said I would bring my fiancée along. You won't mind being my fiancée for one evening?"

On that spring Friday late evening, the activity at the service station was frenetic. Franko found a quiet corner tucked at the back of the lorry park. They were looking for a truck from Holland, he said, carrying machine parts. They did not have long to wait. As it drew in to the furthest corner, Franko moved the van alongside, got out and lit a cigarette.

The driver of the truck jumped out. "That's a bad habit," he said. And Franko grunted and ground the cigarette into the tarmac with his heel. Contact had been established.

Another man and a woman got out from the passenger side of the truck and came to join them. "This is my fiancée," Franko said.

The woman nodded but did not offer her own name. "The cargo is in the back," she said "Five cases as requested." Her English was good but heavily accented.

They were already opening up the back, levering aside massive crates to create a narrow passageway. The woman stood at the entrance, speaking into the darkness in a quiet but authoritative voice, and slowly, one by one, five slender figures, shrouded from head to toe, stumbled out to be bundled unceremoniously into the back of the van. As soon as they saw Minkie they broke into anxious twitters in a language that bore no resemblance to any she knew.

"What the hell's going on?" demanded Minkie.

Ignoring her, the woman said. "So these are the five pieces as arranged. Fine pieces in very good condition – or they will be once they have been washed and fed. I think you will be satisfied. Now we have other cargo to deliver."

As the truck pulled away, Minkie turned on Franko alarmed and angry. Before she could speak he said "Yes, I know what you're going to say and that's why I didn't tell you earlier about the girls. But whether they are from Sarajevo or somewhere else, it's the same: people just wanting a new and better life. For them Bosnia has become the new gateway…"

But she didn't believe him any more. "Where are they from Franko? And what will they do here?"

"These are Kurds," he said. "They will stay a few days with Joshua, and then some one will take them to where they will live and work." He did not meet her eye. "That is all I know. And all you need to know."

Sara – September 1997

On that mid-September morning Sara was on her way to work and feeling on top of the world. As she crossed the Market Place to the garage where she kept her car behind the new Co-op, an unexpected jab of *déja-vu* caused a brief waver in the spring in her step. The leaves on the chestnut tree on the village green were beginning to turn, further mellowed by the September sun. Without thinking, she did a half turn and went to sit on the seat beneath it, the ditty of *Underneath the spreading chestnut tree* jingling unbidden in her head.

Equally unbidden was a wave of nostalgia. Here was a view that represented a microcosm of most of her adult years. Her mind purposefully skirting round any thoughts of Berry, she scanned the countless times she had passed this very spot on so many varied missions: to Sara's Collectibles now seamlessly incorporated into the neighbouring antique centre; to the church hall on press day for the *Chronicle*, now ably masterminded by Amanda; to meet Justin … A shadow flickered in the sunlight. Poor Justin. After two crises in which he had been found unconscious – once by the postman peering through the letterbox, once by Minkie to whom he had given a key – he had bowed to the inevitable and moved into The Fieldings, a retirement home nearer Banbury. It was a very nice retirement home with self-contained flatlets, a communal dining room, visiting speakers and outings arranged ("to keep our brains from atrophying completely, dear girl"), and strategically placed bell-pulls to summon assistance in case of need. Justin had been very good about it. "I shall expect you to visit," he'd said on that last day when she was helping him to pack up. And she had been to see him quite regularly till life got … got a bit too busy. Minkie, and even Azzie, had been more faithful. She'd go next weekend. Without fail.

Polly had gone, too. Little Polly Cuttle, for whom Sara had once been emotional prop and stay, had matured into a surprisingly self-assured mother-of-three. Certainly she had no further need of Sara, would no doubt be faintly appalled at some of the things going on in Sara's life. Minkie called Polly from time to time and would report on the children's latest ailments and achievements. It was quite remarkable how that child, young woman, had entwined herself in all those threads of Daerley Green life and made it her own. There had even been some contact earlier in the year with that cousin of Polly's –a weird reclusive old boy – something to do with finding work for the refugees her handsome young cousin was involved with. Come to think of it, it was quite a while since he'd shown his face.

"Hello stranger," said Amanda's voice, and the next moment she was sitting on the seat beside her. Amanda, once as near to being a close friend as anyone in Daerley, and whom she now hardly ever saw. Turning to smile at her, Sara noticed the fine crow's feet lines at the corners of Amanda's eyes. They were about the same age. She'd better check her own.

"I've been watching you from my office window," Amanda went on, nodding her head towards DG Publishing across the Market Place. "Looking so serene and proprietorial. How is it we don't see each other these days?"

"Both too busy running our little corners of the universe I suppose." Sara said. "But it's easily remedied. Let's go and see Justin on Sunday, then you can come back for supper."

"I'd love to come over. How's Minkie?"

"Frighteningly grown up. Just passed her driving test would you believe."

"And Mike?"

"Away as ever. Afghanistan again." Sara gave a small shrug. "It's the way life is for us, and we've … I suppose we've both adapted to it."

Amanda nodded and repeated. "I'd love to come over." She stood up. "You can bring me up to date with young Minkie and that good looking cousin of hers. And I'll be able to tell you about my very first golf lesson. On Saturday at that golf course run by our Beresford friend – remember him?" She headed back across the Market Place with a backward wave of an arm.

Sara stared after her. The mention of Berry's name so unexpectedly out of context brought a jolt of shock. He was a part of her life so separate, so self-contained, so totally justified within its narrow confines that it no longer needed self-searching and therefore had no relation to anything that went on outside it. Now Amanda's casual reference seemed to bring an undefined threat.

Pull yourself together, woman.

Briskly Sara headed towards the Co-op and her car.

It was just a year since Amanda came back from New York coinciding with Berry's return from Europe. The extreme unexpectedness of the latter had thrown Sara. She and Mike had had a good summer, and doubtless contributory to this was the fact that Berry had been away – though the aching for him had seemed unbearable to start with. It had also helped that Mike did not leave the UK for all of three months. But there was more to it than that. It was as if they had reached an unspoken agreement to step back from whatever brink they had each been approaching, and to take stock. It had been a great summer. Together they had taken on responsibilities: of helping Justin come to terms with his illness, and Minkie to believe that separations did not cause worlds to end, least of all love to die. They had also consulted over decisions, notably Sara's to sell the shop following Polly's move.

"Won't you get bored?" had been Mike's main reservation.

"May be I need to remember what it's like to be bored," Sara said, really meaning perhaps it was time to give herself more space. In the event she had not been bored. Arranging the sale had taken up a lot of time. Mike had some weeks at home and, when back at work, returned most weekends. They had done a lot of things together. She'd cooked meals and run the house;

he'd reorganised the garden, revelling in the hard physical activity. And they made extremely good love on a regular basis. She'd made a good job of compartmentalising her mind and her conscience felt comfortable, free of guilt.

Towards the end of summer, Sara sensed a restlessness in Mike and felt it in herself. From time to time there were letters from Jovanka in Yugoslavia from which Mike read out extracts. He mused aloud that he ought to return there and assess the worsening situation in Kosovo, but when his next major assignment came it was to Pakistan and soon after that Afghanistan. As was his nature, he became totally focussed on everything to do with it. Early on he said apologetically "It looks as though I shall be away quite a bit again."

"Yes, well it's your job."

"I worry about you. It's been good this summer. Really good. But I suppose over the years I've become a bit of a world-crisis junkie. Perhaps I need it to feed my ego? But you're stuck here and now, without the shop … What will you do?"

"I'm thinking of enrolling on a course," Sara said, the idea coming out of nowhere. Then she remembered the new sign she'd spotted outside a shop in Banbury: *Cyber Inc. – the easy way to the World Wide Web.* "A course on the Internet," she added. Then "And by the way, this is my patch and I like being stuck here."

She'd barely known what the World Wide Web was at that stage.

"No probs," she was assured by Pippa Jordan, Cyber Inc's managing director. She was an Australian, wore one nose- and two eyebrow rings, and floated in swathes of Indian cotton print looking as though she had just drifted in from a pop festival. But when it came to computer technology she was ace.

So Sara had done a crash course in computer skills, followed by desktop publishing and web page design. And became completely addicted. Pippa was lavish in her admiration, said she'd never met such a 'natch', and over one of the first of many veggie lunches floated the idea of a partnership in desktop publishing.

She had already invested a great deal in transforming the shop premises in George Street into a light, airy, well-equipped centre for computer technology. For its regular attenders it had become something of a social centre, too, with coffee constantly on the hob, and a small room set aside for imbibing it and exchanging know-how or dumping computer angst. Pippa claimed that her students taught each other as much as she did, which of course was absurd, but there was no doubt that the informal atmosphere attracted many who initially considered themselves as terminally computer illiterate or would have been daunted by more conventional IT centres of learning. In particular Cyber Inc was proving a great draw for a generation of silver surfers who had seen how basic computer skills would help in their community and charity work and, not least, in keeping up with their grandchildren. At the other end of the scale were the young self-employed, increasingly keen to be free of the merry-go-round of redundancies and short term contracts.

Now Pippa was impatient to expand. "With my techie wizardry and your editorial skills we'll be unstoppable," she said.

Upstairs, a couple of rooms needed no more than a bit of carpentry, a few coats of paint and some furniture, to convert into the hub of a potential desktop publishing empire. That was according to Pippa, who thought only in mega-terms. Mike found her amusing, Sara enormously refreshing.

For her the project provided welcome antidotes to her Daerley Green rut and Mike's absences. As for Berry, he had called Sara soon after his encounter with Amanda in The Trumpet to suggest lunch. From her response to his voice, Sara knew the old chemistry still worked and it would take very little to send her hurtling back into the emotional mayhem of that obsessive relationship.

"There's a busy patch ahead – give it a couple of weeks," was all she could think of on the spur of the moment. She could have suggested that it was time to accept they had both moved on. But she hadn't.

A few days later they had coincided at a concert at the Parish Church. They had been standing in the interval talking to friends, Mike's arm loosely round Sara's shoulders. She remembered looking up at him, laughing at something he had said and tweaking his hair, and then glanced across to see Berry watching them. He'd given her that familiar quizzical little smile, a faint shake of the head; and he had not rung her again. She heard his house was on the market, and by early January he had moved out to a village the other side of Banbury "much more convenient for the golf club." In the meantime they had met on a number of occasions: socially, in the street, at the post office. It had all been very civilised, but he had not invited them to his farewell party. She'd told herself she didn't mind and that it was rather childish of him.

By mid-January the conversion in George Street was complete and, following an advertising campaign in the local press, Cyber Inc's editorial department opened for business with a small office-warming party for friends and contacts, mostly Pippa's. Minkie was there with Jesse, newly returned from the States. Sara was particularly glad to have Jesse back. She had only recently surfaced enough from her own preoccupations to observe how edgy and withdrawn Minkie had become in recent weeks. After the initial euphoria of having Franko back in her life, Sara judged him a mixed blessing

At the last moment Mike was there, too. He had called her on her mobile from London to say he had unexpectedly been summoned back following a re-shuffle in the upper echelons of management.

Sara had explained about the office-warming "Which means I shan't be there till later, dammit."

"Fine. Keep a bottle for me and I'll join you. Could do with a bit of light relief. I'll call in at home on the way and freshen up."

"Right. Oh, there's a letter for you from Jovanka. On the hallstand."

"I didn't know you were back!" Minkie had flung her arms round Mike as soon as he appeared. "Missed you."

"Missed you too, Princess." Mike stood back to survey her appraisingly. "And more beautiful than ever." They always looked so at ease with each other. Sara felt the familiar small twinge of envy. "And Jesse. Good to have you back young man." He turned to Pippa, smiling. "And congratulations to Banbury's latest entrepreneur. No wonder the pundits say this is one of the fastest growing towns in Europe."

Pippa was looking spectacular that evening, a supreme advertisement for the Oxfam shop on which she boasted she depended almost entirely for her wardrobe. On this occasion she was in flowing purple and orange: a fantasy bird beneath the exotic bird's nest of her upswept hair. She gave her deep throaty laugh. "Which is my cue to say a few – a very few words. Namely that Sara, my partner, and I have it in our sights to make Banbury the cyber capital of the earthling world, whether you need a flier for the next school fête or a manifesto design for global cooling. Or something like that."

Sara, my partner, and I ... Sara caught Mike's eye across the room and grinned. She remembered feeling so good that evening. It was not until they got home that she remembered the letter. "Any special news from Jovanka?"

Mike fished the envelope, still unopened, from his pocket, slit it across the top, pulled out two flimsy sheets covered with Jovanka's large sloping scrawl. As he scanned through it, Sara went into the hall to extract a local freebie paper from the letterbox and returned muttering crossly "I've told them time and again not to leave these things half sticking out like that." She glanced at its front page with banner headlines about some local residents' protest, and then across at Mike. He was staring at the letter, contained in stillness.

"Anything wrong?" He didn't look up. "Mike?"

He did look up then, visibly re-arranging his face. "Nothing special. Sorry love, I'm bushed. Two continents and a brief teeter on the brink of cyber space are probably enough for one day."

Sara found the letter next morning folded back in its envelope under a book by his side of the bed. She wasn't looking for it. It just fell on the floor with the book while she was tidying up. Mike had been up since before seven. She'd heard him go downstairs, let himself out quietly for this ritual early morning tour of the garden.

By breakfast time he seemed his old self and was planning to go into Oxford to do some research for an article. "Have you seen Jovanka's letter, I seem to have mislaid it?" was his only reference to the previous evening. Only at that point she had not.

It had never before occurred to Sara to read Mike's letters - well, except for that time in the attic; but she had extracted the flimsy pages without pausing to think. The reference was on the second page: *I think I have met your friend Marija. Didn't you say she worked in a restaurant?* That was all, but it was enough: enough to confirm her suspicions that he had never forgotten the writer of that long-ago love letter; enough to show that she was still alive and he knew where she was; enough to resurrect the ghost that had once haunted her.

"I found Jovanka's letter," she said when he got home from Oxford, "by the bed," and knew by his "Thanks love," that it hadn't occurred to him either she might read it.

So what now? A confrontation? That evening as a gardening programme unfolded on TV, Sara's mind was unreeling its own video of disconnected scenes, a pale shadow central stage in blurred settings she could not properly identify. She found that she minded about the ghost more than she would have dreamed possible. There had been a time not so long ago when their lives, hers and Mike's, had seemed to run on tracks diverging so greatly that concepts such as fidelity hardly seemed relevant any more. She'd had that obsessive affair with Berry, assumed that Mike had some kind of relationship going on somewhere and hadn't wanted to know about it. But this past summer had changed that.

"What do you think?" asked Mike's voice. He was looking at her questioningly but relaxed.

"Sorry. About what?"

He put on his resigned face. "Do come back to earth, my love. They've just been demonstrating how to create a wild life garden – encourage a few more creepies and crawlies. Do our bit for the environment."

With a big effort Sara made the quantum leap from fantasising to reality. "You mean just leave a bit of the garden to go wild?"

Mike switched from resignation to extreme-patience mode. "No it doesn't mean that. It means you plant things to attract other things: buddleia for butterflies, thistles for finches are the more obvious. And be a bit less tidy, so hedgehogs have somewhere to hibernate. That sort of thing."

"Sounds good." But, watching and listening to him, she was really thinking there was no way this man could be leading the double life of two relationships, even with half a continent to separate them. Jovanka's reference to this Marija could have any one of a number of innocent explanations. Anyway Jovanka was not to know she, Sara, did not read her letters so would hardly draw attention to someone with whom Mike was having an affair. No, there had to be other reasons and she would put her mind to them in due course; perhaps even ask Mike, gently pulling his leg about this mysterious Marija. But there was no need to do it now.

She went over and gave him a hug in sheer relief.

"Nice," he said. "Any special reason?"

"No," Sara said. "Fancy a night cap?"

Mike was London-based for several weeks. He had been commissioned to write a series of articles on the Balkans for an encyclopaedia on the 20th century, and was in his element shuttling between the School of Slavonic and East European

Studies in London and the Bodleian Library in Oxford. In Banbury, Cyber Inc was doing very well indeed.

"Pippa's absolutely brilliant at exploiting new markets." Sara told Mike over the phone. "We're actually having to turn work away. Mind you, she had the vision in the first place to see that you can downsize computer technology to accommodate the sort of people who wouldn't normally dream of considering it. Made it user-friendly, you know, for small charity groups, clubs, people like that."

"I note you're acquiring all the jargon," Mike teased.

In a way she was glad he was so involved with his research for she often worked late. Not always strictly out of necessity either. "You really are becoming a cyber junkie," Pippa said, looking in one evening to find Sara trawling the net for some special clip art for a brochure she was designing for a local self-help group. The fact was that she was insatiably fascinated by the inexhaustible store of knowledge accessible by a few clicks of a mouse. There was an awful lot of dross, too, of course, but part of the challenge was learning to navigate through and beyond it. And she had become very good at it.

Towards the end of March, Mike went back to Serbia. Somewhere just below the level of a very busy consciousness, Sara felt a flicker of anxiety. The situation in Kosovo had been steadily deteriorating, Mike said, and he was convinced it would implode before long. Franko thought so too. Sara overheard him and Minkie arguing about it and was rather glad that he was less in evidence these days. With her A-levels imminent, she could do without the distraction. In another attempt to make sense of this new Balkans turmoil, Sara dipped among a myriad websites listed under Kosovo by various search engines and emerged more confused than ever. She did note, however, that it seemed quite a long way from Novi Sad.

Unusually Mike did not call her while he was away and when he did return a couple of weeks later it was several days before he came home. Calling her from Plum's flat he was terse almost to the point abruptness. "Hey," she'd protested. "Why are you snapping my head off when I only want to know how the trip went?"

He'd just about apologised, muttering something about the stresses of being confronted with "yet another humanitarian balls-up." And when she had tried to lighten things with some of the day-to-day absurdities of life in cyber space, he made no attempt to disguise his lack of interest. "Sod you Mike Hennessey," Sara said to the receiver as she replaced it. She'd really thought this time they had found sufficient common ground to span the void between their disparate interests. Well, things were different now. She was her own person, with a stake in a business and a commitment to a whole lot of clients. Some of whom, she went on informing the mute telephone receiver, were at least doing their best in a small way to make things better for someone else, even if they weren't out there at the cutting edge of world crises.

"Is anything wrong with Mike?" Minkie asked when he finally did come home.

So she'd noticed it too. "I think he's finding the Kosovo situation very stressful," Sara said.

"Not half as much as the people living there, I bet," Minkie said. It was unlike her to be critical of Mike. "Anyway I thought he'd been in Novi Sad most of the time."

"Oh, I probably got it wrong," Sara said quickly, and felt a shadow like a dark sad cloud.

Early in April, Pippa landed a major commission. There were big plans brewing to develop the canal-side area of Banbury into a major shopping and leisure complex. A northern company specialising in sports equipment was aiming to expand south and wanted a preliminary project plan incorporating the pros and cons of the town and its surroundings for such an expansion. Their marketing director, a blunt Lancashire gentleman, let it be known that he had no great belief in such fancy new concepts as geo-marketing assessments and certainly no staff to spare to indulge in such a thing, but he would pay a tidy one-off fee for Cyber Inc to do it for them in great detail. And quickly.

"Geo-marketing assessment! What sort of animal is that, for heaven's sake?" exclaimed Sara. "And why us?"

"Why us – because we're *good*. As for the rest," Pippa said firmly, "use your imagination, Sara. All they want is a tasteful, impressive brochure full of statistics to back up a decision they've probably already made: i.e., why Banbury is the best place to expand to from the point of view of a fast-growing market, central location, good access, recruitment, attractive living space, etc, etc. We've got all the contacts we need. All we're short of is time. So get on with it, partner."

So Sara had got on with it, compiling charts of every conceivable facility that an incoming company would need, scouring the net for profiles of other towns, and creating a comparable profile for Banbury, researching every imaginable statistic, and then preparing a lay-out to incorporate her findings together with a spread of photographs and sketches by one of their favourite local artists.

She was studying some print-outs one evening when she heard a small sound and glanced up to see Berry standing in the doorway, looking amused.

"The colourful lady downstairs said you were still at it," he said. "I must say busy-executive mode becomes you."

Feeling extraordinarily pleased to see him, Sara said "Well, I don't supposed you came here just to tell me that. So what can we do for you?"

"I have in mind a pretty brochure. We're expanding the golf club to offer limited but very up-market accommodation, with restaurant facilities to match. And of course we want to tell the world about it."

"As long as you don't need it by next week."

He smiled, looked round the office appraisingly. "I don't think timing will be a problem. Something we can discuss, along with other details. Perhaps over a drink? If I may say so, you look as though you could do with one."

She hesitated, but only briefly. "It'll have to be a quickie," she said.

Within a few minutes, Sara was helpless with laughter as Berry embarked on a series of anecdotes on the pitfalls of launching a new instruction course expressly for golfing widows. He had always been good at making her laugh.

Into a moment of companionable silence he said more seriously "You're even more becoming when you laugh."

Sara took a sip of her lager. "I'm not having another affair with you, Berry."

"Heaven forbid," he said so primly that she began to laugh again.

Then she told him about Cyber Inc, about Minkie on the eve of her A-levels, about her concerns regarding Franko.

"And Mike?" he asked pointedly when she paused.

"Mike's expanding his global interests into Afghanistan," Sara said, but had not meant it to sound quite so tart. She looked at her watch. "And I must go. They're both at home this evening for once." She smiled across at him. "Thanks for the drink – though we didn't get very far with discussing your brochure."

"I'm planning opportunities," Berry said. "Strictly business of course."

Minkie and Mike were in deep discussion, curled up at opposite ends of the sofa when she arrived home. Minkie broke off to say "Hi!" and Sara said "Guess who I've just had a drink with – Berry Tremayne, no less."

Minkie unwound herself. "Great – how is he? Why doesn't he come to Daerley any more?"

"Been too busy expanding the golf club I imagine. He wants us to do a brochure for him. But he asked after you, of course."

"Never did understand what either of you saw in him," Mike said in a bored voice.

"May be it's something to do with his sense of

community, not to mention sense of humour," Sara said spiritedly. "I'll go and make us some coffee."

Berry called next morning to make what he termed an 'official appointment to discuss business, perhaps over lunch.' This time they did get down to details of the brochure, its content and timing. Within a few days she had roughed out some ideas, and within a fortnight prepared a dummy of the one he preferred.

"Would you," he said tentatively "consider bringing it round to the cottage?" His cottage he meant, on the outskirts of Priory Downe, just over into Warwickshire. They'd had a drink first, then looked at the dummy, then had another drink. Then they'd gone to bed.

Not actually bed – it was the lambswool rug in front of the big open fireplace that first time. It was a couple of days later – after 'just a bit of tweaking to get the final lay-out right' - that they migrated upstairs to bed. And the chemistry, the sex, the mutual ability to fulfil each other's needs, were as fantastic as ever. "How do we do it?" Berry murmured, leaning on one elbow looking at her. And she'd rolled towards him and proceeded to demonstrate all over again.

Sara did not even enter into a debate with her conscience. If Mike could have his agenda, she could have hers. Berry had a way of bringing her sexually alive in a way she never dreamed; the old addiction for more of the same was back unabated, and the fact that sex, some good laughs and a modicum of shared business interests formed the entire basis of the relationship, seemed of spectacular unimportance. He made her feel beautiful, even apparently look beautiful. "You look great," Minkie commented one morning. "Have you done something to your hair?" But in fact she had done nothing to it at all.

All the same, this time she laid down some ground rules. Apart from office meetings, they would restrict their activities – she grinned at Berry slyly over the word – to his cottage. It would be in the early evenings, never overnight. She would not come to the golf club, and he would not come to see her in

Daerley Green. She had absolutely no intention that this time their affair could in any way impinge on any other area of her life.

"Real clandestine stuff," Berry said, but raised no objection.

In the event, it was hardest of all on her at the end of a session of companionship and lovemaking to collect herself physically and mentally and go back to being a business partner, a foster mother, a housekeeper and occasionally a wife. To begin with she visited the cottage three, even four times a week, later twice, more recently once. Sara told herself that the knowledge Berry was there gave the need to be with him less urgency, that the anticipation made their sex even better. And they were both successful and busy.

Occasionally when she was with Mike, there was a twinge of guilt. But only a twinge. It was difficult to feel loyalty to someone who, once again, was leading an almost totally separate life. It was also clear that something very particular had happened to him on his last visit to Serbia, and it could only be connected with his precious Marija. In which case disloyalty was no longer part of the equation.

And from time to time there were interludes when she could almost persuade herself they were a normal family unit. One of them centred on a dinner out to celebrate Minkie's successful A levels.

"To our brainbox Princess!" Mike had raised his glass in a toast, and Sara saw the pride in his smile.

Minkie looked from one to the other, not raising her glass immediately. She had pulled her long hair back into a sleek knot on the top of her head, and looked quite gorgeous. She also looked very serious as she said, "I don't really know how to say this, Mike … Sara. You have given me something unimaginable and if I speak for a week I shan't find enough words to thank you."

"Not to mention ending up with a very sore throat," Mike

said gruffly, but his eyes were glistening.

Minkie got up, came round the table to give each of them a hug. "I will try to make you proud of me."

Later it seemed she had told Mike of her ambitions to go back to Sarajevo before she made any decisions about further studies. But then Sara had accepted long ago that she always discussed things with Mike first; that to all intents and purposes she'd become the daughter Mike had never had.

Now, following her encounter with Amanda on the village green, Sara reached her office and picked up the phone to Berry.

"Just off to a meeting, sweetie. I'll call you back."

He hadn't called for a couple of days and then it was to say that things had become rather hectic, so could they postpone their next session until next week. He lingered over the word 'session', following it with a low growl.

Sara gave a small laugh. "Fine by me. Things are pretty hectic here too. By the way I bumped into Amanda a couple of days ago. I gather she's getting into golf."

Perhaps she imagined it but she thought she detected the smallest pause. "That's one way of putting it," Berry said. "It's a sort of *quid pro quo* – a lesson or two in exchange for all the help she gave distributing our brochure. Through DG Publishing, you know?" No Sara didn't know.

But then it was none of her business. Was it?

Mike : January 1998

In Priština, student demonstrations were demanding full autonomy for Kosovo, and the self-styled Kosovo Liberation Army had begun to attack Serbian security forces. Back home in Daerley Green on a dank January morning, Mike checked the first green spikes of snowdrops pushing through near the old oak tree and thought of Sonja. As he thought of her often, though no longer every day nor quite so obsessively.

Those moments after he first saw the photograph of her were forged deep into his psyche. He remembered shouting out in shock, though not what he had shouted. He remembered Bogdan's startled face as he turned questioningly to Marija. He remembered Marija's low responses and then Bogdan going out into the small hallway and a moment later the slam of the door of the flat.

"Does he know?" Mike had asked roughly.

She shook her head. "No one has ever known except my Niko. And now you. Bogdan knew her – Sonja – only little. He was away so much." She paused. "Now he goes to visit our friends for an hour. I tell him we have things about your work to discuss …"

"I don't sodding care where he's gone," Mike interrupted. He felt incoherent with shock, anger, grief, a succession of new sensations, all of them hurting. Unbelievably hurting.

Marija said "Unmarried girls in Sarajevo, not nice girls … they did not become pregnant. It was a … a very big shock for me."

"You didn't tell me. Why didn't you tell me?"

"Michael, we were young. I thought I was in love or I would not sleep with you. But your letters were already telling me how you had moved on – moved away. And I am from a proud people. Then there was Niko who said he had loved me for long time, that he wanted to look after me and the child. Everyone thought she was his. He looked on Sonja as his."

"But she wasn't, was she? She was mine. *Mine,*" Mike raged. He repeated "She was mine, and I never knew her." He saw her tears streaming silently, but his own pain was too vast to feel compassion for hers. He sat clutching the framed photograph, and began interrogating her: the colour of his daughter's hair, her eyes, the sound of her voice, her likes and dislikes, hopes and fears. Marija answered him quietly, the tears still flowing, making no attempt to stop them. Sonja had dark hair and green eyes, like Marija herself. No she wasn't pretty. Her face was rather strong for a child, but when she laughed it lit up. "Like yours," Marija said. "Most of the time I thought of Niko as her father; but when she suddenly laughed after some sad time, then it was like long ago touch from you."

She was not good with books, much more interested in sport. A tomboy. Especially swimming. She had swum like a mermaid, come third in all of Bosnia and Herzegovina for her age group. Good on skis too, and loved to go with her father, with Niko that is, into the mountains.

In vain Mike searched for some echo of himself. He stared down at the photograph with that small square face staring back at him, frozen in perpetuity. She had her thin arms round a basket full of something. When he queried it Marija came over to look. And then her sad, tear-stained face briefly lit with a smile. "Wild flowers," she said. "Every time she came home it was with such flowers. She pressed them in big books, looked up their names and wrote about them: what good medicine they made; or vegetables or soup or tea."

It was then that Mike's sorrow surged up from some deep unknowable depth and he put his head in his hands and wept.

In time he became aware that Marija's arms were round him and they were weeping together.

"Did she suffer?"

"No. I promise you. For all of them it was at once."

After a while Mike got up and went to the bathroom to sluice cold water over the hot tight skin of his face. He saw it, twisted with sorrow, staring back from the mirror above the wash basin. When he returned to the living room he said, "I've given you a terrible time Marija. You didn't deserve that."

"I can understand ... the shock. Before I was thinking it was better not to tell you."

"So why did you invite me here?"

"I saw that you were sad for me. I wanted that you know I am all right. With Bogdan. He is a very good man. But I forgot about the photograph. How could I forget that?"

Mike picked it up again. He wanted it as much as he had wanted anything. "Do you have any other pictures?"

"All were destroyed with the mortar. Just this I found unbroken, like a miracle." Perhaps he could get a copy made. "Will you tell Sara?"

Mike went on gazing at the photograph. "I don't know," he said.

He hadn't told her. Sara belonged to a totally different compartment of his life. Sometimes, even long before he knew about Sonja, he looked – really looked - across at her as she chattered away about Daerley's latest affairs and wondered how two such disparate people had come to share their lives in a contract as binding as marriage. For he did regard it as binding; and he had been, still could be, enchanted by her. It wasn't just her attractiveness, though there was no denying that. It certainly wasn't shared interests, though at times they had both made real efforts to accommodate each other's. Sara's need to identify purposes in her life, whether it was the *Chronicle* or Justin's welfare, could be very endearing. It could also make her seem quite vulnerable. That time she had discovered she couldn't have a child - her vulnerability had touched him profoundly. Perhaps it was that extra quality that added to his own purposes in life. At times it seemed like the vulnerability of a child: of the child that they could not have.

There was no way he could tell her about the child he did

have. Correction: *had* had.

And anyway, Sara had lost her vulnerability these days. She had, in her own way, turned professional, with her own objectives and deadlines and colleagues. For a time the previous summer, they seemed to rediscover in each other that extra quality that made them individually feel more whole. For surely at its deepest level that was the ultimate aspiration of a loving relationship: to make the whole greater than the sum of its two parts? But for whatever reason it had not lasted.

He had rung her from Plum's flat on his return to London, finding unnecessary reasons to delay the call; and felt relief when his first attempts were met by the answering machine. He had not left a message feeling a need to be in control, to be sure he had the flat to himself when he spoke to her. When he eventually heard her voice he was surprised at how much lighter it was than he remembered, and then felt resentment at the triviality of her words. Had the trip been difficult? Was he exhausted? They'd been incredibly busy at Cyber Inc. which was going from strength to strength. When was he coming home? He found himself making excuses as to why he would not be returning to Daerley for some days.

After he replaced the receiver he knew he had been abrupt without even remembering what he had said. And that wasn't fair. It wasn't Sara's fault his only child had been snuffed out in some alien conflict; nor that she could not have one herself. He hadn't even asked about Minkie.

God, Minkie!

Mike had buried his face in his hands, grateful that Plum would not be home until much later. Back in Novi Sad talking and talking and talking with Marija, the only reality for several days had been the aching sense of loss for something he had always wanted, never imagined he had and in the end would never know. He found it impossible to discuss it with Jovanka, merely justifying the hours he spent with Bogdan and Marija by saying they were helping him with some non-existent feature he was preparing. He didn't know what excuse Marija gave Bogdan for his constant presence, but he didn't seem to question it. It wasn't even that they talked so much about Sonja; it was simply that he found a nameless kind of comfort in being with those who had been close to her. In the end he told them about Minkie and that helped as it was a subject that could be freely discussed with Bogdan. He had promptly embarrassed Mike by vigorously shaking his hand and expressing a touching gratitude on behalf of all Sarajevans.

"Tell him it's no big deal," Mike said to Marija. "I – we love her. Yes, it *was* pity at first – she was such a waif. But now I can't imagine life without the child." Thinking of Minkie, for a few moments his mind was at peace. He mused "Hardly a child now, of course. Eighteen, and so beautiful." And then he remembered. "The same age as Sonja. Oh dear God, and if I'd known ..."

Marija said sharply "Even if you had known, we would not have let her go. And there is one more thing you must know. Our child was not perfect. That day of the mortar I tell her to take little Niko to friends in another part of the city, where it is safer. But the electricity is on that day and there is a video she wants to see." As Mike gave a small cry she went on "You can tell yourself a million times that perhaps you can save her. A million times I tell myself *I* could save them all if I do not go to the market but stay home and make sure we all go to the safer place. You know nothing, Michael – *nothing* when you speak of guilt."

He had not spoken of it again.

Two weeks later, sitting in Plum's flat with his head in his hands, Mike tried to visualise life without Minkie, and could not.

He went home a few days later. Preoccupied with a rush of work at Cyber Inc, Sara did not appear to notice his boorishness. Not so Minkie. One evening soon after his return, when Sara was working late and Mike was in the living room pretending to read the paper, Minkie had prepared a tray with a large Scotch-on-the-rocks for him, an elderflower cordial for herself, placed it on the coffee table beside him before curling up at the opposite end of the sofa, and said "So tell me about your trip. You've been pretty off-ish since you got back."

He had muttered something dismissive but she had persisted "It's part of my country Mike. Or was. The more I hear about conditions from Franko, the more determined I am to go back. I want to know."

So he had started telling her about Jovanka, and the difficulties of daily living in Novi Sad, with the shortages and soaring prices. And then without planning it, he began talking of Marija and Bogdan and their terrible losses. Not with any reference to himself of course, but as though they were Jovanka's friends. It was only when he saw the tears in Minkie's eyes that he registered what painful memories he must be triggering for her and he paused stricken. "I'm so sorry Princess. What am I thinking?"

"No, it's OK, OK. Sometimes life here feels so insulated – so completely 'other' from everything I knew before – I need to be reminded of where I come from. To remember that the future is up to me. That I've been given a chance when others weren't so lucky."

Mike dredged through his mind for titbits of remembered conversation with Jovanka, spiced with her dry sense of humour, and Minkie was smiling again by the time Sara arrived with her "Guess who I've just had a drink with – Berry Tremayne, no less." As soon as possible he'd pleaded tiredness and gone early to bed.

He took to dreaming about Sonja. She was always in the distance, her back to him, sometimes picking wildflowers in a field, sometimes sitting at an easel so that he supposed it must be Minkie after all. Always he approached her with this great sense of joy mixed with a nameless dread of seeing her face. And always he awoke before he did.

Over the coming days he seesawed between intense

anxiety for Minkie, and irritation when she behaved in a frivolously normal teenage way. The anxiety was initially connected with Franko whom he did not trust and whose visits always seemed to leave Minkie on edge. He put this down to the memories Franko brought from home, and in contrast grew to appreciate the steadying effect that Jesse had. That was when he was not suffering appalling shafts of fear that Minkie's and Jesse's relationship was as serious as it appeared to be and might well provide other causes for excising her from his life.

The anxiety became at times obsessive and, recognising this, he did his best to conceal it. If challenged, he could not have specified what he was actually anxious about, but the ultimate fear was that in some unpredictable, unstoppable way she would dematerialise from his life. Once he had chanced upon Azzie in a Banbury shopping precinct, and grabbed her arm to say "Azzie! I'm glad I've run into you. You're Minkie's best friend. She's all right isn't she? There's nothing worrying her that you know of?"

Azzie had looked quite startled until he realised he was still gripping her arm and let go of it, forcing a relaxed smile. She'd said, "She's fine Mr Hennessey. Well, apart from being a bit stressed out about the A's, but then we all are."

"Yes, of course. Of course – the exams – that'll be it."

It was a relief when his next assignment came: back to Afghanistan whose deprivations and ravaged countryside – not to mention the trigger-happy tendencies of its male population – ensured that his mind was entirely concentrated on the moment. In Kabul, with the strengthening grip of the Taliban, life was reeling back to the dark ages, but the international community was now focussing attention on the Uzbek-dominated north; and not least its charismatic leader, the Russian trained Uzbek General Abdul Rashid Dostum. It was not a comfortable assignment but Mike almost welcomed the deprivations, some of which at least they were obliged to share with the rest of the population. He found himself thinking that life must have been something like this for Minkie in Sarajevo. Then: *and for Sonja.* But at least the dreams of her had stopped.

By the time he returned home early in May he had regained some measure of perspective. Firstly, there was nothing like a bit of deprivation to make one appreciate the comforts of home. England had never looked a more green and pleasant land, and the garden was at its multi-colourful best. Sara was ... well, Sara seemed much more self-contained was the only way he could think of it, and therefore less demanding of him. It certainly made for an easier life. In particular, it was helpful in their combined concern for Minkie who was building up to a pre-exam frenzy. Thankfully, Franko's visits had ceased as, according to Minkie, he had acquired greater commitments in Germany. She seemed surprisingly unfazed by this.

There were small highlights – even major ones such as the sight of Minkie's shining face as she read the results of her A-levels. The three of them had gone out for a celebratory dinner and Minkie had made a touching small speech of thanks for all they had done. That really had nearly choked him. She was still not keen, though, to discuss the future.

"For heaven's sake let the girl have a breather," Sara said. Not wanting to spoil the mood of the evening, he had let it go but at the first opportunity he had tackled her again.

They were in the kitchen, heating up a casserole in the microwave that Sara had left for them in the fridge. The future, he had pointed out, could not be postponed forever. Minkie pulled a face. "You too! Jesse keeps on about it. And every teacher within sight."

Mike said firmly "You're not charming your way out of this, Princess. The point is with all the competition there is for the best places, you should have been putting in applications months ago." He removed the casserole from the microwave, gave it a stir. "I'm not going to let you change your mind about the art studies, and that's final. You're too good."

Minkie grinned at him cheekily. "I like it when your

182

masterful." Then suddenly serious she went on, "Don't imagine I haven't been thinking about it over and over and over again. And talking about it, especially with Azzie. But I need *time*, Mike. Yes, I might be quite good, though probably not as good as you think I am. But I've got to work out a lot of things first." She looked very young and vulnerable. "Sometimes I haven't the faintest clue even where I belong. That's a pretty bizarre feeling. I've got to sort that out before I make decisions that affect the rest of my life."

Mike wanted terribly to hug her, but knew it was important to let her talk her confusion through. He concentrated on dividing up the casserole on two plates and took them over to the breakfast bar as she went on, "So what I'd like – really like is to take a year off ..." She paused and looked at him with a deeply anxious expression before she blurted out in a rush "Get a job and make a bit of money, then go back to Sarajevo for a while ..." She stopped and took a deep breath.

He wanted to hug her more than ever. Instead, he smiled as reassuringly as he could and said "Stop looking so worried, Princess. It's always been understood that you want to go back. I just question whether it wouldn't be better to get the qualifications first – may be take a short trip in the meantime – and then make the life-changing decisions."

She shook her head. "I don't think there's any way I could concentrate on Uni the way I feel at the moment." She picked up a fork, started toying with the casserole; then looked back at him. "Don't you see Mike? I still don't believe Mother is dead. Even if she is, I don't know whether this is where I'm meant to be. And without going back I can't know." She put the fork down again. "And now you'd better hear the rest of it."

And to his growing amazement, she went on to tell him of a whole string of job applications made and some offers received, culminating with the one she was about to accept: with Office Sparklers, a firm of office cleaners in Banbury. As Mike opened his mouth in protest, she explained rapidly that she had settled for this as she could choose her own hours and fit them in with the access course she'd signed up for at the Art College. Yes, she knew she should have discussed it with him and Sara but "I thought you'd try and talk me out of it. Especially you. And you've been away so much, and there was Franko and the exams. And everything. Anyway, what do you think?"

What he thought in terms of astonishment and admiration was inexpressible so Mike confined himself to "I think you're a very remarkable young woman, and I'll back you all the way."

Once informed, Sara was rather more practical. Firstly she checked up on Office Sparklers and pronounced them squeaky clean, not least because they paid well above the going rate and had a low staff turnover, always a good sign. Then she checked the details of the access course, suggesting some assignments for Cyber Inc which might provide useful projects as well as earn her a little extra cash. Mike was surprised and impressed.

It was in September that he began to call Marija from the London flat. He did it when Plum was out and sometimes when Marija was out too so there would be a brief and rather surreal exchange with Bogdan. In that regard at least his conscience was quite clear for his feelings for Marija had undergone a total catharsis. Impossible to think of her as the woman with whom he had made such magnificent and passionate youthful love. She was the mother of his child, and for this she had his boundless gratitude. The sound of her voice each time was an affirmation that Sonja had existed; and anyway he was concerned for her and for Bogdan and little Snežka.

"By the way," Plum said one evening. "You haven't got a bit of fluff over in Novi Sad, have you?"

"Do you have to be so crude?" Mike said. "The answer's no. Why?"

"Thought the phone bill was a touch on the heavy side. Then noticed some unusual numbers on the list of calls. One in particular."

He'd been tempted then to tell Plum, pour it all out so that there would at least be one other person in the world to whom he could mention Sonja's name, wonder about her aloud, how she might look, what she might be doing in an endless succession of 'nows'. But he hesitated too long and the moment passed. "It's some friends of Jovanka," was all he said. "They're having a hard time and I wanted to keep in touch."

He saw Plum did not believe a word of it.

On his return from London just before Christmas, Minkie waved a large envelope at Mike and said, "This came for you. From Jovanka. It's either a b-i-g Christmas card or a small calendar."

Three-and-a-half-months with Office Sparklers had transformed her from pert schoolgirl to confident young wage earner. It was quite astonishing. "You've no idea what pigsties people make of the places where they work," she'd said more than once, deeply disapproving. "When I run my global operation I shall insist on universal order and cleanliness."

"Pity your poor husband," was Azzie's comment.

Now, with a week off, Minkie was making final adjustments to the Christmas tree in the living room. Decorating the tree had become her special annual job. It had began some years earlier when, rummaging in the loft, she found a dusty box of old silver balls and tinsel, some camels carved in wood, a clutch of Christmas elves with tall red hats, and a farmyard's worth of pottery animals. These she had arranged on and around their first small tree, each year adding some new and original items that she had made or picked up at a craft market or charity fair. Early on Mike had started keeping a photographic record, and the tree seemed to grow with Minkie each Christmas as she set out to surpass the previous year's creation. Culmination of the tree's decorations were the white candles, real ones, that she placed on branches weighted down by satsumas or clementines to make them more or less horizontal. The candles were lit on Christmas Eve and then on a growing number of occasions each year as the fame of 'Minkie's tree' spread. Mike loved to watch the pleasure on her face in the candlelight.

He watched her now as he eased the big stiff envelope open. "The tree's looking great, Princess. It's your best ever," he said extracting the contents. And then he froze.

It was neither a card nor a calendar; and it wasn't from Jovanka. It was an enlargement of the photograph of Marija, Niko father and son, and Sonja. Attached to it was a plain card on which she had written *Christmas greetings from Marija, Bogdan and Snežka.*

His small shocked cry was involuntary. Minkie looked up and came to peer over his shoulder. "Oh, but it's not Jovanka."

Mike cleared his throat, swallowed hard. "Her friends. You remember I told you about those friends of hers I met?"

Minkie nodded. "The ones who lost their partners and children?" But how to explain the sending of the photograph? Thankfully Minkie showed no curiosity about this. She was studying the photograph closely. "The lady is very beautiful. And he looks pretty dishy. And the girl – I guess she'd be my age now. Is she the one you met?"

She was still looking down at the photograph and Mike concentrated hard on the dark glossy back of her head. "No, this … this child was killed. The one I met – Snežka -was only a toddler at the time. It's her father Bogdan and Marija, the lady in the photograph, who are bringing her up." He forced a laugh. "It's rather complicated."

"Not by Bosnian standards," Minkie said. "Sometimes I think back to my school friends and whether they were from so-called 'mixed' marriages and what's happened to them. It's not a thing any of us thought about before … before all this." She had never spoken about her school friends before; there were so many areas of her childhood life about which they really knew nothing. When he said as much Minkie's shiny head turned and she reached up to put her cheek briefly against his. "I wouldn't have known how to talk about it in the early days," she said. "It wasn't until I met Azzie that I dared to dredge up some of those memories. And in time the blackness turns to grey, and ..." She gave a big shrug. "You have to get on with what you've got, don't you?"

Such youth and such intuition. Mike smiled. "You're right, my wise Princess."

Minkie smiled back "That's better," she said. She handed the photograph back to him. "Perhaps one day I'll go and see Snežka. After all this Marija did for her what you've done for me, so we have a big thing in common. Which reminds me, I must call Azzie - I promised to meet up with her tomorrow for a last frenzied Christmas shop. Being brought up a Moslem you wouldn't think she'd bother, but of course Auntie's solid C of E, so I suppose she gets the best of both worlds. Or is it the worst?" She went out of the room laughing.

Mike sat for a long time, the photograph on his lap, Minkie's words echoing in his head: *this Marija did for her what you've done for me.* She would never know their significance, for the inevitable next thought was: *and as Niko did for Sonja.* For the first time Mike gave consideration to and came to understand the depth of feeling of the unknown Niko for his, Mike's, unknown daughter.

It was a quieter Christmas than usual and Mike was grateful for it. He was also grateful for some extra assignments on Encyclopaedia 2000 which required additional research and some concentrated days in the Bodleian. Azzie came over for Christmas day for most of which it rained. After the usual excesses of Christmas lunch, they all went for a short, wet walk and then settled down to Scrabble. On Boxing Day, Minkie went to Azzie's and the following day there was an unexpected visit from Polly Cuttle and her small tribe. Throughout it all Mike was aware of Sara's preoccupation. She had mentioned that Cyber Inc was going through a quiet patch, but he did not think that was the cause. Faced with his own preoccupations Mike found he could empathise with Sara's without even knowing what they were. For a few – but only a very few – moments he even considered showing her Marija's photograph – not of course with a full explanation, for that could never be; but just sharing the involvement with that small family. Of course he didn't. He had always been terrible at subterfuge and there was already far more of it in his life than he could comfortably handle.

The fact was, though, that he felt much more at ease with Sara when she wasn't in that top-executive mode she had adopted in recent months. He genuinely wanted her to be happier than she obviously was and during that usual doldrum time that succeeded the celebration of a New Year, he suggested on a couple of occasions they should go out for a meal, a drink, whatever. When she pleaded tiredness for the second time, he decided to go anyway. Avoiding the inevitable bonhomie of The Trumpet, he drove a few miles to an old favourite from their early married days. It was a Monday lunch time and almost empty: no doubt, everyone recovering from the first excesses of 1998.

But not quite empty. In the snug off the main bar the sound of low laughter caught his attention as he paid for his half of lager, and he glanced through. Sitting very close together, indeed almost in each other's laps, were Amanda Heyforth and Beresford Tremayne, apparently about to devour each other. They were far too absorbed to notice him, and Mike retreated to a corner out of their view.

Amanda Heyforth and Beresford Tremayne – who would have thought? Not a pair of names he would have naturally coupled together. But then you could never tell. Minkie had once been devoted to the man, and there was a time when he had even thought Sara rather smitten.

Suddenly he didn't really fancy a drink after all. He pushed it aside and went back out into the dull January day.

No point, he decided, in mentioning any of this to Sara.

Kosovo

From a 1988 Guide to Yugoslavia: "... By far the greatest national group is Albanian, forming nearly 80 percent of the population. After 1945, large numbers of Montenegrin partisans were also given holdings in the area. Albanian and Turkish are official languages in addition to Serbo-Croat, and broadcasting and education are carried on in all three languages. The Albanians are temperamentally quite different from their Slav compatriots, and among some of them blood ties with their relatives in austere little neighbouring Albania run deep, a factor encouraged by the literature in their own language which comes from across the border. A desire for greater independence on the part of an active minority led in the early 1980s to considerable unrest and even violence, and order was only restored by a hasty dispatch of the army. The calm remains uneasy."

By the end of 1990, President George Bush was threatening military action should the Serbs crack down further on Kosovo's ethnic Albanians. Historical movements had resulted in the population of the province comprising 93% Albanian; yet the one belief that united all Serbs was that Kosovo, cradle of their culture, was inalienably part of Serbia.

During the following years tit-for-tat killings escalated as the Kosovo Liberation Army (KLA) gained support and confidence.

In October 1998, as diplomacy faltered, Nato placed authority for air strikes in the hands of the Secretary-General.

Jasminka : October 1998

All was not well in Minkie's world. Azzie was emigrating to join her brother and parents in America: the date now fixed for mid-November. Franko had recently catapulted back into her life and out of it again, leaving her feeling bereft and confused. And, very worst of all, Mike had broken her heart.

Earlier, apart from the deteriorating situation in Kosovo, it had been a good summer. Her growing sense of closeness to Mike had deepened quite sharply in recent months, especially since he had told her of his visits to Novi Sad and about those friends of Jovanka. It was also then that he had spoken for the first time about his own strange childhood, and she had warmed to her vision of the small boy so ill at ease in that free and easy communal living embraced by his odd-sounding parents. What unexpected lives lay behind the faces that had become so familiar to her - far, far more familiar than those of her own family.

She had thought about this a lot, even about how these feelings for Mike compared with those she might have felt for her father. But the comparison was impossible. She had never known her father from any perspective other than as a child. He had been her chief figure of authority: the one she ran to when she felt threatened, but also the one she sometimes tested to see just what she might get away with. Her love for him had been tinged with awe, even fear when she knew she had been found out in some misdemeanour. It was quite different from the love she had for Mother: unquestioning, safe in the knowledge that there she would always find the gentle touch to help smooth the hurts away.

But when it came to her father and Mike, she knew there was no comparison to be made. Her feelings for Mike did not come into the daughter/father category; much more the sister/brother. Older brother. Much older brother and one who also hurt sometimes and needed a word of comfort.

And Sara? There had rarely been a sense of sisterhood

there; more an unpredictable friend. In fairness, Minkie could appreciate now that it must have been hard for Sara to have a self-absorbed foreign child thrust into the familiar busy-ness of her role in Daerley Green. Still she had always been there for her. It was Minkie herself who had taken the first tentative steps of independence that went with forming new relationships: first with Polly, then Justin and Berry but, above all, Azzie.

"I think you're loathsome," she said in something approaching anguish during the summer when it became clear that Azzie's departure was going to happen sooner rather than later.

"It's going to be scary for me," Azzie pointed out. "Having to start all over. Yet again."

"Yes, but with your own proper family."

Azzie caught the wistful note and said "Yes, I know I'm lucky" She went on briskly "Anyway there's no point in starting anything serious in the next few months, so I might as well earn a bit of money to take with me. I thought you might recommend me as a clean, honest and reliable addition to the Office Sparklers team? Auntie's horrified, of course, at the thought of having a charlady in the family, but I think she's given up on me now that I'll soon be completely out of her hair. What do you reckon?"

Minkie reckoned it was a fine idea. A week or two after she had shared her decision to take the job, Mike had waylaid her as she crossed the market place. As always it was being well used as a parking lot and he'd stopped to lean on a bright red Robin Reliant three-wheeler, looking quaint and slightly absurd amidst the more usual selection of Toyotas and Vauxhalls and VWs. She'd laughed and said "That jalopy looks more my style than yours." And he beamed at her and said "Good, because that's just what it is."

She hadn't understood immediately and then when he'd said, "Yes, it's really yours. Get in and see how it fits" she could hardly breathe with excitement. He'd got it for a song he said; after all, who in their right mind would want to chug around the countryside in that; but she could see he was almost as excited as she was.

"Had you actually thought of how you were going to get to work and back? No, I thought not. Anyway, it's taxed for six months. May be you'll have saved up for something better by then."

Still struggling for words Minkie said, "I love it. I'll never ever want anything else," really meaning and believing it.

So she had started the new chapter in her life as wage-earner and car owner. The Reliant was soon christened Robbo and won new friends daily, usually to the accompaniment of ribald comment. And she really loved the job: the independence of it, the being in charge of putting order into other people's daily chaos, of having at her command these important-looking expanses of office world with their desks and electronic equipment and piles of folders and overflowing wastepaper baskets. Sparklers allocated her two small and one larger office suite, all of them on the industrial estate off the Southam Road. Occasionally someone would be working late, but mostly she had the premises to herself and she would create images of the occupant of each desk: the messy ones who left cups with dregs of cold coffee and squashy crumbs and crumpled balls of paper, and the obsessive ones who must have aligned their papers with a ruler to leave them so tidy.

Her routine settled comfortably into a three-hour stint from 6-9 pm three times a week and an occasional Saturday. This dovetailed well with her two days and one evening at College but did little for her social life. Jesse had complained a bit. "So I travel half way round the world and take a crappy job just to be with you and you don't wanna know." She had given him the sort of hug that left him in no doubt how much she wanted to know, and he'd cooled down and "guessed he understood what she had to do." Robbo, of course had helped as they both now had wheels and could more easily snatch meetings in the course of their respective schedules.

There was no problem about getting Azzie on to the team or co-ordinating her work schedule with Minkie's, who picked her up and dropped her home. Sometimes after work they would stop off for a pizza in Banbury, and occasionally when they were feeling more flush round off with a half of lager in the Horton Bar of the Whateley Hotel. It appealed to their sense of the absurd to know they had come straight from their cleaning jobs to mingle with the moderately affluent and upwardly mobile. It was on one of these occasions that Azzie had leaned across and hissed "See who's just come in."

Minkie glanced round in time to see the unmistakable back views of Amanda Heyforth and Berry heading past the oak-panelled bar to a smaller room beyond.

"Did you see – he had his hand on her bottom. He's gross." Azzie pronounced.

"Well, he never was your favourite person," Minkie said, not wanting to admit her own extreme surprise at the sight of them together.

"While you were besotted."

Minkie considered this gravely. "No, that's not fair. He was very kind to me when I was going through a bad time. He went to a lot of trouble for me – and for you come to that. Remember all that involvement with the youth club? I mean it was never really his scene, was it, but he did have some great ideas."

"He also had another motive – like getting closer to Sara through you. And he was obviously crazy about her for a time." Azzie caught Minkie's expression. "All right, that's water under the bridge."

After that they saw Amanda and Berry together several times, once almost in a head-on collision as they came out of their favourite pizza haunt near the Cross. Amanda produced a jaunty "Hello young ladies," and insisted on pausing to check on their health and progress, while Berry stood grinning and looking uncomfortable.

It was a bit disconcerting, Minkie thought later as she drove home, to discover how much relationships could change. There was a time when Berry had been one of the few solid pillars of her life and now it was difficult to feel anything in particular, other than mild curiosity. The train of thought stayed with her through the usual exchange of greetings with Mike and Sara when she got home and as she got ready for bed. It was, she supposed, nothing more complicated than the fact she had grown up.

Her mind turned to Justin. That relationship had changed too, though in a different way. Since his move into The Fieldings, he seemed to have shrunk into his own large frame: as though preparing to become a ghost. Minkie lay in bed feeling a shadow of sadness. She loved him deeply. He had been there for her at her times of profoundest sorrow, had given her the beginnings of a sense of light in a greyness that had once seemed all embracing. She went to see him as often as she could and was rewarded by the way his face lit up as soon as he saw her.

And then there was Polly, the very first of her props: funny, scatty Polly who hadn't even known where Bosnia was. In those way-back days, she had been the one with whom Minkie felt the most comfortable, even forgetting briefly her own misery in her interest in the events forecast by Polly's huge belly. That had given her the first real sense of normality with its memories of the recent birth of her newest cousin in Sarajevo: a sense of the unchangeable on-goingness of life wherever you were and whatever else was happening. Dear once-scatty Polly who could now qualify for a Master's degree in the management of husband and brood of three!

Which brought her to Polly's dotty uncle and his broken down farm. Once Franko was back in Germany, Minkie had been heartily thankful to forget her brief involvement with his dubious enterprise. Her greatest hope was that the whole thing would go away, and in a way it had. On a visit to Polly's in the summer she had felt compelled to ask for news of the old boy.

"Fancy you remembering him! Poor old duffer was carted off to a funny farm. The booze got him in the end." Polly made a sad face. "I went over to clean the place up before it went on the market. You wouldn't believe the filth. I reckon he'd hired the old barns out too for some no-good purpose. There was a load of rubbish, even some old mattresses, as though a lot of people had been camping out for quite a while."

Finally, Minkie's thoughts came round to Franko himself as she drifted into sleep and a vivid dream of childhood days: of a family picnic on the slopes of Jahorina. She had gone off to pick bilberries and become lost. As is the way of dreams, she followed innumerable false trails deeper and deeper into the forest, getting increasingly anxious until she was in a nightmare panic. At that point Franko had appeared. He'd been searching for her for hours, he said, and began to lead her back: only they seemed to get even more lost as the clouds gathered and a storm approached, and when he turned to take her hand, his face had changed completely to the older, streetwise face of more recent days.

She awoke with a dark sense of foreboding.

"So what are your plans for the day, Princess?" Mike asked looking up from buttering toast. Then "Hey, what's wrong?"

"Weird dreams." Minkie pulled a face. "And immediate plans are to go into town for a dental check-up, change library books and pick up some materials for my course."

But the foreboding did not go away and as she approached Robbo across the Market Place and saw a familiar figure leaning against it in a thin haze of cigarette smoke, she could almost believe she had conjured him up.

"I could get you a better one than this, little cousin," Franko said, dropping the cigarette and heeling it into a crack between the cobbles. He dangled a set of car keys from his little finger and nodded towards a sleek silver Audi Roadster parked next to Robbo. Then he held out his arms. "How are you,

195

Minkie?"

She looked at him with a mixture of affection, caution and exasperation. He had put on a bit of weight but was as handsome as ever in a well-cut denim safari suit that certainly did not come from any jumble sale. "Why on earth didn't you come to the house?"

Franko shrugged "I don't think your English family like such unplanned visitors."

"Well may be … But you could have rung." She came round to give him a hug. "It's wonderful to see you – it's just that I could have re-arranged things. Anyway get in and we'll talk on the way into town." She unlocked the car. "And how did you know this was mine."

"I know many things," Franko said, manoeuvring his broad frame into the narrow passenger seat. "I know you are working and you have some studies and …"

"So you'll also know you need to fix your seat belt," Minkie said, starting the engine.

"Oh, how English you've become, with your seat belts and your timetables." He grumbled, but he clicked his seatbelt into place.

They arranged to meet in the Horton Bar at midday, and Franko was already there when she arrived, a Scotch on the rocks at his elbow, a coffee lined up for her. "I did not think you would be drinking and driving," he teased as he kissed her lightly on each cheek.

"And you would be right." Minkie settled opposite him at the small table. "And now you can tell me everything, including why you are here."

"The truth is I'd like your help," Franko said. "I know you didn't like the operation I was involved in before, and I agree it had some bad things. But it is quite different now. The drunk old man you introduced me to has gone, his farm is sold, so there is nothing like that any more. We are now very … I think you say streamlined. We have very good places organised and more

196

people – more and more people all the time – desperate to come. You can help me."

"No I can't, Franko. Even if it is different from last time it's still against the law. And don't tell me again how English I've become, because that's the way I am after nearly six years here."

"It was an observation, not a criticism, Minkie." He reached out to put a hand over hers briefly as it rested on the table. "Like I observed you are a good driver." She waited. "And that's all I want – nothing else: a good driver for a few weeks, and I can promise you more money in a day than you make in a month in that crazy job of yours. And a car to dream about."

Minkie said "I love my car, and I like my job. And *they* are both legal."

Franko sighed. "You have changed my Jasminka." He leaned back in his seat, lit a cigarette, studied her thoughtfully through the first drifts of smoke. "Don't you remember how we were going to change the world? Make things better?"

"I remember it very well," Minkie said quietly. "We were going to make Sarajevo like it used to be, a place where people worked and lived without thinking about the names or origins or customs of our great grandparents or in which building they had worshipped their God. Is that what you still want Franko? Is that why you offer me good money to drive these desperate people from one part of a foreign country to another?"

He went on studying her through the drifting smoke for a moment, then leaned forward and said "Yes, Minkie, now I see the problem. It is not that you have changed. It is the world – my world anyway." He shook his head. "Dear Minkie, I do not think you begin to understand how it is in Sarajevo now. Not just the streets and buildings which are broken or destroyed, or the forests all around which have been taken for firewood. Can you imagine, those beautiful forests? No, the worst thing is the soul of Sarajevo which has sold itself to the devil."

Minkie felt the tears pressing behind her eyes. "Not the soul of the city," she said. "The soul of individuals. May be a lot of individuals. But not the city."

Franko leaned back again. "You are very naive Minkie. It is so when you have not been fighting for every small scrap of survival. I tell you, the only way to live was to become a ... how do you call those big black birds that live off dead things? You have to become like that, and more and more so when you see how others are coming from many many places to make a lot of money from a situation which has nothing to do with them. You can't imagine how many foreigners there are now – not just the United Nations, but advisers and advisers to advisers, and armies of so-called aid people with their lorries full of charity. Yes, some of it gets to the right people, but even more makes easy money for the smart guys who know how to exploit other people's misery." She saw his eyes spark with anger. "Yes, it is so. But it is also possible to make money from helping people to do the things they could not manage without you. This I do. And this I make no apology for."

Minkie hesitated. Momentarily swayed by the intensity of his feeling she began to wonder if he were right. While she had been living here in this quiet ordered place, however hard the initial burden of unhappiness, Franko had lived through the disintegration of the city they had both known as home. While she and Azzie had gone round in school holidays, jollying people into parting with money or goods for dispossessed Kurds, Romanian orphans, earthquake or hurricane victims - even Bosnians - Franko had been at the receiving end. Watching her, he pressed on "Those people trying to make new lives are the same people that were our neighbours, our school friends. So many broken families, so many children without parents. Like you Minkie. But they didn't get a chance to get away."

She must help. Somehow. She began "So what exactly do you ...?" she saw Franko's expression had changed from anger to persuasion and now twin flickers of hope and triumph.

And then she remembered the frightened young women scurrying out of the lorry by the M40. She said "These desperate people, are they all from Bosnia?"

He looked exasperated. "Desperate people are desperate people Minkie. I don't ask for their passports when they want help."

"Only their money," Minkie said. "You seem to be managing rather well on their desperation."

"I take a lot of risks," Franko said. "And I can tell you with me they have a better chance than with many others."

She felt a huge sadness that the ideals and hopes she had shared with him had come to this. She didn't blame him for who knows what she would be doing in the same circumstances? She also knew, not just from what Franko was telling her, but from what she had read in newspapers, seen on television, that Sarajevo was a place far removed from the one of her childhood. But exactly what it was – especially the nature of its soul – was something only she could decide for herself. The need to go back took on a new, almost violent urgency that made her take in a sharp breath.

Watching her Franko said, "From which I gather the answer is no." His face creased into that old infectious grin. "It was necessary to try, and I did very much want to see you."

He was incorrigible. "Yes, well just don't tell me any more about this enterprise of yours," Minkie said. "I'd really rather not know. And please remember the authorities in other countries probably won't appreciate your …er.. your altruism." After a moment she added, "What Mike and Sara have done for me - that really is altruism."

"It is easier to have good motives when you have a roof over your head and a full stomach every day. But I can see they are good people." Franko put his hand over hers again. "So dear cousin, who knows where we may meet again. You know there will be another war before long to stop that madman Milošević from murdering all the Albanians in Kosovo? Hundreds of thousands have left their homes already ahead of the Serb military offensive."

"And what about the Albanians murdering the Serbs!"

He shook his head. "Of course with your half-Serb background it is difficult for you to see so clearly. But you know there has been terrible oppression there for years. The situation is very bad. This time though … this time many people think the West will not stand aside as they did in Bosnia. And if Serbia is attacked …" Franko gave an expressive shrug.

Plenty more desperate people for you to help, Minkie said in her head. Aloud she said, "Jesse thinks the same."

Franko looked surprised. "Your American? Yes, I suppose it could be the kind of crusade that might give that Clinton a … do-good factor."

"Feel-good," Minkie said.

"Feel-good then. He would like better to be remembered for something else than this Monica affair I think."

Minkie drove him back to Daerley market place.

"I'll keep in touch," he said. She knew he meant it, doubted if he would, and nodded. Then she reached up and kissed him on both cheeks and held him close briefly before he turned with a wave of the arm to slide into the Audi. She watched him manoeuvre deftly through the parked cars and swing out towards the main road, standing there for some seconds looking down the road to where he had been.

As she walked back to the cottage she thought, well at least Franko and Jesse would agree on one thing: how terrible the Serbs were in Kosovo. For the moment, though, she had a great need to hear Jesse's voice, renew contact with a stability that was so lacking in Franko. He answered his mobile on the second ring, responding with a pleased and surprised "Hi Hon!" as soon as he heard her voice, sensing immediately her tension.

They arranged to meet by the canal by the Rock of Gibraltar pub. Minkie was there first, sitting on a wall, looking out for the apple green Mini that was his pride and joy. She felt her spirits lift as she saw it arrive, watched him lope towards her, fair hair in its usual disarray. Without preamble she said, "I've had a really bizarre day. Franko turned up unexpectedly…."

"Ah!" Jesse said. He took the hand she held out to him, and joined her on the wall.

"Please just listen, will you? I know you can't stand him, but he'll always be special to me – and he made me understand what life is really like in Sarajevo. So even though he's obviously mixed up in something not quite legal …" She ignored Jesse's sceptically raised eyebrows. "…At least he's trying to help a few people." Whatever else, she had to believe that. "Anyway, we've both changed too much, and I don't think I'm likely to see him again." She pulled her hand away and clasped her head, raking her fingers through her hair, feeling a flood of sadness. "It's the story of my life isn't it? People disappearing. Father – Mother – now Franko. And Azzie. Even Polly earlier on. And if they don't go away, they change. Like Berry and even Justin."

Jesse put his arms round her. "I'm not changing. Or going anywhere," he said. After a while he went on quietly, "I guess it's the things that happen to us and the way we handle them that make us what we are. Franko chose his route, you chose yours. You've had a tougher deal than most Minkie, and I reckon you're near-perfect."

Minkie found she was crying and didn't know whether it was with laughter or sadness. She gave a big sniff and said "You're absurd."

"You are so precious to me, Minkie. I'll be there for you always if you want it."

"And I love you too."

They hadn't said it for a while, both of them taking it for granted. Minkie sat up, fished out a handkerchief, blew her nose. She said, "Franko thinks there's going to be another war. I think Mike does too."

"Kosovo? That's one subject on which your cousin and I

could probably agree."

"And one on which you and I can't."

Jesse stared out over the canal. "You're going to have to face it, Hon. That Milošević is real bad news."

"I'm not arguing with that. Nor are hundreds of thousands of people in Serbia. You've seen the demonstrations on TV."

"Sure. But how long does it take to get rid of him and how many people die in the meantime?"

Minkie said in a tight desperate voice. "I can't make you understand, can I? You don't have any real history in America, so how you can you understand that when something has belonged to you for hundreds and hundreds of years, and is the cradle of your soul…. like Kosovo is for Serbs – you *can't* let it go. And just supposing there is an international agreement to stop him … Milošević … what on earth is the point of having a war to save innocent people by killing other innocent people? And who will take charge? If Sarajevo is anything to go by, it will just be another mess, with a few people doing their best and everyone else lining their own pockets – except the real Sarajevans … "

On the opposite bank a moorhen approached the canal with cautious long-legged strides and plopped into the water. Watching it Jesse murmured "Well, I'd say 'amen' to that." He turned to her. "But I guess at the bottom of it all, the real question, the gut-wrenching one that I can only try and imagine is that you want to go back to Sarajevo and see what's going on with your own eyes. And may be that's what really needs some action."

"That is what I want most from the depth of my soul."

Jesse kissed her gently. "Then let's see what we can do about it," he said.

A few days later he rang her. "I've been putting out feelers about the kind of charity traffic that's going on between the UK and Bosnia. Some of it has more heart than common sense, but I've come across one outfit I'd be prepared to stake my life on. It's run by a guy called Hank – another Yank."

Minkie couldn't resist, "Does he have any other credentials - apart from being a Yank?"

"Grandparents living in Sarajevo for a start, along with an assortment of uncles and cousins. They handle things that end. Hank has been running a one-man scheme with the help of students – raising money, collecting stuff – and hires a truck for a once monthly trip which he slots into his time off from a small translation agency he's running."

"And?" Minkie asked quietly, no longer wanting to tease.

"And he'd kinda welcome a couple of passengers to share the driving on one of his trips – especially one who knows their way around. May be in the New Year."

She said carefully, not daring to believe what she was hearing "Are you saying that he would take me with him? To Sarajevo? Just like that?"

"Well, there'd be a bit more to it – like getting the right papers and checking it out with Mike and Sara. But once they meet Hank.... He's a real regular guy you'd trust your young sister with. And of course I'll be there."

"Oh Jesse. There's nothing I want more in the world."

"So it's going to happen, Hon. You'll see. Sure there'll be a few papers to fill in, but with Mike on your side and all his contacts it'll be like falling off a log. "

He could not have been more wrong.

"You want to do *WHAT*?"

Minkie had joined Mike on his pre-breakfast tour of the estate and it had seemed an ideal time to broach the subject. It was a dank morning, full of the smell of autumn, and aglow too with its colours. The prunus that she had helped Mike to plant that first autumn was now a sturdy tree in a blaze of crimson, and nearby a couple of silver birch shimmered in pale lemon.

Mike was raking leaves as she told him the sequence

exactly as it happened, skimming a bit over her meeting with Franko except for his disturbing account of Sarajevo and then going on to explain how Jesse had met this Hank and the brilliant idea resulting from it.   Absorbed in her own mounting enthusiasm, Minkie did not notice Mike's darkening expression.

Now he said, starting quietly but his voice gaining in anger and strength "Has Jesse completely lost leave of his senses? And you Minkie? Are you both living in cloud-cuckoo land and lost any awareness of what's going on in that desperate part of your world?   Hundreds of thousands of people leaving their homes ... stories of murder, rape ... villages devastated."

Minkie took a step back. She had never seen him so angry. Not at her. "But you're talking about Kosovo," she faltered. "That's nowhere near ..."

"The answer's NO, Minkie. Absolutely *no*. Short of a miracle, like someone obliterating Milošević, the whole region is liable to blow up in the coming months. Pray God it won't be worse than that. And this time the West won't just sit on their hands like before. Jesus, I never thought you could be so stupid."

Hurt and now angry herself, Minkie glared back at him. How dare he call her stupid. How *dare* he control her life, forbid her to do the one thing that was most important to her: the thing that she had yearned for so long, and which at last had seemed a possibility. How dare he act like the heavy father ...

But she didn't mean to spit back "I'm not your kid, so stop treating me as if I am."

It was if she had hit him. Mike flung the rake aside and stormed back into the house. Minkie stood there by the crimson prunus, shivering with cold and shock. She heard a door slam and knew he had left the house even before Sara came out looking worried and bewildered, demanding "What the hell's going on?"

Minkie rushed passed her, into the house, up the stairs, into her bedroom and flung herself on the bed, crying as though her heart would break.

Sara – October 1998

On October 12th a ceasefire was at last brokered between the Kosovo Liberation Army and the Serbs, by Richard Holbrooke, special envoy to US President Clinton. It was to open the way to an international, though unarmed, verification force.

In Daerley Green, Sara had been coming to terms with many things.

Without doubt 1998 had been the worst year in her life – apart, of course, from the long-ago year of her abortion. More than once she had acknowledged bitterly the irony of the circumstances that linked these events across twenty-three years. But as far as more recent events were concerned, she had stopped wondering how she could have been blind for so long, for the answer was quite clear: she had not wanted to face Berry's infidelity any more than he had wanted her to discover it.

The seeds of it were there to be gleaned that landmark Sunday she and Amanda had gone to visit Justin, followed by supper together. It was then Sara had put the question that had been adrift in her mind all week. Casserole dished up, condiments distributed, she said at last "So how did the golf lesson go?"

Amanda had hooted with laughter. "According to Beresford I'm the least promising pupil ever. But he's hellishly stylish isn't he? I think I'll venture another lesson or two."

And Sara had found herself looking at Amanda for the first time, not just as an old mate but as another woman and potential rival. She had always thought of her as poised and personable; now she recognised this did not do her justice. Her auburn hair was immaculate; any grey in it was impeccably disguised. The hazel eyes, always candid and expressive, gained emphasis from a touch of eye shadow. The forest green suit was casually elegant, the chiffon scarf a perfect match for her hair. There was no argument that Amanda's time in New York had given her a flair for making the most of herself that had not been there in her teaching days. She was indeed an attractive and youthful forty-two. Well, she'd made no secret of an affair or two while she'd been away, and there was nothing like an affair to make you review your image. Sara could vouch for that.

"There was a time when I thought he rather fancied you. Weren't you at school together?" Amanda said now.

Sara said quickly "He could be pretty objectionable in those days. But I agree he's improved." She nudged the casserole dish over. "Have some more."

It was nearly a week before she saw Berry. In the interval, and during the course of interminable head conversations, she came to the conclusion that she would know immediately from his behaviour and demeanour if he were embarking on another relationship. Then would be time enough to ask questions, make decisions. But their hours together the following Saturday were as deeply satisfactory as they had always been. The way they spoke to each other, looked at each other and, above all, made love – all of it perfect; if possible more perfect because of the longer than usual interval since their last meeting and the exquisite re-discovering of what they both already knew so well. Yet, happy and relaxed as they lingered over a last glass of wine, she could not resist "So how is Amanda getting on with her golf lessons?"

He'd given an amused snort. "I guess it's about the same as yours might be, only you have the good sense not to try!"

The best way to avoid unpalatable truths was to look in the opposite direction and the message Sara took from Berry's response was precisely what she wanted to hear. It had ever been thus. Sara's path rarely crossed Amanda's these days unless one of them contrived it, and Sara was not in contriving mood. Anyway, there was not much time for introspection. Business was brisk at Cyber Inc.; and other things were going on. Minkie had started her cleaning job and Mike had bought her that absurd little car; the relationship with Jesse really did seem serious and she only hoped it wouldn't all end in tears. And Mike himself seemed to have pulled back from his strange and unpredictable moods the previous year. She assumed that whatever had gone wrong in Novi Sad had now righted itself. That was something else to avoid examining too closely. It was sufficient that it made him much easier to live with.

Through the spring and early summer of 1998 she had been purposefully occupied. Her meetings with Berry were less frequent but, as she kept reminding herself, they were both busy. Every time they did meet, the old magic renewed her determination to keep the relationship going. It was like a drug again. She needed her fix of desiring and being desired, and busy-ness filled the gaps in between.

She took a couple of more advanced courses on web design and multi-media, and Pippa now left the entire desk-top publishing side of Cyber Inc. to her.

"I'm really impressed," Mike said, dropping in unexpectedly on a Monday early in July to take her out for a bar snack before he left for London. His initial reservations at her venture into computing had given way to a genuine interest in the development of the company, and her contributions to it. Sometimes he made suggestions of his own. The one he made that day over bowls of carrot and coriander soup and glasses of Chilean red was the most startling yet.

"Why don't you make a bid for producing the *Daerley Chronicle*?"

She'd laughed, assuming he was joking, but he went on quite seriously "May be you're not quite as *au fait* with Daerley intrigue as I am for once – The Trumpet is a great hotbed of local gossip, some of it no doubt quite libellous, but I'm sure this is genuine. The *Chronicle* is aiming to go high tech."

"OK, but then why wouldn't Amanda use DG Publishing? After all she works there and it would keep it in the community?"

"But Amanda's giving up. Hasn't she told you that she's decided to give up being editor?" Heaven knows what Mike read into her expression for he leaned forward to put a hand on hers.

"Hey, we're not talking World War Three, just a change of editor for the village rag!"

Sara forced a smile. "It just shows how I've slipped off the village grapevine. Still Amanda might have dropped a hint. After all the *Chronicle* was my baby for quite a while."

Later she couldn't decide why the news came as such a shock, but something about it felt wrong. When she rang her that evening, Amanda merely said, "I thought the whole world knew. You must remember how it goes – suddenly you can't face another club report or school sports day or endless bickering in the Parish Council. I just suddenly needed to move on. Fortuitously a fairly new couple to Daerley seem interested. Both of them with kids at the school and involved in the PTA, badminton club, history society, and all that. *And* techie-inclined. Quite honestly I think Cyber Inc. would be a bit out of their range, but no harm in trying." There was a small pause. "I'm really glad the company is doing so well. And you? Are you OK? And Mike and Minkie?"

Sara had the oddest sensation of a conversation with an acquaintance rather than an old friend. "We're all fine." Another pause. "How's the golf?"

Amanda laughed. "I survived half a dozen lessons then we both agreed to call it a day."

Sara had to ask "Do you see anything of Beresford these days?"

"We have the odd drink, meal. He's good company. In fact .. er .. I'm just off to meet him. I've been giving him a hand with a golfing book– coffee table stuff – you know the sort of thing, fabulous photographs and famous faces. What you'd expect from Beresford."

It was then that Sara knew: not from what Amanda had said, but from the proprietorial way she said it, and a warmth in her voice as she spoke of Berry. They were having an affair. Without any shadow of a doubt. Or almost.

She found an excuse to end the call and sat on the edge of

her bed, rigid with tension, anger, confusion. And shame. She must have sat there for a long time for when she at last became aware of laughter outside, the summer evening had deepened to old gold. She registered the carefree sound of people going about their normal business, probably on their way to or from The Trumpet. As she looked out at that meaninglessly normal world, she noticed the last rays of sun catching the top of the church tower. She glanced at the alarm clock on her bedside table. Nearly ten o'clock. Mike was in London, Minkie overnighting with Azzie. Impossible to stay in the house with these terrible thoughts and still that small glimmer of uncertainty. She made herself get up, go downstairs, brew some coffee. Then at eleven o'clock she went out.

It was a warm breathless July night and quite dark by the time she reached Berry's cottage. As soon as she reached the top of the short drive leading to it, Sara saw Amanda's car tucked into a grassy space near the gate: the same grassy space where she had parked so often herself. The cottage was in darkness downstairs, but the lights were on in the bedroom she knew so well: the soft glow from the lamp that Berry had brought back from Portugal spreading over the bed. The window was open. If she went closer she would probably hear them.

Sara turned the car round and fled.

Through a sleepless night, she went through a succession of scenarios in which she confronted Berry. She was almost certain Amanda was as unaware of his duplicity as she had been until a few hours ago. Equally she knew she could not tell her, not only for what might be regarded as altruistic reasons but because of what it would reveal about herself. For the first time Sara faced – truly faced - the lie she had been intermittently living, the shouts of *you lying cheating bastard* that filled her head suddenly ricocheting back at her.

She sobbed herself through anger, self-pity, remorse, hysteria and finally into a calmness that was devoid of any emotion. After breakfast she rang Berry and told him the affair was over. "There's too much at stake. For Mike. For Minkie." It was an argument that didn't make any more sense now than at any other time in the past three years but she didn't care.

After a short silence Berry said "Hey sweetie, you can't do that." His voice became warm, persuasive. "Let's meet and talk it through …"

"No!" Sara said sharply, and replaced the receiver.

The following week Amanda caught up with her on the Market Place. "Time for a drink? I need to talk." A few moments later, in a quiet corner in The Trumpet, she went on without preamble "I want you to hear this from me first: I'm renting out the cottage for a while, and moving in with Beresford."

So, not a moment wasted. "We-e-ll, you've kept that pretty quiet." Sara forced a smile. "Are congratulations appropriate?"

Amanda grinned. "Isn't Beresford supposed to get those? But I'm very happy." She looked it too. "In case you're wondering, I don't have any illusions, you know, that fidelity is high up on Beresford's list of qualities. But we're both free and the arrangement suits us. He makes me feel good, and I think I do him." She took a sip of lager. "I really wanted to talk to you about it before, but for some reason Berry was set on completing some project before we became, as it were, an item in the public domain."

Sara thought *I bet he was.* She swallowed hard. "Well, as long as you don't have illusions. He's had quite a reputation in his time."

"I think he's met his match," Amanda said.

In retrospect Sara could remember very few details of the following weeks except that she seemed to continue to function in all outward respects quite normally, like a well-programmed automaton. Around her she noted that the world continued to go about its affairs. Minkie was psyching herself up to be miserable at Azzie's impending departure to the States; but the prop of

Jesse was never far away, and there was her subtly deepening relationship with Mike.

If Mike noticed any change in Sara he kept it to himself, but two other people did not.

"You're not happy, dear girl," Justin said, making it a statement rather than a question on one of her visits soon after Amanda's announcement.

"I'm fine."

He'd gone on looking at her thoughtfully. "I hear Amanda is moving in with Beresford."

"You don't miss much, do you? I expect you'd like a cup of tea."

He'd dropped the subject until she was about to leave. "If ever you want to talk … about anything … I'm not quite senile yet, you know, dear girl."

Pippa had been more forthright. After a brainstorming session on a new project one late afternoon she had observed "Is your current broodiness the result of something I should know about, or just a symptom of mild mid-life crisis?"

"I'm not broody."

"Excuse me but you are. If it's something serious I'd rather know – for example, that handsome husband of yours has walked out, or you're pining for a lost lover …"

Wretched, shrewd Pippa. "Stop being dramatic. I tell you I'm fine."

"Well," Pippa said, shuffling papers busily. "If you say so. But try and look it, will you, when the customers are about?"

Perhaps it was her caustic disbelief that had prompted Sara to accept an invitation to be on the team of a Daerley Green website proposed by one of the newer members of the Parish Council. It was a good team with bright ideas. Sara flung herself into the project with her customary 110%.

There had been a meeting the previous evening and, as she set the breakfast table that October morning, Sara was mulling over a suggestion that the website should incorporate an on-line forum, when Mike crashed through the house and out again. Moments later Minkie had stormed upstairs.

Sara could hear her sobs from downstairs. They were heart-wrenching: the sort of sobs that start deep in the gut and well up to choke your throat, one after the other after the other in a shuddering uncontrollable succession. She went up the stairs, stood outside Minkie's room for a moment. The sound was unbearable. She opened the door quietly.

Minkie was sitting on the edge of the bed, doubled up so that her black hair covered her arms and legs like a shining blanket. The whole of her shook in a series of convulsions. Sara sat beside her, rested an arm round the heaving shoulders, then put a hand out tentatively to stroke the shiny hair as she murmured "It's OK, Minkie my pet; it's OK" over and over again without knowing what it was that had not been OK.

The convulsions went on and on. Sara watched her hand moving over Minkie's hair, noticing how extraordinarily beautiful it was. Without any plan of what she was going to say she began "When I was about your age – no, a year or two younger – something happened to me that felt like the total end of my world. It wasn't a big thing like a war, like you've been through; it was something I allowed to happen, something in a way that I did to myself; but I knew – or I thought I knew – it would mess up my life for ever."

She paused, her hand resting on the glossy head. "I was wrong. The thing that happened didn't change of course. That would always be there, is still there. But the world went on turning and other things went on happening. And one of the things that happened was Mike."

She paused again. The convulsions had eased a little; the glossy head shifted a fraction and a choked voice said, "Go on talking. Please."

Sara went on, explaining it now as much to herself as to Minkie. "Mike made this thing seem much less important, even though he didn't know anything about it. There was suddenly a reason for being alive. You must have the same feeling about Jesse." She stopped. "Was it about Jesse, the row?"

The dark head shook vigorously, then slowly lifted. Sara couldn't see her face past the curtains of hair, but she handed her a handkerchief and said "You don't have to tell me unless you want to."

Minkie blew her nose several times, pushed back her hair but went on staring at her feet. "I suppose in a way it *was* about Jesse. But really it was about me going to Sarajevo. Jesse found out he could fix a trip with a charity lorry – it's a really properly organised one, with absolutely no risk involved. Mike was so angry. I've never seen him so angry. But he treats me like a kid. I'm twenty for God's sake. He said we were both crazy and I must be stupid ..."

"It's because he loves you to bits, you must know that. And because he knows the situation is likely to blow up again into something pretty nasty. And quite soon." She took one of Minkie's hot damp hands in her cool ones. "He couldn't bear the thought of you being hurt. You see, he thinks of you now as the daughter he ... we never had."

"Oh." Minkie turned her swollen tear-stained face to look at Sara. "And I yelled at him I wasn't his kid and to stop treating me as if I were."

God, how that must have hurt. Sara felt a shaft of pain for Mike as she gave Minkie a hug. "Tell him how you really feel, that's all you need to do."

Hours later, she was in the kitchen when she heard Mike come in. He looked drained. She went to put her arms round him, then stood back holding his head in her hands. "Minkie has something to say to you," she said. She gave him a quick kiss. "She's in the living room. Be gentle."

From the kitchen she stood listening to the murmur of voices: Minkie's first, becoming quite agitated, breaking off for a few tears; then Mike's deeper tones, followed by the two voices alternating at a more even level. It sounded as if it were going to be all right.

Then it occurred to Sara it was a very long time since she had spent so many hours thinking about something other than her own misery.

Mike – May 1999

Following new escalations of violence, Serbs and Albanian Kosovars were summoned by world leaders to peace talks at Rambouillet, near Paris, on 6th February. The Albanians reluctantly agreed to settle for autonomy within Serbia's boundaries; the Serbs refused to accept the unfettered movements of peace-keeping forces on their sovereign territory. Nato prepared to bomb them into submission. Bomb us, the Serbs warned, and there will not be an Albanian left in Kosovo. As Yugoslav armed units began to drive thousands more ethnic Albanians from their homes, Nato air strikes were launched on March 24th.

Two months later, as Serbia at last began to crack and Nato ambassadors approved a substantial force for peacekeeping duties only, Mike stood by a grey Danube staring at one of Novi Sad's destroyed bridges.

He was staying with Jovanka again and the bridge - Most Slobode, meaning Freedom Bridge - was quite near her flat. It had been hit by three missiles one evening some weeks earlier.

"Would you believe that a car was actually crossing it, and the driver managed to back off in time," Jovanka said. It was indeed hard to believe, for the bridge had been sliced through the middle, its six lanes now plunging to a watery terminus. Mike had heard a lot of bomb stories since he arrived a few days earlier. The one people most liked to tell was how they had gathered in their hundreds on the bridges and challenged Nato to come and bomb them *now*. But the one that stuck in his head was of the young man who, after a night of partying, and, desperate to get back to his pregnant wife, crossed another bridge against the warnings of the military police. It was hit while he was half way across.

As he turned away from Freedom Bridge and began to follow the riverside walk back towards the main part of the town, Mike thought of Sara and Minkie. They had both pleaded with him not to come, though by now this wretched conflict was clearly approaching its conclusion. Though she had often expressed concern before he headed for one of the world's hot spots, Sara had never actually asked him not to go.

There had been a quite remarkable change in her in recent months. A marked change in Minkie, too, and in the relationship between the two of them. It dated from that terrible row he'd had with Minkie over her announcement to return to Sarajevo with some charity outfit discovered by Jesse. Quite apart from any question of permits, it was clear that neither she nor Jesse had thought it through, either in relation to the worsening situation in Serbia or the continuingly volatile one in Bosnia. He had been so afraid for her and he acknowledged his anger had flared to a level quite beyond reason.

Mike did not easily lose control and he would not forget that day Minkie had informed him with such coldness "I'm not your kid" and he had slammed out of the house and found himself, tense and shaking, driving down the M40 at speeds not only illegal but exceedingly irresponsible. He'd got off the motorway as soon as possible, parked near some woodland and walked and walked himself back into some kind of control, though not into inner calm. He had driven home with a heavy heart, quite unclear how to handle the situation only to find, amazingly, that Sara had handled it for him. She had hugged him and said, "Minkie has something to say to you. She's in the living room," and pushed him gently towards the door.

Perched on the edge of the sofa, fingers twisting, head hanging, staring at her feet, Minkie had apologised. Then she had begun to cry and looked up at him not trying to check the streaming tears. "I don't know where I belong any more," she said. "I feel as though I've been waiting forever to go home. But I know this is home too, and I just take it for granted that I can belong equally to both. But I can't, can I? I'm *never* going to be like everyone else with a place I have a right to be, however much I love you … and Sara of course…"

It was all Mike needed to hear. In one stride he was beside her, arms round her, saying into that shiny black hair as she buried her face in his shoulder, "You silly goose of a Princess. You will always have a right to be here. In a way more of a right than if you were born here. Can't you see that? You're here not by accident of birth, but by a choice that we made. Whether you continue to belong will always be for *you* to decide. That will be your dilemma my sweet. Not whether you belong, but whether you choose to belong."

Thinking back over the conversation now from the far away banks of the Danube, Mike recognised that, as an argument, it would not have stood up to too close a scrutiny. At the time the words had just come from that well of emotion that was his love for the girl. Logically, she was right. Any ultimate sense of belonging would depend on many other things, not least how she felt after she made that longed-for return to Sarajevo. But just then, logic had not been relevant. The real relevance was Minkie's expression of love for them and, allied to it, the surprising and welcome presence of Sara in the process of reconciliation.

The incident seemed to have a curiously softening effect on Sara too. Before that she had for some time been at home much more than usual, but so edgy and withdrawn that she might just as well have been absent. He assumed at first that Cyber Inc was going through a quiet patch, but was cheerfully corrected by Pippa when they met by chance in town. Once or twice, glancing across at Sara's shut-in face, he had wanted at least to try and find some words to draw her back from whatever dark place she was in; but they had drifted too far apart for him to be sure how welcome such an intrusion might be. He played safe and kept quiet.

Then from one day to the next she had become involved with a small group in Daerley on a community website. Some bright spark on the Parish Council had come up with the idea, his main motive being to upstage one created by a neighbouring parish. Whatever the motivation, it seemed to provide the right trigger for Sara who flung herself wholeheartedly into the project.

Out of the catalyst of the 'Minkie incident', the three of them seemed to forge a new closeness. Christmas had been particularly good: the quietest and, as far as Mike was concerned, the best he could remember. Jesse had joined them for most of it, and they had fought fiercely and amiably over some confrontational computer game, before choosing to 'go into retro' as Jesse put it, and wrangle happily instead over Scrabble and Monopoly. It was a blessed relief to opt out of the usual festive party round: one in particular.

"By the way," he had said one evening, "I bumped into Amanda on the market place delivering invitations for some Christmas beanfeast she and Beresford are having. She said she'd appreciate our moral support to cope with a deluge of golfers."

"No thanks," Sara had said with brisk finality.

"How about you Princess?"

Minkie pulled a face. "I think I'll stick with my ageing guardians." After a moment she added "It's really bizarre how couples get together, isn't it? I mean Amanda and Berry - who would have thought? Still, maybe it's no more bizarre than how I used to think he was the best thing since sliced bread; and now he seems ... well, just ordinary."

All three were in the kitchen at the time, Minkie peeling potatoes, Sara slicing peppers for a ratatouille. "It's called growing up," Sara said. "Painful at times too. At thirteen or fourteen I remember falling in desperate love with the milkman. But it's also a time for forging life-long friendships, you and Azzie for example."

The lightning advances in computer technology had brought with them all the pluses and minuses of being within a few clicks' reach of anywhere in the world at any moment of the night or day. Mike could now work as easily at home as at the office and that winter had often chosen to do so. It was early in

December that, checking his email, he found the first one from Jovanka; he had sent her his email address some time ago 'just in case'.

Our school now has this email thing, she wrote. *It is a big mystery for me, but I think it could be helpful in keeping in touch with any friends we still have out there. My soul is weary-through with the thought of another war. Have the West gone mad?*

She would not, Mike knew, have seen newsreels of endless lines of fleeing Albanian Kosovars; and if she had she would probably have reminded him of similar wretched lines of Serbs fleeing from Croatia a few years earlier. God, what a mess. He emailed her immediately, deeply thankful for the tenuous link it would also provide with Marija's family. Jovanka still reported seeing her from time to time. Snežka was now coming to Jovanka's school and proving a receptive pupil, including in English.

He showed the emails to Sara, waiting for her to say, "Who is Marija?". When she did not, he produced the answer he had already prepared anyway: "Extraordinary coincidence. Marija was someone I met when I was in Sarajevo ... way back. In my student days. Seem to remember I rather fancied her at the time. Couldn't believe it when she resurfaced in Novi Sad all these years later."

Well, as far as it went, it was true. He fished out the photograph to show her: Marija, Niko, Niko junior, and Sonja, and told her of the tragic circumstances that had brought Marija and Bogdan together. Sara had gone on looking at the photograph for a long time and asked a lot of questions: what sort of place the family lived in, their jobs, and about Snežka. He had been quite surprised by how interested she was. It was a huge relief to be able to talk about them openly; almost now without any sense of guilt for that youthful passion was finished, gone, and in any case it was before he and Sara even met. As for Sonja, whose hopes and potential he would never know and would never be fulfilled - that loss was an ache he would have to bear alone.

As the situation worsened, Jovanka's emails became increasingly worried. *It's not for myself. My life lost real meaning when I left Sarajevo. It is for the children, especially those who have already been through war, and so many have – in Croatia or Bosnia, or leaving their homes in Kosovo afraid of what is coming. We are already bursting with refugees and now they want us to give up more land.*

Mike had not shown these emails to Minkie. She was already distraught with the growing threat of Nato bombing. On an impulse Mike went to see Justin whose frailty had no way impaired his alertness of mind as he listened to Mike's concerns for Minkie and his friends in Novi Sad.

But he had little comfort to offer. "I can give you no easy phrases to help them, dear boy. All I can present is a fairly well reasoned argument as to why the Serbs and Albanians both feel they have divine right on their side in their claims on Kosovo, and why in one way or another all of us have contributed to that situation through our own history. But it won't help Minkie or your friends, and it won't change the situation one iota. Some of our venerated leaders, not all with motives as altruistic as advertised, are on a Messianic mission that has irredeemably predetermined who are the goodies and baddies. And whether you and I like it or not, a mighty stick of dynamite is about to be used to crack this particular relatively small nut."

"Small nut? Potential genocide?"

"The Holocaust was genocide. And Rwanda. Of all people you, as a scribe, must have noticed how words lose their real meaning through misuse? This is ethnic cleansing by forcible expulsion on a large and ghastly scale. Exceedingly ghastly, but not genocide. Bombing Belgrade is hardly likely to help the poor devils much and will certainly make the Serbs more vengeful than ever."

Once the bombing had started Jovanka's emails gave terse

accounts of flattened factories, destroyed bridges. Early in May she wrote *Last night was terrible with dozens of explosions. The refinery was hit and the sky was on fire. A black cloud of smoke covered everything like night until at last the sun rose out of it at nine o'clock. I had to do something so I took a ferry across the river, but then there was another alarm so there were no more ferries and I was stuck on the other side for hours.*

It was quite soon after this that the power stations were hit, too. Jovanka's emails ceased and his to her were returned '*undeliverable*'. When he discovered that Canary Wharf had no intention of sending him back there, he took a couple of weeks of overdue leave and went anyway, using a circuitous and tedious route overland from Budapest.

From Belgrade a crowded bus took him next morning through Vojvodina's green and productive plains to Novi Sad and its devastated bridges. He went first to Jovanka, who opened the door to him with only the briefest involuntary flicker of surprise.

"You are a good man," she said, immediately proceeding to heat water for coffee. Then added with that touch of irony that always had appealed to him "I suppose you will be visiting Marija and Bogdan while you're here?"

A few hours later, it was Bogdan who opened the door. He seemed touchingly pleased to see him, clasping Mike's hand in his own beefy paw and repeating. "Good, very good. Good you come."

Marija came out of the kitchen, wiping her hands on a towel and saying "Yes, it's wonderful to see you Michael. Come in, come in."

He hardly recognised her: except, of course, for those unchangeable green eyes. Her new swept-back hair style, with the henna tints so popular among Balkan women, made her appear older but if anything even more striking. She wore a caramel trouser suit that emphasised her slim figure; and clearly she had found a new confidence. And a toughness. Not least, her English had improved beyond recognition.

As they moved into the living room the first thing Mike noticed was that the family photographs had been replaced by two more recent ones: one of Marija and Bogdan laughing at Snežka who was perched, perhaps for the first time, on a bicycle; the other a studio portrait of an older Snežka alone, blonde curls now darker and cut short as she gazed steadily, seriously into the camera.

"It seems a lot has happened," Mike said, not attempting to hide his surprise; and, over a fiery injection of plum brandy, she told him.

"I decided it was time to stop being a victim. That is an expression very much liked by the psychiatrists here. We become sick because we see ourselves as victims. So I decided to stop. A big help was when I discovered one of my professors from the University in Sarajevo had come here and also decided to stop being a victim. He began many classes for former students and other people too. I found this soon after your last visit, and so I went to his classes and took a degree in English. Then when so many important people began coming to Yugoslavia …" She paused. "Former Yugoslavia I think you call it now. Anyway with all these important people coming, they needed more and more interpreters. And it is much better paid than serving drinks to other victims."

All the time Bogdan watched her proudly, almost as though he understood everything she said. When she had finished, he said something and she turned to smile at him in that special way Mike remembered from his last visit.

"Bogdan wants you to know he has changed his job too. He had some problems with his back and must stop the heavy loading work that went with his truck driving. Now he is a night guardian at a factory, which gives him time to study too. I am teaching him some English." She put out a hand to touch him.

"And Snežka?"

"Ah, she is also learning English, and a very good pupil Jovanka tells me. Though her motives are perhaps not the usual ones. She is very busy preparing letters to President Clinton and Prime Minister Blair to explain to them how wrong they are to bomb us."

As if on cue, the door opened and Snežka appeared holding a single white rose which she presented to Mike. She had grown into a tall slender eleven-year-old with a thin serious face, mature beyond her years. He took the rose. "Thank you."

"It is for peace," she said. She stood looking at him unwaveringly for some moments before turning to say something to Bogdan. He responded quite sharply, but Marija laughed and said, "You'll be glad to know that Snežka doesn't think you look like a killer!"

Over a fish soup supper, Mike said "Something had to be done Marija. This Milošević. You probably haven't seen the newsreels of what's been happening in Kosovo – the mindless killing, the unspeakable misery."

"And have your bombs made it any better? Is it less mindless because you are many thousands of feet up in the sky and can't see the results of your killing?" Marija pushed her plate away. "Earlier, you must have seen the protests in Belgrade and other cities against Milošević – hundreds of thousands of people. Before the bombing. After it started, no one was going to protest any more. We would have managed it our way in time."

He needed Justin there to put it all into context, Mike thought. But really there was no point. The war would end, the bombing would stop, Kosovo would be crawling with peace-keeping forces just as Bosnia was, the refugees would go home, there would be old scores to settle and the unsolved problem would fester below the surface until some new trigger acted as a touchpaper. There was already unrest in neighbouring Macedonia, which was bearing the brunt of the fleeing hordes of Albanian Kosovars with imbalances resulting in their own population.

Marija went on "I remember when we first left Sarajevo. We were transported in a broken-down old bus to Serbia, not one of us a complete family any more. All of us missing husbands or wives or children. Worst were the children missing both parents. We came through some villages. One of them was a Bosniak village, all the houses destroyed and women and old men trying to lift stones or timbers, looking for things, some of them weeping. Even though I had stopped caring about anything much any more, I thought 'why do we have to do this to them'. Then we came through a Serb village and it was just the same. Only now I felt a terrible anger." She shrugged. "It is so: that you want to protect your own whatever else is happening to anyone else."

Snežka had been looking from one to the other, clearly trying to understand. Now she said, very seriously "I think only old people like war. I and my friends will make things good." Though there was no physical resemblance at all, she put Mike very much in mind of Minkie who, after all, had only been about a year older when he first saw her. It must be that shared indefinable Balkan gene descending through generation upon generation of being a football in other people's playing fields: part fatality, part determination. Only Snežka already had a poise completely unknown to poor, lost little Minkie on that bleak day of their first encounter in the children's home.

"Minkie said much the same when she first came to England. In fact, she still says it, and is quite determined to go back to Sarajevo."

Marija turned to explain in Serbian to Snežka who Minkie was, adding in English "Perhaps they are right these children ... these young women."

"Perhaps I come to England and explain to the people there," Snežka said. "Perhaps I go to Sarajevo with Minkie."

Bogdan interjected in Serbian, clearly wanting to know what was being said. Mike watched them as they talked. In particular he watched Snežka, trying to impose on her that squarish faced image of Sonja, the only one he would ever have of his lost daughter. He glanced at Marija, wondering where on earth she had found the reserves of strength to survive, and now to move on. Finally he looked at Bogdan who could be nobody's idea of a knight in shining armour; wondering how he, Michael Hennessey, might have shaped up in those circumstances.

Wondering suddenly how ... *if* ...he'd shaped up enough to meet Sara's times of need.

Overview : June 2000

A year after the war, hundreds of thousands of Albanian Kosovars had returned to their homes; tens of thousands of Serb Kosovars had abandoned theirs. Reconstruction had begun, but official reports spoke of minorities suffering continued violence and insecurity. A long way to the east, the refugee problem in Afghanistan was now estimated to exceed two million. And Minkie was visiting Daerley Green.

This was her first weekend at home since moving in with Jesse into the tiny flat in Oxford off the Woodstock Road two months earlier. And, yes, she did still regard it as home. Much as she adored every nook and cranny of her life with Jesse, it was a bit special to be back in her old room, with her own space. Not to mention the extra attention.

She had joined Mike on his pre-breakfast tour as he was attacking a profusion of morning glory seemingly intent on strangling a trellis of honeysuckle. "So how is life in a *ménage à deux,* Princess?"

"Magic. I never thought I'd actually enjoy housework. Not that there's much house to work. And I'm having to train Jesse out of some pretty disgusting bathroom habits."

"I don't think I want to know about those." Mike tossed a tangled pile of offending vegetation into the wheelbarrow.

Minkie grinned and linked an arm through his. "Only stuff like soggy toothbrushes." After a moment she added seriously, "I'm desperately happy, Mike."

"And I'm desperately glad for you." She squeezed his arm. It hadn't escaped her notice that Sara had taken the wanting-to-move-in-with-Jesse announcement much more in her stride than Mike had. But he'd been great about not wanting to spoil it for her.

"Well it's not a major surprise," Sara had said. "As long as you've both considered all aspects."

"I shan't get pregnant if that's what you mean."

226

"It's not what I mean – I take it for granted you both have more sense. I was thinking of the level of commitment, and what it would mean to either of you if the other found it wasn't what you wanted in the end. You're not exactly an ordinary young couple – Jesse with his roots in the States, yours in Bosnia."

It had been surprisingly foresightful, coming from Sara. Mike had said "Sara's right. There's a lot to think about. And what about your work?"

Minkie said "Well, I think I've had enough of being an office cleaner. Anyway, now I've completed the art course, I reckon the chances of a job with some kind of art content are better in Oxford than most places. As for commitment, we've talked and talked and talked. The agency where Jesse's working is expanding and has offered him a year's contract to start a Special Interests department called Meaningful Breaks. Dire isn't it? you know the sort of thing - in search of the last surviving blue nosed skink in Australasia, for example; or the social content of 5th century cave art in Mongolia. And that's something I could help him with, at least on the art side. Or may be as general research assistant. Then ..." She broke off, looked from one to the other, and said "Then at the end of the year, we both have major decisions to make. Jesse thinks he ought to get back to the States and I know I must go to Sarajevo. I'm not sure how either of us will cope with that when the time comes." She gave a small smile. "In the meantime we're giving ourselves a sort of sabbatical."

There was a lot of other stuff she hadn't mentioned at the time: like how much she missed Azzie, now in the bosom of her family in Utah; and how much Azzie was missing her, with resulting pleas for her to go over and visit. All in all, America was exerting a strengthening pull. It was getting harder and harder to connect with that childhood world of Sarajevo. Especially now that the Meaningful Breaks project was developing well. When she allowed herself to, she could envisage ever more imaginative programmes for years to come and an expanding global network.

"And how about you?" Minkie asked now. "Sara said something about changes in Canary Wharf and probably Cyber Inc. But she's looking great, isn't she?"

Observant Minkie. Mike said "Yes, there's plenty to tell you. About a lot of things." He paused and glanced towards the house in response to a distant summons to breakfast. "Over toast and coffee, I suggest."

It had not been easy to hide how much he hated the idea of Minkie moving in with Jesse – not because he had anything against Jesse, nor because he didn't, if reluctantly, accept that 'moving in' was what the young did these days. No, it was something far more subtle and difficult to encapsulate.

"It'll be the father-daughter thing," Plum had said – the only person to whom he had even tried to explain. But then Plum was the most self-contained and asexual person Mike had ever come across and had, to the best of his knowledge, never indulged in more than the most fleeting of relationships. All the same, he was probably right. Ever since that devastating discovery that he had fathered a daughter he would never know, Mike was aware he had transferred much of that sense of kinship into his feelings for Minkie: feelings which had in any case deepened over the years. One result was that he cared for her too much to be a cause of her unhappiness. Sara had put it in perspective in a couple of sentences. "Just let's be profoundly grateful that all we have to deal with is a young couple who appear genuinely in love. No drugs, no late-night drunk-outs. Would that I'd had as much sense."

She had become surprisingly good at putting things into perspective.

There were other matters to preoccupy him. Canary Wharf was undergoing a major shake-up. A new Sunday paper had been launched amongst much razzmatazz and failed rather spectacularly soon after. There had been some reshuffling among a couple of tabloids and the fall-out was just beginning to infiltrate Mike's editorial management. Suddenly there were a lot of new kids on the block, some of them both talented and pushy.

"Doesn't half make you feel middle-aged," Mike complained to Sara one evening.

"Well you .... we are middle-aged. It's not a disease you know; just a statistical fact." She looked at him severely. "It's also a state of mind. I know middle-aged 20-year-olds, and adolescent octogenarians."

He smiled across at her. "Statistical middle age seems to suit you anyway. You don't look a day over thirty. But states of mind also result from external forces. Like being told from one day to the next that a need to reduce our overseas reporting staff happens to coincide with some vacancies on the subbing desk. The implications of that were put to me a few days ago in a way that was not ... let us say, exactly subtle."

"Oh," Sara looked concerned. "That's pretty bloody ungrateful after all these years of devoted service."

"Gratitude is not a word that figures large in Canary Wharf vocabulary. Perhaps I should be grateful to be part of a reshuffle rather than on a redundancy list. But I'll hate it, Sara. Hate the lack of freedom, hate the work, hate the unsocial hours...."

He hadn't expressed such bleakness for a long time. Sara came over to kneel beside him and gave him a comforting hug. As she settled at his feet she said "Have you thought of perhaps packing it in, trying something else?"

"Like what? It's all I'm good at – poking my nose into other people's business, trying to make some sense of ever-perpetuating new bursts of global mayhem." He paused, then added brightly "Oh well, they said it was only a temporary change, so let's give it a whirl. And when they see what they're missing ...." He bent to kiss the top of her head. "Odd, isn't it, how life can suddenly turn into a rather disturbing game of musical chairs. Minkie moving in with Jesse. All this unrest at work."

"Canary Wharf would never be anyone's first choice for an ordered and predictable career," Sara pointed out. "Have we ever known for sure where you might be in a month from any given moment?"

"That kind of unrest I can cope with." Mike leaned back, one hand smoothing her hair where it curled over her shoulders. Idly his fingers separated a few strands, began coiling them loosely. They were both silent. The warmth of Sara leaning against his leg felt good and he was aware of the first stirrings of desire. His pulse quickened, but it was so long since they had ventured outside the conventional norms of lovemaking within bedroom hours, and not so very often at that, that he let his hand stay. Instead he said "Anyway you have your own worries my sweet. Is Pippa still keen on going 'dot com' with Cyber Inc?"

"Mm," Sara said. He waited for her to expand. After a moment she said quietly, "Don't stop." She reached up and guided his hand gently to the nape of her neck, backwards and forwards, rubbing against it. Then she tipped her head back against his knee and looked up. "Let's go to bed," she said.

It was a long time since she had taken the initiative; a long time, too, since they had held each other afterwards in that unhurried companionable way. After a while Sara had said into his shoulder "We're all right, aren't we", more as a statement than as a question.

"Very all right."

"I was afraid for a while."

"Me too. We'd drifted a bit." He kissed the top of her head. "It happens."

"I suppose I was jealous. Of you being away so much. Of your commitment to things, people, I didn't know. Selfish really. I think basically I am a selfish person. May be ..." She stopped.

She had tensed in his arms, like a coil taughtening before it sprang. Suddenly Mike wanted her to stop, fearful of where the train of thought was taking her; fearful that this developing and good mutual awareness was still fragile .... too fragile to withstand analysis, even self-blame.

He tightened his hold on her. "It takes two to drift," he said. "And two to want the drifting to stop. I love you, Sara."

"I love you too, Mike." After a moment he felt the tension ease and in a few minutes Sara was asleep in his arms.

"So have you got used to it?" Minkie asked over breakfast that weekend when Mike had told her of the changes. He had been a month in the new job and, no, he had not got used to it, hated it as much as ever. It did, however, have one advantage. His working hours, if unsocial, were regular; he knew precisely when he would be home and, once home, his mind was uncluttered by the next story, the next overseas trip.

"So it's really rather nice to be able to plan things for a change. I mean together, " Sara said.

"In which case you'll be able to plan a visit for dinner with Jesse and me." Minkie reached out for more toast. "And what about Cyber Inc? Did I hear rumours of expansion?"

"Pippa's idea. She wants to go dot com."

"And why not?"

Sara pulled a face. "I've always been a big-fish-in-small-pond-person and left the wider world to Mike. And maybe you in due course?"

It was an interesting thought: even a direction in which circumstances appeared to be nudging her. But for the moment Minkie could not see beyond the next few months. She demanded to be updated on all other gossip: "Starting with Justin."

Sara made a sad face. "He's not coping very well. Since his eyesight started to go he seems to have given up. And what can you say to someone whose whole life revolves around reading?"

"When one of my uncles went blind we used to take it in

turns to go and read to him. He always rewarded me with some *loka* – sort of Turkish delight. I'll go and see Justin this afternoon. Take some papers to read to him. Poor Justin – I'll never forget how he seemed to know just what to say when I felt so lost and alone."

""I should have thought of that," Sara said, cross with herself. "I could manage half an hour most days without much problem."

"Don't forget to take some tabloids to make him mad. It'll do him good to get mad. So who else is there? Oh what about the love birds?" Minkie asked. And when Sara had brought her up to date with the Amanda-and-Berry saga, she gave a snort of surprise and then echoed Mike's view that they had each probably met their match.

It was about a week earlier that Amanda had called Sara at Cyber Inc. and, over lunch, announced "Berry and I are getting married. Next month to combine with some golfing junket in the States. Yes, I know he's not the most reliable guy in the world, but we're both footloose and we're good together."

She looked marvellous: happy, vivacious, attractive. Sara waited for the shock: all that subterfuge, all that passion, all that exhausting, demanding desire.

"Say something, for God's sake."

She felt only relief "Let me get my breath back! I'm gob-smacked. Well, in a way." Sara smiled. "You look stunning and I'm really happy for you Amanda. And hope that he'll continue to deserve you. And that it'll be third time lucky for Berry. I reckon if anyone can keep him under control it's you."

"Yes, well I think he's been as honest as the poor darling knows how. He's even confessed to fancying you like crazy for a while. Said he'd carried a torch for you since you were in the Sixth Form. "I bet he was a dishy teenager."

"And he knew it." Sara said. "That at least hasn't changed."

It was only a few days after Minkie's visit that Jovanka emailed Mike with her small bombshell. *A school charity organisation has invited a group of children from Novi Sad to visit Oxford at the end of June. It is especially for children who have lost a parent in the war and we will be a group of fourteen, including Snežka. I will be leading them. Never in my dreams did I imagine such a possibility. This is why I did not tell you until I see the tickets. Snežka wrote straight away to ask for an appointment with Mr Blair! But I think she would also like to see you. And also meet Minkie.* All at once the scattered threads of his past seemed to be homing in on him.

He was in London and called Sara straight away. "Your past catching up with you," she said, echoing his thoughts, but her tone was teasing. "When's it happening."

Mike scanned the email again. "End of this month. No date. Jovanka never was one for precision."

In the event it was sooner than they thought. Mike was still in London and Sara had just got in from work when the phone rang and an unfamiliar voice said "Mrs Hennessey? I have a lady here from Serbia who would like to speak to you."

And then another unfamiliar voice. "This is Jovanka speaking. Please is Mike there?"

There had been a mix-up over the arrangements, she explained, and they were here a week early. This had made a problem with the accommodation so they were spending two nights in a church hall while it was sorted out. Everyone was rather tired from the journey and uncertainty.

"I'll be with you in an hour," Sara said.

The church hall was just off the Woodstock Road, not far from Minkie's and Jesse's small flat. Sara arrived to find a small army of volunteers clearing up after a makeshift meal and a gaggle of children rummaging among their belongings. Someone directed her to a small cubbyhole of an office where a willowy and anxious–looking girl was in deep converse with a rotund woman of middle years.

"I'm Sara Hennessey," Sara said, and the rotund woman's weary expression lit with relief.

"You are so kind to come," she said. "It has been big muddle. First our coach was double-booked for next week. Then they find new coach but we must be ready in two hours! Can you imagine, with all these children?" No, Sara could not imagine. "And no one tells them here in Oxford ...."

"So we were caught completely on the hop," the willowy anxious girl said defensively.

"I think it was a very big hop," Jovanka gave a big shrug. "It is so in my country."

Sara said. "Anyway, it looks as though the children have at least been fed and provided with somewhere to sleep."

"They will eat and sleep here today and tomorrow. Then they'll go and stay with the host families we'd allocated them to originally," the girl said.

Sara went with Jovanka to check the arrangements. The hall had been turned into a dormitory of camp beds, boys along one side, girls the other, with a chair by each one. Someone had been extremely busy. The children were settling down into groups of two or three, but all began clamouring with questions as soon as Jovanka appeared. She raised a hand for quiet and, after she had given a few crisp instructions in Serbian, they went back to their places to sort out their scattered belongings.

"I'd suggest you came home with me," Sara said, "But I imagine you'd prefer to stay with the children."

"Not prefer," Jovanka's tired eyes were suddenly twinkling, humorous. "But it is my place here. Come and meet Snežka. I think Mike has spoken of her?"

She was sitting alone, dark curly head bent over a book. In response to Jovanka, she stood up and held out her hand, and Sara found herself being scrutinised by brown eyes she would have judged far too serious for a twelve-year-old if she had not become familiar with Minkie's those years ago. "Hello Snežka. Mike is looking forward to see you again." She took the small, cool hand. "And welcome to England."

"Thank you." Snežka withdrew her hand. "But why did you send aeroplanes to bomb my country?"

"Jovanka was furious with her," Sara reported to Mike over the phone later that evening.

Mike was curious "And what was your answer?"

"Pretty inadequate. That I was as much in the dark as she was."

"Yes, well I think she's the sort of child that would appreciate honest ignorance. Thanks for coming to the rescue – I've re-arranged schedules so that I can get back tomorrow."

"Good. I've invited them over for their free slot the next day. Minkie and Jesse too."

It turned out to be the best kind of English summer's day for an oddly uneasy gathering. Sara settled for a barbecue in the garden, and Jesse took charge on the pretext that only Americans really knew about barbecues; but Sara suspected it was as much because he wanted legitimate occupation. She had not expected tension, but in retrospect it was foolish of her not to anticipate it, with such disparity in backgrounds, ages, and baggage of experience. She watched Snežka observing, taking it all in, appraising rather than participating in a way that was far from normally child-like. She also watched Mike trying too hard to put her at her ease. But it was the interaction between Snežka and Minkie that was the most unexpected.

As soon as she arrived with Jesse, Minkie had come to greet Jovanka with smiles and hugs and a torrent of Serbian. Then she had gone over to Snežka, hands held out. Whatever it was the child responded tersely in Serbian, it clearly took Minkie aback. Jovanka had intervened, speaking sharply to Snežka, who shrugged and turned away.

At that moment, either fortuitously or intentionally, Jesse called for assistance and Minkie went to join him, her expression tight.

"What was that about?" Sara asked of Jovanka.

"That child is too old for her years in experiences and too young in her understanding." Jovanka said. "Minkie said she wanted to hear all about home, and Snežka I'm afraid told her that since she had turned her back on it, she was not in a position to call it home. I am very angry with her. But when I see Minkie it gives me much hope. You have made a miracle, you and Mike, with that sad little girl who left my care all those years ago. Thank you Sara."

"Minkie is largely responsible for the miracle herself," Sara said. "Don't be too angry with Snežka. It must be a huge adjustment for her." But her heart went out to Minkie. Of course Snežka was just lashing out from her own hurt, poor child, and would not begin to understand the depths of Minkie's struggles over the years. But she saw with relief that Jesse, as always, seemed to have found the right words and soon had her smiling again. She also noticed Snežka observing them and wondered if she would similarly try to freeze Jesse out.

But it was impossible to freeze Jesse out. For all his time in England he had not lost that disarming American self-belief that it was beyond reason for anyone to disapprove of him. He prepared a plate of choice titbits from the barbecue, took it over to Snežka and squatted beside her. "Minkie tells me the best lamb in the world comes off the spit in Bosnia."

"And pig," Snežka said.

"Pork. We call pig meat pork. Don't ask me why."

"Can you tell me why you bombed my country?"

"Snežka!" Jovanka said sharply.

"It's OK," Jesse said, and sat down on the grass beside the child. "I can tell you what we were *trying* to do – and that was to stop people killing each other in another part of your country. Not everyone agreed it was the right thing to do. Not everyone thinks we got the best results. But at least the intentions were good. And at least there is peace now."

Snežka studied him for a few moments in silence. "It has

been very bad for us." She picked up a fork and speared a piece of meat. "But you are first to make answer."

"So now you can do something for me. I want you to come to spend an evening with Minkie and me so we can get to know each other better."

"Perhaps Minkie not want."

"I think ... I know Minkie wants very much."

The meeting was arranged for later in the week. Jesse was held up by a late meeting that afternoon, but Minkie went straight from work to pick Snežka up from her digs.

"We'll need to go to the supermarket on the way home," Minkie said. "Do you like fish?"

Snežka shrugged, and Minkie mentally kicked herself, remembering now how much she had hated the bombardment of choices facing her in her early days in England.

She was in the process of rummaging through packages of special offers in salmon tail fillets when she realised Snežka was no longer with her. It took her several minutes of mounting alarm before she found the small figure standing motionless before a series of freezer displays. Something about her touched a memory, and then she was back seven, nearly eight years on a similar shopping expedition with Sara when the impact of such abundance of choice had completely overwhelmed her. As she approached Snežka she heard her say angrily in Serbian over and over again "too much, too much, too much..." Then she saw the tears streaming down the child's face, took her hand and led her out of the store.

"We were half way home before I remembered I'd abandoned my trolley next to the frozen fish," Minkie told Jesse some time later, as they sat down to a scratch meal from left-overs in the fridge. Jesse was the one who had prepared it in their tiny kitchen while Minkie and Snežka talked in the living room. Talked and talked. They spoke in Serbian so he understood nothing but he saw Snežka's despairing expression begin to lighten as she shared her burden of unhappiness.

Over supper, the talking went on and on: about the past, how things were and the huge question mark over what might be. They spoke in a mixture of Serbian and English, but once Snežka turned to Jesse with her characteristically direct look and said "Sorry, I was bad. Not understand. Minkie is very good people."

"I think so too, Snežka."

Later she turned to him again. "Minkie and I … we can make good things for Sarajevo one day." She looked back at Minkie. "You make promise?"

There was an unspoken appeal for understanding in Minkie's expression as her glance met Jesse's; but "Promise," she said.

Sarajevo : September 2001

Jasminka : September 11

In Kosovo, reconstruction continued as did ethnic discord with minority Serbs, Turks and Gypsies now the principal victims. In neighbouring Macedonia, rising ethnic tensions during the summer had sent thousands of Albanians fleeing into Kosovo. And in Sarajevo, Minkie and Jesse were standing at the living room windows of an eleventh floor flat overlooking the infamous Sniper Alley of the war years.

"There's no way you could imagine this without being here," Jesse said, his voice very quiet.

"It was even more surreal when you had all the sound effects." Minkie said.

Nowadays Sniper Alley - formerly Vovjvode rad putnika, now rechristened Bulevar Meše Selimovića – had reverted to its role as busy dual carriageway carrying the main weight of motorised traffic to and from the outside world. Separating the two carriageways were twin strips of grass and trees, and between them the tramlines that, via several stops, would take them to the city centre. Beyond this broad thoroughfare and the buildings crowding from all directions were the mountains, homogenised into smooth continuous contours by the early autumn haze. But it was neither the thoroughfare nor the mountain skyline that caught their attention. It was the shared characteristics of all the high rise buildings in the immediate vicinity: the pockmarked walls, the glassy rows of apartment windows punctuated by blackened holes where mortars had scored direct hits, each obliterating yet another home.

After a while Minkie added "They seem to have changed all the street names. It's not my city any more." Her face crumpled. "Oh Jesse."

He put his arms round her and she buried her face in the gaudy check shirt they had bought together on Oxford Market a few days before leaving. She sensed that in his own way he was as overwhelmed as she was by the rollercoasting last few weeks, the preparations, the journey, and now the being here. At least she'd had some idea of what to expect. Sort of. It wasn't surprising he couldn't find the right words.

But she was wrong. Gently, Jesse eased her away. "Go make some coffee," he said. "And don't be so defeatist."

Snežka's bitter little comment at the barbecue the previous summer had bitten deep. Minkie's initial reaction had been hurt, then anger. Who was this kid to make judgements on what she was or was not entitled to call home? Later, she acknowledged at least to herself the extent of the subtle shift in her own priorities. She had never felt happier, more settled, than in the undemanding day-to-day minutiae of her life with Jesse. While he was beginning to champ at the restrictions of their very small flat, she adored its compactness. For her, every new book, each new ornament or gadget they added contributed to its cocoon-like security. And while Jesse periodically bemoaned the lack of challenge in his agency work – for it appeared to be gaining huge success with almost no effort on his part – she rejoiced in the affirmation of their effectiveness as a team (for she was now working for the agency full time herself); and tended to shy away from any proposal that could possibly ruffle the smooth tenor of the status quo.

In one sharp sentence, Snežka had brought these facts to her attention. And then the child's tears in the middle of the supermarket had really reminded Minkie of where she came from. She saw that this resentful kid, in many ways so much more streetwise than she had been at the same age, was riven by the same vulnerabilities. Similar backgrounds, too, both losing a parent in that futile war.

"It was even worse for Marija; she lost her husband and two children," Snežka said once. "But I was too little to remember them."

Once she asked "Did you know that Marija knew Mike a long time ago? Isn't that weird?" And Minkie remembered the photograph Mike had shown her and thought yes, it did seem a bit weird.

Finally, there was Snežka's determination to be part of a better future for Sarajevo – which she still referred to as home. It had triggered in Minkie those forgotten - dormant? - dreams of all that she and Franko had once believed.

They had met several times before Snežka returned to Novi Sad. "Your Serbian's improved no end since I came," Snežka informed her with the uninhibited candour of the young. They had been discussing the first tentative ideas on how to give Sarajevo and its inhabitants back a sense of place and identity: initially, they thought, through multi-ethnic networks in the schools, workplace, communities. "But," Minkie pointed out "we can't make much progress from so far away."

"You're right," agreed Snežka. "It will have to wait until we get back before we can do anything practical. And I don't think Marija and Dad will agree to me going home, not properly going home, till I've finished school. But may be I could go to Uni there – and before that we could meet up in the holidays?"

So Minkie observed with a twinge of unease that already, in Snežka's eyes, their futures were interlinked. And if she thought the girl would forget these pipedreams once she returned home, she soon had to think again. A few days after Snežka's departure the first of many emails arrived: chatty messages about her life and activities and aspirations, and a string of questions about Minkie's that could not be ignored.

"I got to thinking," Snežka wrote, "it could be we knew different generations of some of the same families." For the first time for many years Minkie began to picture long-ago faces and try and imagine how they might have matured - supposing they had survived.

Summer-autumn-winter-spring. And then another summer. Small tremors came to shift the foundations of all that she had assumed to be unchanging and unchangeable in Daerley Green. Mike had finally broken free of Canary Wharf at the beginning of the year, taking a cut in salary to become features editor of a new current affairs monthly. Sara had sold her partnership and worked on a freelance basis for Cyber Inc, now part of a multi-national dot com enterprise in which Pippa continued to thrive. Occasionally Mike would call Minkie unexpectedly and take her out to lunch in Oxford, treasured occasions when she briefly reverted from being a competent young career woman in a modern relationship to his Princess-and-almost-daughter.

It was about mid-June when Jesse said over supper "I had a call from New York today."

Something in his tone made Minkie pause, fork half way to her mouth and lower it again. "I have a feeling I'm not going to like this."

He gave her one of his wide reassuring grins. "On the contrary, it's great news. Or could be. Depends on which way you look at it. On the one hand ...."

"I'll throw something at you."

Jesse bowed his head in capitulation. "It's great news that requires some serious thought. And decisions. It seems that our launch of Meaningful Breaks and its expanding success has made quite an impression across The Pond. A certain major travel enterprise would like to have the benefit of our expertise. Imagine that! To such an extent that they want more or less a clone of it transplanted to somewhere in Middle America."

"God, we're brilliant!" Minkie dropped her fork and flung up her arms in triumph. "So for a nice fat fee we get to train some fresh-faced kids from Milwaukee or Massachusetts ...?"

"No-o-o-o." Jesse took a deep breath. "The idea is that we should run it – as in you and I – after training someone to keep the operation going here."

Minkie lowered her arms, stared across the table at him in silence.

"Your mouth's open," he pointed out.

"So decision time has come," Minkie said quietly. She swallowed panic.

"Well, we knew it would sooner or later. And I guess I've been treading water for a while now, Hon. Maybe thinking life has gotten kinda too comfortable."

"I don't want things to change. Ever."

"Yes you do. You want to change the world. It's just which bit of it you ... we need to decide on." Jesse said. "Do you want to call Mike?"

Yes, Mike would know how to weigh up all the arguments. Minkie hesitated, but only for a moment before she said "It's not Mike who has to make the decision."

They talked far into the night. Jesse admitted he had been feeling increasingly restless for some time. "But then every time I see – really see – your head on the pillow beside me, or look across the breakfast table at that sleepy, grumpy face; or the bright sparky one peering round the office door; or hear your voice unexpectedly on the phone .... and then try and imagine my life without any of that ..." He paused and took a deep breath. "Then it's like being on the brink of a black bottomless abyss."

"For me too."

"And yet ... and yet recently more and more I've been feeling the pull of home. Not just the bricks and mortars of it, but the life style – you know, what Mike would call the razzmatazz, the get-up-and-go. When this call came through today..." He paused, leant forward to cup her face in his hands. "... it was a bit like something, I guess, almost spiritual."

Minkie met his gaze steadily. "Then this is what we do," she said. "We make a trip to Sarajevo, as we always planned. In September when things are quietening down here. And anyway, we've got a good team going now." Her voice lightened as new vistas opened up. "Hank's always saying he can do with some extra drivers for Balkanaid. Maybe Mike and Sara could join us over there? And New York can surely wait a few weeks. Then we decide."

Now, a few weeks later, Minkie went into the kitchen to make coffee as Jesse switched on the television in the eleventh floor apartment of Hank's main contact in Sarajevo. Seconds later she heard a shout. Or not so much a shout as a wail, almost an animal sound of pain and bewilderment. She rushed into the living room. Jesse was standing white-faced staring at the TV screen from which voices jabbered incomprehensibly as news shots showed a plane ramming into a skyscraper and black smoke pouring out.

"What's happening, for God's sake what's happening?"

From the confusion of voices, Minkie understood this was a live broadcast of events unfolding in New York. Even as they watched another plane appeared, moving steadily, unstoppably towards a second tower.

"N-o-o-o-o!" Jesse yelled.

Sara : September 13

It was a pleasant room in a second floor flat just off one of the main shopping streets. A great relief, too, after the bus ride in from the airport which had left Sara deeply dismayed. Whatever visions she had conjured from Mike's and Minkie's talk of Sarajevo, they had not been dominated by ugly forests of high-rise flats on a day of implacable rain, the clouds rolling down invisible mountainsides to hang over the head of the valley as leaden-seeming in weight as in colour. Though it was hard to summon up much emotion after the events of two days ago.

The phone had been ringing as Sara let herself into the cottage that Tuesday afternoon. She hardly recognised Mike's voice as he rasped harshly "switch on the television and stay on the line."

The second plane had already hit and then, in horrendous slow motion, the first tower began to collapse, disintegrating into itself as voices rose into ever shriller pitches of horror and disbelief. *What sort of obscene joke is this* was the first flash of thought before Sara understood this was no joke, that hundreds, probably thousands of people were dying as she watched.

They must have stayed on the phone half an hour, sharing the historic awfulness of the moment, hardly speaking. Finally Mike said, "I'll be home asap."

She had just put the receiver down when the phone rang again: Minkie, barely comprehensible through her sobs. "People … throwing themselves out … of windows .. thousands dying … it's unbearable."

Sara had talked to her quietly, giving out a reassurance she did not feel. Order would be restored. Once the smoke and dust cleared, perhaps it wouldn't be as bad as it looked. Jesse came on the line, his voice shaking. "What kinda sick people do things like that, Sara? And there's another hit on the Pentagon. Jesus, what's going on?"

"I don't know, Jesse, I don't know. We'll have to wait. Stay calm. Take care of each other." A thought struck her. "Oh God, do you have any family in New York?"

"I guess not. I called Mom in Paris and Auntie in Missouri. There could be cousins, friends, I can't think straight right now." A pause. "We're both desperate for you and Mike to be here."

"We'll be there just as soon as we can."

They'd talked late into the night, she and Mike. A minor office crisis was obliging him to delay his departure by a couple of days. Under other circumstances Sara might have delayed hers, too, but they agreed she should join the young people.

"Though it won't change anything, will it? Especially for Jesse – I feel so desperately sorry for him. The Americans aren't used to being violated."

"You're presence will help make things seem more normal."

That had made Sara smile. It was a novel thought.

The young man from the accommodation agency had met her at Sarajevo bus station and brought her here to meet their hostess Nana, and explain that the English lady's husband would be arriving a few days later. Fortunately the rain had eased. Many people rented rooms, the young man said as he manoeuvred her suitcase on wheels between mammoth puddles along the broken pavement. It was a way to earn some dollars or Deutschmarks. Everything was very expensive.

The room was fine: a double bed with heavy hand-woven drapes, big carved wardrobe, table, two chairs, and a cubbyhole housing loo and shower. Mike had booked the accommodation over the Internet. "You'll get a much better feel of the place if we go private," he said. But since "My name is Nana," seemed to be almost the extent of their landlady's English, Sara began to have doubts. However, she had hardly opened her suitcase to start unpacking when Nana tapped on the door to announce "Coffee."

So Sara had sat on a sofa piled with embroidered cushions in the small living room that had a minuscule kitchen-alcove, and sipped from a tiny handle-less cup at her first genuine strong, sweet *turska*. And soon learned you could communicate surprisingly well with a few words, some gesticulations and goodwill on both sides. It was Nana who did most of the communicating. After a brief reference to the terrorist attacks in America, accompanied by a few disbelieving shakes of the head, she clearly wanted to focus on the sufferings of her own city. Sara had already sensed that foreigners – at least foreigners in no way connected officially with the rebuilding of Sarajevo – were still rarities in this city, and for some of those who had survived the terrible war years there was an almost pathological need to speak of their experience, regardless of whether or not it was understood.

With her round homely face and matching figure, her quick nervous gestures and expressive Balkan shrugs, Nana reminded Sara quite a lot of Jovanka. She guessed, though, that neither of them would welcome the comparison for, amongst Nana's mimed explosions and shows of sorrow, there was much sombre reference to Četniks, that derogatory epithet for Serbs. Sara was glad that Minkie was not there. A huge diagrammatic map marked *Sarajevo 1992-1995* was produced showing the city and its encircling mountains, each topped by menacing ranks of tanks and guns. "Četniks, Četniks," Nana said, savagely jabbing a finger at them. Damaged buildings were graphically highlighted, and little stick figures shown racing along the streets, large pink splodges marking the street intersections that were in a direct line of fire. Other stick figures were humping firewood down from the once thickly forested slopes. A few prone ones emphasised that not everyone had made it.

From the map Sara saw now how exceedingly long and straggling the city was, the ugly high-rise suburbs spreading along the widening valley away from the more solid architecture of the town centre and finally, huddled into the valley head, the crowded little streets of the bazaar area, punctuated with mosques and other distinctive buildings from the centuries of Ottoman rule. Then abruptly Nana gave another big Balkan shrug, folded the map away, collected up the coffee tray and went into the tiny kitchen.

Sara returned to her unpacking and had almost finished when she heard the phone ring and soon after Nana tapped on the door. "Phone please. Englishman."

"Thank God you've arrived safely," said Jesse's very un-English voice. "We're on our way to pick you up."

They knew of a small restaurant specialising in Bosnian food just round the corner from Sara's accommodation. She was shocked by their pallor, Jesse's even more than Minkie's.

"It's as though I've been wandering around in some wonderful daydream all my life and suddenly woken up to find that reality is a nightmare. Part of me wants to be here helping Minkie, another part wants to get on the first plane home and be part of whatever the hell's going on there. And then I get angry because everything here's so normal, everyone going about their business, working, shopping, filling the coffee shops, talking, *laughing*." He stopped. Sara saw he was close to tears. "So what kinda animal does that make me, thinking of this place as normal? All those broken buildings and people in pieces?"

A young waiter brought them menus. Jesse made an obvious effort to get himself under control and a great show of ordering paradise salad followed by Bosnian hotpot, *paradajz* turning out to be the local name for tomato. But none of them was hungry.

Sara said "Give yourself time, Jesse. There's nothing practical you can do."

"Except be there, sharing the pain. That's what Pop implied." Sara thought, *well, he would, wouldn't he?*

"There's pain here, too," Minkie said. "My daydream's biting the dust as well."

"Yeah, and I'm not helping," Jesse said.

Minkie was too preoccupied to hear him. "Did I really think everyone would welcome me like some kind of returned prodigal daughter? They've all gone, Sara. Or rather they've either gone or don't want to know. It's like Franko said, but I didn't take it in, didn't want to hear. All the kids from mixed families..." She stopped. "Mixed*!* Like mine. Do you know I never thought of myself as a mongrel before? Anyway most of these mixed families split, like Franko said, along ethnic lines, the children usually going with the mother. So all those with Serb mothers moved into the Serb outskirts of Sarajevo or other areas of Bosnia; the Bosniaks stayed here. But of my group of friends nearly all have moved away or are dead. And the few I've tracked down who are still here look on me like – like some alien being. One told me she didn't think we really had much to talk about. The others are mostly cousins on my father's side. I found one about my age was working in a cyber café in town. He wanted to know with exaggerated interest every detail of what it had been like all that time feeling warm and safe and well-fed."

Sara stopped pretending to eat, put her fork down and said firmly "You probably won't want to hear this, either of you, but I think you should both stop wallowing in circumstances beyond your control and concentrate on the things you can do. Jesse, you could make some more calls home and find out how practical your help would be if you went home. Minkie, you're going to have to develop a tougher skin to cope with the rejection you're obviously feeling, and keep on digging. Your mother can't have dematerialised without leaving any trace."

"I think you're being a bit hard on Jesse ..." Minkie began, as Jesse started saying much the same about her. They stopped, glanced at Sara, understood what she was doing and smiled for the first time.

Jesse said "I'll make some more calls as soon as we get back. It'll be lunch time at home."

Minkie picked up her fork and began nudging at her salad. "You're right Sara. This is still my city every bit as much as anyone else's. And just because I have been away, may be I'm better able to remember what it was and could be again. There are still plenty of glimpses of it. I'll show you. Tomorrow."

Next morning Jesse rang to excuse himself. From his calls the previous evening he'd learned that one of his girl cousins had been in New York for a job interview, and a couple of close friends doing Broadway. There were frenzied efforts going on to try and trace them. He wanted to stay by the phone.

Sara was relieved to get out of the flat. The TV was on non-stop, tuned in to a CNN channel for her benefit, with Bosnian sub-titles. The sequence of planes ramming into the Twin Towers and their subsequent disintegration, of fleeing crowds pursued by lethal clouds of dust and debris, were playing over and over again.

Minkie arrived, pale but determined to show Sara 'my city', the core of it tucked into the valley head, where the river Miljacka emerged from a ravine, and the old suburbs clambering up the lower slopes of the mountains. The narrow alleys of

Baščaršija, the bazaar quarters, were crowded with little shops, most of them now modernised but some still crafting the wares they sold – silver and coppersmiths, tanners, wood carvers, potters. The main mosque of Gazi Husrev-bey was under repair but men in its wide courtyard were preparing for prayers. Later the call to prayer was taken up from one to another of the minarets that punctuated the old town's skyline. They wandered through the old covered market converted into a complex of boutiques. An old caravanserai was now a fashionable restaurant. Serious young men wandered in and out of the Medresa, the religious school. For a while the horrors of New York seemed marginally more distant.

Along the quayside bordering the river they passed the devastated old Town Hall and Library. Further down on a corner by a shuttered museum Minkie said "See how they've even removed Princip's footsteps."

Sara looked enquiring. "Gavrilo Princip," Minkie explained. "The one who shot the Archduke Franz Ferdinand when he visited here in 1914, and started the First World War. There used to be footprints sunk into the pavement showing where he stood when he fired the weapon. He was only eighteen."

Sara thought aloud "Young for an assassin."

"Or a freedom fighter. Bosnia wanted to be free, like Serbia already was. Anyway there would have been a war one way or the other, even if they hadn't found Serbia to blame. Justin said they were all desperate to use all those huge armies and piles of armaments."

Well, at least her mind was off today's horrors. Sara said "My feet are killing me. I need coffee."

Over coffee she went on "At least I can understand now why Mike so loves this place."

Minkie cast her a grateful look. "And he'll understand why I'm not going to give up on it, too. I can't wait for him to arrive."

But he doesn't have a magic wand to wave either Sara thought.

Mike : September 17

He had driven across Europe like a maniac, almost non-stop. It was hard to shut out those newsreel pictures of the Twin Towers belching smoke and showers of debris, some of which might be human; the screams of people racing away from the advancing wall of asphyxiating dust, and most poignant of all, the sound of ringing mobiles that would never be answered. It was only after he emerged from the Karavanke tunnel out of Austria and into Slovenia that he turned off the main road and headed into the mountains for a few miles. There by the embryo Sava river, he found a guest house with balconies bright with petunias and geraniums. He installed himself on one of them and, with a couple of ice-cold lagers, let the images and sounds of death dissipate from his head out into the foreverness of the mountain peaks. He noted the highest tops were brushed with the first of the coming winter's snow.

It was a long time since he had been in Slovenia, now a little republic in its own right, only a decade earlier the northernmost of Yugoslavia's six federal republics. He had forgotten how very beautiful it was.

Later he had pork ragout with dumplings, sweet pancakes dripping in chocolate sauce. The accompanying bottle of Riesling was probably a bit over the top after the long drive and the lagers, but he began to feel human for the first time since entering the Channel Tunnel. The last few days had brought such a barrage of changed plans, shock and anxiety, there had been no time to think anything through; and the causes for the anxiety had still been distant. Now they were only a few hours' drive away. He could hear the weariness in Sara's voice over the crackling line as she summarised for him how it had been since she arrived in Sarajevo.

He thought what a challenge it had been for her, coping with Minkie's and Jesse's deep but disparate concerns, and how magnificently she seemed to be coping. Then he thought that this probably was the first time they had ever faced together such major uncertainties, likely to affect the rest of their lives.

"Poor love," he told her over the phone. "I didn't know what I was landing you with all those years ago."

"Landing *us* with," she corrected. "I guess it's a bit easier for me to stay detached."

She was surprising him more these days than she ever had. He sent a kiss down the phone. "Be with you as soon as I can."

He had news of his own to impart too, but this wasn't the right moment. Marija had called on the eve of his departure. Snežka, it seemed, had been pestering the life out of them ever since she learned that the Hennesseys were going to Sarajevo. She had managed to talk her father into arranging for her to stay for a few days with an old colleague and his wife in Sarajevo. But they were an elderly couple. Could Mike possibly meet Snežka off the bus in Sarajevo on September 20th, and just keep a general eye on her? It was an awful lot to ask, she knew, but she would be so very grateful, it would take a great worry off her mind, etc., etc. Mike thought it was a complication they could have done without. But there it was.

His usual approach to Sarajevo in the past had been from the coast. Now he crossed from Slovenia, through undulating swathes of Croatia and into the rugged ranges of northwest Bosnia. The signs of the recent war were still much in evidence, put into even starker contrast by the rash of new buildings, bright brickwork, gleaming glass, polished tiles. He stopped only once for *čevapčići* and a gritty *turska*. It rained intermittently, at times heavily, but had eased by the time he reached Sarajevo in the late afternoon.

"God, I'm glad to see you." It was Sara who had opened

252

the door of the flat to him. Nana was out collecting a grandchild but had left a thermos of coffee and some extremely sweet pastries to greet her new guest. They sat over these in the small living room, while Mike gave a quick resume of his journey. "But it's you I want to hear about."

Sara gave him as full an account as she could. "In a way I'm more concerned for Jesse at the moment. He's clearly ripped apart between wanting to support Minkie in what's proving a deeply painful probe into her roots and his desperation to get back to his own traumatised country." Sara poured another coffee. "My guess is that, now you've arrived, he'll probably leave as soon as he can. It'll be hard for Minkie. In a different way she's equally torn: one minute a foreigner in her own land; the next more determined than ever to recreate whatever dream vision she has in her head." Sara hesitated before adding "I'm afraid she's set high hopes on your arrival, though I'm not sure what she thinks you can do."

Mike gave a wry smile. "Poor, poor Princess. After so many years of hoping and waiting, I've always been terribly afraid for her: how she'd cope with the reality instead of the images in her head. No news of her mother of course?"

Sara shook her head. "Though today for the first time there have been glimpses of the old Minkie. She popped in this morning to say she'd been contacted by an aunt of a school friend. The friend is living in Canada, but the aunt had heard Minkie was here and got in touch through that charity outfit they're involved with. The first person to take the initiative I may add. Anyway she was off to meet someone this afternoon, and will no doubt erupt at any moment to tell us all about it."

"And you? You look sort of ... crumpled."

Sara laughed. "Thanks. I feel as though I've been through a mincing machine." She leaned her head back against the bank of embroidered cushions and reached a hand out to interlink her fingers through his. "It's been what you might call a huge learning curve: like travelling through time and back again.

On the one hand, knowing what we know, it's hard to credit the surface normality of this place. On the other, you see those broken apartment blocks – forests of them used as target practice for months, years. And then realise that the tiniest thing that we take for granted, like filling a bucket of water or buying a bag of potatoes, could and did cost people their lives. Against all that, the appalling events in the States take on a slightly different context. Though not, of course, for poor Jesse." She raised her head. "I suppose what I'm saying is that for the first time I get an embryonic understanding of the world you've been in and out of all your working life."

Later, she sat on the edge of the bed watching Mike unpack, then they went for a meal in the small nearby restaurant Sara had come to regard as her 'local'.

"Have we ever talked so much?" Sara wondered aloud.

"Have we ever had so much to talk about?" Mike returned, his next thought being *it wasn't the topics that had been lacking but the willingness to discuss them.* And then he remembered about Snežka.

"It's a complication we could do without," Sara commented when he had told her, echoing his own first reaction. "But it could be a good thing – give Minkie a new focus." For a few moments she seemed fully occupied in dissecting the trout that had just been put before her, but her concentration must have been far removed from it for she suddenly said, without looking up "How will you feel if Minkie decides to stay here?"

"I'll be devastated," Mike said, and to his horror felt his throat tighten, the tears welling, not just at the thought of losing Minkie, but for the whole mess of the past and the grief for the daughter he had never known. He cleared his throat, fished in his pocket for a handkerchief, blew his nose. "Sorry darling. I guess I'm more tired than I realised. And you have quite a disconcerting way these days of hitting nails on heads. If Minkie stays here, I suppose we'll just be like most other couples with a daughter living away from home."

"Well, it's closer than America," said Sara. She glanced across at the door. "I'm surprised she hasn't erupted on us yet – I said we'd probably eat here."

She still had not come by the time they went to bed. Next morning at breakfast Jesse rang in a frenzy of concern. Minkie had gone out the previous afternoon and had not yet returned.

Jasminka : September 17

The Home seemed much smaller than she remembered it: presumably because she was that much bigger herself. Minkie paused as soon as it came into view at the end of the long drive of lime trees planted, she seemed to remember, by some Austrian nobleman who had built the place as his hunting lodge.

That afternoon she had waited until the rain stopped, and then walked. It was much further than she had calculated and it was already late in the afternoon, but now Minkie completely forgot her tiredness. The hour ahead might well reshape the rest of her life. Sitting on a rock at the end of the drive, she slowly absorbed the scene in its entirety. The drive had been resurfaced recently and the grass verges cut. When she looked back, the city was quite hidden though there were clumps of rooftops a mile or so away marking a village that had become absorbed by the city suburbs. It was hard to believe that the sound of the mortars could have sounded so loud from here; so threatening at times that Jovanka would hustle them in from the yard, a clucking hen rounding up her chicks.

Minkie held her breath, feeling the freshness of the air on her skin, listening to the silence here, away from the city. Not quite silence. There was a faint whine of traffic, a purposeful hum of bees spurred into activity by a few late shafts of sunlight, rural rustles and twitters, the distant drone of an aircraft.

At once the sound re-activated the memory of those TV images and sounds precipitated into homes all over the world from New York. After the initial shock and her helpless empathy for Jesse's bewilderment and grief, she'd been aware of a first small jab of resentment. The ghastliness of the attack on the Twin Towers was too huge to cope with: like those tens of thousands perishing in some distant earthquake – or more comparably since it was human-inspired, the ungraspable hundreds of thousands in the Rwanda genocide. She couldn't begin to get her mind round such events; they were almost as unmanageable as some cataclysm in outer space. All she could grasp was its effect on Jesse whom she loved, and how it was turning him into someone else.

"I've gotta to go home, Minkie," he'd told her last night, his face grey. "You understand that, don't you?"

She did and she didn't. She understood he needed to know what happened to the several relatives and friends he'd discovered had been in New York at the time of the attack; but she didn't understand why he couldn't wait for the news here. It felt as though her problems had been diminished in some way by the New York atrocity. She realised that was entirely self-centred of her, but she couldn't stop feeling it. What was one mother's possible death or survival compared with the snuffing out of countless wives, husbands, lovers, sons, daughters, friends? The only thing they had in common was that they were all victims of inhuman acts.

A new sound reached her through these dark thoughts: the full-throated solo of a song thrush. Minkie smiled, anticipating its familiar phrases, each repeated twice, three times, then a pause before starting again. Mike had introduced her to it in her earliest days in Daerley Green. Of course she must have heard it many times before, but it was not something that impinged above the noise and fear of warfare. She had grown to love the sound and felt a sharp pang of homesickness. Except *this* really was her home. Had been. Could be, should be again.

She turned to look down the drive: no longer a Children's Home, but a Rest Home for the Elderly so she had been told. It was the aunt of a long-ago school friend who had told her and who had triggered this visit. "There is a woman called Katja running this new home," she had said. "She helped me once when I fell in the street during a mortar attack. Later I met her sometimes at the market and I remember her speaking of Jovanka. I think earlier in the war she sometimes went to help her with the children. One day after the war I visited an old aunt in the new rest home and there was this Katja. She may know something."

It was the slenderest thread but anything was worth trying. Suddenly aware of a drop in temperature, Minkie fished a sweater out of her knapsack and turned towards the home. Even allowing for the different conditions and the passage of time, she would never have recognised the place. The walls were newly plastered, the woodwork freshly painted. Bright cheerful curtains matched the jaunty upholstery. All no doubt financed by some charitable group in towns like Banbury somewhere in the West. Minkie followed the murmur of voices, the clink and clatter of cutlery and dishes, and came to a large dining room. She didn't recall such a large room so it was probably two rooms knocked into one. A miscellany of old people sat at several long tables tucking into bowls of soup. There were baskets piled with bread, big dishes of salad, vases of fresh flowers. For some reason a cameo flashed into her mind: of Justin, hunched and grumpy in an armchair in the common room at The Fieldings. "Infernal artificial flowers! You'd think they could manage the odd bunch of real ones to remind us there still is life out there." After that she'd always taken him fresh flowers for his room.

A young woman, her long hair tied back in a ponytail, was helping an old man to break up a hunk of bread. One elderly woman was snoozing quietly over her soup, but otherwise the chatter was animated. Far more animated than her last memories of the place.

Minkie stood in the doorway watching them. An old lady noticed her and beckoned her in, but she smiled and shook her head, not sure what her next move should be.

A voice behind her said "Are you looking for someone? Can I help you?"

Minkie turned. A middle-aged woman with a sad face and kind eyes stood behind her, holding a basketful of apples.

How strong those apples smell and *I think I'm going to faint, but no I mustn't* Minkie thought in the nano second before the woman said again "Are you looking for someone?"

Minkie struggled for breath, managed at last to gasp "Yes, someone from long ago."

The older woman put the basket of apples down on the nearest table and smiled sympathetically. "Come through to my office and we'll see what we can find. Is it your grandmother? What's her name?"

Minkie followed her into the small office, so very much smaller than she remembered it. She murmured "I've been away from Sarajevo a long time."

"Have you?" The woman went over to a desk. "But your grandmother's name?"

"Not my grandmother. My mother. And I think you know her name."

The woman turned sharply, choked, recovered and said calmly "I am Katja Lazić, the director here. I don't know what is troubling you young lady, or why you are here. But if you will tell me what it is you want, I will try and help you."

"You are Branka Račić, born in Mislići, married to Ismet who was killed by a mortar in 1992, and you have a daughter called Jasminka who went to England. I am that daughter."

The woman's face might have been carved in stone.. "I don't know who you are with your strange ideas, but I must get back to my work. Where I am needed." She pushed almost brusquely past Minkie and hurried down the hall back to the dining room. Minkie saw her put a hand briefly up to her forehead before she picked up the basket of apples and disappeared from view.

Minkie did not remember finding the chair by the window, or sitting down, or looking out at the dying day. She just became aware that darkness had come and the sounds of the meal progressing down the hall had stopped, though she had no recollection of other noise or movement. From the jumble of incomprehension in her head, one idea emerged quite quickly and clearly. Her mother had simply shut out the awfulness of the past and recreated herself. For a while Minkie toyed with the idea that she had suffered some kind of amnesia during the war; but that was the convenient stuff of books. Real life, Minkie already knew, was much less obliging.

"But I'm not going away Mother," she said aloud. "However inconvenient it may be."

She was surprised how calm she felt. How often she had tried to imagine what those first moments of reunion might be like; had dreamed of them, sometimes had hideous nightmares about them. Not one of them had been remotely like the reality. But then, eight ... nearly nine years of uncertainty, alternating with conviction against all odds, had just abruptly ended. That surely was cause for calm. The cause too for embarking on a brand new mission: to oblige this Katja Lazić to admit that she was, after all, Branka Račić, not only with a daughter but with a whole history that she could not ignore.

Having reached this conclusion, it seemed sensible to leave her mother time to recover from the initial shock which, Minkie now saw, she had been wrong ... thoughtless ... in springing so precipitately upon her. She should have been more subtle in her approach. Of course it had been a shock for her, too. But not such a cataclysmic shock for she, at least, had come in search of her mother and had always known deep into her innermost being that she would find her. For her mother it had been quite another matter. One moment she had been bereft of a daughter, the next confronted by a totally strange being purporting to be that person. Of course she needed time to adjust to such a monumental change of circumstance. In a little while,

Minkie would find her and make it all right.

In the quietness, she projected into a succession of scenes in which they would gradually rediscover each other. She had seen amongst her own friends how the mother-daughter relationship could be at its best: like friends, like sisters. A series of videos in her head had the two of them wandering around Oxford, Banbury, this or that Cotswold village, sitting on the bench in Whirling Wood. She smiled at the vision of her mother poking among hygienically packaged supermarket vegetables, heard her caustic wondering whether any of them had ever known the feel of the sun or the wind or the Good Lord's earth. But it was the mother of her childhood she was visualising, not this stranger. No, Minkie told herself firmly, she had to accept that it was going to be far more difficult than she had ever imagined. For both of them. There were all those war horrors to learn about, the growing up years to share and …

Minkie caught her breath. The very first thing they must do was to go together to visit Father's grave.

"You're still here?" Minkie blinked as her mother returned to the office and switched on the light. She stood in the doorway, hands thrust deep into the pockets of her jacket. "I must ask you to go now."

"I have no idea why you are lying to me," Minkie said quietly. "But I'm not going anywhere until you tell me the truth. Or if I go, it will be to find Mike and bring him here so that he will tell me the truth."

The woman gave a sharp intake of breath. "He is here? Mike Hennessey is here?"

So there could be no more pretending.

"Yes, Mike is here. And his wife Sara. And my American boyfriend Jesse."

An expression – curiosity? hope? regret? – briefly flickered across Branka Račić's face. Then she drew herself up. "So Jasminka, that is where you should be. With your English father and your English mother and your American boyfriend. I

260

will arrange for one of the girls to drive you back to the city."

"No," Minkie said sharply. "I need to know my mother."

Branka Račić came a few steps closer, stood looking at her, not as mother at daughter, but as stranger at stranger. "You are making it very difficult, child. Don't you understand that I sent you to England because you reminded me of too much? It set me free to live again. I am happy you have a good life. It is what I hoped and I'm sure these English people love you." Then she said slowly so there could be no mistake. "You must understand, I don't want you here."

Minkie stared back at her. She whispered "I don't believe you."

Branka Račić turned away. "Then that is your problem Jasminka. I will find one of the girls to take you back."

Mike : September 18

Soon after Jesse's call that morning, Nana left for her job in a local store and found Minkie huddled on the steps at the entrance to the flats. Catapulting down in response to Nana's urgent call, Mike's frenzy of fear for Minkie and anger at her thoughtlessness moderated as soon as he saw her hunched figure, dark hair cascading from her bowed head over her folded arms and knees. Mike dropped down beside her, an arm round her shoulders.

"We've been absolutely frantic. Are you hurt?"

The dark head shook from side to side. After a moment she moved a little closer under the shield of his arm.

"Let's go inside and talk. Get you warm. Ring Jesse." Minkie did not move. Mike held her closer for a moment, said gently "Come on Princess. We can't stay here. Let's go inside and you can tell us what's wrong."

"What's wrong is that I found my mother and she does not want me." Minkie said slowly and distinctly, lifting her head to stare at Mike with large, tired, dry eyes. "It seems I get in the way of her freedom, so she sent me away."

For a moment he couldn't take it in. "You found your mother? How? Where?"

"She has another name now, and is working in an old people's home. A fine place," Minkie went on conversationally, "just outside the city boundaries. You have been there. We have both been there – only it's changed beyond recognition." She began to laugh. "Just imagine that – my mother is working in the same place where you first saw me. The place where she sent me because it was safer, or that's what we all thought. Isn't that a joke?" She was shaking with laughter now, only suddenly it turned into big gulping sobs and at last she let Mike lead her into the flat.

By the time Jesse arrived, Minkie was emerging from a shower, still looking wan but much less dishevelled. He was not able to control his anger.

"How *could* you just go off like that. Disappear. Not a word to say where you were."

"Leave it Jesse," Mike said quietly. "She's had a hard time."

"*She's* had a hard time! I've been waiting at the end of the phone all night for news of whether people I care about have been blown up by some crazed maniacs the other side of the world. And here, the woman in my life goes walkabout. OK so your mother didn't know her lines for the return of the prodigal daughter scene. Jeez, you arrive out of nowhere. What did you expect? And where have you been all night?"

"Leave it," Mike said again, more firmly. "This isn't helping."

"No, it's reasonable he ... you all should want to know," Minkie said. "I *was* thoughtless. I suppose this was a sort of endgame of nearly ten years of not knowing." She put a hand out to touch Jesse's cheek. "Suddenly I didn't have space left for anyone else's pain but my own. So may be I got my just reward: like, total rejection. Once that had been made quite clear, this girl from the rest home dropped me off in the centre of Sarajevo, near the Orthodox Church. Yes, I should have come and told you. But you would have tried to make it seem all right. I couldn't bear to hear the words you would say that would try and make it seem less unimaginably awful than it is. So I went into the Church and lit a candle for Father, and tried to talk to God; but He didn't seem to be listening. Then I walked about a bit and found a cyber café and had some coffee and got talking to a really nice man who saw I was upset. But after a while I realised he wasn't so nice after all and told him to go away. And I just sat there drinking coffee and listening to music that was so mind-numbingly loud, it was impossible to think. And then I came here."

Mike ached for her. She was right; he would have scoured his being for the right words to ease her pain. But when you hurt at that level there were no useful words. Remembering Sonja he knew that.

But at least Branka Račić was alive. An idea began to take shape.

Jesse's anger had dissipated. He moved across to put his arms round Minkie, rocking her gently. "Jeez, I'm so sorry, Hon. I know how much your heart has been set on this journey… on finding your mother. All these years. And you're right. There's only so much pain anyone can take. Everything's got blurred at the edges for me, too."

Mike thought *'you're talking too much, Jesse. It's not what she needs just now'*, but Jesse went on, unstoppable as a fully-wound clockwork toy. "Whatever else happens, you've gotta remember how much you mean to all of us here, and back home in England. Mike and Sara who've always been there for you. And me. When this nightmare is over, I'll be there for you as long as you want me." The words went on and on coming as he rocked Minkie to and fro. Instinctively she had put her arms lightly round him to keep her balance. Her face was hidden but suddenly she looked up at Mike, her expression pleading. His first thought was *'God, how I love her';* he slammed his mind shut against the second *'so I don't have to lose her after all'.*

It was Sara who took charge. "There's enough emotion here to launch several soap operas," she said firmly. "I don't intend to tackle *turska,* but somewhere in my bag there's a precautionary jar of pleb 'instant'. It might inject some clearer thinking into the proceedings."

Mike followed her through into the minute kitchen, mainly to give Jesse some time and space with Minkie.

"Poor Jesse. He's completely out of his depth, and the sooner he can get himself back to the States the better," Sara said quietly. "It's so bloody cruel." She didn't expand on what was so cruel, but Mike guessed it was the way the young couple had both been catapulted into life-altering circumstances at the same time. He felt a twinge of guilt at his own relief: that whatever direction Minkie's life was taking it wasn't likely to be across the Atlantic in the foreseeable future.

Sara went on "And Minkie ... She seems quite out of reach in her distress. You're closest to her. What do you think?"

Through the frosted glass panel that separated them from the living room, Mike could see the two figures sitting close together, heard the murmur of voices, mainly Jesse's.

He made up his mind. "I think the first thing is for me to go and see Minkie's mother and find out what the hell's going on." Sara nodded as though she had expected as much. "Then we'll just have to see." They both stood watching the steam gathering momentum from the saucepan of water. After a moment he added "I can't believe I didn't anticipate how much this trip might affect her."

"Who could have predicted the odds-on chance of her mother being alive and Minkie ever finding her?" Sara countered. "Let alone a more or less coinciding terror attack on New York?" She had distributed coffee into the cups and was pouring the hot water into them when Mike saw a flurry of movement through the frosted glass, heard Jesse's raised voice

"Why are you shutting me out for Chrissake?", then Minkie's quieter "I just need space, is that so hard to understand?"

By the time Mike had followed her out into the little hallway she had already slipped on her outdoor shoes and was shrugging on her coat.

"I just need space, Mike," she said again. "I'm OK. Really. Just a bit of space. I promise I won't disappear again. It wouldn't have happened before if I hadn't completely lost it."

He nodded and stood at the door a moment, watching her disappear down the stairs. When he returned to the living room, three cups of coffee were on a tray on the table and Sara was saying in a matter-of-fact voice "Why don't you call the airport and check the earliest flights that'll get you home? Do it from here. Nana won't mind."

Jesse looked from one to the other, his usually open face puckered in distress. "I already have. There's a flight to Vienna tomorrow morning connecting with one to New York. I've booked through. It's one of the reasons why I was so mad at Minkie – thought I might not even see her before I left." He ran his fingers through his blonde mop. "I can't believe we were so close all those years, and now I hardly seem to know her. All those years growing up together, then being together; kinda thinking it would always be like that ..." He gave a big helpless shrug.

"None of us could have anticipated this, Jesse – least of all Minkie finding her mother, and such devastating rejection."

"Yeah, well, you know how things are with me and Dad. I just can't grasp how Minkie has this big deep thing for a Mom she hasn't seen for nearly ten years and who now says she doesn't even want her."

"It's so new and raw," Sara said gently "Give her time Jesse."

"It's not time that's the problem," Jesse said. "It's Minkie's sense of identity – where that takes her. I love her like crazy; but there's no way I could live here with all this unforgiving emotional baggage." He got up and thrust his hands deep in his pockets. "I guess I'll go back to the apartment and pack. And do some thinking. And waiting. You'll call me if she comes back here?"

Some time later, somewhere along a steep narrow lane, Mike paused in recognition. Glancing down, he almost expected the T-shirt with the red heart and the torn slogan *I love Sarajevo* still to be there, crumpled in the gutter. The building in whose doorway he had stopped to look back over the city's roofscape almost exactly nine years earlier had been rebuilt. From inside he could hear a radio belting out the sort of jungle music you might hear anywhere in the western world. Children's petulant voices were raised in a dissent that was abruptly quelled by a woman's sharp intervention. It was as though the remembered chill background sound of mortars had never been.

He allowed himself a few moments of irony: mentally journeyed back to his earlier visit and its totally unpredictable outcome; then fast-forwarded to today's representing the reverse of all he wanted. Only Sara knew of this current mission. It was self-imposed through the love he felt for Minkie and, if successful, would be the cause of him losing her. No one would know if he abandoned it. Briefly he toyed with the temptation. In time Minkie would recover from the hurt; be absorbed back into the cocoon spun round her in Daerley Green; New York would heal its wounds and the young people would fall back in love again; Minkie would go off with Jesse to America; see her friend Azzie; marry Jesse and become an upstanding citizen of Middle America …

No! Startled by the stridence of his own voice, Mike looked round. There was no one to hear. He resumed his upward trek coming eventually to the straggle of houses of a farming community now scooped into the city's boundaries.

Behind him the sounds of the city gradually merged into an urban hum. A couple of teenagers catapulted from nowhere towards him on an overladen motorbike, and were gone leaving blue smoke, the thick smell of diesel and a harsh tremor on the air. Ahead, the layered mountains waited and watched as they had always waited and watched. He could see now more clearly how thoroughly the slopes least vulnerable to mortar fire had been denuded of their trees.

He reflected that however much you anticipated a range of options and outcomes, you were rarely prepared for the reality when it came. There had been times when he had deeply feared Minkie's love for Jesse as an inevitable cause of her disappearing from his life. Now he was as convinced as he could be that this was not where the danger lay. In the last few hours he had seen how that relaxed sense of communion she and Jesse had developed over the years and which, yes, he had found himself deeply envying on occasions, had belonged to a world whose demands fitted into a very different framework. That morning Mike had witnessed Jesse's total incomprehension, and felt for him. The significance of what Marija had once described as 'blood feelings' was quite alien to the young American, not because he did not want to empathise but because its infusion into the historic gene of a people was beyond his experience.

Mike reached the avenue of limes and approached the home, recognising as Minkie had a few hours earlier how much it had changed. It was late morning and a girl with a ponytail opened the door to him, assuming he had come to visit a relative and pointing him towards the sound of voices. On the way he passed an open door, looked in, saw Branka Račić at a desk in a small office, checking accounts. It was a few moments before she was aware of him watching her from the doorway and glanced up with a small questioning frown.

"I am Mike Hennessey," Mike said.

"Ah." She put down her pen, inclined her head in a gesture more of resignation than of surprise. "Yes, I think you will come."

"In which case you will probably know why."

As she turned to face him more squarely, she visibly took a deep breath. "I do not have the words to thank you for what you do for Jasminka."

Mike sat down uninvited on the only other chair in the austere little room. "I didn't come to be thanked."

"But these are the only words I can offer, and they are from my full heart. I cannot ... I do not want her back."

He had rarely felt such a depth of anger. "Mrs. Račić, Jasminka is not a bag of apples you can keep or give away according to convenience." He saw the pain on her face, but went on relentlessly. "I think you forget that I came to see you during the war, before taking your daughter to England." Purposely he put emphasis on the words *your daughter*. "You were very ill, but I remember that you thanked God for this opportunity. I don't believe for a minute that you were thanking God for getting rid of your daughter ...."

Branka Račić interrupted. "I send Jasminka with you because Jovanka tells you are a good man, but now you say terrible words. You speak of things you cannot understand."

Mike softened his tone a little. "But I think I can. If I say things that hurt, it is only because I love Jasminka like my own daughter. I have watched her grow from a frightened, lost child to a beautiful young woman who probably has too many ideals for her own happiness. I have heard her deny against all the evidence – the total silence, the hints and rumours – that her mother was dead. I have listened to her plans to save Sarajevo's soul, if necessary single-handed ...."

"Stop! You must stop!" Branka Raćić said. Almost shouted. There were no tears but her face was contorted with grief. Finally she covered her face with her hands.

Mike said. "It gives me no pleasure to make you unhappy. I can only tell you that your daughter is in the same state, but in her case it is a desolation caused by your rejection."

She uncovered her face, looked up. "That time in the war when Jasminka goes away, my only want for her is to be safe.

My world then is finished, but for her there is still hope if she is away from here. I do not think about the future. For me there is no future – only hate and death and bombs and cold and hunger and more hate. My Ismet is dead, my daughter is away, friends do not speak, or they are sick, or they die. Many times I wonder what is reason for to live? Then sometimes things become better. The bombs stop for some days. The foreigners come and there is more food. Also more problems with black market, but some of them try to help very much. I begin to think one day I will see Jasminka again." She stopped, shaking her head. "It is not easy to explain in English after so many years."

"Go on," Mike said gently.

"One day I meet a friend; we have not seen for long time. She is Bosniak and like me her husband dead. He was Serb. For the first time I can speak with someone of many things that are ..." Branka Račić clutched her head to indicate how these thoughts were trapped, unable to get out. "Later we meet many times. I speak of Jasminka. Her son is away and she knows nothing about him. She says she hopes he will never come back to find how his world, this wonderful city, has become a place of hate .... Then I think that is what I must want for Jasminka so that she can be free. And when I hear rumours I am dead, I say nothing. With so many people dying, coming, going, it is not difficult to become someone new."

Her hands were on her lap. Mike leaned forward and took one of them in his and they sat there for a long time in silence. At last he said "How many aspects there are to love."

She nodded and after a moment asked "You have children?"

"No, it was not possible for us, for Sara and me."

"Then it is more hard for you if Jasminka stays here."

"It will be very hard. But it will be hard whenever she goes." Mike gave a wry smile. "Who would have imagined all this could begin with one visit to a children's home to make a story for a newspaper!" After a moment he went on more briskly   "I must tell you Jasminka is known as Minkie in England. This is what her school friends called her first, and then everyone else."

Branka Račić said experimentally "Minkie. Yes, that's nice name." She stood up and went over to the window. "It was a big surprise how beautiful she is. Ismet would be very proud." She turned back. "This American, is he good man for my Jasminka?"

Mike noted the possessive pronoun. "He's a serious young man who loves her very much. But of course at the moment he is quite distraught – after the terrorist attacks on New York, Washington." She nodded her understanding. "Like Minkie, he has a lot of ideals for making a better world, though I suspect he would choose different ways of achieving this. I think she is rather more mature than he is. Eventually I think he'll want her to go to America, but she wouldn't make any decisions before she had revisited Sarajevo."

"And you, what do you like?"

What did he want? He thought, *well Sarajevo at least is closer.*

She stood looking at him. He wondered what she could be thinking about this stranger who knew so much more about her daughter than she did. When he didn't answer her question, she rephrased it. "So what is the best thing for our Minkie now, Mike Hennessey?"

Jasminka : September 18

She had to be on her own. Bewilderment had been writ large on Jesse's face when she rejected his offer to come with her; but she had enough hurt of her own to cope with.

Without knowing it she followed the same route that Mike had taken many times on his assignments to Sarajevo: climbing up from Baščaršija along the narrow street where *Dve bela goluba* restaurant had now been replaced by a mini-market. Quite soon on these steepish slopes she began to shake off the urban sprawl.

After a while she stopped to get her breath, leaned on a wall looking down on the city. Here and there among the packed rooftops a clearing indicated a garden or park here, a cemetery there. The gravestones of the cemeteries gleamed white in the September sun. Of course there were gravestones all over the city now, hurriedly placed during the war on any available open ground for hasty burials between, sometimes during, mortar attacks. But these older cemeteries – Moslem, Jewish, Orthodox, Catholic – marked the centuries when Sarajevo absorbed all comers.

If bridges could not be rebuilt here ....?

Minkie resumed her climb. For the second time since that dreadful confrontation with her mother she felt a glimmer of peace. No, not so much peace as of a sense of being in the place where she should be. Even in her wretchedness the previous night when God appeared to abandon her in the Orthodox Church and that awful man started pawing her in the cyber café, even then she had felt herself beginning to yield to the essence of Sarajevo: a drop of water being soaked into a sponge.

"Hey Zvonko, put a bit of muscle into it!" A voice interrupted her thoughts: a close-by voice accompanied by the chink of some implement on stony ground.

Struck by the voice's unusual cheerfulness, Minkie stopped and looked over a wall. A group of about a dozen people were at work on what appeared to be an allotment. Four of the men were wielding spades. Some women and a gaggle of children were filling a couple of wheelbarrows with stones. The man with the cheerful voice issuing instructions leaned on a crutch. Minkie saw he had only one leg.

Noticing her, he called "We could always do with an extra pair of hands!" Minkie smiled, shook her head, but climbed over the wall to join them. She saw now that the allotment was quite extensive and well tended, with plenty of neat rows of vegetables: onions, carrots, late lettuce, early cabbage, others she did not recognise. The group seemed to be preparing new ground.

"That looks like quite a challenge," Minkie said, briefly recalling the clean friable soil of Daerley Green.

"You are not from here," the man said: a statement not a question.

"Oh but I am," Minkie said indignantly. "I'm Jasminka Račić. It's only that during the war I had to go away...."

"We all have war stories here," the man interrupted, but not unkindly. "I'm Bozo. The one with the spades are ..." He reeled off the names of all his companions, names that Minkie recognised immediately as covering the full range of ethnic diversity. When he'd finished Minkie said "I'm quite good at picking up stones."

Bozo nodded, called across to the others "Hey everyone. Meet Jasminka Račić who's quite good at picking up stones."

It was backbreaking work and Minkie threw the whole of herself into it, forgetting her tiredness, the awfulness of imminent choices to be made. "You're a goer, aren't you?" Bozo said, and the hint of admiration was better than the biggest bouquet. After a couple of hours he called a halt. A long table had been prepared under some trees at the far end of the allotment, and dishes of dried ham, salami, salad, tomatoes, olives, gherkins, bread, spread out, along with bottles of water and home brewed wine.

"So who does all this belong to?" Minkie asked, hungrily attacking a hunk of bread and a wedge of salami. It was a long time since she had felt so ravenous.

Bozo explained that it was a community gardening project organised by some American outfit, with the aim of bridging gaps between the communities. "It's the second year," he said. "And, believe me, it's not been easy. Not for any of us. But we've all been through our own hells and some of us want something better for the next generation."

Just what she'd always said. Minkie muttered "Only making war is often an easier option than making peace."

Bozo looked at her with interest for a moment, then went on "We all come from very different backgrounds. Zvonko, for example, is an accountant. Faruk is a farrier, Mila a teacher …."

"And you?"

"Before this," Bozo tapped his stump "I ran a restaurant. Destroyed of course. You will have passed it – a mini market now. Anyway for a while I gave up in favour of becoming a professional victim. Now I'm thinking we could do with some more decent restaurants to show these foreigners what real Bosnian cooking is like. So who knows ….?"

Minkie munched away in silence for a while, listening to the snatches of conversation round the table: whose kid was doing what at which school, how especially tough it all was for the old'uns, how the rebuilding of this or that house was progressing.

"I'd like to find some work here," she said.

"No problem as long as you don't have a high subsistence threshold." Bozo looked at her thoughtfully. "You've come back here to live?"

"It's the general idea, though you're the first one to actually offer any encouragement."

"Don't judge too harshly," Bozo said. "It's not easy to stop being a professional victim."

He gave her the address of the office of the American outfit in town and told her she could find him on the allotment any day. "We have different groups working, but I'm always here. Foreman in charge. Cushy job." He grinned. She liked him a lot.

It was as she headed back to the guesthouse that devastating tiredness hit her. Not surprising after a virtually sleepless night and enough emotion, as Sara had said, to float several soap operas; not to mention more physical exercise than she had done within memory. But there was a new lightness of spirit too, nudging back the heavy darkness of Mother's rejection to just beyond range of immediate thought. It was only when she reached the guesthouse that she realised her first instinct was to share her amazing new experiences, not with Jesse but with Mike.

It was Mike who opened the door of the flat. His look of deep anxiety lifted as soon as he saw her. "You're filthy," he said. "And there's someone to see you."

She slipped off her shoes, went into the small living room. From the sofa next to Sara, Branka Račić greeted her daughter with a smile.

Mike : September 20

It was raining. Again. Mike stood in the booking hall of Sarajevo bus station and stared out at the rain slamming against the windows like water jets from some massive hose: the steady drum of it and the cascading rivulets blurring the outside world.

He glanced at his watch. Ten o'clock. Snežka's bus was due in half an hour. She'd be exhausted after the overnight journey. He'd already checked out her hosts' address in one of those god-awful blocks of flats, just off Sniper Alley. They spoke a little English, seemed a nice old couple if a little bemused at how they had landed themselves with a just-teenager they barely remembered. Mike suspected he and Sara would take charge of her for the few days she was here: for the last few days before they themselves said goodbye to Sarajevo … and Minkie.

He swallowed. It was hard to credit how much their lives had been turned round in the last 36 hours.

About an hour after he had brought Branka Račić back to the flat Minkie had returned. They had made yet more coffee, he and Sara, while Minkie and her mother, amid a torrent of Serbian, talked and wept and laughed and wept again.

Mike had told Minkie of Jesse's plans to return to

America, but from her reaction – "yes, well I guessed he'd go back some time soon" – he knew she had not registered the immediacy of his going. They had telephoned Jesse, but there was no reply. Eventually they had all gone to see the allotments. Her eyes feverishly bright, Minkie insisted on it. Mike and Sara had both looked questioningly at Branka Račić who'd said "We go and meet this Bozo. I don't think Jasminka sleeps until we do. And she must sleep." What a sensible woman. And what a relief to have some one else to defer to.

By the time they reached the place, it was late afternoon. A sizeable new patch of freshly turned, almost stone-free soil marked the day's efforts, and some of the group were already heading for home. Bozo was in discussion with a couple of the men, with much arm waving to indicate the boundaries of the next part of the project. He turned as Minkie called his name. Then he had noticed Mike, his face puckering in a puzzled frown. He had swung a step towards him on his crutches. "You?" he said.

It had been one hell of a shock to recognise him and be recognised, but it had also been one of the most positive things that had happened since Mike's arrival. The bitterness of the one-legged man he had met outside his shattered restaurant those years ago had gone. Today, Bozo was unarguably someone with a purpose. Mike had told Minkie to translate to him the news that Marija too had made a new life, that her young stepdaughter would be arriving in Sarajevo the very next day. Bozo grasped his hand as if he had just been given a priceless gift.

"What an extraordinary coincidence," Sara said, obviously struggling to make sense of any of it.

"Not a coincidence, a sign," Minkie said. "It's a sign that everything will work out."

Her voice was unnaturally shrill and Mike had exchanged anxious glances with Sara, but it was her mother who firmly took her arm and, speaking quietly, led her away. And Minkie, without protest, had allowed herself to be taken back to the flat and put to bed in Nana's tiny spare room where she crashed out almost as soon as she was horizontal.

By then Jesse had telephoned on his return from "a long, long journey into my head". As soon as he opened the door to him, Mike saw the old Jesse was back in control. He greeted Branka Račić warmly and was "real excited for Minkie", but in a way one might be pleased for the good outcome of an old friend's dilemma rather than if it were of immediate personal concern.

"So I guess that amazing faith has been answered after all these years," he said, when Mike had summarised the events of the past hours. "I am happy for her." He smiled at Branka Račić. "And for you."

"It will not be simple or easy," she said. She had been watching him intently, following every word, movement, change of expression. "Perhaps not for you too."

He said quietly "I guess for a while Minkie and I were two other people: became what we each wanted the other one to be. I've never known her as she is here, and may be she's becoming the person *she* needs to be. I'll always love her to bits; but I guess it took a thunderbolt in my life to make me appreciate the kind of loving needed to live out someone else's crisis like your own. Maybe when I get back home I'll finally find out who I need to be too. Sure as hell I don't know at the moment." For the first time his voice wobbled. Sitting next to him against the pile of embroidered cushions, Sara took his hand in hers.

He turned and produced his old grin for her. "I'll be fine. Minkie knows how restless I've been getting in recent months. Yeah, I adore her – always will, and I love Oxford. But I've been feeling the call of my own spiritual home: the get-up-and-go society, which I sometimes sensed she kinda disapproved of and which, for good or ill, is what I understand and represents where home is for me. Maybe … one day … who knows?"

"Did you manage to track down your cousins in New York?" Mike asked.

"Yeah, one of 'em , Suzi. She's meeting me at JFK

tomorrow. In fact, I think I've called just about everyone I can think of. First priority is to check out just who's still not accounted for. Then, of course, I've gotta sort out Meaningful Breaks – Hank says he'll o/c the Oxford office for as long as it takes, and I guess the idea of expanding into the States will be put on hold for quite a while." He drew a deep breath. "And once everything's sorted, I fancy being footloose again for a while. See what's round the next corner, and the next." He grinned again, but there was wryness in it as he said "I'd almost forgotten it's how I used to be, always moving on. "

"It's going to be hard for Minkie," Sara said.

Jesse shook his head slightly. "It'll be a different ball game now she's found her Mom. Not to mention a whole city to put to rights." As he rose to go he said "I'll call in on my way to the airport tomorrow. Say goodbye." His face crumpled a little as he turned away.

After he had left Branka said "He makes good decision; it is necessary to be with your people at these times. A very nice young man, but not right for my Jasminka. Now I must go. Tomorrow we see how she is. Perhaps she change her mind again."

But of course she hadn't. It was Jesse, returning next morning, who went in to wake her. He was in there a long time, and when he came out his eyes were red. "Her Mom was right. No way is it simple or easy. It's better I go now. For Minkie. For me." He came over and enveloped Mike and Sara each in turn in a bear hug. "I'll write, call, email, whatever," he said, and was gone.

Mike said "Poor Princess," and Sara had given him a little push. "Go in and see her."

Minkie was sitting on the edge of the bed, snuffling into a handkerchief. "Don't you dare be sympathetic. I'm so dried out with crying I've got ..." she paused for a loud hiccup " ... hiccups." She started to giggle, then cry, then hiccup some more.

Mike took the glass of water by her bed and kept his voice

carefully under control. "The best way to get rid of hiccups is to try drinking from the side of the glass furthest from you." He gave a demonstration and handed her the glass.

She eyed him suspiciously through several more hiccups, then tried to follow his example. There was some spluttering and some spilt water, but the hiccups had stopped. She gave him a watery grin.

"I know," he said. "I'm amazing. Now get dressed while I make some more coffee. There's a lot to do."

Both he and Sara had gone with her to the office of the American charity in the centre of town. There was a lot of sitting around, drinking ever more *turskas*, while they waited for the local director of operations to come out of a meeting. He was a Bosniak American and proceeded to conduct a quite serious interrogation of the who, how and why of Jasminka Račić's interest in their scheme.

"We get a lot of spontaneous enthusiasm that's not backed up by much staying power," the director said apologetically. "Not to mention the hornet's nest of unsavoury folk engaged in every kind of trafficking you'd probably rather not know about. So, if there's one thing people here need now it's stability."

"Oh I can vouch for the staying power," Mike said, studiously ignoring Minkie's signals. "This young lady's been planning Sarajevo's revival since she was twelve."

"That's good to hear." The director smiled. "Now the community garden scheme has had two successful seasons, it looks as though we're getting the local authorities on board, which means more land will be made available, and hopefully a reduction in endless red tape."

They left Branka Račić's telephone as a contact number and he said he would be in touch very shortly. Out on the street again Minkie said "Is it OK if I go and tell Mother? I'll be back this evening and we can plan something for Snežka's stay. It's tomorrow she arrives isn't it?"

They had left her at the tram stop. How easily the word

Mother had slipped into her vocabulary, Mike thought. Perhaps Sara thought the same, for she had reached out and taken Mike's hand. "I imagine this will be the last day we're on our own for a bit. Let's be tourists."

It had been a good day pottering in and out of museums, art shows, craft shops. Over lunch Sara had said "I can't believe how so much has changed in a few days." He knew she was thinking of Minkie and Jesse in particular.

"Yup. I'm afraid there'll be a reaction when the frenetic purposefulness of it all begins to become more routine. But at least her mother will be there to keep the perspective." He'd hesitated before going on "I suppose the same applies to us – the delayed reaction, I mean. Daerley Green without Minkie ..." He felt his throat tightening and stopped.

Sara said, "It's going to be surprisingly bloody difficult all round. Well, maybe not surprisingly for you – what you two had was something quite special. I doubt if Minkie will realise quite how special until you're no longer around. But Minkie and I – well, it wasn't always easy and that must've applied even more to her than to me. There was no way we could become replacement parents but at least in your case, with the awful loss of her father, she wasn't faced with divided loyalties. With me ..." Sara shook her head "I must have been a daily reminder of how she'd lost the only security left in her life, and now I've met Branka, I can appreciate the loss she must have felt even more. But I know I'm going to miss that young woman like crazy." She stopped abruptly, frowned. "Sorry. Don't know where all that came from."

"You always were too much into self-deprecation."

"How do you distinguish between self-deprecation and fact-facing. Now that's something I've really never been good at."

He saw she was serious, leaned forward and touched her cheek gently. It triggered a momentary memory of Bogdan touching Marija's cheek and the exclusiveness of it. As he met

Sara's troubled gaze, he was startled by an unexpected flood of caring.

"I guess," he'd said "the main distinction is how good or bad it makes you feel about yourself; and I'm not sure you're always the best person to make the right judgement."

She'd put a hand up to touch his. "Wouldn't you think you'd have learned all that by 40-something?" she said.

Back at the flat that evening as he poured out a couple of glasses of a pale, dry Žilavka from Mostar, Sara said "This is probably going to sound a bit way out, coming from me. After all, you're the one who gets spooked by places and finds hidden messages in strange situations. But I've got this really weird feeling that all this – everything that's happened -" She waved her arms in a wide all-embracing circle. "has a significance beyond the obvious. A sort of starting-again significance. Well, that's obvious. Of course we're starting again; but how we do it – I mean whether we just pick up the threads or make new beginnings separately or together ..." she trailed off. "I'm floundering."

"It's not just significant. Bloody vital, I'd say."

And then she'd shot at him " So what was that business about, with Bozo and Marija?"

He'd met her eye steadily. "He was a great friend of hers. Ran the restaurant where she and I .... we spent time together."

"It's all right," Sara said. "You said you fancied her."

If he didn't come clean now he never would. His heart began thumping in his throat. It was like standing on the top board, waiting to dive into a pool for the first time. "I didn't just fancy her. I was in love with her – with all that intensity of first love, the wonder of it, the whole unrealistic bag of tricks. Long before you and I met of course."

She nodded, looked at him thoughtfully for a long moment before saying, "I don't think I ever had that sort of first love. A bit of lust here and there, but .... I really wish I had. So why didn't you go back to her?"

"It was the only thing in my mind when I left Sarajevo to go home. But I got that job on the paper, and gradually it didn't seem so urgent. Then there was a bit of a redheaded bombshell in the office who let it be known she wouldn't be averse to my attentions ..." He leaned his head back and closed his eyes. "Right little Lothario wasn't I?"

"Not quite the first description that comes to my mind." Sara got up and went over to the window. "For a while I thought you'd found her again. Marija that is. Were having an affair."

Mike hadn't moved. Truth time. Nearly-truth time. "I can't say it didn't cross my mind, especially after I bumped into Bozo that first time, and learned she was still alive. It was a period when Daerley Green made me feel like some kind of alien. Everyday life there was so far removed from all those other terrible everyday lives I was reporting. Not just far removed, but apparently indifferent."

He opened his eyes, surveyed Sara's back. It did not move as she asked "Including me?"

"It's not a question of blame; it's a question of where we felt our respective priorities lay at the time..."

"That's not what I asked."

"OK. Well then, yes. Including you. You once told Minkie that you were better at being a big fish in a small pond than a little fish in the ocean, or something like that. And in Daerley you were a big fish. The *Chronicle* and all that it represented dominated your life – or that's how it seemed to me. So, when I heard Marija was alive, it almost felt like a sign. One of those hidden messages you were just on about. Even more so when I heard that her path and Jovanka's had crossed in Novi Sad."

That had made her swing round. "Jovanka knew about this?"

"Just that she was someone I'd met long before the war." Mike went to join her by the window. Between buildings, there was a wedge-shaped glimpse of park and beyond it traffic, shoppers, workers: an everyday scene in post-war Sarajevo. "Only, as you know, after losing her husband and two children, Marija met up with a fellow victim … And even if she hadn't, life had turned us both into very different people. No unrealistic bag of tricks could survive that."

"I remember the picture you showed me. She was very pretty," Sara said.

The picture with Sonja … Mike snapped his mind shut and said "They'd been through hell, both of them. Yet seeing them together, Marija and Bogdan, I found myself actually envying what they had: that very special quietness between them which didn't allow anyone else in. Isn't that sick – to envy them that after all they had been through?"

"I sometimes felt a bit like that watching you and Minkie," Sara said. "I suppose in a way it was a similar thing, you and she sharing at least a common background of experience."

"Dear God." Mike remembered resting his hands on her shoulders. "Why didn't we have this conversation a long time ago?"

"I suppose because I was busy in my pond and you in your big sea." Sara met his gaze steadily for a moment, suddenly bit her lip, looked away. "Remember when we were doing our cleaning-the-slate exercise all those years ago? Well, you mentioned the red-headed bombshell then, and a couple of blondes I seem to remember. But not Marija." They'd stood in silence, a little apart, for a while. He sensed she hadn't finished. "That could've seemed hugely significant except that I hadn't come completely clean either. I didn't tell you about the brief wild time I'd had in my last term at school." She'd dropped her voice so that he had to really concentrate as she came out in a rush with. "Or that it was with Brett – you'll know him as Beresford Tremayne. And for a while … for a while we picked up where we left off."

He'd closed his eyes, drawn her towards him until they

were just standing, like two storm-blown trees, propping each other up.

After a while Sara's muffled voice said "Sorry. The damnedest thing is that I didn't even *like* him, not in the go-to-the-ends-of-the-earth-with sense. No way. But he was great company, made me laugh when I was down. Made me feel attractive. He was really good at that." He felt her arms come round him, tightening. "And Minkie adored him when she was younger – he was really good with her too, and that was genuine."

Mike had been acutely aware of the lengthening silence and the fact he could find no words to help her.

"For God's sake say something," Sara said at last.

"I can't find the words," was all he could manage. He had meant he couldn't find the words to express the depth of his regret at the hurt they had managed to inflict on each other. Or to encompass his own limbo of unanswerable questions: how were things going to work out for Minkie? And for him without her there as part of his life? Sara had misunderstood, reading blame into his wordlessness, and said sadly into his shoulder "Perhaps it would have been different if we'd had a kid of our own." And then he had wept.

Someone touched his arm, spoke to him in Serbian. He shook his head, murmured apologetically *"Sam Englez."*

It was a relief to be back in the present. Only five minutes to go - if the bus were on time. Suddenly he was glad that Snežka was coming. Minkie had said she would help show her round. For a few days yet they would be a kind of family. And later perhaps Snežka might come to England, perhaps even do some studies there.

He had pleaded tiredness in explaining his tears to Sara; that and the parting with Minkie, which God knows was a real enough reason. He dreaded it. Sara seemed to accept the explanation.

A bus with an *iz Beograda* placard on its windscreen was drawing in to the bus station. He thought, whatever else, he and Sara no longer needed to live with their lies. Not the total truth yet. Maybe never. But perhaps when you loved beyond a certain level, it was necessary to accept the burden of some untruths

The bus had stopped, people were shuffling stiffly out, collecting their luggage, looking for waiting friends. One figure was smaller than most, with curly dark hair and oval face and a serious expression that suddenly lit up. "Mike, Mike!" called Snežka, who had once shared a home with his unknown daughter. "I am so happy to see you."

Sara : September 20

Sara glanced at her watch. Two minutes past three. Two minutes later than when she had last looked at it on this day of interminable waiting. Mike had called to say Snežka had arrived safely. They were at the flat where she would be staying and would be with Sara around four. Snežka was bursting with excitement to "be home".

In the end, Minkie had not returned the previous evening, phoning to say was it OK if she stayed with her mother. She had called again twice that day to check arrangements. "I'll join you all for supper. It'll be great to have so many positive things to tell Snežka," she said, her voice bright, optimistic. An incredible change from less than 48 hours ago.

Why on earth hadn't she gone with Mike to meet the child, Sara wondered irritably? She had spent the morning pottering round Baščaršija, buying 'Sarajevo-the-place-to-be' T-shirts for Polly's kids and one of those war maps of the city which might still fascinate Justin. It had struck her how oddly at home she was beginning to feel in this city that had seemed deeply alien so short a time ago. Especially once the rain eased and a slant of autumn sunshine caught domes and minarets, brought texture to the encircling mountains.

She had stuffed vine leaves and fruit juice in a café and got back just after lunch to find Nana had returned unexpectedly from work. She was watching television and had pulled a face, miming a headache. Sara saw that the TV was still endlessly showing re-runs of aeroplanes ramming into tall buildings, as though the repetition of the horror might somehow alter the ensuing sequence of events. Or was it that people were caught up in the vicarious sickening thrill of it. She couldn't bear to see it again and had taken her restlessness into the privacy of their bedroom.

She riffled through a small pile of local brochures and postcards that had accumulated on the table. Well there were always postcards to write: *Berry – Don't wish you were here; Dear Justin* ....what on earth could she say to dear, dear Justin who was about to move on to whatever there was to move on to?

Anyway how could she think rationally about a place which seemed light years away? Which is how it must have often felt for Mike. She sat on the edge of the bed, lightly balancing a postcard showing a general view of Sarajevo, its skies blue and clear, its mountains sharp, its scars invisible.

It'll be great to have so many positive things to tell Snežka Minkie had enthused over the phone. A 22-year-old and a just-teenager linked by a common background of tragedy and purpose. By the time she'd reached Minkie's age, Sara thought darkly, the most far-reaching event in her own life was being impregnated by Berry and all that had reverberated from that. Years of reverberation when she really thought about it – right up to yesterday when she had heard herself say "Perhaps it would have been different if we'd had a kid of our own". And Mike had wept.

And, remembering, she had nearly wept with him.

Sara saw that she had let the postcard fall and her hands were clenched in her lap. She unclenched them, spreading the fingers out as far as she could across her knees. There couldn't be that much difference between one generation and another surely? May be it was simply that hers had not had to cope with enough demands. Or the wrong sort of demands. Maybe if insufficient demands were imposed on you, it was necessary to find some to impose on yourself.

Or maybe the real trick was just facing up to reality: like she'd screwed up her life in return for a bit of adolescent flattery; like meeting Mike had given her a second chance and she'd almost screwed that up too.

What was it he'd said "You always were too much into self-deprecation?"

The fact was that in the early days she'd never felt she'd matched up to his expectations, or her idea of what his expectations were. And that was the trouble, being sure of your lines in this on-going party game of life. Her success with Sara's Collectibles had truly surprised her, given her a boost of confidence. She discovered that dealing with people was fine if you didn't have to get too close. Later, as editor of the *Chronicle,* she knew what was expected of her. But as foster-mum to an unknown Bosnian child, she'd found she was right out of her league.

And then Berry.

Ah Berry.

His expectations were unambiguous. He wanted her to be available for him and to be good in bed. The first had taken a while, the second hadn't been a problem. But in the end it wasn't enough.

And now? In a few days, she and Mike would return to a Daerley Green still no doubt reverberating a little in the after-shock of September 11 but almost certainly beginning to settle back into its own parochial rhythms. There would be murmurs of concerned interest about the absence of Minkie, but no first inkling of the void it left in their, especially Mike's life. A few would remember "that nice young American" and wonder at the traumas faced by young couples in today's world. Mike would go back to feature editing because that's what he did these days. And she would pick up the threads of her reduced commitments: the village website, commissions for Cyber Inc, visits to Justin for as long as he was still around. No doubt there would be approaches for new commitments "now that you've got more time on your hands."

All that hard-earned experience would become part of history, hers and Mike's.

Yet, between them, they had something unique to offer.

She thought of Snežka's dark unruly mop and accusing eyes – "Why did you bomb my country?" Perhaps, just perhaps, they could offer this unique something to her. Allow the past to become part of the future.

In the distance a bell rang, once and then again more insistently. She heard voices, smiled at the sound of Mike's deep familiar one, and then caught the excited higher pitch of a young girl. She stood up, ran a hand over her hair, and went out to greet them.